Christmas Revels VI

FOUR REGENCY NOVELLAS

Kate Parker

Louisa Cornell

Anna D. Allen

Hannah Meredith

SS

Singing Spring Press

CHRISTMAS REVELS VI : FOUR REGENCY NOVELLAS

ISBN: 978-1-942470-11-3 (Print)
ISBN: 978-1-942470-10-6 (E-book)

Published by Singing Spring Press

Table of Contents

Her Ladyship Orders
A Christmas Tree

by

Anna D. Allen

Her Ladyship Orders A Christmas Tree

The falling snow could not stop Mrs. Treadwell from her rounds in the village... or from relaying her bit of news. Basket in hand, shawl wrapped tight about her plump figure, she hurried across the green, now ankle-deep white, past the great equestrian statue of Richard the Roundhead, and headed straight to the butcher shop.

"Her Ladyship has ordered a Christmas tree!" announced Mrs. Treadwell without preamble to the assembled customers as she entered the shop.

Everyone stopped their chatter and stared at her. After a silence lasting the space of several heartbeats, a small voice spoke up.

"A what?"

"A Christmas tree," repeated Mrs. Treadwell. "There we were, in the kitchen, having our breakfast, when who should come walking in without so much as a by-your-leave or a knock at the door but Sam the potboy from up at the Hall with a note telling the new man he was to find a *Christmas tree* for Her Ladyship."

Everyone spoke at once.

"Well, I never."

"What's she want to go and do a thing like that for?"

"Humph." That was Old Mr. Phelps.

From behind the counter, Mrs. Cunningham, the butcher's wife asked, "So Her Ladyship has returned home?"

"No, no." Mrs. Treadwell waved aside the question as a ridiculous notion. "She's still in Cheltenham. But the Coburgs are coming home with her and will be stopping by on their way to Brighton for Christmas with the Prince Regent."

Murmurs of shock, surprise, and approval rippled through the clutch of customers, *the Coburgs* being common parlance for the heir to the British Crown, Princess Charlotte of Wales and her new husband, the German Prince Leopold of Saxe-Coburg-Something-or-Other that no one in the shop could quite remember. Nor in the nation, for that matter.

Now the butcher piped up. "Don't you think that should've been the first thing you said, woman?"

"No. I don't, Henry Cunningham," replied Mrs. Treadwell with her fists on her ample hips. "Everyone up at the Hall will be worrying over the Coburgs, but it'll be left up to us to find this... this Christmas tree to impress them."

"'Tis true," observed Old Man Phelps, "Not like we'll be the ones wining and dining with the toffs up at the Hall. We'll just be expected to line up and cheer, tugging our forelocks and waving our handkerchiefs. God save the King. La dee da."

In the midst of glares directed at Old Man Phelps— practically treasonous, that one—a small voice asked, "What's a Christmas tree?" It came in the nick of time, as Mr. Cunningham was about to come around the counter and box Old Man Phelps's ears and toss him out. But thankfully, answers came in rapid course.

"Pagan idolatry."

"A papist plot. That's what it is."

"Surely not?" asked the quiet voice.

"I don't like it. Not one bit."

"The Coburgs are not papists," Mr. Cunningham attempted to explain, with little success, "They're proper Protestants, like the rest of us."

"Where is Coburg anyway?"

"Does the vicar know about this?"

That question—or more precisely, the pondering of the possible answer—silenced everyone, glances passing amongst them. An instant later, the customers tumbled out into the lane, leaving behind a baffled Mr. and Mrs. Cunningham and a grateful Mrs. Morris—she of the small voice—who no longer had to wait to purchase a bit of mutton for her dinner.

The clutch of customers—now transformed more properly to a gaggle of gossips—marched their way down the slushy thoroughfare to the vicarage and presented themselves at the doorstep of the Reverend Mr. Elijah Haywood.

The housemaid answered the bell and, upon their inquiry as to whether or not Reverend Haywood was receiving yet that morning, stated, despite already knowing the answer, "I'll see if he is at home," and motioned them all inside to wait in the hall.

"Is it the French?"

They heard the frail old voice in a nearby room. Some recognized it—Old Mrs. Edmondson, the vicar's aunt.

"They've landed, haven't they?" she continued.

"No, Aunt Sophia." A strong, female voice reassured the elderly lady. "Napoleon's imprisoned at the bottom of the world."

"They said that in fourteen. They did. And he came back, he did. Didn't he?" It really wasn't a question.

Silence filled the house, then movement. Someone was coming, but instead of Reverend Haywood arriving to greet his parishioners, his daughter, Miss Emily Haywood entered the hall in his place.

"I'm afraid my father has gone down to Portsmouth," she informed them, "but may I be of some service?"

Most of the gaggle managed to hide their disappointment over the vicar's absence—not that any of them disliked Miss Haywood, no, not at all. But she was just a female, after all, and what would a female know of books and learning, especially matters of theology, such as a Christmas tree? And then, there was that other matter. Oh, Miss Haywood ran her parents' household to perfection. No one could deny that. And one had to dine at the Hall to get a better meal than one served at the Haywood table. But no one ever looked at Miss Haywood quite the same after her younger sister ran away to Gretna Green with that midshipman. *Midshipman!* Not even a lieutenant!

"Oh, no, that won't be necessary," said Mrs. Treadwell to Miss Haywood before addressing her companions, "We can just go talk to them up at the Hall."

But no one wanted to go up to the Hall to talk to anyone, not even just to Hobson, the butler, or the new man. In truth, they wanted someone else to deal with the matter, someone like the vicar. And then there was the walk. Through the snow.

"Well, in that case," said Miss Haywood with a pleasant smile, "please come into the drawing room and warm yourselves before trekking all the way to the Hall." She motioned them toward that room and said to the housemaid, "Mary, please bring tea. And I think Mrs. Foster still has some hot buns."

Oh, yes, thought several of the villagers, *that would do nicely*. Others, however, lamented not coming later, perhaps during luncheon, while Mrs. Treadwell wished for cake rather than hot buns.

The drawing room possessed plenty of chairs for everyone, it not uncommon for the vicar to invite friends and parishioners to dinner or tea or an evening's reading of the Bible. And soon, everyone found themselves seated in a wide half-circle about the ancient hearth. The tea tray came, and Miss Haywood poured each of them a cup of tea—*Milk? Sugar?*—on the fine Haywood blue and white imported china, while the housemaid, Mary, served the hot buns.

A long silence fell over them. Some poured their tea into their saucers and blew on it. Others fidgeted, unaccustomed to sitting in such a fine room or using such expensive dishes.

"And how is everyone today?" asked Miss Haywood, breaking the silence.

A jumble of voices answered. Yes, they were all quite fine, although Old Mr. Phelps's knee bothered him something frightful—a sign of more snow, no doubt—and Mrs. Williamson's sister had the ague. *Oh, dear.* An appropriate amount of sympathetic head-shaking followed.

"And what is this matter you wished to discuss with my father?" asked Miss Haywood.

"Her Ladyship has ordered a Christmas tree!" blurted out Mrs. Treadwell.

"Oh, how splendid," replied Miss Haywood with a great smile.

"But it's not."

"It's not?" asked Miss Haywood, now quite baffled. She had read of such customs in the books her father sometimes borrowed from Sir George Sayre, and she always thought these foreign traditions sounded so charming.

"Don't you see?" asked Mrs. Williamson.

"Pagan tree worship," said Old Mr. Phelps, scrunching up his nose, "that's what it is."

"Papist idolatry," said Mrs. Treadwell, speaking over Old Mr. Phelps.

Confused how such a request from Her Ladyship could lead to this outrage, Miss Haywood raised an eyebrow and suggested, "Perhaps you should explain it to me." When all of them spoke at once in an eager effort to help her understand, she clarified with, "Mrs. Treadwell."

The woman in question proceeded to relay the events of that morning: of how Sam the potboy arrived in the home farm kitchen with news that the Coburgs would be stopping by the Hall on their way to spend Christmas with the Prince Regent in Brighton; of how Her Ladyship wished to have a Christmas tree on display when Prince Leopold of Saxe-Coburg-Something-or-Other arrived; of how that task was directed to the home farm—as if anyone at the home farm knew anything about Christmas trees; of how Mrs. Treadwell had left Mr. Treadwell conferring with the new man about how best to acquire this Christmas tree while she hurried into the village to tell Mr. and Mrs. Cunningham the news... uh, to get a bit of fillet for their dinner. That was the real purpose for going to the butcher's, and they all just got to chatting while waiting their turn, they did.

"The Coburgs are coming here?" asked Miss Haywood,

thinking this fact much more relevant than the ordering of a Christmas tree, as strange and exotic as that might be.

Mrs. Treadwell waved that aside. "Yes, but the Christmas tree. We can't possibly…." She shut her mouth and shook her head with a shrug.

"But Mrs. Treadwell," pointed out Miss Haywood, "You and Mr. Treadwell are Her Ladyship's employees. You can't very well take her money and then refuse to do what she has paid you to do."

The mood of the room grew pensive, with several of the villagers wisely nodding their heads.

Mrs. Treadwell, however, shook her head again and said in protest, "You don't understand. We can't possibly do something so…"

"Immoral," supplied Old Mr. Phelps.

"Oh. Is that it?" said Miss Haywood, "You find the Christmas tree immoral?"

A collective sigh of relief issued from the small assemblage. At last, Miss Haywood understood the difficulties of the matter at hand.

"Well, then," continued Miss Haywood, "if you can't participate in the acquiring and decorating of this Christmas tree—they are decorated, you know?" There were nods or shakes of heads all around. "Well, you can't very well take the money Her Ladyship is paying you."

Mrs. Treadwell's mouth formed a small O as everyone realized the quandary in which they found themselves.

Mrs. Williamson shook her head. "You can't take money for work you haven't done."

"That would be theft," said Old Mr. Phelps, "pure and simple."

"Now you needn't worry," said Miss Haywood, "because I don't think a Christmas tree is all that immoral."

Eyes widened with her words. She might as well have said she believed in free love or doubted the divine right of kings or that gentlemen should take up professions.

"No," she continued, "it is not as bad as all that."

"But... but, it's a *pagan* thing," whispered Mrs. Treadwell in a conspiratorial fashion.

"Yes, that may be," replied Miss Haywood, "but it makes no matter."

The villagers glanced from one to another, their suspicions confirmed; females didn't understand spiritual matters. They should have waited for the vicar.

Miss Haywood continued, seemingly unaware of the tension in the room. "Just as the old pagan temples of Rome were converted into Christian churches, other pagan things were adapted for Christians. Such as the day Christ's birth is celebrated."

A gasp sounded in the room. It was Mrs. Williamson.

Miss Haywood looked directly at her and said, "As any good shepherd will tell you, lambs come in the spring, not in the dead of winter. And all those shepherds abiding their flocks by night had the good sense not to be out in the cold. So it must not have been *that* cold."

"'Tis true," said Old Mr. Phelps, and then repeated to his companions as if none of them had heard it the first time, "Lambs come in the spring."

"Oh," said Mrs. Treadwell with longing in her voice, "don't a bit of roasted lamb sound good about now?"

"With mint jelly," someone else said.

"And fresh peas," added another.

"Or maybe lamb stew."

Hums of approval followed.

"Yes," interrupted Miss Haywood, struggling to contain an exasperated sigh, "that does sound good. But as I was saying, it was not uncommon for the Christian fathers to incorporate pagan ideas into the Christian faith, for practical purposes."

"How's that, miss?"

"You mean like the pagan mass?"

"Papist mass," someone quietly corrected.

"That, too."

"No, no. I mean, well…" Perhaps this was the wrong path, thought Miss Haywood, as Mrs. Williamson looked quite distressed by the whole concept. "Converts might be reluctant to give up traditional festivities, more so for the merry-making rather than the old beliefs. Like in New Spain—they didn't want to give up their annual rites honoring their dead ancestors, but this wasn't a problem. They now honor the memories of their ancestors on All Souls' Day. And even *we* celebrate All Souls' Day, don't we?" Although, celebrate wasn't quite the right word. Her father did hold a special service that day and prepared a *mostly* new sermon for the day, but fewer parishioners filled the pews than on any given Sunday. Maybe *recognized*?

More nods and murmurs of agreement followed.

"And undoubtedly," continued Miss Haywood, "the Christmas tree is an example of this in the lands of Germany."

The villagers sat quiet again, pensive looks on their faces. Whether they contemplated her words or roasted spring lamb, Miss Haywood couldn't tell. Then Mrs. Treadwell smiled and shook her head.

"It's a shame you're a female," she said, "otherwise you'd have made an excellent minister."

Praise indeed.

"Well, there you go," said Miss Haywood with a silent sigh of relief. Crisis averted. "More tea, Mr. Phelps?" she asked, lifting the teapot.

Old Mr. Phelps, eager for more, held out his cup. But never received another drop, much to his disappointment, for right at that moment, the housemaid rushed into the drawing room.

"Miss," she said, "Miss Haywood. There are some men in the churchyard." She moved toward the window and pushed aside the curtain. "They look to be up to no good. Carrying axes and shovels, they are."

Miss Haywood rose from her chair but reached the window only after everyone else, except for Mrs. Treadwell, who stopped to ask the housemaid if there might be any biscuits.

Lacking all decorum, they huddled at the wide window, their eyes straining, their mouths gaping, in an effort to see the expected spectacle of *men up to no good* in the churchyard. But over the snow-covered shrubs, across the stretch of white lawn, to the enclosed yard of lopsided gravestones, they saw exactly what the housemaid described—men with axes and shovels. Two men, to be precise.

"Is that...?" Mrs. Williamson hesitated. "Is that Tom Hinton?"

"No, no," replied one of the others, "Tom Hinton's much taller than that."

"Fatter, too."

"It's that Tuttle boy."

"Which one?"

"The one with the red muffler."

Miss Haywood choked back a laugh.

"Don't be daft. Which *Tuttle*? Harry Tuttle the charcoal maker over in Ashton Wood or George Tuttle, Her Ladyship's tenant?"

"George Tuttle, Her Ladyship's tenant. That's his oldest."

"Oh. Right." Everyone tried to peer closer. "The one who nearly drowned in Widow Talbot's pond."

As the villagers verbally tussled over which Tuttle was which, they all watched the two men in the churchyard—the still unidentified one and George Tuttle's oldest boy—trudging about, as if in search of something, until they stopped before a conical-shaped yew shrub about the height of a tall man. They looked it over, seemed to discuss it, and then....

Miss Haywood suddenly realized their intent.

"That's Eliza Throckmorton's yew!" shrieked Mrs. Williamson, and out the room she ran.

The unidentified man raised his axe, as Miss Haywood struggled to open the window. A burst of cold air rush in upon them, and Miss Haywood called out, "Stop! Stop right this instant!"

To her surprise—and immense relief—the men heard her and stopped, the unidentified man in mid-swing.

"I'll be there presently," continued Miss Haywood, before turning to face the gaggle of gossips. "Mr. Phelps, could you go and make sure they don't do anything until I get there?" Although, she could already hear Mrs. Williamson fussing at them. "I must put on some proper shoes first."

Mr. Phelps tugged his forelock and hurried off.

One of the other men piped up. "You needn't bother yourself, miss. I can deal with this."

"No. No. Please don't concern yourself," replied Miss Haywood, moving quickly to the hall, "It is a church matter, and my father left me here to..." She shrugged. "Well, to deal with any problems that might arise." But with those words, she witnessed the glances and knew everyone clearly recalled a previous occasion when her father left her in charge. And look how that turned out.

In truth, Miss Haywood would have preferred to leave it to others. She had more pressing matters to deal with—Aunt Sophia for one. Keeping her calm could be trying at times. There was also the preparation of their own Christmas dinner. Her parents planned to be back before nightfall tomorrow—Christmas Eve—and there was still the matter of her father's sermons for Midnight Service, as well as Christmas morning service. But if Miss Haywood did not deal with this issue of the Christmas tree now, well, no doubt the villagers would be burning the pope in effigy by nightfall. What a happy Christmas that would be for Her Ladyship and the Coburgs.

Much to Miss Haywood's gratitude, Mary, as usual, was two steps ahead of her, and presented her half-boots, gloves, and muffler in the hall. The villagers headed outside, undoubtedly to eavesdrop in plain sight on the tongue-lashing Old Mr. Phelps would unleash on two unsuspecting laborers.

Miss Haywood had just finished putting on the garments, when Aunt Sophia came tottering out from the morning room, her stick tapping the wooden floorboards as she stepped gingerly. Her nurse followed close behind.

"Emily. Those men," she said, her voice shaking, and pointed in the general direction of the church. "Those men, Emily. They've come to take Eliza Throckmorton's yew. In the churchyard."

"Yes, Aunt Sophia," replied Emily, reaching for her cloak and throwing it about herself, "I see them. Don't worry. I'll deal with it."

She hurried outside and trudged through the ankle-deep snow—crunch, crunch, crunch—to the churchyard where several villagers and the two men stood around the tall yew shrub. Now she could clearly see the other man with George Tuttle's boy. It was Young Mr. Phelps, who was hardly young. He had more than a decade on her, but looked like he had two. His kept his head lowered… because Old Mr. Phelps was upbraiding him.

"That a son of mine would be involved in such a thing." He shook his head. Everyone else shook their heads. "The procuring of a Christmas tree. And Eliza Throckmorton's yew, at that." He shoved his gnarled forefinger toward the crooked headstone with the dearly-departed lady's name carved on it beneath grey and green lichen.

"Rest in peace," continued Old Mr. Phelps, "That's what it says."

"In Latin," pointed out one of the villagers.

"It says it in Latin," repeated another.

"Written. It don't say anything."

"How is *this* resting in peace?" asked Old Mr. Phelps.

Emily glanced at the stone. That was what was written—*requiescat in pace*—along with a death year of 1564 and *aetatis suae 89*. Never mind no one alive ever knew her or even remembered anyone who ever knew anyone who knew her. She was a revered village fixture, like the statue of Richard the Roundhead—who had the good sense to die before the Restoration and was succeeded to the earldom by his Cavalier son. Everyone entering the church on Sundays had to pass by Eliza Throckmorton's stone next to the tall yew. Twice, if one counted exiting the church, as well. She was, for all intents and purposes, a friend and neighbor. The fact that she was dead made no difference.

"What is this all about?" asked Emily, calmly entering the fray, as it were.

George Tuttle's boy let out an enormous sigh. Relief filled his eyes, as if she had just saved him from the mob. Young Mr. Phelps raised his chin and stood up taller with his father no longer berating him.

"Her Ladyship ordered a Christmas tree," explained Young Mr. Phelps, "We thought this one looked good."

"When Her Ladyship sent you out to find a Christmas tree…," began Emily, only to be interrupted.

"It weren't Her Ladyship. It were the new man."

"The new man?" she asked, "The new land steward?"

"He's Scotch, you know," whispered someone behind her.

"Scots," someone corrected.

"Half-scotch."

"Half-Scots."

"Still foreign, if you ask me," grumbled Old Mr. Phelps.

"Yes, well, be that as it may," Emily attempted to continue, "I hardly think Her Ladyship or anyone else intended for you to cut down Eliza Throckmorton's yew. Besides, they're poisonous, you know. I doubt this is the kind of tree appropriate for using as a Christmas tree, especially with children about." She couldn't pause long to draw breath; if she did, one of the gaggle would put in their two pence again, and then where would they be? "Besides, this is church property, not His Lordship's land, and to take the yew would be theft, unless my father gave permission, which he can't because he's in Portsmouth. Otherwise, you'll have to write to Lambeth Palace to get permission to cut it down."

In truth, she had no idea. But it sounded good, and she knew it would delay the matter until her father returned, hopefully tomorrow. Still, everyone stared at her with wide eyes and open mouths, with George Tuttle's boy and Young Mr. Phelps slowly backing away from Eliza Throckmorton's yew, as if it were corrupted with the pox. Old Mr. Phelps, however, gazed at her with narrowed eyes and furrowed brow, one hand scratching the back of his head.

"But Miss Haywood," protested Young Mr. Phelps, summoning up his courage, "the new man said we were to bring back a tree."

Oh, bother! She should have left well-enough alone. Now, she would have to go deal with the new man. If she didn't, well, undoubtedly she'd be blamed for any ensuing disaster.

"Leave the new man to me," she volunteered. Reluctantly. The relieved faces told her it was what they all wanted—someone else to unravel this muddle.

"I can take you over in my cart," offered Old Mr. Phelps. He glanced up at the falling snow. "But we'll have to hurry, as it might not make it if the snow keeps coming down like this."

"Thank you, Mr. Phelps," she said, grateful for the assistance, despite the fact that it was only half a mile to the home farm. She turned to Young Mr. Phelps and George

Tuttle's boy. "Until we settle this matter, best not to cut down any trees. Otherwise, my father might read your names in his next sermon, and none of us want that, now do we?" She thought she heard Young Mr. Phelps practically growl, but George Tuttle's boy's eyes widened with stark fear.

It took only a moment for Old Mr. Phelps to bring his cart around—pulled by his donkey, Penelope—and they were on their way down the lane toward the home farm, just outside the village. Of course, Penelope moved along at about the same pace as Emily did when walking the route, but still it saved her the effort and kept her half-boots and skirts dry.

"What you said back there?" asked Old Mr. Phelps, "'Bout having to write to the Archbishop and all? Is that true?"

"I've no idea," admitted Emily, "but it stopped them."

"So you fibbed."

"Yes, I did." But was a fib a lie, she wondered. And what she said *could* have been true, although she doubted one would have to write the Archbishop of Canterbury to get permission. Maybe the Bishop in Salisbury would suffice.

Penelope trudged along, slow but steady, until in short order they arrived in the yard of the home farm. Old Mr. Phelps helped Miss Haywood out of the cart and then hurried off to find the new man while she waited.

The snow fell steadily around her, the sound strangely quiet and loud all at the same time. She supposed the snow insulated any noise, which in turn augmented the sound of millions of snowflakes hitting the earth. She even thought she could hear each and every individual snowflake, and she closed her eyes to the stillness and peace.

Only to hear beneath it...

By by, lully lullay.

A rich voice singing.

...thou little tiny child, by by, lully lullay.

She knew the carol well, one of her favorites, and she looked about to see from whence it came.

This poor youngling, for whom we sing...

She followed the song to the stables, the doors wide open. And there she saw a grey-haired old man in his shirtsleeves, cloth in hand, polishing an ancient red sleigh.

Herod the king in his raging... The man sang, a perfect tenor, without the usual tremor so often heard in the singing voices of the elderly. Miss Haywood let him sing, not wanting to interrupt him. But then he caught sight of her and stopped, both song and work, with an abrupt start.

He stared at her, dark eyes wide, a blush creeping across his smooth face. He wasn't old at all. He was a young man— or at least close to her own age—his thick shock of hair not grey but a mixture of dark overrun with premature white, thereby making it appear grey at first glance... and making him appear older. He brushed a lock of hair from his forehead and reached for his jacket.

"My lady," he said, clearly embarrassed as he put the jacket on, "I beg your pardon."

"Oh, no. No." Emily raised her hand, as if to stop him. "You're mistaken. My father's the vicar."

He breathed an apparent sigh of relief, his body relaxing. "I thought you were from up at the Hall. They said Lady Margaret might return ahead of her mother." She heard no trace of a Scottish accent in his voice.

"We've never been introduced," said Emily, "but I've seen you on Sundays. Briefly."

He nodded and looked down at the cloth in his hand.

With a quick shrug and a tilt of his head, he said, "If only we had a master of ceremony to do the honors." He went back to polishing the sleigh.

Before Emily could reply—or determine whether he spoke in jest or with undue seriousness—Old Mr. Phelps came shuffling in. "You found him, I see."

The new man tossed aside the polishing cloth and addressed Old Mr. Phelps. "Mr. Phelps, if you would." He motioned toward Emily.

Old Mr. Phelps glanced from one to the other, confusion in his face. Then he brightened and said, "Oh. Right." He stood up taller and cleared his throat. "Miss Haywood," he said with a dignified nod to her, "may I present Mr. Lachlan Reed. The new man."

Mr. Reed bowed to her. "Miss Haywood."

"The vicar's daughter," added Old Mr. Phelps.

Despite the farcical sense of the moment, Emily gave a polite curtsey. "Mr. Reed."

"There," said Mr. Reed, with a grin, a spark of mischief in his eyes, "We have been introduced. Now, is there something I can do for you?"

She found his gaze... intimidating? No. But disconcerting, nonetheless. While she wished to look shyly away, she met his gaze without flinching.

"Young Mr. Phelps and George Tuttle's boy," said Emily, "You sent them to get a Christmas tree?"

"That I did."

"Well, they clearly didn't know what they were doing as they attempted to cut down Eliza Throckmorton's yew." Emily feared she sounded as if she were scolding.

Confusion sprang up in Mr. Reed's eyes. Not literally, of

course, but Emily saw it nonetheless, and she could well-imagine his thoughts; he envisioned an ancient tree, twisted and gnarled, not the man-sized shrub standing sentry beside Eliza Throckmorton's gravestone.

"A yew?" asked Mr. Reed, furrowing his brow.

Old Mr. Phelps spoke now. "And it nearly caused a riot in the village."

"Is that so?" Mr. Reed raised an eyebrow, clearly skeptical of the claim.

"Yes," replied Emily, but then she faltered. "Well. Nearly so."

"And now you think I should go apologize to Mrs. Throckmorton, is that it?"

"Oh, no, I don't mean...."

"She's dead," Old Mr. Phelps helpfully provided.

"She's dead?"

Old Mr. Phelps glanced upward and squinted. "Winter of 1564, it was."

Eyes widening and mouth nearly gaping, Mr. Reed stared at the old man, and Emily knew his thoughts in an instant. He deemed them all mad, every last one of them. And she wasn't so sure she disagreed.

Still focused on Old Mr. Phelps—the way one might do with a dangerous animal—Mr. Reed turned his chin toward Emily and asked, "So, how does this concern me?"

"You were tasked with finding a Christmas tree by Her Ladyship, were you not?"

He turned wary, crossing his arms over his chest and facing her. "I was."

"And what do you know of Christmas trees?"

"Absolutely nothing."

At least he was honest, thought Emily. "Yet you sent Young Mr. Phelps and George Tuttle's boy to find one? What did you expect them to bring back?"

"A tree."

Emily sighed. "Given that none of us has any inkling of this Teutonic tradition, perhaps inquiries should be made first. Before we go cutting down trees willy-nilly."

"And how do you propose I do that? Her Ladyship and the Coburgs are expected tomorrow or the following day. That's not much time to make *inquiries*."

"Sir George Sayre has an extensive library," offered Emily, "Perhaps you should inquire with him as to an appropriate variety of tree suitable for a Christmas tree."

"Can't."

"Why ever not?"

"We haven't been introduced."

Old Mr. Phelps chuckled, while Mr. Reed looked quite pleased with himself. But Emily felt quite put upon. After all, this wasn't her problem. It was Mr. Reed's problem. She needed to be home. It was nearing noon, and Aunt Sophia would be wanting her luncheon. Her day wouldn't be right without luncheon served at the appointed hour.

But the Christmas tree... And the Coburgs expected in a day or so. If Mr. Reed didn't find an appropriate tree—whatever that might be—it would reflect poorly on His Lordship, Her Ladyship, and the entire village. And if everyone found out she simply went home rather than assist Mr. Reed....

"I could accompany you and introduce you to Sir George Sayre," she offered, hoping Mr. Reed would decline the suggestion.

"Good. Let's go."

"Now?"

"Well there's not much time, now is there?" Mr. Reed pointed out.

"He's right," said Old Mr. Phelps, "After you consult Sir George, you still have to find a tree, cut it down, haul it back to the Hall, and get it ready for the Coburgs." And then he quickly added, "Not that I approve of this sort of thing," scrunching up his nose and shaking his head.

You? When did this become her problem?

"Besides," said Mr. Reed, "I need to take the sleigh out. Wouldn't do to have it fall off the runners the first time Her Ladyship drives out in it. Or worse, the Coburgs."

"Ho! Ho!" cried Old Mr. Phelps with great delight. "Probably a hanging offense, that one."

"No time like the present," continued Mr. Reed, and he vanished deeper into the stables.

Emily, uncertain if he intended to return, followed after him, peering in the dim light down the length of the stables to see where he went. But then she heard a slight cough. She turned to see Old Mr. Phelps standing beside her.

"I've been thinking," he said, "Correct me if I'm wrong, Emily, but New Spain, what they're now calling this Mex... Mex..?"

"Mexico?"

"Precisely. That belongs to *Old* Spain, and Spain is papist."

Oh, dear.

"Obedient to the Pope," continued Old Mr. Phelps, "Not even to their own king, let alone to a proper English king."

Emily resisted the urge to point out that King George

was, in fact, quite German. And as for *proper*, she doubted any member of the royal family or the courtiers surrounding them resembled anything remotely akin to *proper*.

Old Mr. Phelps seemed to ponder a thought and asked, "Does Spain have a king? What with that Bonaparte brother now being gone and all, well, I've quite forgotten."

"Yes, yes," replied Emily, "of course, Spain has a king."

Old Mr. Phelps gave a little laugh. "Of course they do. Everyone has a king." Then he grimaced. "Except those bloody Americans. Oh, beg your pardon, miss."

"Quite understandable, Mr. Phelps."

"I'm just saying..." He leaned in close and whispered in a conspiratorial fashion. "I don't think we should be following the example of papists with this Christmas tree. That's all."

Emily didn't have an answer. Worse, she didn't have any tea and biscuits with which to distract Old Mr. Phelps while she thought of something—hopefully, something very clever and erudite... but without sounding too much like a bluestocking. It would require further consideration.

Old Mr. Phelps, however, awaited a response.

"Well," replied Emily, struggling for words, "That is..." She tried to think, and managed to say, "Well, our Lord was a carpenter."

Oh, brilliant, she inwardly groaned.

"True, true," said Old Mr. Phelps, "but what does that...."

And thankfully, at that moment, Mr. Reed, leading a horse, returned via the open stable doors having gone the long way around.

"Mr. Phelps," he called out as he harnessed the bay to the sleigh, "Mrs. Treadwell's back and said she's putting on the kettle should you be wishing a cup of tea."

So the new man had already learned that trick. Or perhaps that trick worked the world over.

Old Mr. Phelps's eyes gleamed and he clapped his hands together. "Oh, that I would. Thank you." And with a tip of his hat to Emily, he trotted off to the kitchen.

Mr. Reed said not a word as he went about his business, but he eyed her warily. Emily, for her part, watched him carefully. He was tall and lanky, more like a boy of seventeen rather than a man nearing... What? Thirty-five, forty? The lines around his dark eyes told her that much, but the white hair threw off any easy estimate. But whatever the case, he could stand to gain a few pounds in her estimation. Mrs. Treadwell would see to that, no doubt; although, she was hardly the best cook hereabouts. His mode of dress—buff knee breeches and boots—were decidedly outdated but practical, especially for a land steward.

He tossed her a wool blanket, which, thankfully, she managed to catch without making a fool of herself; having five brothers held some advantages. Then, Mr. Reed placed a bundle of rope in the sleigh behind the seat.

"Why the rope?" asked Emily.

"In case we come off the runners and end up upside down in a ditch somewhere."

"You jest?"

"Not in the least."

Emily considered the sleigh—and this whole venture—again. Her life as a cautionary tale passed before her eyes, the vicar's daughter who allowed her sister to run away with a midshipman—*not even a lieutenant!*—to Gretna Green. *Whatever became of her? The daughter, not the sister,* the gossips would ask. *Oh, she broke her neck when His Lordship's sleigh fell off its runners in the winter of '16. She was with the new man—you remember, that half-Scotsman without an accent. The one that could stand to gain a few pounds.*

On further thought, perhaps she should just return home. But instead, she asked, "Should I be concerned?"

"No."

For some reason, that succinct answer reassured her.

Mr. Reed took an overcoat and blue muffler down from a peg on the wall and put them on. A pair of gloves appeared from somewhere on his person, and he motioned to the sleigh.

"Shall we?" he asked.

Emily glanced down at the leather seat. A moment of schoolgirl panic rose up in her. They would be alone together. Someone might see. Then she remembered her age. Well, if they were seen, it would at least entertain the gossips.

She climbed in and sat down, Mr. Reed joining beside her. At least the seat wasn't so small that they were pressed together.

"Right," said Mr. Reed with a snap of the reins, "Sir George Sayre and his library it is."

The sleigh moved forward a fraction and lurched to a sudden stop.

"Should I get out and push?" offered Emily.

"No. At any rate, not now. Maybe later." Mr. Reed snapped the reins again, simultaneously making a clicking sound with his mouth. This time, they moved, slowly at first, out of the stable and across the yard, and soon headed down the lane at a brisk pace.

Emily—who'd never been in a sleigh before—expected

something out of fairytales or the myths of ancient Nordic gods… over hill and dale, through forests deep and dark, alongside still-babbling brooks. That sort of thing.

It was better.

The sleigh raced along, just like in song and stories, but the speed of the sleigh made the snow fly faster, snowflakes gently pelting Emily's face, and she resisted the urge to shriek and laugh like a child. Up hills, they slowed, but then moved faster downhill, the horse tossing her head and prancing, her delight matching Emily's.

Then she noticed, despite their rapid progress down the lane, the stillness of the snowy world. A slight wind brushed the trees overhead, sparking creaks and groans amongst the branches, like the squeak of a door in need of oil. Emily pulled the blanket tighter about her against the cold, Mr. Reed silent beside her, his gloved hands clutching the reins. On they went, alongside snow covered hedgerows, hazels and brambles, asleep and waiting for spring.

"How about a holly bush?" asked Mr. Reed without warning, his voice louder than the swoosh of the runners.

"I beg your pardon?"

"It's a Christmas sort of thing."

She realized he referred to the Christmas tree.

"To us," replied Emily, "but maybe not to Germans. Do they even have holly bushes in the Germanic lands?"

He hummed, as if pondering her question, but gave no answer.

As the silence lengthened, she asked, "Lachlan? That's an unusual Christian name."

He glanced over at her, those dark eyes briefly fixing on her, before he returned his attention to the road.

"My mother's maiden name," he said.

"You're half-Scots."

"Quarter. My grandfather was Scots. Borderer, at that." He glanced at her again, and this time, she thought he grinned... or maybe it was a grimace. "In Scotland, that might as well be English. Never been there myself."

She wondered if that explained his lack of an accent. And then she thought of his words, and of the words earlier when the villagers had variously labeled him Scotch and then half-Scotch. And she realized, here, in England, they thought him Scottish, but in Scotland, they would have thought him English. And she felt a pain of loneliness, of hidden sorrow in him.

Or perhaps it was only her own imagination at work.

ᘓᘔ

Sir George Sayre lived in a house of red brick and ideal proportions, a cube full of large windows and topped with a round, white cupola. Attached to one side, however, was a long glasshouse, throwing the sense of symmetry of the carefully designed house completely off, all for a passion greater than architecture.

Horticulture.

The sleigh pulled up before the brick façade, the occupants impressed by the gentleman's home but also feeling a tad small. As they climbed out of the sleigh, a squeaky French window slid open in the little afterthought connecting glasshouse to manor house.

"Ahoy," cried the white-haired gentleman with a wave of his hand, "Ahoy, Miss Haywood. As your brothers might say." He laughed, and then moved aside as Thomas the head gardener's boy—Sir George had a full staff of gardeners—

climbed out the window.

The boy, all eager smiles, rushed to the sleigh to take the reins from an equally amused Mr. Reed.

"If it falls off the runners," said Mr. Reed to the boy, "come find me."

"Don't doddle, Thomas," continued Sir George from his perch in the window, "and tell Cook to send up something."

Emily and Mr. Reed trudged through the ever-deepening snow to the French window.

"Inside, inside. Hurry." Sir George motioned them. "The cold air's getting in." He held out his hand to Emily and helped her clamber over the low sill, Mr. Reed following with ease.

"How delightful," proclaimed Sir George as he slammed shut the window, "How delightful, indeed." He took Emily's hand again and bowed over it, as he always did with ladies. Emily had thought him handsome since the beginning of forever, even when a child and too young to recognize such things. Still slender with only the faintest trace of a pot belly underneath his embroidered waistcoat, he seemed to age faster with each passing year. His once black hair, cut in a Brutus style, was all white, contrasting sharply against his black eyebrows. And she noticed she no longer had to look up to him when speaking, his once great height slowly diminishing with the advancement of time.

"Sir George," said Emily with a smile, "may I introduce Mr. Reed, His Lordship's new land steward."

"Oh, yes. Right," said Sir George. He hesitated a moment, as if suddenly shy, and then clasped Mr. Reed's hand. "So you're the man to see about those rhododendrons on the north side of the Hall. I'd dearly love to obtain one. Old Evans wouldn't hear of it, and His Lordship is so rarely here I hadn't the chance to discuss the matter with him. I suppose I could write to him, but it seems such a trivial matter. You know, I hold with Salisbury—are you familiar with Salisbury? Such a disagreeable man, but I agree with his idea that rhododendrons and azaleas are…"

They found themselves in a small room with a tiled floor and potted palms. Emily knew from previous visits that the door to the right led into Sir George's library. Sir George, however, led them to the left, into the warm, moist air of the glass house. No one knew which Sir George loved most—his books or his plants—but he reveled in each with equal abandon and devotion.

"…But I suppose we should hold off any discussions about it until the spring," continued Sir George, "or at least until the snows melt." He suddenly became aware of his surroundings. "Oh, do forgive the mess. Making boughs of holly," explained Sir George at the sight of holly cuttings scattered about the floor around the garden furniture he used as a substitute for a sitting room.

Emily, however, realized Mr. Reed barely noticed the mess. Instead, his eyes strayed down the length and breadth of the glasshouse, and she knew that, rather than the chaos of bough-making, he now experienced a glimpse of Eden.

An intoxicating perfume of camellias filled the air—so out of place for that time of year—the red and white flowers in full bloom. Surely, thought Emily, that was the smell of Heaven. The tall spikes of pineapple plants fanned out behind the camellias, Sir George still endeavoring—but still failing—to produce a pineapple fruit. But, as he would eagerly tell anyone who might listen, he lived in hope, foolish as it might be.

A hundred shades of green, lush and verdant, interspersed with splashes of red, white, orange, yellow, and purple, stretched to the end of the glasshouse. Orange trees and lemon trees reaching to the ceiling, the light diffused through a light blanket of snow.

Sir George, perhaps long accustomed to the reaction, became aware of Mr. Reed's admiring reverie. He smiled but it soon faded, and he said, "How unfortunate you cannot see my bird of paradise in bloom. You must make a point to visit in the summer. Or better yet, I'll send for you when it blooms, and you can be sure to see it then."

The tea tray arrived. Followed by another tray. And another tray. All carried by McCall the butler, the footman, and the downstairs maid. In short order, the jumble of holly and ribbons were moved aside, coats and gloves were dispensed with, and the tea table was laden with a culinary bounty. And they were soon seated to the generous repast of tea and cake and sandwiches and more cake and some scones, too, with strawberry jam and cream. All of which would have been much to the delight of Mrs. Treadwell had she been there but she wasn't and that was that and she was the less for it.

At length, after Sir George described the building of the glasshouse and the problems the glazier was currently having with that one pane up there—See it just there?—it dripped something terrible, and oh, how he admired Her Ladyship's rose garden, but Heavens, would never trade his own for all the world, and do you prefer chicken or cow, for roses, that is... oh, more cake? Well, eventually, Sir George asked, "So, what brings you both here today? And on such a day as this. Frightful. I can't recall it ever being quite this...."

"Christmas trees," said Emily as quick as she could.

"Christmas trees?" exclaimed Sir George in astonishment.

"Her Ladyship has ordered a Christmas tree," said Mr. Reed.

"Why on earth would she do something like that?" continued Sir George.

Emily explained how the Coburgs were coming, and Mr. Reed explained how he had sent George Tuttle's boy and Young Mr. Phelps to find a tree.

To which, Emily interrupted with, "They were endeavoring to cut down Eliza Throckmorton's yew!"

"Oh dear," said Sir George with subdued decorum, "*Taxus baccata*." Seeing Mr. Reed's confusion, he continued, "This tall, that wide. Really a lovely specimen." He shook his head. "I imagine that caused quite a stir. Young Mr. Phelps wouldn't know a steer from a milch cow. And as for that Tuttle boy... More tea?"

Emily held out her cup. "The thing is," she said as Sir George poured, "we know next to nothing about these Christmas trees."

"Not much worth knowing," replied Sir George, "A quaint custom, I'm sure, but so much bother."

As I am well-aware, thought Emily, but she said instead, "Yes, but I recall you had a book."

"Oh, most certainly," exclaimed Sir George with a joyful smile, "I have a book on practically everything."

"This was a book on holy days in foreign lands." She tried to recall the book in her mind. Red Moroccan leather, she thought, or maybe green? "It was illustrated." That she remembered quite clearly, with delicately painted engravings.

"Oh, yes. I think I know the one." Sir George hopped up and hurried from the glasshouse.

In the gentleman's wake, Mr. Reed, taking another sandwich, said, "He's a bit of a talker, isn't he?"

"You must forgive him," said Emily, "He spends his days here alone, with his books and his plants, with no one but the servants and his gardeners for companionship. And while they are all very good people...."

"They're only servants?"

"No. They have duties for which they are well-paid. They can ill-afford to sit around chatting with Sir George while things pile up."

"You're right, of course," said Mr. Reed, "and I imagine while his gardeners can discuss botany with him at great length, no one in this house can converse the minutiae of books with him."

Minutiae? It wasn't a word she expected from the mouth of a land steward.

"They hardly have time to read for their own pleasure or enlightenment," he continued, "let alone to amuse Sir George with their literary erudition."

"Nor should they," said Emily, the idea disturbing her for some reason. "It seems a kind of sacrilege—reading merely to satisfy another's pleasure." Although, she often read to Aunt Sophia and sometimes even her parents, but that was equally for her own pleasure as theirs.

"He must be lonely," said Mr. Reed, "with no one of his own...."

The door through to the house opened, the glass panes

rattling, and Sir George called out, "I found it." And he raised the heavy green tome for his visitors to see.

Standing before them like a minister in a pulpit before his congregation—or a madman on his box on Speaker's Corner—Sir George removed his gold-rimmed spectacles from his breast coat pocket and put them on. He opened the book and read aloud from the title page: *Curious Continental Customs Pertaining to High-Days, Holy-days, Ceremonies, and Celebrations, Complete in Three Volumes with 48 Illustrations and 9 Maps*. Compiled by The Right Hon. Thaddeus Fletcher Foyle, MP. Volume Two.

He looked up from the page. "Do you know this Foyle? Really, a remarkable fellow. Served as secretary to the Ambassador to Bavaria."

"Well, then," said Mr. Reed, "he should know what he's talking about when it comes to Christmas trees."

"Isn't Coburg right above Bavaria?" asked Emily.

Sir George paused in his flipping of pages and briefly glanced upward, as if considering the question, before replying, "Yes, I believe so. Although, I do have an atlas. A marvelous edition, with hand-painted...."

"No," interrupted Emily, "that won't be necessary. Pray, continue with Mr. Foyle's observations."

Sir George began flipping through the pages. "I don't see a mention of Coburg...."

"No matter. Bavaria shall suffice well enough."

He flipped through the book, occasionally licking his fingers to turn the pages, until he exclaimed, "Ah, yes. This is it!" He turned the book to Emily so she might see the illustration. "It is it, isn't it?"

"Yes, that's the one."

She hardly had a chance to even glance at the black and white engraving—not even one of the hand-painted prints—before Sir George turned it away to study it some more.

He shook his head and scrunched up his nose. "I don't know what kind of tree the artist intended, but it wasn't drawn from life, that's for certain." He shrugged. "Well, no species I've ever seen, at least. Gracious, I hadn't realized they hung them upside down from the ceiling."

"How's that?" asked Mr. Reed, leaning forward with more animation that he'd previously shown.

Sir George handed him the open book, and both Mr. Reed and Emily huddled together over the page to consider the image. It was a drawing of mediocre quality depicting a sad little tree, spindly and limp, hanging upside down.

"Oh, yes, upside down," said Sir George, taking up his seat again and pouring another cup of tea, "And then they display all manner of bows and trinkets and whatnot upon them, all with candles aflame. That doesn't seem too bright, if you ask me. Might as well just set the house alight while one's at it."

Mr. Reed turned to Emily, his brow furrowed as if struggling with some complex mathematical calculation. "I believe Her Ladyship wishes to display the Christmas tree in the hall. It must be thirty feet to the ceiling. It's not possible to hang a tree from that ceiling."

"Maybe the ballroom would be more suitable?" asked Emily.

Mr. Reed shrugged. "I can't see how we could hang a tree from *any* ceiling—unless it were a small tree and we hung it from a chandelier hook."

"Hardly what Her Ladyship intends to impress the

Coburgs. Perhaps we can forego that particular aspect of the tradition," suggested Emily.

"And display it upright? In the hall? Would that be acceptable?"

"It will have to be," said Emily, "Besides, Her Ladyship would undoubtedly prefer a large, impressive *upright* tree in the hall to some scrawny little thing hanging upside in the ballroom. Don't you agree, Sir George?"

"Oh, undoubtedly," he replied, "Undoubtedly."

Mr. Reed sat back and rubbed his chin. "Then what kind of tree do we need to *impress*?"

Sir George pointed at the book. "Clearly, it's some kind of fir."

"Is that the kind of tree we need?" asked Mr. Reed, "A fir?"

"Hmm, yes," replied Sir George. He seemed momentarily distracted, as if his mind were elsewhere—which was not uncommon when dealing with him. "Or maybe a spruce. Yes, a spruce might do as well."

Mr. Reed rose. "I should be on my way, then. So much to do." He turned to Sir George and said, "I'm sure to find a spruce or fir somewhere on the estate."

"Oh no," countered Sir George with a grave shake of his head, "there's nothing like that on His Lordship's lands. Four hundred years of careful mismanagement has seen to that. Oaks, beeches, chestnuts, poplars, sycamore, yes, but nothing like this on His Lordship's lands. You know, I'm related to His Lordship. My third cousin, twice removed, on my grandmother's side. You'd think that'd count for something, don't you? At least, when it comes to decisions regarding the garden. Someone would come seeking my advice. Oh...," he hesitated, "...but I suppose you are seeking my advice." And he laughed merrily at the realization.

Mr. Reed, for his part, sat back down with a heavy sigh. Emily thought he looked dejected.

"Don't trouble yourself, Mr. Reed," she said.

"Yes, Mr. Reed," said Sir George, "one of your neighbors will have exactly what we are looking for, have no doubt. We just need to figure out whom."

We? This was becoming an ever-growing venture.

Sir George, lost in thought, tapped his forefinger against his lips. "You know," he said after a moment, "I think I know where there might be the perfect tree. A lovely *Picea abies.*"

He hopped up again and hurried to the door leading into the house. Opening it, he motioned to his guests, "Come through, please," and disappeared into the darkened room.

Emily and Mr. Reed followed. From the bright, airy, green world of the glasshouse, they entered a dark, closed space, their eyes taking a moment to adjust. Emily knew what to expect, but it still delighted, while Mr. Reed audibly gasped at the sight before him.

Sir George's library.

A two-storey world of books, leather, and polished wood. A fire burned in the hearth, and there, next to the mantel, Sir George rang the bell.

Emily leaned close to Mr. Reed, pointed toward the door at the top of the spiral stairs, and whispered, "I'm told that doorway leads to his bedchamber." She nodded when Mr. Reed looked at her in amazement. "Oh, yes. He spends his days in the glass house and his evenings in here, and never has to venture too far if he doesn't want to."

"Does he ever loan his books?" asked Mr. Reed, like a

hungry man.

"He does. As many as you wish. But he makes you write your name in a ledger, and if you don't return the books, he will find you." She nodded again. "He took Mr. Hollander to court for failure to return Mr. Walpole's *Castle of Otranto*." This time, she shook her head. "Imagine. Having your name dragged through the courts over *Castle of Otranto*. It's not worth it."

"You didn't like *Castle of Otranto*?"

"Rubbish."

Sir George joined them. "Is she complaining about Walpole again?" He laughed. "Well, it was an excellent edition. Worth six shillings, if not more."

"I refer to the contents," said Emily, "not the quality of the binding or printing."

"I shall never recover its loss," continued Sir George.

Mr. Reed shook his head. "You don't like Walpole?" he asked Emily.

"I think it gave her nightmares." Sir George smiled.

"It did no such thing. It was preposterous, that's all."

"Then who do you recommend?" asked Mr. Reed of her, "Mrs. Radcliff, perhaps?"

Sir George let out a laugh, while Emily said, "No, no. Of course not. More Gothic drivel."

"She prefers this Scott fellow," supplied Sir George, "and that lady authoress."

"Oh, yes," said Emily, "she is very good. Have you read...?"

McCall the butler appeared at the library door. "Sir?"

Sir George raised his forefinger to the butler and turned back to Mr. Reed. "Now then," he asked, "Is there room for three in that marvelous contraption of yours?"

"Three?" exclaimed Emily, realizing Sir George intended for her to accompany them in this ongoing quest for a Christmas tree. "But I need to get back to Aunt Sophia. I've already missed luncheon, and she will be worried."

"We'll send a note." Sir George motioned McCall further in the room as he continued speaking to Emily. "Your aunt will understand."

Emily shook her head. "Sir George...."

"Have no fear," Sir George assured her, "A note will satisfy her more than anything. She can reread it each time she wonders where you are and will be reassured each time. Tell her you will be home for dinner."

Clearly, Emily thought, Sir George had his mind set, and without further debate, she asked, "And where, exactly, are we *three* going?"

"Widow Talbot's," replied Sir George, "Assuming there is room for three in His Lordship's sleigh." He turned to Mr. Reed, raised his eyebrows, and cocked his head to one side in a querying manner.

"Yes," said Mr. Reed, "Yes, of course. Although, it might be a tight squeeze."

Oh, wonderful! All three of us crushed up together in the sleigh. Emily hoped this was worth it. She doubted it, but not helping would be even worse.

"Splendid!" cried Sir George, "McCall, my coat. We're going to visit the Widow Talbot. And tell Thomas he's doddled long enough. The others will help him when they get back, but those boughs of holly need to be finished." Sir George turned back to his guests and gestured toward the library table. "Pen and paper, Miss Haywood." He smiled, vaguely reminding Emily of the proverbial cat. "I have oranges to pick."

With that, Emily and Mr. Reed found themselves left alone in the library.

"Is he usually like that?" asked Mr. Reed.

"No," replied Emily, taking up a pen, "Well, yes, but today, he seems... more so."

"More so?"

It was bizarre, Sir George's behavior. And then it dawned on her in a flash. "Oh, my." She couldn't help but smile at the mere idea of the gentleman and....

"What are you smiling about?" asked Mr. Reed.

"Sir George," she said, "Widow Talbot. She put off her mourning at Michaelmas."

"What? You mean he..." A grin broke out across his face. "At his age?"

"There is nothing wrong with his age!" protested Emily, "Any respectable lady would be a fool not to accept his suit if he came a-calling." She raised her eyebrows. "He does come with this library."

She burst out laughing. To her relief, Mr. Reed joined in.

"Ah, if only we all had such a library to commend us," he said.

With that, an uneasy silence fell between them. Emily wrote her note informing Aunt Sophia that she was going to see Widow Talbot and would arrive home in time for dinner.

Sir George returned to the library, all smiles, with a basket of oranges for the Widow Talbot. A few minutes more, and Emily found herself, once again, bundled up against the cold and racing down the road in the sleigh. But this time, she was wedged between Mr. Reed and Sir George, with barely enough room to breathe, her feet propped up on the coil of rope. It seemed colder, too, the snow falling heavier than before, and all three shared the blanket. But Sir George was laughing and talking away, telling of this house and that tree and *Oh, was that Young Mrs. Phelps?* He waved his hat. *How Young Mr. Phelps ended up with such a bright wife, I'll never know.*

It certainly wasn't for his library, thought Emily, biting back a laugh. For a moment, she thought she heard Mr. Reed laugh. But surely not. She must have been mistaken.

ೞೞ

The Widow Talbot—sometimes known as Mrs. Talbot; sadly, there was no one left alive who called her by her Christian name but she signed documents as *A. Talbot*—lived several miles north of the village on extensive lands inherited from her father and her husband. She had numerous tenants and a lucrative flouring mill.

All of this, Mr. Reed and Emily learned from Sir George on their short journey. It left no doubt in either of their minds as to why Sir George would wish to court such a lady. For given their ages—Widow Talbot being a grandmother—it surely could not be for warmth of affection, or, dare one say it, love. As all and sundry knew, *old* people were past such frivolities and only acted with reason in matters... until, of course, senility set in.

The ancient Tudor manor with its exposed beams stood just beyond the mill on an acreage of leveled land above the mill pond, which was more aptly a lake, complete with a small island and a Grecian folly that few ever visited.

It just so happened on that day as the party in the sleigh came up the drive, a calamity befell the Talbot family. Emily saw it occur, while the two men only recognized the danger when she cried out.

There was nothing unusual in seeing boys sledging down a snow covered hill—albeit on their grandmother's silver tea tray. And, in keeping with boys of all ages, Frederick, Geoffrey, and James Talbot had mounded up the snow in one particular spot half way down their hill so that, if they hit it just right on the silver tea tray, they would leap into the air and fly for a moment. It didn't matter that their mother had told them not to. It didn't matter that their grandmother had told them not to. It didn't matter that they knew they could break their necks while doing so—or worse, put an eye out. No. It was fun. And nothing anyone said would stop them.

Unfortunately, for the littlest Talbot boy, James…, he hit the mound of snow wrong. Instead of landing to the left and sliding down to the level tree-lined embankment, he flew off to the right.

Down he went.

Toward the ice encrusted lake.

He screamed.

His brothers screamed.

Emily screamed.

The older boys ran after their brother, shouting all the way. James endeavored to stop, a futile effort, his hands finding no purchase in the soft snow.

Mr. Reed managed to pull the sleigh to a stop. Emily did not wait but practically bounded over Sir George in her effort to get to the boys.

James hurdled onto the ice and slid some distance until, with a sickening crack, the ice broke and the boy fell through with a scream and a desperate splash.

"Get the rope," shouted Emily as she rushed down the hill.

James buoyed up, struggling to climb out of the water and onto the ice, only for the ice to crack and break further. The more he moved, the more the ice broke up, until it was nothing more than a watery stew of ice. Boys who grew up next to mill ponds learned to swim, and thankfully, such was the case with James. No, he wouldn't drown because he couldn't swim. He would drown because of the extreme cold as his body went numb. But it would take a couple of minutes, perhaps giving them enough time to reach him.

As Emily reached the frozen water's edge, Frederick Talbot, all of nine years, moved to head out onto the ice to save his younger brother. Emily pulled him back.

"No, I'll go," she said, pulling off her coat and muffler. And then she shouted, "Hold on, James. We're coming."

Mr. Reed arrived with the rope, Sir George following close behind.

"What are you doing?" asked Mr. Reed as he removed his own coat. "I'll go."

"No. I will go." She knew, regardless of whom went for the boy, people rarely survived icy water. Even rescuers succumbed to frigid death. Getting to the boy was one problem. Getting back was another. Anyone who managed to swim out to him would never make it back. The boy had one chance, and she didn't have time to stand there and argue with the two men who thought they knew better.

"Tie the rope around me," she continued, "and I'll swim out...."

"I can't let you do that."

There wasn't time for this. Already wrapping the rope around her torso under her arms and tying it with a sailor's knot as her brother had taught her, she stared up at Mr. Reed and as emphatically as she could muster, said, "*You* can pull us back. I can't. *You* can get us to the house. I can't. Even with Sir George's help. If you go out there, someone dies, probably both of you. No more discussion."

She didn't give him a chance to protest further. She was already walking out onto the ice, the rope trailing behind her. Knowing that she needed to keep her weight evenly distributed—although, it'd do little good for long—she quickly got down on her stomach and began to crawl across the ice. However, it little resembled crawling; more like slipping and sliding, pushing and attempting to grip.

Until an elbow broke through the ice.

A moment later, her gloved hand went right through into the frigid water. Her chin hit the ice, hard and painful. And then, as she knew it would, the ice gave way and she went under to a barrage of freezing daggers.

She came up immediately, gasping for air, and for the briefest heartbeat—brief indeed giving its pounding—she felt the line tighten, only to slacken. She spotted James, still churning about, but not for long. She didn't have long either.

"James," she called out to the boy, "swim toward me." If he could meet her even part way, it might make all the difference.

Pushing against the ice, Emily swam, breaking the ice further as she went.

But James was losing his end of the struggle. His movements slowed, his face pale, his lips blue. And just as he sank beneath the water, Emily reached out and grabbed his jacket. Her fingers hardly worked, but she managed to drag him into her arms.

"I've got you, James. I've got you."

She pulled him even closer, draping his arms about her neck. Drawing on her remaining strength, she kicked her legs and, with some effort, floated onto her back, cradling James atop her.

To her surprise, she didn't have to call out, as she expected. Before she even opened her mouth, she felt a gentle tug, and then she was moving slowly through the slushy wash, until she butted against the more solid ice. She closed her eyes. She couldn't help it. The next thing she knew she was sliding over the surface, faster now.

She realized James no longer lay atop her, hands now lifting his limp, seemingly lifeless body.

"He's breathing," someone cried out. Sir George, she thought. There were screams—women—and shouts. Someone was crying. A child. More than one child. Not James. She opened her eyes and saw Sir George carrying James, rushing with him toward the house, up the snowy slope.

Someone carried her as well. Her cheek rested against a neckcloth.

Mr. Reed.

He smelled like... like soap made with lavender.

He looked so serious, she thought. His jaw tight with... anger? Fear? Determination, she decided. With relief. She didn't have to worry anymore.

Of course, the silver tea tray now rested at the bottom of the lake. Oh, well. At least no one would blame her for that one. And she closed her eyes again.

80C8

When Emily next opened her eyes, Mr. Reed was carrying her through the kitchen, Widow Talbot leading the way to a sitting room. So many people crowded about, rushed about—the Talbot's footman, the Talbot's maid, the Talbot's housekeeper, Widow Talbot, Young Mrs. Talbot, even younger Miss Talbot, Frederick and Geoffrey and their sisters, everyone shouting, orders given for this or that—someone called for the surgeon—and there was Sir George, holding poor James as they stripped the boy of all his wet clothing before a blazing fire. Emily could see his eyes struggle to open, and he attempted to look around, probably confused by all the fuss, only to slip back into sleep or unconsciousness, his head lolling back.

She found herself seated before the fire and slumped in a settle. Someone was pulling off her glove. Mr. Reed, she realized. Other hands tugged at her. Where was her muffler? She couldn't remember taking it off. It must've ended up in the lake. With the silver tea tray. Why did she keep thinking of the silver tea tray? Poor James would certainly never hear the end of that one.

Young Mrs. Talbot scolded her older sons, Frederick and Geoffrey, one of them crying, for sledging on that particular hill when she told them not to for this very reason. Widow Talbot kept saying *Boys will be boys* and *It's not as bad as all that*, to which Young Mrs. Talbot pursed her lips and clinched her jaw and somehow held her tongue although she clearly wished otherwise. Emily almost laughed; perhaps Sir George would find success in his pursuit of Widow Talbot.

Towels and blankets and tubs were all carried in, followed by steaming cans of water. Poor James, with his fussing mother and pacifying grandmother and crying brothers hovering, found himself thoroughly dunked in a laundry tub and left to soak in hot water.

Emily's half-boots were gone—*Did Mr. Reed do that or the housekeeper?*—and she sat in her soaked chemise with her frock bunched around her hips. Someone was pulling her up—*Surely not Mr. Reed?*—and another pair of hands pealed the half-frozen garment down to mound at her feet.

"No, no," said Mr. Reed to someone, "Leave it." And he swept her up and lowered her down, still in her chemise, into a copper tub. "Is that better?" he asked her.

Emily could only nod as she sank down, hot water lapping at her chattering chin.

Mr. Reed nodded as well, letting out a satisfied sigh of relief, and he gave her a small smile. But then it faded. Lines creased his brow and he turned away.

"All right, all right," he said to the chaos about him, "Yes, now then, let's clear out." And he herded the others—the maid, the footman, the two no longer crying boys, Sir George, even Widow Talbot—out of the room, leaving poor James and Emily with Young Mrs. Talbot and the housekeeper.

෨෬

Sir George and Mr. Lachlan Reed were not provided with so fine a room as the housekeeper's sitting room. They were led to the scullery. Of course, they were merely wet from carrying the invalids to the house, and much of that was only coat deep. Still, Widow Talbot insisted they partially undress—each layer of clothing examined for the least trace of dampness—and she brought them muslin shirts belonging to her late husband.

With blankets about them, they settled before the kitchen fire to warm up from the day's turmoil with mugs of mulled cider. Two gentlemen—well, one gentleman, and, despite whatever good qualities Lachlan might possess, he did not qualify as a gentleman—in their shirtsleeves was not appropriate attire for the drawing room.

The Talbot's cook seemed to take little notice of their presence in her domain. She busied about, ignoring them, and eventually presented them with bowls of beef stew with hunks of crusty brown bread which was leftover from the Talbot family luncheon and would serve as dinner for the servants.

A line of laundry was strung up before the fire on which dried their coats and their jackets and their shirts and neckcloths, along with all of poor James's clothing and Miss Haywood's coat and muffler—retrieved from where she had discarded them by the lake—and her frock. After a while, the housekeeper added Miss Haywood's stockings to the line as well. Yes, it was a very long line with all that—two lines, really, with one higher up and one lower down—but it was a large fireplace, one of those ancient varieties found in half-timbered Tudor houses with a Medieval core. And it was a large kitchen, perhaps even once serving as a kind of a hall in some bygone forgotten time.

Lachlan sat staring at Miss Haywood's white stockings. Really, the housekeeper shouldn't have put them there. Such things were more appropriate for the scullery. But there they were, and of course, Lachlan's eyes were naturally drawn to them and the vision of them wet and clinging to Miss Haywood in her nearly transparent chemise.

Sir George, on the other hand, sat uncommonly quiet. And Lachlan, to break the silence between them, asked the foremost thought—well, second most thought—in his head.

"Why isn't she married?" asked Lachlan, "Miss Haywood?"

Sir George's face brightened. "Well. Yes. That." But then he pursed his lips, furrowed his brow, and said, "Let us say she suffered a tragedy. In her youth."

"Oh?"

Sir George cocked his head to one side and seemed to prevaricate. "Not so much a tragedy but a scandal, which might as well have been a tragedy for Miss Haywood for all the good it did her." He leaned forward as if to impart a great secret and whispered, "Her younger sister ran off to Gretna Green." He sat back and nearly shouted, "With a midshipman! Ha!"

Lachlan wondered which part was the tragedy... or the scandal. The Gretna Green part? Or the midshipman part?

"Not even a lieutenant!"

At least that answered one question.

"Reverend Haywood barely kept his position as the village vicar," continued Sir George, "and that primarily because His Lordship would not allow his removal. Still the curate gave the sermons for several weeks. Have you heard him speak? A nice enough fellow, to be sure, but the man cannot string two words together when he gets before the congregation. Better off as a clerk, if you ask me. For a while there, I feared Reverend Haywood would not be coming back—he gives very short sermons, you know. None of this fire and brimstone nonsense. Except on rare occasions, like when the Cunningham boys tied Mrs. Williamson's line of laundry to the tail of a pig and chased it down the lane and right through Mrs. Haywood's roses." Sir George laughed at the memory.

"What happened?"

"Oh, well, after Mrs. Williamson got done with them and Mr. Cunningham got done with them, they still had to endure Reverend Haywood's trial by fire sermon…."

"No, I mean Miss Haywood. What happened with her?"

"Oh. Right. Yes. Well, I feared the parishioners might never let Reverend Haywood back, but it soon became apparent that they blamed Miss Haywood for the entire incident."

"Miss Haywood?!" How was that even possible?

"Yes, Miss Haywood!" continued Sir George, "She was responsible for her sister, Miss Katherine, you see." He laid aside his empty bowl and poured another mug of mulled cider from the jug left heating on the hearth. After a careful sip, he continued his tale. "The Reverend and Mrs. Haywood had gone to London. Some church matter or other. Miss Haywood, being the eldest and over twenty-one, as I recall, was left in charge of the house. When who should come home on a leave of absence but their brother, young Lieutenant Haywood, with his new friend, the infamous *midshipman*."

Lord, preserve us!

"A fortnight later," continued Sir George, "Middle of the night. Miss Katherine and the midshipman take Reverend Haywood's gig, and off they go to Gretna Green—a three-day trip in the best of weather." He raised his eyebrows. Lachlan understood. Where did the lovers spend those nights prior to their marriage? "Thankfully, the chit had the presence of mind to leave a note stating their intentions. Otherwise, half the village and every constable between here and the Arctic would have been out searching for her, I can tell you."

Sir George took another cautious sip of the mulled cider

before resuming. "Everyone involved or even remotely connected to the lovers would have been ruined, but His Lordship intervened. The Reverend kept his position. The midshipman did not lose his commission, as we all expected. Even the Haywood boys managed to navigate through the scandal unscathed without any harm to their careers."

"How many Haywood brothers are there?"

"Five. No, six. I always forget about Matthew. Ginger. Spitting image of his father, otherwise there'd be talk about that ginger. He's in Lincoln's Inn these days. A barrister. All the rest serve in the royal navy." He shook his head. "Not a clergyman in the bunch. Mrs. Haywood came from a navy family." Then his face brightened. "And what of the midshipman, you may ask." Sir George gave a friendly tap on Mr. Reed's shoulder. "Captain now. Ship of the line, no less."

"You jest?"

"I kid you not. And Miss Katherine just delivered their sixth child. That's where Reverend and Mrs. Haywood are now. Portsmouth to see to the Christening of the new babe. Oh, yes, the midshipman has done quite well for himself."

Lachlan heard the sardonic edge in the comment. Yes, the midshipman had done well, but what about Miss Haywood?

"But what does Miss Haywood have to do with this?" asked Lachlan.

Sir George shrugged. "After something like that, it's not as if a respectable gentleman would come a-calling, now is it? Miss Haywood may be a very decent sort, but who's going to trust her with their daughters, given all that's happened? She showed bad judgment, letting those two fall in love under that roof while charged with her sister's care, even if it turned out all right in the end."

This was absurd. "And how many years ago was this?"

"Oh," pondered Sir George, "Twelve, fifteen years ago. Give or take."

"That's terrible!" proclaimed Lachlan. He glanced around, aware of how loud this voice echoed in the kitchen, and lowered his voice. "Miss Haywood had nothing to do with the actions of her sister and *she* is made to suffer for it?"

"Yes. Atrocious, isn't it?" Sir George shrugged again. "There was some talk of her going to London to stay with a family friend—she might have found a husband that way. But nothing came of it. Besides, someone has to stay home and take care of Old Mrs. Edmondson, don't they?"

കൈൗ

Emily must have fallen asleep there in the tub, at least for a short while. She awoke to find the village surgeon taking her pulse. A screen had been brought in to provide her with some degree of privacy, and beyond it, she could hear poor James protesting *But I don't want to go to bed, I'm all right. Really, I am!*

The surgeon noticed she was awake. He smiled and asked her to wiggle her toes. When she did so with ease, he pronounced her none the worse for wear and ordered she eat a good meal, preferably with some strong red wine and beef.

When he left, the housekeeper returned, bringing several clean articles of clothing. Alone now, she assisted Emily out of the bath and helped peel the wet chemise from her skin. After drying with a towel, Emily slipped into a borrowed chemise and dressing gown, a pair of slippers much too large for her feet, and then wrapped herself in a blanket.

Despite having just awakened—presumably—she felt sleepy. But most of all, she was incredibly hungry.

She shuffled out into the kitchen in the hope of finding one of the servants. To her surprise, she discovered Mr. Reed and Sir George sitting before the fire, while the Talbot's cook busied about. Both men rose at the sight of her. She could well imagine how she looked, in over large slippers and a borrowed dressing gown—hardly appropriate attire, but at this point, it hardly mattered. *Oh, good Lord!* Her hair! She hadn't given it a single thought. She quickly reached up and felt the side of her head... and realized someone, in the midst of everything, had plaited it into a single, damp braid. With that knowledge, she moved further into the room and close to the fire.

Mr. Reed retrieved another chair for her. "How do you feel?"

"Famished," she replied, sitting down. She wanted to add *tired*, as well, but kept that to herself.

"It's because of the cold," said Sir George.

"And the swimming," added Mr. Reed as both men resumed their seats.

It occurred to her that only two hundred years before, that little trick might have sent her to the stake. She nearly said as much, only to notice all her undergarments spread out before her on a line to dry, including her chemise and stockings! Before the two men! How mortifying!

But she couldn't very well say anything.

Thankfully, a distracting cup of steaming tea appeared before her nose as if from nowhere—held by the Talbot's cook, of course. That drove all thoughts of embarrassing undergarments from Emily's head, and she accepted the cup with deep gratitude.

"How about some stew?" offered the Talbot's cook with an eager smile.

"Oh, yes, that would be wonderful," replied Emily, cradling the warm cup of tea and breathing in its inviting aroma.

The fire popped, but otherwise, they sat in silence for a long while, all seemingly deep in thought as the Talbot's cook readied some beef stew for Emily... when Sir George rose abruptly and nearly shouted.

"My oranges!"

In all the excitement, they had nearly forgotten their reason—perhaps *reasons* was the more accurate word—for visiting Widow Talbot: their search for a Christmas tree.

"Has anyone seen them?" continued Sir George, "Surely they weren't left in the sleigh?"

That was the last time Emily had seen the oranges, but she assumed, quite naturally, that the Talbot's groom had taken care of the horse and sleigh and anything left with them.

"Oh," said the Talbot's cook, as she handed Emily a bowl of beef stew with crusty bread, "I think they're in the hall." She pointed in that direction. Without another word, she headed that way, and Sir George, blanket about him and in his stocking feet, followed her, leaving Emily and Mr. Reed alone by the fire.

"Do you think he has a chance?" asked Mr. Reed.

"Ah. You noticed that too." Emily smiled. And then shrugged. "A lady in her position has no need to remarry. With sons and grandsons aplenty, she has no need of a gentleman's protection." She took her first bite of the overcooked beef and the underseasoned gravy, but it didn't matter. It satisfied the rumbling in her stomach.

"There are other reasons to marry," Mr. Reed pointed out, "Companionship. Common purpose. Affinity. Love."

"True."

A commotion somewhere in the house interrupted them, thumping footsteps and then more overhead, all followed by the sound of poor James complaining of his treatment yet again.

But I don't need any medicine!

Emily agreed. He needed sustenance and a day to play in the nursery with his soldiers and hobby horse.

"I do hope he will be all right," she said.

"He will," replied Mr. Reed, "and he'll have a thrilling story to tell his grandchildren—of flying through the air and crashing through the ice and being rescued by the vicar's daughter."

The vicar's daughter. Yes, that was it. *She* had gone into the water for the boy while two equally capable men had stood by on shore, all on her insistence.

"Are you angry?" she asked.

Taken aback, he replied, "No. Why would I be?"

"Because I usurped your male prerogative of being the hero."

He stared at her, wide eyed.

Oh, dear. Now, she had really offended him.

But then he burst out laughing.

"I'll survive," he assured her, and then, calm once again, said, "And you were right. It was easy to pull you back. Although, I had to be careful not to pull too fast; I didn't know how good a grip you had on the boy."

He poured some more mulled cider for himself, offering some to Emily as well—she declined—and then he asked, "How did you know?"

"Know what?"

"How to save the boy? How did you know that, if I went in after him, you and Sir George, no matter how capable he might be, probably wouldn't be able to get us out of the water and to the house before it was too late?"

"I am very well read."

He raised a single eyebrow. She could not get away with such an answer, even if it were fairly accurate.

"I have six younger brothers," she said instead, "and this was not the first time I've had to pull a boy out of a questionable body of water—although, it was never frozen water before now."

"And you can swim!"

"Five of my brothers are in the navy," she said, "Do you have any idea how many sailors drown simply because they don't know how to swim?"

Mr. Reed shook his head.

"Our father wouldn't let any of them enlist without first knowing how to swim," she continued, "and I made sure they knew how."

"Well, for what it's worth," said Mr. Reed, "I am thoroughly impressed. And grateful you had the presence of mind to reason it all out before I jumped in without any plan for getting out of the water."

Emily sat silent, too stunned to respond.

"I've embarrassed you," said Mr. Reed, "Well, at least the color has returned to your cheeks."

She shook her head. She felt nothing but shame.

"I didn't want to come," she said, "I didn't want to help. With finding this Christmas tree. I wanted to stay home. I have enough problems in our own household without dealing with the insecurities of half the village."

"Then why did you come?" he asked, calmly and sounding truly curious, "Why seek me out?"

"The Coburgs are coming." She spoke with too much animation. "This is the biggest thing to happen in the village since... since..." She couldn't think of a great thing that'd happened in the village. True, Charles II dallied with Goody Fletcher in the porter's Lodge at the Hall in 1679, but that wasn't spoken of in mixed company. And Henry VIII had the monastery destroyed, but technically, that wasn't in the village. "...since Edward IV marched through on his way to Tewksbury."

"Ah, well. Tewksbury," said Mr. Reed, "very exciting, that."

She suspected he would've been more impressed—or at least entertained—by the Charles II and Goody Fletcher story, especially as one of Goody's fourteen children looked nothing like Mister Fletcher.

"Yes, well, the Coburgs are coming," continued Emily, "and it will have an impact on the village, even if it is only superficial and inconsequential to the rest of the world. People here think it important. The room where they stay will be renamed the Coburg Room, and a hundred years from now, the housekeeper will be guiding curious visitors through the Hall and saying 'This is the bed where Queen Charlotte slept during her visit with the Prince Consort in 1816.' The Hanovers will be long gone, and the country will be ruled by the House of Saxe-Coburg-Something-or-Other." Really, she needed to find out the name of this family, especially since they would be the future monarchs of the land.

"Yes, I know all that," replied Mr. Reed, "but why did you come find me? Why are you searching for this Christmas tree? You could have just let Young Mr. Phelps and George Tuttle's boy cut down Eliza Throckmorton's yew and been done with it."

"Been done with it?" Emily nearly shrieked. "I couldn't very well do that. For one thing, that yew did not belong to them or to His Lordship. For another, the villagers were a pitchfork away from becoming a mob."

"And you put a stop to that?"

"Well, we can't have a mob burning the pope or the Prince Regent in effigy when the Coburgs arrive, now can we?"

"No, of course not," replied Mr. Reed, "but you have other things to do. You have tried to return home several times, I've noticed, always to be easily dissuaded. Couldn't you send someone else to deal with this matter?"

"No," she replied after a long pause. Then quietly, she added, "I knew if something went wrong, I would be blamed." She took a deep breath. "So, you see, my motives have nothing to do with saving the village or Her Ladyship from embarrassment. It was entirely selfish on my part."

"Because of what happened with your sister?"

"Ah, yes. Even the *new* man has heard the tale."

He reached out and took her hand. "And you think I am doing this for altruistic reasons? I have no desire to be dismissed." He gave her a small smile. "If not for your supposed selfishness, that boy would be dead. And there was nothing selfish about going in after him. You did what needed to be done. Just like with the Christmas tree."

Before she had a chance to reply, Sir George returned to the kitchen with Widow Talbot carrying his basket of oranges in her arms. They were laughing together. The oldest Talbot grandson, Frederick Talbot, trailed along behind them.

Upon spotting Emily and Mr. Reed in her kitchen, Widow Talbot reacted as if seeing them for the first time. She held out the basket of oranges.

"Did you see the beautiful oranges Sir George brought me?" she said, more proclamation than question as they rose. "Of course, you did. You came with him." She laughed, setting the basket down on the kitchen table. She had always been a beautiful woman, and even now, with grey hair hiding faint traces of once ginger locks, she was still considered handsome. It was easy to see why Sir George wished to pursue her.

"Whenever you have need of oranges," said Sir George to her, "please, do not hesitate. I will happily bring you a basket myself. It's no trouble at all."

As Sir George and Widow Talbot continued their flirtation, Frederick Talbot surreptitiously stole an orange from the basket. He tucked it into his pocket before stealing another one.

Emily cleared her throat and asked, "The Christmas tree?"

For a moment, Sir George looked confused. Then recognition covered his face and he said, "Oh. Oh, yes. The Christmas tree."

But Emily had a strange suspicion nudging at the edge of her mind. Something wasn't right.

Sir George turned to Widow Talbot and said, "That lovely *Picea abies* you have just by the stables." When Widow Talbot looked at him askance, he corrected himself. "The Norway Spruce."

Still looking quite confused, Widow Talbot shook her head.

"Fifteen, twenty feet high," continued Sir George, "Her Ladyship needs it."

Understanding flashed over Widow Talbot's face. "No, no. It came down in the storm of year six. Remember? Nearly fell on the stables."

"Oh, what a shame!"

Yes, wasn't it just.

"Well," continued Sir George, "while our endeavor has been thwarted, at least it wasn't a trip in vain."

"No, no," said Widow Talbot, "indeed not. You must stay for dinner."

Before anyone could accept or decline the invitation, Frederick Talbot piped up. "What do you need a tree for?"

His grandmother tried to shoo him away—*seen, not heard*, that sort of thing—but Sir George, ever eager to chat, explained about the Coburgs coming to the Hall, that Her Ladyship had ordered a Christmas tree, and that they were tasked to find a suitable specimen.

"Oh," said the boy as if learning all the secrets of life, "We have lots of trees."

"Well, we need a coniferous tree," said Sir George, "About fifteen feet tall. Or more."

"A tree that eats meat?" cried the boy with an odd mix of

fascination and horror.

Widow Talbot shook her head, fear in her eyes. "I don't like the sound of that."

Sir George smiled with amusement. "Coniferous, not carnivorous. An evergreen."

The boy looked disappointed with this new-found knowledge. His grandmother, however, breathed a great sigh of relief.

Sir George, for his part, slapped his hands together and said, "Well, then, my boy, show us some of your trees."

Inwardly, Emily shuddered. She had spent enough time on this venture. And while she was grateful she happened to be present when the crisis came, she now needed to be home. Aunt Sophia waited for her. The snow continued to fall outside, light and gentle. The hour grew late, and on these darkest days of winter, twilight would be upon them soon enough.

But she didn't need to say a word.

Mr. Reed spoke up. "I fear we have taken Miss Haywood away from her aunt for too long already. She did promise to be home for dinner."

"Oh, Miss Haywood," said Sir George, "I completely forgot. Do forgive me."

Emily gave him a polite smile and nod.

"So I will take her home," continued Mr. Reed, "and we can continue this effort tomorrow when the light isn't fading."

"Of course, of course," said Sir George. He turned to Widow Talbot and said, "If you could spare me a horse this evening, I would very much like to accept your invitation to dinner."

Widow Talbot beamed at the words, and while their backs were turned, Emily quietly gathered her clothes from the impromptu line. As her undergarments were still quite soaked, she left them; she could send for them tomorrow. The frock was dry, as well as her half-boots, which surprised her. She wondered how long she'd sat—and slept—in that warm bath. Her coat and muffler waited on a peg for her.

She slipped back into the housekeeper's sitting room and dressed behind the screen, her clothes smelling of wood smoke from the kitchen fire. The housekeeper kindly loaned her a pair of stockings, and when no trace of Emily's gloves could be found, Widow Talbot lent her a muff.

By the time Emily emerged from the sitting room and back into the kitchen, Mr. Reed was ready with the horse and sleigh. Goodbyes were said, along with sincere words of gratitude, and once again, Emily found herself beside Mr. Reed in the sleigh, rushing down the snow-covered road.

They had travelled on a circuitous route from the home farm to Sir George's house to the Widow Talbot's farm. As a result, Emily pointed out, the quickest way back to the village lay in the opposite direction from whence they had arrived at the farm. Mr. Reed, being new to the district, followed her suggestion without question.

Somewhere, behind grey banks of snow clouds on the horizon, the sun was setting. The snow had stopped, the sky above clear, but those clouds promised more to come. It felt colder too, but that might have been the air rushing past as they sped down the road. Emily, with her hands clutched together inside the muff, snuggled down under the lap blanket and, unintentionally, closer to Mr. Reed.

"Do you think that was his plan all along?" asked Mr.

Reed, "Sir George, I mean. That he knew the tree was gone but wanted an excuse to call upon the Widow Talbot?"

"With us acting as chaperones?" added Emily. "Yes. I do think he deceived us." And I thank God he did, she thought to herself. Otherwise poor James Talbot would be dead. The mere idea saddened her, despite her actions preventing it that afternoon. So she said, "But you'll return tomorrow to find a tree."

"Truth be told," he said, "even if we did find a tree tomorrow, there's not enough time to cut it down, haul in to the Hall, and decorate it before Christmas. And that's after we figure out how to display it—upside down, right side up, and with what?" He shook his head. "I fear Her Ladyship will be disappointed with our efforts." He sounded worried.

Emily was reticent to query further regarding his private affairs, but she pressed on. "Are you really concerned about being dismissed?"

"I do not believe His Lordship would dismiss me," said Mr. Reed, "but I am unacquainted with Her Ladyship. How much sway does she hold over her husband?"

"Little to none," replied Emily with no need for much consideration of the matter, "If that. I shouldn't worry about His Lordship dismissing you based on Her Ladyship's word. He's more likely to do the exact opposite of what she suggests."

"Are they not on friendly terms?"

"I believe they've come to a mutual understanding; one will never be in the same location as the other except by royal decree."

"Really?"

"A *ton* marriage. Sad. But there it is." The greying world

slid past them, and after a silent moment, Emily asked, "So you were acquainted with His Lordship before coming here?"

"I oversaw his estate in Surrey. Before that, I worked on a neighboring estate."

And that was the end of conversation... at least so far as that particular subject went. She didn't mind. It made for a nice change from her neighbors.

Another thought kept coming back to her regarding the afternoon's events. It was disconcerting enough to contemplate what might have happened had she not gone to Widow Talbot's that day, if she had insisted on staying home and not involving herself in the villagers' concerns over the Christmas tree. Add to that, though, an unshakable trust she placed in Mr. Reed as they stood there by the lake. Where it came from, she couldn't say, but she had known, without reservation, that he would pull her from that icy grave. If it had just been her and Sir George or Old Mr. Phelps or Young Mr. Phelps, for that matter, she doubted she would've entered that water. She would have been too afraid. And poor James would've died.

But for Mr. Reed.

She turned and looked at him, at his profile against the diminishing day. "Thank you," she said, "Thank you for pulling us... pulling me out of the water."

He looked over at her and replied, "Anytime you decide to go for a swim in a frozen lake, I am at your service."

They lapsed into silence again, the runners swooshing beneath them through the drifting snow. Emily sank deeper down beneath the lap rug and enjoyed the ride.

After a moment, she realized where they were. It had been some years since she had come down this particular road across His Lordship's lands. She had forgotten how close it went by the Hall, but there she saw the porter's lodge by the gates, and in the distance, the Hall itself, lights blazing as the servants, no doubt, prepared for the Coburgs.

And then she saw it.

And then another one.

"Stop," cried Emily, pointing beyond the lodge.

Mr. Reed pulled on the reins, and the sleigh slowed and came to a standstill.

"What is it?" he asked.

"There," she replied, still pointing, "What was that tree Sir George recommended?"

"Norway Spruce."

"Aren't those Norway Spruces?"

Mr. Reed looked out across to where she pointed to the dozen or so tall Norway Spruces just beyond the lodge. He nodded his head.

Emily continued, "I thought Sir George said there wasn't anything on the estate that could serve as a Christmas tree?"

"Mmmm," hummed Mr. Reed as if contemplating the question, "I don't recall his exact words, but that was what he implied, at least. But these won't work, either." He shook his head. "They're too big. They'll fill the space, all right, but it'd be impossible to get one through the doors. We'd have to strip the branches, and that would defeat the purpose."

For a moment, Emily didn't respond. She just sat there, staring out at the trees. And then she shook her head. "Then don't cut one down. Pick one and decorate it right there."

"Right there?"

"The Coburgs will go right past the trees as they go up the drive. And in this snow, a decorated tree would be beautiful."

"But I think the point of the tradition," said Mr. Reed, "is to bring a tree indoors."

"And how would we know that?" asked Emily in the most addlepated manner she could manage, while attempting to flutter her eyelashes. "After all, we're just country peasants. What would we know of these fancy Continentals ways?"

Mr. Reed laughed, as she had hoped he would, and he asked, "Are you suggesting we play ignorant?"

"Why not?" She shrugged. "It's not as if any of them would think otherwise of us, even if we managed the perfect Christmas tree."

"That is harsh."

"But true." She gazed off over the snowy landscape. The flurries had finally stopped, and to the east, the clouds had cleared enough to see the first faint traces of stars. "If we muddle it up completely," continued Emily, "the worst that can happen is the Coburgs will say 'how quaint' before moving on to Brighton and laughing about it over the dinner table, which I suspect frequently occurs at the Prince Regent's table."

"But what about Her Ladyship?"

Strange, Emily thought, but she really didn't care if Her Ladyship thought ill of their efforts. They were doing the best they could, and if Her Ladyship didn't appreciate that, well... "She'll survive."

Mr. Reed contemplated the evergreen trees for a long while before admitting, "It does solve our problem." He shrugged. "I don't know; which one would you pick?"

Emily considered for a moment and then pointed to the

one nearest the drive. It wasn't the tallest or the finest specimen, as Sir George might say, but snow frosted the green branches like sugar icing, and she could imagine it glistening with candlelight. "That one."

He gazed at it for a long moment and then nodded. "I'll tell everyone and we'll get to work on it first thing tomorrow. In the meantime...," he turned and looked at her, "we should get you home. Your aunt will be worried."

And with a flick of his wrist, they were once again heading down the lane toward the village and the home farm. The horse must have known their direction, with an imminent return to her stable and a bucket of oats, for she trotted along, merrily, tossing her mane in expectation.

Perhaps they took the curve too fast.

The horse followed the road. The sleigh, however, did not.

Something underneath it gave way—rusted iron, rotten wood, a lose nail—followed by a hard thump when one corner crashed down. Emily, with a cry, was flung against Mr. Reed as the sleigh fell off kilter. Neither horse nor driver panicked, and the listing sleigh came to a slow, grating stop against a snow bank.

The world stilled, except for the racing of Emily's heart—and undoubtedly Mr. Reed's as well. Light from the waxing moon low reflected bright off the snow between intermittent clouds, thereby making it possible to see their surroundings.

"Are you all right?" Mr. Reed held her by the shoulders and endeavored to set her right.

"Did we come off the runners?" asked Emily, disoriented. She blinked her eyes a few times and looked around.

"I'm not sure," replied Mr. Reed, "One of them, maybe. Are you hurt in any way?"

"I don't think so. Are you?"

"No." He managed to extricate himself from the sleigh—a tad cumbersome given the awkward angle at which it rested—and then lifted Emily out with an ease she never expected. He looked back in the sleigh and then said, "The rope. I forgot it by the lake."

"Shouldn't the sleigh be all right here until you can come back for it in the morning?"

He stared at her for a moment, a strange look of astonishment on his face. "Yes. But... we'll have to walk the rest of the way."

"Oh. Is that all?" she replied, wondering if he really had intended to make repairs here and now, in the dark. "I think we can manage that, don't you?"

"We could ride," he suggested, gesturing toward the waiting horse, "That is, if you don't mind riding together."

She glanced from the horse to the man standing there, tall and slender, white hair bright in the moonlight. She might have been past her prime but her heart still skipped a beat at the thought of being close to him. She should have said no, that they could walk, but that was ridiculous when there was a perfectly good horse they could ride. "I don't mind at all."

Mr. Reed set to work unharnessing the horse, and while they didn't have a proper saddle, he draped the lap rug over the horse's back.

And then Mr. Reed held his hand out to Emily.

She reached out to accept it and took a step forward.

Only to slip on a patch of ice.

Her feet slid out from under her, and with a yelp, she landed in the deep, drifting snow with a poof, and fell back, her eyes looking up at the stars.

ℰⱤ

Miss Haywood, in Mr. Lachlan Reed's opinion, was the most amazing lady he'd ever met.

Or was she a woman?

Did vicar's daughters qualify as ladies? She certainly behaved like one. And her brothers were all officers in the royal navy... plus that one brother who was a barrister. Barristers were gentlemen. Weren't they?

But yes, Miss Haywood was definitely a lady. And extraordinary.

Her efforts to help find a Christmas tree, regardless of her motives, demonstrated considerate diligence, despite her preference—and need—to be at home tending to her aunt. But then she had gone into that water without the slightest hesitation. She had stood up to him and left him without a defense. Watching her swim out to the boy had disturbed him; it felt unnatural letting her go out like that. It angered him, too, leaving him feeling somehow like less of a man.

Until the moment came for him to act. He hauled her back and pulled her out of the water... and he knew. She was right. She couldn't have saved him from the water, not even with Sir George's help. Maybe the boy would've survived, but Mr. Reed doubted his own survival after that. Or worse, both of them could've toppled over trying to lift him, and they all would have drowned. He'd heard of such things happening.

As he had carried her, half frozen, her eyes fluttering open then closing, to the house, he had realized something more. She had placed her entire trust in him, a near stranger.

To save one life, she trusted her own life to another.

He felt honored, given such a privilege.

He was just a land steward, as his father had been before him, and he couldn't imagine wanting to do anything else. He knew that somewhere, generations ago, there had been a viscount's younger son or such—at least, that was what his grandfather claimed—but his present family could be considered minor gentry by only the most liberal definition. But he knew, if anything, he wanted to be worthy of this lady.

Now, in the wake of this disaster with the sleigh—really, he shouldn't have taken it out with a passenger, or at the very least, he should have inspected it more thoroughly beforehand—Miss Haywood readily agreed to *ride* back to the village. With him. Together. How irksome any lady might find it, but she didn't hesitate to acquiesce to the suggestion.

He held out his hand to her, and she reached out toward him and took a step.

And down she went, landing in a snow bank in a wave of white.

Lachlan rushed to help her...

...and found her laughing.

"You're all right?" he asked, leaning over her.

"No," she laughed, "I've injured my pride." And she laughed even harder. Then he noticed her bare hand rubbing her hip—her *pride*.

When she stopped laughing, she said, "Family humor— *Pride goeth before the Fall*. The part that hits first when you fall. Of course, it's not funny if you have to explain it."

"No, no," he said, "I understand. But if you hurt yourself, it can't be very funny."

"I assure you, I'm all right."

He held his hands down to help her up. But instead of taking his hands, she said, looking up at him, "I'd forgotten how much fun snow could be." But then he realized she no longer looked at him but past him. "How extraordinary the stars are," she said, her voice filled with wonder.

He turned his head and looked up. She was right—yet again. The clouds had cleared overhead and stars filled the sky, too numerous ever to count, the crescent moon low in the black sky. And before he allowed himself to think about it fully, he plopped down in the snow bank beside her and stared up at the sea of stars.

Despite the cold, he wished he could remain like this with Miss Haywood for the rest of the night—quiet and still, with only the sound of their breathing, the world at peace, or at least, seemingly so—two people on the edge of infinity. He longed to reach beside him and take her hand so he might gently raise it to his lips and kiss it. But then he remembered her hands were bare, and the night was frigid, and the horse stomped his impatience for a warm stall and a bag of oats.

Lachlan sat up. "Your aunt will be worried," he said, and rose.

This time, when he reached down to help her up, she took his hands. He pulled her up, and for a brief moment, as a misty cloud of her breath enveloped her, he felt the urge to kiss her. He resisted—it would be a betrayal of her trust—and stepped back.

Lachlan mounted the horse and easily pulled Miss Haywood up before him—none of this indelicate pushing and shoving of backsides—and they were once again heading down the road toward the village.

The ride, like much of their time together, was quiet,

with few words spoken in a comfortable silence. Lachlan instinctively held one arm about her waist for fear she might slip off the horse. Miss Haywood didn't look at him but kept her face forward.

The lane they followed back to the village completed a circuitous route. They entered from the opposite side from the church and vicarage. From the houses and shops, lights blazed in windows and glinted off the snow, but few villagers moved out of doors, due to the cold and it being the dinner hour. They rounded the green—now deep in snow—past the equestrian statue leftover from an earlier age.

"Who was this Richard the Roundhead?" Lachlan blurted out. The base remained uncarved, the statue nameless, for all intents and purposes, but the villagers, he'd noted, always referred to the leaden green sculpture as Richard the Roundhead.

"His Lordship's ancestor," replied Miss Haywood, "the Fourth Earl."

"If he were a Roundhead," pondered Lachlan, "why is there a statue commemorating him?"

"It was there before the Civil War," explained Miss Haywood, "With the Restoration, the villagers wouldn't allow its removal, and the Fifth Earl didn't care one way or the other if it stayed or went." She shrugged. "But he was a Cavalier, and there were no reprisals against the village. The old earl was dead, after all."

"Was he one of the regicides?"

"He was conveniently ill and, therefore, absent from the trial," said Miss Haywood, "but if he had been present, there's no doubt he would've sided with the rest of them to execute the king. And then he had the good sense to die a month later.

But since his son went off to Holland and France with Charles II, no one paid much attention to the infamous life and ignoble end of Richard the Roundhead."

"Except the villagers?"

"He was well-liked here."

Lachlan couldn't help but smile. "Like Eliza Throckmorton."

"Exactly."

He could hear the amusement in her voice. He suspected if either Richard the Roundhead or Eliza Throckmorton walked through the village that night, they'd find it essentially unchanged from their own time—maybe a few *new* structures from Queen Anne's time, but little more.

The vicarage was one of those newer buildings, only a hundred years old or so, with plenty of straight lines and not an exposed timber to be found.

At the vicarage doorstep, Lachlan dismounted and then lifted Miss Haywood down with ease, his hand lingering about her waist for a tad longer than appropriate, he feared. She didn't appear to notice.

He stepped back, away from her, fully intending to say goodnight and then wait until she had safely entered the house. But instead, the door abruptly opened, and there stood one of the servants.

"Oh, Miss Haywood," cried the woman, "We thought you wouldn't make it home in time for dinner. Mrs. Edmondson has been so very worried."

"I'm perfectly all right," replied Miss Haywood, "It simply took longer than...."

"Emily?" came an aged voice from within. And from behind the domestic appeared an ancient figure, withered and grey, tottering along with a stick. Lachlan recognized her as Old Mrs. Edmondson, whom he'd seen at church on Sunday. "Dinner is waiting on the table...."

But as her bespectacled eyes sighted Lachlan, her face brightened. "Henry. There you are. I wondered where you'd gone off to. Your dinner is getting cold."

Miss Haywood turned to Lachlan. "I'm so sorry. She does this to every slender man who comes to the house. She thinks you're her son. I should have warned you beforehand."

"It's all right," he assured her, "No harm done. Is this Henry dead?"

"Not at all." She spoke low. "Just can't be bothered to tend to his own mother. Ran off to London or Bristol or Newmarket. Wherever a reprobate might lose all his money."

"Henry?" called out Old Mrs. Edmondson again as the domestic endeavored to bring her back into the house, "Your dinner."

"Don't worry," said Miss Haywood, "Ride around toward the stable, and I will tell her you are stabling your horse. By the time we sit down to dinner, she will have forgotten all about you."

Lachlan knew she was lying—to be kind. He was familiar with Old Mrs. Edmondson's illness and knew once the sufferer caught hold of a thought, they did not let it go but dwelled on it incessantly, to the detriment of those who cared for them.

"No," he said, "I can stay, if you don't think it impertinent to invite myself to dinner."

The look of relief on her face was unmistakable. "Yes. Yes, you are very welcome to join us."

"In that case," he said, giving her a smile, "I will take the horse around to the stable and rejoin you shortly."

And as he led the horse away, he heard Old Mrs. Edmondson, her voice filled with distress. "Where is Henry going? Is he coming back?"

"It's all right," assured Miss Haywood as the three females went inside, "He'll be back in a moment."

He knew he should just continue on back to the home farm. He should have just said goodnight and been on his way. But he didn't want that.

And he welcomed any excuse to remain in Miss Haywood's company.

ဢဢ

To Emily's surprise, Mr. Reed stayed quite late, the three of them—Aunt Sophia, Mr. Reed, and herself—lingering at the table long into the evening. All the while, Aunt Sophia prattled away, speaking to Mr. Reed as if he were, in fact, her son, Henry. Emily sometimes thought Aunt Sophia's senility was a way to deal with the fact that Henry had abandoned her. She dwelled in an idealized past with her darling boy, but Emily remembered a very different Henry. He'd been a horrid child, until he grew to become a contemptible man, wallowing in wine and women and gambling, a prodigal son who never returned. He fit in quite well with the Prince Regent and his ilk, although he could no longer afford such lofty circles.

Mr. Reed, for his part, played along, or seemed to, anyway. Emily noticed he never lied outright to Aunt Sophia. He just didn't correct her or dissuade her fantasy. But when she asked about where he had been and what he had been doing, he described farms and houses and villages in Surrey, places Emily knew Henry wouldn't be caught dead in. Mr.

Reed, however, spoke with pride and admiration of the ordinary lives of His Majesty's subjects.

He told humorous tales of dogs purloining mutton joints and spindly vicars ringing bells, of sheep-shearing races and drapers going courting with bolts of cloth. Aunt Sophia laughed long and hard, but whether it was because she understood the stories or simply suffered from a case of infectious laughter, Emily didn't know... or care, for that matter. For once, Aunt Sophia wasn't declaring the French had landed or distressing over the arrival of her next meal.

Until, at length, as Emily and Mr. Reed discussed the advantages of keeping pigs in the apple orchard, Aunt Sophia drifted off to sleep in her chair after the coffee arrived. The pair only noticed when her gentle snores interrupted them.

Emily rang for the nurse, and moments later, Aunt Sophia was heading to bed, her queries about breakfast trailing behind her. Emily found herself alone with their guest.

Alone with Mr. Reed.

Well, the dining room door was open. That made it all very appropriate.

Emily thanked Mr. Reed for pretending to be Henry, and then she apologized for necessity of such a farce.

Mr. Reed shook his head and waved aside her apology. "My first employer was similarly afflicted in the last years of his life," he explained, "He always thought I was his brother, which infuriated his son. At first, it bothered me as well— someone refusing to recognize the person I was, albeit without intentional malice on his part—but then I realized, despite not knowing who I really was, he was always pleased to see me, and he treated me well. I think, on some level, he knew that I was, at least, a decent person."

"And his son wasn't?" asked Emily, "A decent person, that is?"

"Heavens, no." He took a sip of coffee before continuing. "First thing he did when his father died was sack me. When His Lordship learned of it, he hired me immediately."

"That's quite the compliment."

"I suppose you're right. I hadn't thought of it that way before." He smiled. "I was simply grateful. And even more grateful His Lordship asked me to come here when Evans died."

Emily, likewise, found herself grateful His Lordship asked Mr. Reed to replace the late land steward. They talked of his plans for improvements to the estate and the tenant farms and all manner of farming matters that should have bored her to tears but didn't. And in the midst of that, she learned he was an admirer of Mr. Wordsworth, and so, naturally, the conversation lapsed into poetry and novels and plays.

In truth, Emily had no idea how long they sat there at the table. She only noticed the lateness of the hour when the maid came to clear the dishes and jumped with a start at the sight of them still sitting there. They both leapt up from their chairs, as if they had been up to no good—when they clearly hadn't.

Emily, ever mindful of her duties to a guest in her home, suggested they move to the drawing room for a glass of brandy. Mr. Reed appeared to hesitate but then accepted. Emily led the way into the hall, where they discovered, by way of the clock there, that it neared midnight.

They both looked at each other. Emily knew Mr. Reed,

like all men who worked the land, rose early, well before dawn. Did he have to milk the cows? No, Mr. Treadwell did that, along with his sons, but she suspected Mr. Reed helped out also and finished a day's work before any of them sat down to Mrs. Treadwell's breakfast.

Mr. Reed began to make his apologies, but Emily spoke over him. "The groom is gone. He went with my parents to Portsmouth. You can sleep in his room." It was half a mile back to the home farm, in the cold and dark. And it was snowing again. It would be safer to ride back in daylight.

Again, he hesitated, but then he nodded.

Emily led the way to the kitchen and pointed in the direction of the groom's room, just beyond the fireplace and Mrs. Foster's room. Then they said goodnight to each other.

And that was that.

As Emily ascended the stairs to her own bedchamber, it all felt so anti-climactic. Thinking over the day, she realized it had been such a wonderful day, despite the dip in the lake and the problem with the villagers. But now, she felt like the cinder girl from the French story, and the ball was over.

There would be no prince for her. Nor, for that matter, a prematurely white-haired land steward.

ဆဩ

When Emily woke the next morning—Christmas Eve morning—she learned Mr. Reed had already departed. Of course. He was a man with duties and responsibilities, and he had spent the previous day gallivanting about the county with her.

Only, that wasn't entirely true. *She* had spent the day with *him* in his efforts to find an appropriate tree to satisfy Her Ladyship's request. Never mind that her thoughts dwelled on the man, as if she were some school girl. She knew such a fixation was simply because he had noticed her and spoken with her. Really, it was silly. And now that the problem of the Christmas tree had been resolved, well, that was done. Life would return to normal routine.

Especially as she also discovered her parents had returned. She had slept much later than usual—probably due to all the activities the day before—and she found them breakfasting in the dining room with Aunt Sophia.

"Made it as far as Cranston yesterday evening," explained her father, the good Reverend Haywood, "and we stayed with Reverend Michaels. You know, I think Reverend Michaels lays almost as good a table as we do. Although, his cook's puddings do not compare to Mrs. Foster's."

"But they didn't give you any breakfast?" asked Emily as her mother dished up more eggs and her father slathered marmalade on a fresh bun.

Her father laughed. "Just a trifle."

"We left at the crack of dawn," added her mother.

"Much to do today," continued her father, "Christmas Eve, you know."

"Is Henry up yet?" asked Aunt Sophia to no one in particular. Emily wondered if Aunt Sophia thought of her own son Henry or the white-haired Mr. Reed.

"He's in London," said Mrs. Haywood to Aunt Sophia. It was a lie, of course. No one ever knew where Henry was until he showed up asking for money.

Aunt Sophia looked askance at Mrs. Haywood, a faint flicker of distrust in her faded blue eyes, but then she nodded and said, "With the Prince Regent, no doubt."

"That's right," said Mrs. Haywood with a condescending

nod.

Emily returned her attention to her father and said, "You have two sermons to write."

"One," he replied, "Reverend Michaels and I put our heads together last night, and we're each giving the same sermon at Midnight Service—it's really quite good."

"If you say so." Emily smiled.

"I do. So did Reverend Michaels. Shepherds' abiding. Watching their flocks until their Lord summons them. All that good stuff." He took a sip of coffee. "That only leaves tomorrow."

Christmas Day.

"So much to do," said Mrs. Haywood.

Yes, there was.

"Do you think Henry will come?" asked Aunt Sophia.

"You never know," replied Mrs. Haywood. At least that was the truth.

As Emily ate her breakfast, her mother talked of nothing but the new baby... and the other grandchildren... and the former *midshipman*... until, in the midst of a brief pause to order more coffee...

"Did anything significant happen while we were away?"

"Her Ladyship ordered a Christmas tree," said Emily as nonchalantly as possible.

Both Reverend and Mrs. Haywood raised their eyebrows.

"Oh?" said her father.

"Eliza Throckmorton's yew," said Aunt Sophia, seemingly apropos of nothing.

Emily nodded. "The villagers are quite put out about it. Think it's pagan idolatry or some papist trickery. I've had quite a time of it."

"No doubt, my dear," said Reverend Haywood.

"A contingent showed up here wanting to speak to you about it," continued Emily, "I didn't know what to tell them."

"Oh. Well. Christmas tree, you say?" Her father seemed just as baffled as she was about it. "I'll have to think about it."

"Our Lord was a carpenter," said Aunt Sophia.

They all looked at her, silent. She appeared quite pleased with herself.

Reverend Haywood nodded and said, "True. True." And that was that.

Emily didn't tell her parents of the previous days' events. Not that it was something shameful—no, indeed, quite the opposite. But it felt like something to be kept private, almost sacred, between her and Mr. Reed.

Through the dining room window, Emily spied movement at the church. She rose to investigate and saw men arriving with sledges filled with holly and greenery. And there was Mrs. Treadwell, hopping down from one of the sledges and running off toward the shops.

Turning back to her family, Emily said, "The greenery for the church has arrived."

With that, breakfast was over.

Reverend Haywood retired to his study, while Emily and Mrs. Haywood prepared to go to the church to begin the works of decorating the sanctuary. But Aunt Sophia would have none it. She neither wanted Mrs. Haywood to leave nor did she wish to accompany them to the church. Instead, she talked of nothing but Henry. She had caught a thought and would not let it go.

They—Emily and her mother—decided Emily would go

ahead and Mrs. Haywood would join her once Aunt Sophia was settled.

So Emily departed. But instead of walking over to the church, she headed out across the green first toward the shops. She needed to confirm with Mr. Cunningham the butcher their order for Christmas Day. It wouldn't do to be without a goose.

The butcher shop buzzed with voices, but the instant Emily stepped inside, an uneasy hush fell over the room. Every eye stared at her.

"Good morning," she said, putting on a brave smile.

The smattering of responses was barely audible, and as she glanced about, she discovered eyes were quickly lowered rather than meet hers. The company parted as she made her way to the counter, and as she confirmed her order with Mr. Cunningham—*yes, two geese*—Emily could feel the eyes boring into her back.

When she turned to leave, Mr. Cunningham stopped her.

"This Christmas tree," he asked.

Oh, blast and blazes! Were they still harping on the Christmas tree? And without another thought, Emily blurted out, "Our Lord was a carpenter."

"I beg your pardon?" said Mr. Cunningham. Confused glances passed amongst his customers.

"Nothing," said Emily, "Just something I was thinking. Carpenters, wood, trees."

"Well, this Christmas tree," continued Mr. Cunningham, "Mrs. Treadwell said they found one near the Lodge."

"Yes. It should do nicely."

An uneasy stillness fell over the clutch of customers, and into this silence, a small voice—Mrs. Morris, it turned out—

asked, "Is it true you saved poor James Talbot from drowning?"

They all waited with bated breath, until Emily replied, "Well, I had help."

"From the new man?" piped up Mrs. Cunningham from behind the counter. Furtive, knowing glances passed amongst them all.

"And Sir George," added Emily.

Polite nods followed, but it didn't sit right, and Emily felt a growing dread as she realized it was already too late to quell any rising gossip. She made her way to the door, opened it, and before stepping outside, she turned back to the watching customers and said, "Good morning," again with a smile.

The moment she shut the door behind her, Emily heard the customers inside burst out in a cacophony of... presumably gossip of pernicious delight. She really didn't want to know but feared it boded ill.

She hurried back across the snow-covered green, to the church. Whatever the gossip was, she'd find out soon enough, but in the meantime, she had work to do. Holly would not string itself.

She entered the church where, every Sunday, her father gave very short sermons, except on those rare occasions when he found necessary a didactic lecture of fire and brimstone, usually to put an end to some bit of tomfoolery. All her ancestors were probably interred there, either inside the church in plain tombs or beneath slabs of stone or else out in the churchyard, subterranean neighbors to Eliza Throckmorton, probably since Adam and Eve... or at least since the Saxons invaded, but barbarian hoards did not sound as elevated as the first man and woman.

Her mother had not yet arrived, but Old Mr. Phelps and his son sat on the step before the altar, hard at work making boughs of holly. Emily crossed the nave—a short walk when compared to a cathedral but long enough—and joined them.

The interior of the ancient building was barely warmer than outside, and Emily removed only her gloves as she sat down on the step to assist the men.

Just a moment passed before Old Mr. Phelps said, "Yes, indeed, this Christmas tree is much on my mind…"

Oh, good Heavens! They were all as bad as Aunt Sophia, every last one of them, fixated on a thought they could not let go, as if afflicted by a monomania.

"… And I can say, I don't like it."

"Me, neither," quipped Young Mr. Phelps, "Not one bit."

"I know you said…," began Old Mr. Phelps before launching into her previous explanations.

She remember very well what she'd said, thank you very much, and she was tired of trying to find a reason that would justify a Christmas tree to the satisfaction of the villagers.

"…but I just don't like it," repeated Old Mr. Phelps.

"Especially as we're the ones who have to decorate it," added Young Mr. Phelps.

She really wanted to shout *Our Lord was a carpenter!* and be done with it, as if that might miraculously explain all. Instead, she said, "Wood."

"I beg your pardon?" asked Old Mr. Phelps.

In that moment, a new idea came upon her, and she spoke before the idea slipped away. "The cross is a tree, of sorts, and…" She hesitated, searching for the right words. "…represents the Tree of Life…"

Both men stopped mid-motion and stared at her, Young Mr. Phelps gaping like a dead fish.

"...The source of all sin," she continued. In for a penny, in for a pound. "And Christ died for those sins." *Too esoteric?* she wondered.

Old Mr. Phelps just nodded, without any real understanding in his face. Young Mr. Phelps, on the other hand, looked thoroughly baffled. Definitely too esoteric. Neither said a word and resumed their work. In silence.

Some moments later, out of the blue, Old Mr. Phelps spoke, his voice echoing in the vast space of the church and giving Emily a start.

"So, you're saying," said Old Mr. Phelps, "a Christmas tree is the Tree of Life? The one with the snake and the forbidden fruit? And all that?"

Oh, dear. When put that way, it sounded completely asinine.

Emily gave a heavy sigh, and instead of trying to find some reason to explain away a Christmas tree, she said, "Her Ladyship is our neighbor. Our friend even. She employs many of the villagers, and she is good to us. She has requested a Christmas tree. Who are we to deny her this gesture of kindness and consideration to her guests? That should be enough reason for us to do it." And Emily realized that truly was the best reason of all.

With that, both Old Mr. Phelps and Young Mr. Phelps nodded, seemingly satisfied, and continued on with their work.

She stared at them for a moment, shocked that such a simple answer had done the trick. If only she'd thought of it sooner, it could have saved her a lot of trouble. But then, she might not have become better acquainted with Mr. Reed.

The door burst open, the sudden sound filling and echoing through the cold church, and Emily expected to see her mother enter. Instead, she witnessed Mrs. Treadwell marching up the middle aisle toward them. She looked like the proverbial cat but with some fat bit of gossip.

"The new man has gone to see your father," announced Mrs. Treadwell there before the altar.

Emily refused to take the bait, despite a rush of concern. Instead, she nodded and replied, "Oh?"

Mrs. Treadwell looked triumphant and said, "You were seen, you know?"

Emily calmly replied, "I beg your pardon?" but inside, she panicked. Seen where? And doing what? She tried to recall the details of the previous day with Mr. Reed, and everything she remembered had been completely appropriate, even when he carried her from the lake and assisted in undressing her. After all, they had been chaperoned the entire time.

"Yesterday," continued Mrs. Treadwell as the two men listened intently, "With Mr. Reed."

"Oh, that," said Emily, nonchalantly, "Yes, well, a great many people saw us yesterday. And no doubt, they also saw Sir George with us."

"And last night?" asked Mrs. Treadwell. So that was her ace; at least she didn't know about the undressing bit. "You were seen...."

There was only one way to deal with this. Emily quickly rose to her full height, thankfully standing on the altar steps so that she towered over the busy-body gossip.

"Not another word, Mrs. Treadwell," said Emily, "Or you

will commit a slanderous lie. Before witnesses and in the house of God." Emily stoically collected her gloves and said, "Shame on you, Mrs. Treadwell, for spreading malicious tales."

And Emily marched out of the church, leaving two grinning Phelpses and one flabbergasted Mrs. Treadwell behind her.

Emily needed to talk to her parents, tell them about yesterday with Mr. Reed before they heard the gossip. She strode off through the snow toward the vicarage. Yet as she neared the house, she happened to glance down and notice the numerous tracks going away from the house. Her own, undoubtedly, counted among them, going from the vicarage across the green toward the shops. Perhaps her mother or Aunt Sophia had needed something.

Then, an odd set of tracks—not in keeping with the others—caught her attention. They led from the house and down the lane away from the village. And there, in the distance, she saw the retreating figure of Mr. Reed carrying his hat in his hand.

She fought the urge to rush after him, to ask what had happened. Instead, she hurried into the house, fear mixing with worry over what rumors and innuendo waited inside for her.

"Ah, there you are," greeted her father as she entered the house.

"What has happened?" asked Emily, removing her coat, "Why was Mr. Reed here?"

Her father motioned her to come through to his study. Once there, he plopped down in his chair before his desk and asked, "Why didn't you tell us he stayed here last night?"

Oh, dear.

"And for that matter," he continued, his voice softening, "why didn't you tell us about rescuing poor James Talbot?"

Emily slowly lowered herself to the overstuffed chair opposite her father. She felt like a child who'd been up to some mischief and caught by her elder.

"I didn't want to upset you," she said, knowing it was not entirely true... Well, it was true—she didn't want to distress her parents, especially after the fact when all was over and done with and the danger was past—but she wasn't entirely honest either.

Yesterday did feel like something private, between her and Mr. Reed. But also, the rescue of poor James Talbot... she only did what any decent human being would have done. She didn't want any fuss about it. She didn't want the attention it brought on her. And besides, she had not acted alone.

She said as much to her father, then added, "Mr. Reed and Sir George helped as well. It wasn't just me, all alone."

"So I've heard."

"I was trying to help Mr. Reed locate a Christmas tree for Her Ladyship." She explained about the incident with Eliza Throckmorton's yew and how Mr. Reed needed someone to introduce him to Sir George. "I couldn't very well let Mr. Reed, so new to the district, go gallivanting through unknown country by himself, without a friend or guidance."

"No, of course, not." Despite her father's words, she sensed amusement on his part as she endeavored to explain. "Something could have happened."

"Something did happen." His voice took on a grave tone. "Next time, my dear, play the shrieking female and leave the heroics to someone else."

"But poor James Talbot would have died…."

"Just nod and say 'Yes, Papa,' and I'll pretend to believe you, and that way, neither your mother nor I will worry."

Emily nodded. "Yes, Papa."

"Good. Now. As for your Mr. Reed…"

My Mr. Reed?

The vicar tapped his forefinger against his lips. "You know, he doesn't have any trace of an accent."

"He's not Scottish."

"Oh. I thought someone said he was Scottish."

"Quarter Scots. His grandfather was Scottish, Mr. Reed is not."

"Well, you seem to have learned quite a bit about the man while we were gone."

"Papa, why was Mr. Reed here?"

"You will not believe it!" he said, "It's really quite amusing, and I can well see why everyone is talking about it. Are you ready?"

"Do tell."

"Mr. Reed came to ask for your hand in marriage. Ha! Isn't it astounding?"

Emily frowned. "And what's so astounding about that? Why shouldn't he or some other gentleman…" Mr. Reed wasn't, strictly speaking, a gentleman, but no matter. "…come and ask for my hand?"

All amusement disappeared from her father's face. "Oh, my dear, do forgive me. I didn't mean to imply anything. It's just…" He shrugged. "You barely know the man."

"And what reason did he give you?" asked Emily, as if not fully hearing her father, "For wanting to marry me, that is."

"Oh. You haven't heard?"

"Heard what?" she asked, filled with panic and dread at the possibilities.

"I thought that's why you came back."

She shook her head. "I came back because Mrs. Treadwell said Mr. Reed was coming to see you, and she insinuated something nefarious."

"That woman!" The vicar took a deep, calming breath before continuing. "Well, someone saw you and Mr. Reed arrive home last evening. True to tell, you were seen with him several times yesterday. Alone."

"I am not some schoolgirl cavorting with a rake. I'm an old maid. Hardly worth notice except by gossips with nothing better to do."

"Now, Emily, that is harsh."

"But true, nonetheless." Now it was her turn to take a calming breath. "Pray, continue what you were explaining about Mr. Reed's visit."

"Someone saw Mr. Reed leave this house this morning…"

"Oh dear." It was worse than she'd feared.

"…And Mrs. Treadwell—who never misses a thing, I might remind you—knew Mr. Reed had not slept in his own bed last night. She confronted Mr. Reed about it and, no doubt, is telling all and sundry about it as we speak. But do not distress yourself, my dear. Mr. Reed came and assured me all was propriety itself—which I already knew—and then he asked for your hand in marriage."

So the proposal of marriage was to save her honor. She was simultaneously impressed and appalled, each emotion battling for a superior position with neither winning any ground.

"He assured me," continued the vicar, "that he had slept in Caleb's room. Mrs. Foster has confirmed this and that she fed Mr. Reed breakfast in her kitchen this morning. I sent her round to the butcher's to purchase... something..." The vicar gave a flick of his hand in the direction of the shops. "...and to gossip to her heart's content about Mr. Reed sleeping in Caleb's room just opposite hers."

Emily nodded. "That should do the trick."

"Yes, but that still leaves Mr. Reed."

Yes, it did. He had asked for her hand in marriage. "What did you say to him?"

"I said any question of marriage was between you and him."

Emily smiled. And probably blushed as well. The very idea that someone had asked for her hand, well, it was unimaginable. And for her father to give such an answer to the man. "Thank you."

"Of course," the vicar continued, "I told him if you wished it, I'd give my blessing."

"You did?" *What happened to barely knowing the man?*

"Not a bad looking fellow once you get past the white hair and realize he's not an old man but quite in his prime. Seems decent. And His Lordship promised him the old Weir place should Mr. Reed wish to marry."

Impressive. That alone might convince many a female to marry a man.

"And along with his wages," her father whispered, leaning forward as if to reveal some secret, "he has 100 pounds a year from his late father. With your 200 pounds... well, the two of you could do quite nicely with that."

She gasped at him.

He sat back in his chair and resumed his normal mode of speaking. "Well, it's best to be practical about these matters." He was right, of course. His body shifted, no longer as relaxed, and he assumed a somewhat more formal pose. Emily knew the topic of discussion was at an end, as far as he was concerned. "Now, was there anything else we need to discuss?"

No. She couldn't think of a thing.

"Well, then, you should probably get back to the church, and I should get back to this sermon. Your mother should join you anytime now."

"Where is she?"

"Aunt Sophia wanted to go to the shops. Said she wanted something for Henry. I tried to explain that...." He shook his head and picked up his pen. "Off you go, my girl."

Filled with the thoughts that someone asked to marry her, even if just to save her honor, Emily hurried back to the church, where, much to her relief, she discovered Mrs. Treadwell was gone. Not that it really mattered—other than Emily would not have to deal with her—as Mrs. Treadwell had her tidbit and would spread it high and low regardless of Mrs. Foster's version of events. Thankfully, Mrs. Foster was known to be a more accurate source of salacious information and would be believed, but still, Emily didn't like the suggestion of impropriety on her part when all she did was what every villager had done: offer a bed to a guest due to the lateness of the hour and inclement weather, a common enough practice. And Mr. Reed had slept among the servants—as if Mrs. Foster would allow any tomfoolery in her domain.

In place of Mrs. Treadwell, Emily found her mother at

work with the two men, while Aunt Sophia and her nurse sat in the second pew—Aunt Sophia's preferred spot.

"Have you seen Henry?" asked Aunt Sophia as Emily went passed her.

"No," said Emily, turning back to her, "I haven't. Not today." Technically, it wasn't a lie. She hadn't seen her cousin Henry that day, or for several years, for that matter. But she knew Aunt Sophia was thinking, in a muddled way, of Mr. Reed.

Aunt Sophia held up a blue muffler. "Henry left it this morning. He'll catch cold without it."

"It's all right," said Emily, hearing the distress in her elderly aunt's voice, "We'll see him later, and you can return it to him then."

That answer seemed to satisfy her. For now.

୫୬୯୧

They worked until luncheon, which Aunt Sophia mentioned several times so they wouldn't forget. When Emily and her mother returned to the church—without Aunt Sophia, this time—neither of the Phelpses were there. Instead, a few women from the village came to help finish the work, along with a few tall boys and a ladder. It seemed they worked quickly and finished in no time, but when they left the church, Emily realized it was late afternoon.

Twilight would be upon them soon, and with it, Christmas Eve.

As she followed her mother toward the vicarage, Emily noticed an odd movement out of the corner of her eye. She turned to look and saw Mr. Jessop, the publican, hurrying passed Richard the Roundhead, with a wheelbarrow full of... crockery?

At that moment, Emily realized none of the villagers were going 'to and fro' as was their wont at this time of day as they hurried home or about the shops to make last minute purchases before closing time. Instead, everyone she saw headed toward the lane leading out of the village and toward the Hall. And all of them carried something—a basket, a bundle, a lantern.

And then Emily spotted the sleigh waiting outside the vicarage.

Her heart leapt up.

Silly thing.

Especially as Mr. Treadwell sat there holding the reins.

Aunt Sophia and her nurse came practically tumbling out of the house, the vicar following close behind with coats and blankets.

"We're going on a sleigh ride," cried Aunt Sophia at the sight of Emily. The nurse struggled to get Aunt Sophia into her coat.

"What's this?" asked Mrs. Haywood. She glanced from her husband to Mr. Treadwell.

"Old Mr. Phelps 'as got everyone helping at the Christmas tree," explain Mr. Treadwell, to Emily's astonishment, "and the new man says I was to collect Mrs. Edmondson and bring her. Her Ladyship is expected to return at any moment."

The Coburgs.

Heavens! This was going to be a disaster, Emily feared. They'd all rush over to the porter's lodge to wave and cheer as royalty flew by in a blur, only to have their pathetic efforts at a Christmas tree go unnoticed, or worse, scoffed at.

Emily, however, did not give voice to those particular

concerns. Instead, she pointed at the sleigh and asked Mr. Treadwell, "Is that contraption repaired?"

"Yes, miss," replied Mr. Treadwell, "Me and the new man worked on it this morning. Perfectly safe now."

"Emily," interrupted Aunt Sophia, holding up the blue muffler, "Henry needs his muffler."

Emily nodded, but she knew the sleigh would not hold all of them. "You and nurse go ahead. We'll come along shortly."

Aunt Sophia didn't protest but hurried to the sleigh and, with many hands endeavoring to help her, climbed into the conveyance.

Once the sleigh sped away, Emily and her parents returned to the house to ready themselves for a cold evening, and in short order, they, too, were on their way to the Hall, on foot, with the rest of the household following close behind.

The walk was pleasant, despite the cold. A light snow fell, clouds covering the sky, and the light began to fade. It would be dark when they made their way home later, but the vicar had thought to bring a lantern, which, for now, remained unlit.

They soon reached the low, stone wall marking a boundary to the parkland adjoining His Lordship's estate. It led to the porter's lodge, but even as the ancient house came into view, they could hear voices and shouting and laughter from among the conifer trees beyond the wall. A moment more, as they passed the copse of trees, they saw the source of merriment.

A frozen fairyland, twinkling and sparkling in the falling snow, spread out before them. Lit lanterns hung from posts with garlands of holly strung up between them, all along the drive up to the Hall in the far distance.

A small fire burned in a clearing, while men and women congregated around it for warmth. Additional braziers were set here and there. But many villagers busied themselves about the tall tree Emily and Mr. Reed had selected the night before. But now, instead of being merely a Norway spruce, it was becoming a Christmas tree, hung with burning lanterns and tied with ribbons.

Mostly, children worked on decorating it—even poor James Talbot had been allowed to come—all of them directed by Sir George. He walked about with a basket of oranges and kept handing the children oranges tied with ribbon to hang from the branches.

"Please, everyone," he cried out, "take an orange. Please, take one for home, too." Beside him walked Widow Talbot with another basket of oranges.

From the little Emily knew of Christmas trees, she suspected this was nothing like the German traditions, but it was lovely, especially in the growing twilight and the falling snow, with the flickering lantern flames.

"Highway robbery!" cried her father in a sudden burst of outrage.

Emily glanced about to see what irritated him so to warrant such a reaction. Then she saw Mr. Jessop. He had set up a board covered in waiting cups and tankards. A kettle of mulled cider brewed atop a brazier, the distinct aroma of alcohol mingling with cinnamon and clove. A large crockery bowl had been requisitioned to act as a wassail bowl filled with spicy hot ale and frothy cream. All those familiar smells made it feel like Christmas, despite the oddity of the tree. A bit of slate listed the price of a sixpence for a tankard of cider or a cup of wassail.

Beside her husband, Mrs. Jessop poured cups of coffee for a tuppence each, a farthing more for sugar and milk.

"No doubt, weak and watery, as usual," whispered the vicar to his wife and daughter, but Mr. Jessop, as usual, did not lack for customers. Nor, Emily noticed, did it stop her father from purchasing a tankard of cider.

Leaving her parents behind, Emily approached the tree, all the while wondering where Mr. Reed might be. Then she saw Aunt Sophia standing amidst the children and hanging an orange on a slightly higher branch. Emily also noticed the blue muffler was gone.

"Aunt Sophia?" asked Emily, "Did you lose the blue muffler?"

"No," replied Aunt Sophia, as if Emily spoke nonsense, "I gave it back to Henry."

Henry? Emily glanced around. She didn't see Mr. Reed anywhere. Maybe Aunt Sophia had christened another man *Henry* in the meantime. "Where is he?"

Aunt Sophia glanced around and then pointed and smiled. "There's Henry!"

Emily leaned slightly and saw Mr. Reed descending from a ladder on the other side of the tree. He spoke to someone opposite and then turned toward her, only to stop as he spotted her.

Then he smiled.

Emily's heart did not leap up.

It swelled and then pounded, while her stomach made an unsettling kind of summersault that felt decidedly like nausea. Some other part of her—she wasn't sure which;

something respiratory probably—gave a little whimper and then a gasp as she lost the ability to breathe.

Good Lord, that a man should have such an effect on her!

He moved toward her.

Only to have Sir George come up to him and ask with a grin, "*Henry*, did you get an orange?" as he offered one from his basket.

"Thank you," replied Mr. Reed, accepting the orange without looking at Sir George. Instead, he gazed steadily at Emily, and the moment Sir George moved on, he hurried over to her.

"Miss Haywood," said Mr. Reed upon reaching her, "we really must speak."

"Yes. Yes, of course."

He drew her aside, away from eavesdroppers but still within sight of everyone. He seemed to hesitate, as if uncertain of himself. Then he said, "Miss Haywood, earlier, I spoke with your...."

A shout went up.

Everyone, including Emily and Mr. Reed turned to see what caused the commotion. Then, through the falling snow, Emily saw a liveried outrider racing down the lane toward them. As he neared and reined in his horse, Emily recognized the man—Jack Wilcox, one of Her Ladyship's grooms who'd travelled with her to Cheltenham.

The villagers hurried toward him, and he called out over them, "The Coburgs aren't coming. They've gone to Windsor. It's just Her Ladyship."

A collective groan of disappointment rippled through the crowd.

Except for Emily.

A sense of relief washed over her. At least they wouldn't embarrass themselves. Or Her Ladyship. *But oh, how disappointed Her Ladyship must be.*

Turning back to Mr. Reed, Emily noticed that he, too, appeared relieved by the news.

Before she could say a word to him, the sound of horses and a carriage coming down the lane interrupted them.

Her Ladyship.

This time, everyone rushed for a place along the drive so they might see her as the carriage sped past, handkerchiefs in hand ready to wave. Even Old Mr. Phelps stood among them and pulled his hat from his head out of respect.

But to the surprise of everyone, rather than speeding past, the carriage drew up and stopped before the gathered villagers. The two footmen climbed down from the back and within a matter of minutes, dropped down the hood, thereby turning the vehicle into an open carriage.

There sat Her Ladyship alongside her maid.

White-haired and aged, Her Ladyship wore a fashionable bonnet—that is to say, one of an outlandish color, too many feathers, and unaccountably tall. It was much remarked upon. Mrs. Williamson declared it stunning, while Mr. Cunningham laughed behind his hand at the sight of it.

With the help of both her maid and her stick, Her Ladyship rose and announced with a strong voice, "I'm afraid the Coburgs are not coming."

"Yes," someone said, "we know."

"You know?" asked Her Ladyship, looking over the gathering for verification. When nods here and there confirmed the information, she continued, "Then why all… this?"

"For you," said another.

"And for all of us as well," said Old Mr. Phelps.

Her Ladyship stood there in wonderment for a moment and surveyed the scene before her. Then, her brow furrowed and she demanded, "Is Jessop watering down the cider again?" Laughter erupted from the crowd. "Jessop," she continued, locating him among the villagers, "give them back their money. I'll cover the cost of refreshments."

Cheers of *Huzzah!* went up here and there.

And then, much to the amazement of all, Her Ladyship climbed down from the carriage and asked for a cup of wassail, before walking over to inspect the Christmas tree she had ordered.

Emily found herself standing between her father and Mr. Reed, when her father turned to them both and shook his head.

"While I find this all perfectly innocuous," he said to them, "I really don't see what it has to do with Christmas."

No, no, no! Inwardly, Emily groaned but could not contain the rising moan and said, "Not you, as well, Papa?"

"Yes, but...."

Mr. Reed leaned forward. "It's an evergreen—like holly—representing everlasting life through Christ, who is born this night."

Both Emily and her father stared at Mr. Reed.

"Like holly?" asked the vicar.

"Crown of thorns, pearls of blood. Really, if you ask me, we should decorate with holly at Easter, not Christmas."

The vicar broke out in a joyous smile. "Oh, that is excellent, Mr. Reed. I must use that tomorrow in my sermon. I hope you don't mind."

"No, of course not."

"Really," continued the vicar, "all I could think of was 'Tree of Life' and 'Our Lord was a carpenter.' Not much to work with."

Someone called over to the vicar, and he excused himself, leaving the pair, for all intents and purposes, alone. In the midst of a crowd, of course.

Emily continued to stare up at him. It must have been in an accusatory manner because Mr. Reed apologized and explained, "I only thought it this afternoon while stringing up all those boughs of holly."

"Too bad you didn't think of it yesterday. It might have saved me a lot of trouble."

Someone nodded to the Christmas tree and asked, "So what do we do now?"

Mrs. Williamson suggested, "Maybe dance around it like a Maypole?"

"I don't know," another replied.

A stillness filled the air, the lights from the lanterns filling the night and reflecting off the snow. Everyone looked at each other. And a lone voice went up. Old Mr. Phelps.

Good King Wenceslas looked out...

And another voice joined him.

...on the Feast of Stephen.

That was all it took before everyone was singing.

But neither Emily nor Mr. Reed joined in. Instead, Mr. Reed leaned closer to her and said, "Miss Haywood, I really must speak with you."

Emily nodded, and they moved away from the villagers to stand by an abandoned brazier.

"Miss Haywood," he said, again faltering as he had

earlier, "About what is being said. I was horrified to hear of it..."

"It's quite all right, Mr. Reed," said Emily, "My father asked Mrs. Foster to tell everyone the truth."

"Yes, so I heard," said Mr. Reed, "but, well, I asked your father if I might have your hand in marriage."

"I know."

"He just laughed," continued Mr. Reed, as if she had not spoken, "But then, after I explained, he said to discuss it with you." He took a deep breath. "So I am asking you. Will you marry me?"

He sounded sincere—he truly wished to protect her honor and reputation—and as much as she wished it otherwise, Emily couldn't allow him to sacrifice himself, not for her. Besides, what kind of marriage would it be? Marry in haste, repent at leisure. No, she couldn't marry him, but she didn't want to hurt him, either. "I am honored that you would do this, Mr. Reed, but there's no need. Really."

"Yes, I know that...," he said.

"I am honored that you should ask, that you would wish to protect...."

"Miss Haywood," said Mr. Reed, his tone firmer, "You don't seem to understand. I'm asking because I want you to be my wife. This gossip has simply provided me with the perfect reason to broach the subject."

He was right. She didn't understand.

"Yesterday," he continued, "was extraordinary. *You* were extraordinary. You took on the villagers—that could've turned into a mob..."

"Not really."

"And you helped a stranger when you didn't have to," he

said, "You wanted—no, needed—to return home to Mrs. Edmondson, but you carried on, to help me and then Sir George, in his slight-of-hand courting of Widow Talbot. You saved that boy. You never hesitated, even standing up to me in order to do what you knew to be the best chance for his survival. And then you put all your trust in me. And this morning, I did not want to leave your house. I wanted to see you and be with you all the days of my life."

He barely paused for breath before continuing. "I thank God for yesterday, because otherwise, I never would have known what a wonderful person you are. And I thank God for the gossip, because it gave me the impetus to speak to your father, without fear of the answer. Otherwise, I would have dithered for months before summoning up the courage. So please, I am sincere. Will you marry me?"

Emily could hardly speak, and she felt the wet of tears in her eyes. Then she realized she held her breath, and as she let it go, she said, "No."

Mr. Reed's entire body seemed to slump.

"But," she continued, "you are more than welcome to court me." Mr. Reed immediately brightened, and Emily added, "If your intentions are honorable." She smiled.

He returned an eager, happy smile. "Oh yes. Yes, they are. And then, if you are willing, after some time has passed, I may ask again?"

Emily nodded. "If you still feel the same."

He looked relieved, and Emily realized a joy filled her, a joy unrelated to Christmas. The villagers sang another carol. Neither of them said another word. Nothing more needed saying.

Instead, in their silence, they walked back toward the

others. And as they did, Mr. Reed—Lachlan—slowly reached out his hand without glancing at her but just knowing she was there beside him. Emily, in a motion so natural it shocked her, took hold of his hand. And together, hand in hand, they rejoined the villagers singing around the Christmas tree.

About Anna

Anna D. Allen fully admits she has little knowledge of plants beyond the edible varieties, and given the current state of her vegetable garden, even that is questionable. She holds a Bachelor of Science and a Master of Arts in Language and Literature. She is a recipient of the Writers of the Future award and a member of Science Fiction and Fantasy Writers of America, but she also has a great passion for Regency Romances. It is generally acknowledged that she spends way too much time with the dead and her mind got lost somewhere in the 19th Century. Case in point, her website:

http://beket1.wix.com/annadallen

Along with her contributions to the six *Christmas Revels* Regency anthologies, her available works include the Regency Romance novel *Miss Pritchard's Happy, Wanton Christmas (and the Consequences Thereof)*; the Regency Romance novelette "A Christmas Wager;" the novel *Charles Waverly and the Deadly African Safari*; and three short story collections: *Mrs. Hewitt's Barbeque, Lake People,* and *Lady de Kiernan's Headache*; as well as some boring scholarly stuff about dead people. Currently, she is finishing her first Victorian mystery novel, *The Drowned Girl,* which she freely admits is Holmes and Watson fanfiction... but then, Sir Arthur was writing Edgar Allan Poe fanfiction, so Anna is in good company.

In the virtual world, she can be found on Facebook.

"The Play's the Thing..."

by

Hannah Meredith

PROLOGUE

Early December, 1812. The headmistress's parlor at the Claridge Academy for Young Ladies. Two ladies seated in facing chairs before the fire.

Rachel Grant stifled the impulse to either squirm in her chair or leap to her feet and pace. She was simply *not* good at waiting. She frowned at Amelia Langston. Whatever was taking her friend and employer so long to read a two-page letter?

"I think it would be a mistake to accept," Rachel finally said, flinging her voice into the overlong silence in place of the need to move. Drat it! She'd meant to get Amelia's opinion before offering her own. But the suspense had forced her to prompt some sort of reaction.

Amelia looked up, removed her reading glasses, and rubbed the bridge of her substantial nose—while Rachel continued to wait. "Why ever would you think that?" Amelia asked. "This Christmas gathering sounds like a wonderful opportunity. You've been at sixes and sevens about what to do for the long holiday, and the Duchess of Newley's house party would fill the bill nicely. I'm still just so sorry..."

"Don't be," Rachel blurted out. She wanted to stop Amelia before *that* discussion was revisited... again. In the past, Rachel had stayed with Amelia's family for the long school holidays, but this arrangement was now impossible. Last month, Amelia's youngest brother, Stephen—who had been oh-so-respectfully courting Rachel for the past two years—suddenly married the seventeen-year-old daughter of one of his parishioners. Rachel's presence in a household that included the newlyweds would be awkward in the extreme.

In hindsight, Rachel wondered if the extreme respectfulness of Stephen's address had signaled a lack of mutual attraction. The potential match had been a logical one, perhaps advocated more by Stephen's parents than Stephen himself. As a vicar's daughter, Rachel would have made an excellent vicar's wife, and Stephen definitely needed help managing his parish.

But there had been no spark between them. Stephen was kind and considerate, but also bumbling and, honesty forced her to admit, boring. But she suspected Stephen was probably her last chance at having a home and family and so had been willing to trade her energy and organizational skills for security and a life she found comfortable.

Although both the faculty and students at Claridge still held hushed discussions about her *disappointment*, Rachel found she was primarily disappointed she would not be joining Lord Langston's large and boisterous family for the Christmas Season.

"We've been over this, and things have a habit of working out for the best." Rachel put a forced smile on her face. "And, as you said, the Newley's invitation might be a wonderful opportunity."

"But I can tell you have reservations."

"Of course, I have reservations." Unable to stop, Rachel

bounced to her feet and began circling the room. "I would be spending the entire holiday with people I have never met. At a duke's residence, of all things. I'm plain Miss Grant, a vicar's daughter who now teaches for a living. What would I have in common with anyone else attending a house party there? Well, except for someone's companion or a stray governess who accompanied a family with children."

She'd come to the end of the room and reversed her direction, so she could see Amelia take a breath to begin a rebuttal. "No, not a word until I have mentioned all my doubts, the greatest of which is whether I'm supposed to be a guest or an employee. The duchess wants me to oversee the production of the Harvest Festival play I wrote for the girls here—with 'seasonal adaptations,' whatever that means. She mentions this will be an amateur theatrical, with the parts being played by those attending the house party. So, am I considered one of the amateurs who are guests, or am I a visiting professional, in which case, I would basically be an employee?"

Rachel turned to retrace her steps and saw a grinning Amelia waving a piece of paper in each hand. Rachel stumbled to a stop. "What in the world are you doing?"

"I'm sending semaphore signals for you to dock your ship. I'm having difficulty talking with someone who is sailing about the room."

"Oh, good Heavens. Are you a dignified headmistress or a ten-year-old?" Rachel rolled her eyes and flopped back into her chair in a manner that would have garnered a reprimand had she been a student. "I don't think you're taking my concerns seriously."

"I am—but I think most of your apprehensions are

without merit."

"How can you say that? Did you actually read the letter or just use the pages as signaling flags?"

Rachel's irritation increased as Amelia's face settled into the mask of patience she often wore with the school's slower students. "I've read your letter from the duchess with great care," Amelia said, "and am using what she says as the basis for my confidence that you're needlessly worrying about imaginary problems. So, first to your greatest concern... It is obvious to me that you have been invited as a guest. Her Grace is most laudatory about your talent and praises the cleverness of your play."

Rachel suspected the bulk of her cleverness had been in assigning one of the major roles, the Harvest Sprite, to the Duchess's daughter, Margaret, and then seeing to it that the girl didn't embarrass herself—something Margaret normally tended to do with consistency.

"As far as doing some 'seasonal adaptations,'" Amelia continued, "well, it shouldn't be hard to work in some Christmas references since the theme of the story is that kindness leads to understanding and harmony."

"Amelia," Rachel drew out the name in her own version of put-upon patience, "all of the characters who teach this lesson are animals. Do you honestly see any adult who's attending a house party at a ducal estate wanting to be cast as a wise hedgehog?"

Amelia laughed. "I can think of a number of peers who could be hedgehogs without a costume. Having them appear wise, however, might be much more difficult."

"Easy for you to laugh since you will not be the one trying to convince these people to take a part in a play designed for young girls. I can't see my being particularly persuasive since I don't fit into this segment of society. These are your type of people. Not mine."

Amelia suddenly leaned forward and slapped the two pieces of cream stationery into Rachel's lap. "Just answer the letter in the affirmative. Then go and have a wonderful time. Meet new people. And stop whining about not fitting in. You're the granddaughter of a viscount, for Heaven's sake. Not a washer woman."

"A viscount I have never met. A man who disowned my mother when she had the audacity to marry the local vicar rather than a man of his choosing. I have no desire to claim kinship with such a person." Rachel frowned at her friend in irritation.

Amelia already knew Rachel had no contact with her grandfather. They had discussed Rachel's tenuous connection to Society when she'd taken the teaching position at the Claridge Academy six years earlier. Amelia promoted the school by telling the parents of prospective students that all the teachers were related to peers—a fact which helped both to attract the daughters of wealthy industrialists and to reassure those of the aristocracy. Rachel had reluctantly agreed there would be truth in this statement about her as well.

But being included in a general statement about a group of teachers was not the same thing as presenting oneself at a ducal doorway with such dubious credentials.

"Well, then there's also the problem that I have nothing appropriate to wear." Although this was a tangible concern, Rachel wanted to cringe at voicing what sounded like a typical feminine lament. In this case, however, it was true.

Teachers had neither the funds nor the need for more than one dinner dress—and one was exactly how many Rachel owned. Her trusty mauve had seen her through every occasion that called for something more elegant than a day dress ever since coming to Claridge Academy. From the first, the dress had been more classic than stylish, and now it was simply out-of-date.

"Easily addressed by using the Abandoned Closet and enlisting Mrs. Gibbs." Amelia gave her a satisfied smile.

"But the Abandoned Closet is for the use of our scholarship students." Rachel had long been impressed with Amelia's efforts to make Claridge more egalitarian. Students' use of titles was forbidden, and there were a number of bright students whose parents could not have afforded the fees if Amelia had not arranged for benefactors to help with the payments. But regardless of these efforts, financial and social positions were readily apparent in clothing.

And so, the Abandoned Closet had come into being. At the end of every term, students left clothing in their wardrobes and chests. Out-grown, deemed unfashionable, or disposed of because the garment no longer appealed, the collection of discarded dresses, pelisses, and undergarments was staggering. This was where Mrs. Gibb's skill was needed. The diminutive, gray-haired seamstress could magically transform a castoff item into something fashionable that was unrecognizable to the original owner.

"I was thinking of the dresses Lillian Taymor left here, two years running," Amelia said. "The materials and styles were much too sophisticated for any of our students, but would be ideal for a mature woman."

Rachel gave her friend a rueful smile. "Thanks for

reminding me I qualify as *mature* by any definition." At twenty-six, Rachel probably qualified as on-the-shelf—a spinster school teacher whose last chance at having a home and family had disappeared when a balding, disorganized vicar became enamored with a mere child. So, perhaps, she was a bit disappointed. Maybe, just maybe, a ducal house party would provide her with a different perspective.

"I was thinking of that wonderful green velvet," Amelia said. "So inappropriate for a girl of seventeen, but perfect for you. I think we can be happy that, while Lillian's mother had poor judgment in what a young girl should wear, she also had a good deal of money."

Rachel remembered the green dress and smiled. "I think we should repair to the Abandoned Closet," she said, sliding her arm through her friend's and pulling her toward the hallway.

ACT ONE

Scene One
Three weeks later. An opulent bedchamber at the Duke of
Newley's estate. A gentleman holds a bedpost while his valet
attempts to lace up his corset.

Harris gave another mighty pull, and Captain Lord Alexander Kingston decided he had had enough. "Bloody hell, leave off. You're not reefing the topsail before a blow. I have to be able to breathe." The last word came out as more of a grunt as Harris gave a final mighty tug and started tying off the tapes.

"Captain, if I'm supposed to get you into any of these fancy clothes, then you've got to be trussed up like this." Harris backed up to survey his work. "This is no tighter than it was earlier."

Alexander released his hold and wondered if the elaborate carving on the bedpost had left a matching imprint on his hands. His estimation of the fair sex had risen in the last few minutes. Ladies had to endure this torture daily, proving unequivocally they were the stronger gender. "Harris, remember to call me Mr. Kingston, or this charade will be for naught."

"Right you are, Ca... eh, Mr. Kingston." Harris held out a

shirt the size of a sail. "But I must say, all of this padding you up and then slimming you down seems a bit unnecessary."

Alexander could not have agreed more. But then, this entire assignment was ridiculous. The Admiralty had unceremoniously jerked him off the *Wheatley* and plopped him here in the middle of Lancashire tasked to determine if any of the guests at the Duke of Newley's holiday gathering were secretly supporting the American cause. He was chagrined that his superiors thought this was the best use of his abilities. That he had been personally chosen by Melville, the First Lord of the Admiralty, did nothing to assuage his irritation.

The *Wheatley* had been his first command of a ship of the line. Yes, she carried only eighty-four guns, but he'd been proud of every one of them and had looked forward to meeting the French with those guns blazing. Instead, he was sent back to London where he was given the *honor* of spying on British peers who may or may not be aiding the fractious former colonials in what was, to his thinking, a minor campaign. Alexander felt this was a waste of his experience, proving once again the dry-foot sailors at the Admiralty were asses.

Those fools in London felt he had the necessary qualifications—he would be unknown to the other guests and he would understand implications of merchant ship movements if they were discussed. These were qualifications? They would apply to half of the serving officers in the Royal Navy. His name must have been drawn from a hat.

He was the fourth of six sons of the Marquess of Hallingford, so it was true he could easily get lost in what was generally referred to as Hallingford's Litter. And he'd been aboard a ship since he was twelve, a fact that meant he didn't travel in society. This evidently qualified him as *unknown*, and being pulled away from potential battles assured this was how he would remain.

As for ship movements... did those in the Admiralty think someone would say, "Oh, by the way, here's how I'm getting American cotton around the naval blockade to supply my mills in Manchester," while playing billiards? Idiocy! Of course, the entire American war was idiocy and a drain on resources needed to fight the French, but what could England do when the former colonies tried to take over Canada while the British were otherwise occupied?

"Let's see if we can squeeze you into these," Harris said holding up a pair of dress trousers sized to fit someone playing Falstaff. The damned cheeky man was grinning. Of course, had their positions been reversed, Alexander would probably have viewed this whole debacle as a lark. At least he had confidence that Harris would keep his mouth shut when they returned to the *Wheatley*. If the man had been less loyal, he could have dined out for months on the retelling of getting Captain Kingston dressed.

As it was, getting into the trousers was a bit of a struggle. "Those London gents made your arse too big," Harris said, pushing on the horsehair pads that covered his rear.

All this bother to make Alexander appear harmless. If the Admiralty wanted *harmless*, they should not have chosen a man with his height and powerful physique. It must have been the bloody hair that had convinced his superiors he would make a perfect buffoon.

It was difficult for the world at large to take a man with bright red hair seriously, and he'd had to work doubly hard to prove his worth. For years, he'd kept his hair clipped close to his head. For this assignment, however, he'd been ordered to let it grow, and it was now a riot of ridiculously red curls.

Finally arrayed in a blue coat and garish waistcoat, Alexander surveyed himself in the cheval mirror. The effect was... well, the only word was comic. "Would anyone actually walk around dressed like this?" he asked.

Harris looked up from folding one of the four cravats he'd irredeemably wrinkled before finally mastering the elaborate pattern that now adorned Alexander's neck. "In my opinion, not if he could help it. But I guess there's those who do, or those London gents wouldn't have kitted you out like they did. At least your waistcoat goes with your coat, unlike some they sent along do."

"That's because this bloody waistcoat contains every color known to man." Alexander frowned at the offending article.

"Well, you should thank your lucky stars you aren't wearing breeches and hose all the time, like was first suggested. At least this way, you get a new pair of boots for day wear.

"And comfortable boots, they are," Alexander said. "Although I suspect they are the only tangible good that will come out of this mess. Well, other than I'm unrecognizable and so won't have to live down this escapade if I should ever again meet any of the people here."

After another look at the creature he'd become, Alexander swung around to face his clerk-turned-valet. "Harris, be careful to stay in character below stairs. There's a hierarchy among the servants at a grand house such as this that's as stringent as the one aboard ship, and visitors take on the rank of those they arrived with. So, while valets rank above many other positions, you will be mostly disregarded since you arrived with a mere mister who has no connections."

"I remember the instructions," Harris said. "Keep my head down, my mouth shut, and my ears open."

"Which are opposite from mine, except for keeping my ears open. Part of my *harmless* guise is evidently to talk as much as possible but to say nothing."

Harris laughed. "To be convincing, then, you're going to have to stop scowling. But playing the part of a fribble should be easy. Just pretend you're Lieutenant Powell."

Alexander had made Harris his clerk because the man was sharp, and so, unsurprisingly, his suggestion was right on target. Poor, hapless Lieutenant Powell would be a perfect model, less all the padding, of course. The man was rail thin, but his mouth flapped constantly, spewing forth words on totally inane topics of no interest.

"Good choice," Alexander said. "Now I just wish I could remember some of the subjects Powell tends to go on about."

Harris shrugged. "I certainly can't remember any, but that is probably the point. Just think of something you know that no one cares about and drone on about it."

Again, solid advice, but Alexander's greatest knowledge was about sailing, and he was sure no one would ever find *that* boring. "What about the habits of insects? Before I became a midshipman, I had a tutor who was enamored with insects. We caught them and studied them and mounted them into collections. I might have to visit Newley's library to get specific facts that have become hazy over time, but I can't imagine anyone wanting to discuss insects."

And so, with flies and beetles and wasps buzzing in his head, Mr. Alexander Kingston left his room to join the party assembling for dinner.

Scene Two

Fifteen minutes later. The large drawing room at the Duke of Newley's estate, festooned with Christmas greenery. A lady in a blue dress stands hesitantly just inside the door.

Rachel Grant looked around the large room filled with beautifully dressed people. She had to remind herself to breathe. She was in a duke's drawing room, and no one had pointed her out as an interloper. Never had she been so thankful for the Abandoned Closet. Even though her lady's maid—the idea that such a person would be assigned to her was still a shock—had seemed dismissive of her limited wardrobe, her dress didn't mark her as different. And at this point, blending in was her goal.

"Miss Grant, how wonderful to see you. I hope your journey was comfortable." The Duchess of Newley appeared next to her while she was gawking at the beautifully decorated room and the assembled people resplendent in their holiday finery.

Rachel felt the flush of embarrassment stain her cheeks. She should have immediately sought out her hostess instead of loitering at the door. She dropped into a well-practiced curtsey. "Your Grace, I'm delighted to see you again. You were so kind to send a carriage. It made my journey very comfortable." Definitely more comfortable than traveling by stagecoach, Rachel's intended mode of transportation, but she didn't want to mention that tidbit in a room where she assumed everyone else was only acquainted with a stagecoach because they'd seen one drive by.

"I'm just sorry you were unable to arrive before most of the others," the Duchess said. "I was anxious to see the changes you'd made to your charming play. But now we only have a week until Twelfth Night, when it will be performed, so we will need to begin casting and practice tomorrow if we are to be ready."

Alarm chased her embarrassment away. Heavens! Evidently, she was supposed to have arrived before anyone else so she could get the changes to her play approved by the duchess. This seemed to put her in the position of being an employee. While no financial remuneration had been mentioned, and she'd been given the most luxurious room she'd ever slept in—not to mention the services of a lady's maid—her role was to provide entertainment.

And here she was congratulating herself on how well she could blend in. All the other guests, the real ones, probably knew she was there to supply a service. She was the only one who had believed she was here to simply enjoy the party. She would not have succumbed to that fantasy had Amelia not assured her that she would be a guest. When she returned to Claridge, she was going to find some real semaphore flags and beat Amelia about the shoulders with them.

"I'm so sorry I misinterpreted when you needed me here," she said. "I am completely at your disposal. I'd be happy to run up to my room and retrieve a copy of the edited play right now, if you'd like me to. Or I can give you a copy when we meet tomorrow."

"Tomorrow will be sufficient," the duchess said, but her eyes were focused on someone behind Rachel who had captured her attention. The duchess had graciously greeted her but was now ready to return to her true guests. This thought was born out when the duchess said, "Please excuse me. I see a late arrival I need to attend." And then she deserted Rachel, who was left standing near the door like an idiot. She wondered if everyone could see she was a spinster school teacher with no background, dressed in a remade, castoff dress, and pretending to be someone she was not.

Rachel straightened her shoulders and raised her chin. She had long counseled her students that the appearance of self-confidence was almost as good as having self-confidence. She walked across the room with a purposeful step, as if her direction held a specific goal. A few people in the conversation groups she passed caught her eye. She smiled at them and pressed onward until she was near the far border of the room. There she stopped and turned to face the room, her face carefully displaying an imperious expression.

The Duchess of Newley was in an animated conversation with a large man by the door. A singularly odd, large man. Now there was someone who had made no effort to blend in. Even from a distance, the cacophony of colors in his waistcoat was nearly blinding. And while he wore the standard black evening trousers, his coat was blue rather than the black of all the other men in the room. Whoever had dressed him had done him no favors.

The poor man could do nothing about the form that God

had given him, however. He towered above everyone there and had startling orange-red hair that circled his head in unruly curls. As pleasing as his height and breath of shoulder might be, the illusion of handsomeness was shattered by his girth. He was obviously a hearty trencherman. He had to weigh well over twenty stones.

Oh, drat! The man had raised his eyes and saw her staring at him. She quickly looked at a conversation group nearby and acted as if someone there had caught her attention. But her view was broad enough to note the man said something to the Duchess of Newley. Then, to her horror, they walked directly toward her as if an arrow had been painted on the glorious Axminster carpet underfoot.

Rachel wished there were a large piece of furniture or the proverbial potted palm to hide behind. There being nothing, she tightened her spine and continued with her appearance of surveying the room. When the pair were almost upon her, she looked directly at the duchess and gave her a welcoming smile... which was thankfully returned.

"Miss Grant," the duchess said, "may I present Mr. Kingston. Mr. Kingston, this is Miss Grant."

"Miss Grant," the man acknowledged. His voice was deep and melodious.

Rachel curtseyed and Mr. Kingston bowed. In the process, his large fundament nudged the table behind him. A holly-filled vase that sat on the table's surface began to wobble. Rachel and the duchess inhaled in concert, anticipating the china container would crash to the floor. Instead, a large square hand reached out and righted the vase. The speed of the movement was astounding.

"Please excuse my clumsiness," Mr. Kingston said. He

looked chagrined.

"Don't concern yourself. No harm was done." The duchess was gracious and Rachel liked her better for her kindness toward this awkward man. The older lady shifted her attention to Rachel. "We'll soon be called to dine, and I wanted you to be introduced since I've asked Mr. Kingston to take you in. He's newly arrived from London where he's an associate of Viscount Melville in the Admiralty."

"Delighted to meet you," Rachel said, since there was no other comment possible. They would enter the dining room and be seated by order of precedence, which meant that Mr. Kingston would be seated next to her and was, therefore, as lacking in social importance as she was.

Having done her part, the Duchess of Newley left them to their own devices as she saw to other duties. For a moment, she and Mr. Kingston stood in awkward silence. Rachel was tall for a woman but still needed to tilt her head back to look into Mr. Kingston's face. If this were all one saw of the man, he would be considered handsome in a rugged, windswept way. His features were symmetrical. His cheekbones sharply sculpted. He had the ruddy complexion typical of a fair man who spent a great deal of time out of doors. His eyes, a mixture of moss green and golden brown, were bright with intelligence.

All in all, Mr. Kingston's face was at odds with the rest of his body.

Distracted by this realization, she floundered for a conversational topic. "Did you have a pleasant journey?" she finally asked.

"Yes, especially for this time of year. Cold, of course, but fortunately dry. Kept the roads passable. Did your journey go well?" When he smiled, fine lines radiated from the corners of his eyes.

"The duchess sent one of the Newley carriages to pick me up. I had a short trip, but I traveled in luxury," Rachel said.

"Oh, are you a near neighbor? I did wonder if most of those here came from close by."

Rachel shook her head. "No, I live in Highmot. It's about two hours away. I teach at the Claridge Academy for Young Ladies. Lady Margaret, the Newley's middle daughter, is one of my students."

For some reason, the man looked impressed. That he would be impressed by her being a school teacher reinforced his oddness.

"Then your being invited to this holiday gathering is a singular honor," he said.

She stifled a laugh. "I was asked to help with the amateur theatrical the duchess has planned." Then she had an inspiration. Perhaps she had found her hedgehog. "Do you by any chance act?"

Unlike her, he did laugh aloud. A low roll of thunder that attracted some surprised looks. "I have never tried. But I suspect I would be very bad at it."

"Do you never go to the theater?"

"Not since I was a boy, although I do remember enjoying it then. I have been out of the country a good deal as an adult and haven't had the time to attend."

"Out of the country?" Mr. Kingston didn't have the look of a military man, although the duchess had mentioned the Admiralty in her introduction. "Where have you been?"

"Most recently Africa. My passion is entomology and I

was there to study..." He looked around as if to determine if they could be overheard. Then he leaned down and whispered, "Dung beetles."

His breath on her ear made her feel strangely shivery. The sensation certainly had nothing to do with dung beetles.

Then the dinner bell rang and the assembly began to form up in order of precedence. Mr. Kingston offered her his arm and they strolled toward the back of the line. His arm felt surprisingly muscular beneath her hand.

Scene Three

Later that evening. The same bedroom as seen earlier, but it is now draped in shadows. Two men sit at leisure before the fire, glasses of brandy in their hands.

Alexander stretched his feet toward the fire and released a heavy sigh. "Lord, I can't tell you how wonderful it is simply to breathe. I had no idea the corset would be so constricting. I really don't think I can keep up this charade."

"I didn't think you had any choice." Harris looked at Alexander over the rim of his glass. When Alexander had promoted Harris to be his clerk, he hadn't realized he was also gaining a friend. There was loneliness in being a ship's captain, and Alexander appreciated having someone he could talk to who would give him unbiased opinions.

"There's always a choice," he said, "but for every choice, there is also a price. I'm not willing to pay the price of not following my orders—and those who sent me here know that. I've worked for the past twenty years, since I was a midshipman of twelve, to get where I am. I'm not willing to jeopardize that. But Lord, I hate this bloody assignment."

Harris chuckled. "I think what you really hate is all the padding and the costume."

"In that, you're probably correct," Alexander admitted. "I loathe pretending to be someone I'm not, and the outfit I'm forced to wear is ridiculous. I certainly hope I'm not expected to sneak around someone's room looking for incriminating papers, since the damned corset makes a sound like a tortured ghost if I bend the wrong way. It's the reason I had to beg off going with a group to ride over the estate tomorrow morning. Besides being damned uncomfortable, I decided I would be unable to overhear anything of note over the whining and wailing of my support pieces."

Harris got up and, unasked, added two more fingers of brandy to Alexander's glass. "Did you find anyone who might be aiding the American cause?"

"Not a soul who seemed in the least suspicious. I have no idea who the Admiralty thinks is involved in illegal activities, but whoever it is, they're not obvious."

"Perhaps you should question the duke, specifically about where he magically obtained this fine French brandy," Harris said, settling back into his chair.

Alexander chuckled. "I did that after the ladies left the dining room and the tantalus was brought out. Newley was very specific that he'd laid in a large supply years ago."

"And you believed him?"

Alexander shrugged. "Let's just say I'd believe my father if he said the same thing, which I'm sure he would. I'm looking for blockade runners who are aiding an enemy's cause, not a few Englishmen who enjoy smuggled brandy."

Harris shook his head and may have muttered "toffs," but it was said low enough that Alexander couldn't be sure. "So, what are your morning plans?" Harris said aloud. "Your hard-working valet has to ready the appropriate clothing."

"Since it takes so long to get me wrapped in all the padding, I'll be up before the sun, which, fortunately, is what we're both used to. After breakfast, I need to visit the library to come up with some more information to support my *passion* for entomology. I've exhausted all I can remember about dung beetles and spiders. Later, I'll join those who didn't go riding and continue my useless snooping. And then, at some point, I'm going to help with an amateur theatrical."

Harris jerked back and began coughing as if he'd inhaled rather than swallowed a sip of his drink. "Never tell me you're going to act?" he finally got out.

"I suspect that is what the lady in charge of the production has in mind," Alexander said. "And if so, I'll take a part. The lady is... very persuasive. I suspect it will just be a continuation of the role of fool that I'm already playing. She can only have a comedic part in mind for me. With all the padding, I could hardly be considered as the romantic hero. Which reminds me—Is there any way to diminish the size of the stuffing over my arse? I bowed this evening and nearly cleared a tabletop of bric-a-brac."

Harris's subdued coughing turned into a full, unabashed laugh. "I'll see what I can do." He set down his now empty glass and stood. "But presently I need to chose your motley for tomorrow." With a grin that said he enjoyed turning his captain into a fool, he picked up one of the candelabras and wandered to the wardrobe.

Alexander leaned back in the large chair and looked at

the fire though his glass. The amber liquid turned the flames into a kaleidoscope of subdued colors that reminded him of Miss Grant's hair. His comment about her being very persuasive was true, but he wasn't sure if everyone was affected or if her ability to convince was specific to him.

It had been years since he'd been this attracted to a lady. Of course, he hadn't been exposed to all that many. While there had been women in various ports, those had mostly involved a financial arrangement, not attraction. When he was home on the occasional leave, his mother had presented nearly every young lady living near his family's estate. But none had called to him until Miss Grant—and he had no idea why.

She was attractive without being beautiful. She had regular features and soft looking skin. Brown hair and brown eyes. At first glance, she looked like a myriad of others he'd seen. But by the end of the evening, she did not. She'd become unique.

She was tall for a woman, which he found appealing since it kept him from feeling quite so oversized. On closer examination, her eyes were a dark gold, sparkling with wit and good humor. Her brown hair was a mixture of honey and treacle. And her features were not as regular as he'd thought. Her mouth was too big, or maybe it just looked that way since she was always smiling.

Miss Grant was without artifice. She did not mince or glide; she strode through a room as if intent on getting someplace rather than putting on a show. Most importantly, however, she was kind. Alexander knew what he looked like in his present guise. Most ladies would have avoided him if possible. But Miss Grant acted as if she were interested in him. She'd even asked questions as he'd droned on about beetles and spiders and other crawly things the fair sex tended to avoid but which were dear to young boys—and hence, firmly planted in his memory.

When the gentlemen had rejoined the ladies in the drawing room, he noticed how so many eyes noted him and then darted away. Miss Grant, however, had given him a welcoming smile. It seemed she could see the man within rather than what was presented. He'd had a powerful desire to kiss her, but knew that was beyond the pale even if he'd been wearing his own skin and clothes.

Simply put, he liked the woman and wished she had gifted him with her first name to take with him into dreams.

ACT TWO

Scene One
After breakfast on the second day of Newley's house party. The duchess's private sitting room. Three ladies sit at a small, circular table in a broad window bay. Two are reading. One is fidgeting.

Rachel folded and flattened the same corner of the paper in front of her. Folded and flattened again. Waiting for the duchess and Mrs. Goodchild to finish reading her play, now titled *The Christmas Promise,* was like being attacked by midges. It was nearly impossible to sit still.

The only thing that held her in place was the sound of appreciative chuckles that came at different times from the two readers. Rachel had to believe both ladies were enjoying the story. Finally, Mrs. Goodchild placed the last page upside-down on her stack and gave Rachel a grin and a wink, but she remained silent until the duchess did the same.

Rachel continued to fold and straighten.

"What a delightful tale," Mrs. Goodchild said as soon as the duchess's final page joined her others on the table. "I can see why you were so enthusiastic to have it performed here, Elizabeth. It will be a perfect end to your festivities, and it is almost as if the story were written to take advantage of the usual participants."

The Duchess of Newly beamed at her childhood friend. The fact that they *were* friends, casually using their first names, Elizabeth and Emma, had given Rachel a different perspective on the duchess. The duchess behaved with such consequence that Rachel would never have guessed she came from the landed gentry, where Emma Goodchild still remained. In her mind, Rachel was already casting the smiling and exuberant Mrs. Goodchild as the Christmas Sprite who, as the narrator of the play, explained scenes impossible to present on stage and kept the action going.

"The credit is all due to Miss Grant," the duchess said. "She conceived of the play as part of Claridge Academy's Harvest Festival and now has done a masterful job of adapting it to the Christmas Season."

"Adapting it?" Mrs. Goodchild gave Rachel a curious smile. "I would never have guessed this had ever been anything other than a Christmas play. I love the use of the animals as characters."

"You don't think adults might not want to portray a wren or a fox or some other woodland creature?" Rachel asked, suddenly uncomfortable with the praise. She still harbored the fear the entire project would collapse once they attempted to cast the play.

Mrs. Goodchild emphatically shook her head. "Oh, Heavens no. I can guarantee that anyone Elizabeth asks will be thrilled to take part. Being asked to be one of the players in the Newley theatricals is an honor."

"And since I was familiar with the play and knew who would be attending our house party, I've already come up with a list of potential actors." The duchess reached into the reticule lying on the table and with a flourish, pulled out a single sheet of paper. "Tell me what you think of these ideas, Emma."

She consulted her list. "Lady Anne Pierce for the Rebecca Wren and Lady Elwin for the Marjorie Magpie."

"Oh yes. Lady Elwin is a particularly brilliant choice."

Rachel tried place Lady Anne and Lady Elwin. Lady Anne was young and petite, and Lady Elwin, if she had the right woman, had worn a rather garish dress at dinner, so both were being cast to type. Rachel had hoped she would have had a hand in choosing the actors for the parts, but it now looked doubtful she would be involved. So far, she could understand how the duchess had arrived at her choices.

"I'd originally thought Lord Milton might make a good Horatio Hedgehog," the duchess continued, "but now that I've met Mr. Kingston, I think he would be perfect. My only concern is whether he'd be offended to be offered a part where the character is a portly as Mr. Kingston actually is. What do you think, Miss Grant? You sat next to him at dinner last night."

Rachel was pleased her opinion was being sought… and she *had* thought quite a bit about Mr. Kingston, although much of this musing had nothing to do with the play. She was not about to tell anyone that, however.

"I found him to be affable and kind," she said. "I think he is comfortable in his own skin and not the type of person who would easily take offense. And to be honest, the character of the hedgehog popped into my mind when I first met him. So, with both of us imagining him in that role, I think we should ask him. He always can say no."

The duchess gave a nod of satisfaction and made a

notation on her list. "I'll act as if his role was the duke's suggestion. This is always the easiest way to enlist the men. Of course, this means the duke needs a part, and I was thinking of The Tree."

"That's not a very large part," Mrs. Goodchild said.

"But a pivotal one," the duchess replied.

The two women then went on to apportion the remaining roles, leaving Rachel with little to do other than indicate her assent. This is not what she'd envisioned as her role, but it was obviously the one she'd been assigned. The only time she demurred was when the duchess assigned herself the role of the Christmas Sprite.

"I thought Mrs. Goodchild might like that part," Rachel said.

"Oh, no, I don't act." Mrs. Goodchild seemed embarrassed at her admission. "I like to stay behind the scenes."

The duchess reached over and patted her friend on the hand. "Emma is very creative when it comes to costuming. She uses the actors' personal clothing and then does the simplest things, and almost by magic, the character is quickly recognizable. We always press her into being our costumer."

The smaller woman blushed at the praise. "I was thinking that since all the characters are animals this year, headdresses might be a good way to go. Black and white feathers for the magpie, leaves for the tree, things like that. What do you think?"

"Absolutely brilliant," the duchess said.

Rachel's agreement quickly followed. It *was* a very good idea—and one she wished someone at Claridge had suggested. It would certainly have simplified the costumes they'd created for the harvest play.

The duchess tapped on her paper and brought them back to the business of assigning roles. "Well, we're now down to the villain, Walter Weasel. I was thinking the perfect candidate for that role would be..." she paused dramatically and looked at her smiling friend.

"Viscount Ambrose," they both said together and laughed.

Rachel's reaction was different. Caught in the middle of the smoothing action, her hand pushed across her paper with too much force, tearing the abused corner from the rest of the page. Viscount Ambrose? Good Lord! Her grandfather.

"Is Viscount Ambrose in residence?" Her voice must have been louder than it should have been, since the other two ladies gave her a startled look. But the idea she could have seen him last night and not recognized him left Rachel feeling decidedly unsettled.

"Not yet," the duchess said. "He lives nearby and likes to make an entrance on the second night."

"We must remember to be kind to his new wife," Mrs. Goodchild suggested.

"New wife?" Besides not knowing what he looked like, Rachel had no idea where he lived or anything about his family situation.

"Oh, yes. Poor dear." Mrs. Goodchild shook her head in commiseration. "She'll be a fish out of water. Lord Ambrose's third wife is the daughter of a mill owner in Manchester, painfully young and shy, but she came with the requisite funds, so the viscount was pleased to give her a title for needed money."

"From the rumors I've heard, the man was sailing close

to the River Tick," the duchess added. "His marriage was a timely rescue. He's heavily invested in importing cotton and has lost a number of ships to the conflict in North America."

"But one has trouble feeling sorry for the man," said the smaller woman. "He really does fit the role of the weasel to perfection and is a hard man to like."

"But will he agree to that part?" Rachel asked, her voice now small.

"Of course," the duchess said. "He'll do whatever 'The Tree' suggests." Both women chuckled.

But Rachel couldn't even manage a smile. She imagined her play becoming a shambles. There was a good chance that the viscount would *not* take the directions of a disowned and unknown granddaughter if he should, by some chance, recognize who she was. Or should she identify herself when she was introduced to him and stare him down?

Nervous energy pulled her to her feet. "I must finish up a few of the scripts for the individual characters," she lied. And then she fled the room and sought a quiet place to plan how she would meet a man she was predisposed to hate.

Scene Two
Evening of the same day. A crowd of people have gathered in the main salon of the Duke of Newley's home. A young woman stands stiffly next to a large gentleman, stage left.

Alexander tried to salve his self-esteem by using his present padded shape as the reason for Miss Grant's inattention. Since he'd reached his present height at seventeen, he'd never stood next to a lady and been so ignored. And this was the lady who less than twenty-four hours ago had seemed to hang on his every word, even when he was talking about dung beetles.

She had not seemed like the type of lady who judged a man on his waistline, or, in his case, his expansive derriere. He hoped his assessment of her character had not been amiss because, much to his consternation, he *liked* the woman.

Tonight, he'd come prepared with descriptions of the butterflies and moths of Madagascar, a topic designed to appeal to a lady, or at least, so he'd hoped. But evidently his research in the duke's library would be for naught. Miss Grant seemed fixated on those entering the room. She was obviously waiting for someone—and since he was standing next to her, Alexander was sure it wasn't him.

When he was confused by what his superiors wanted, he simply asked them to explain the situation, so he reverted to form and blurted out, "Are you waiting for someone specific, Miss Grant?"

A blush spread over her cheeks. "I'm sorry, Mr. Kingston. I'm a bit preoccupied this evening. At the duchess's suggestion, one of the parts for my play has been assigned to a gentleman who is arriving this evening, and I'm nervous that he will not be right for the character."

Which meant that Alexander was "right" for a hedgehog. A lowering thought. This would be more demeaning, however, if he'd not read over the part and quite liked the character. "Who is this mystery actor?" he asked, leaning over to speak close to her ear, part of his mind admiring the woodsy scent of her hair while a larger part was irritated her eyes had once again strayed to the doorway.

"Viscount Ambrose." She glanced up at him with this statement, and he was surprised to see she wore the look normally seen on a green midshipman right before the shelling began. Without considering the impropriety, he took one of her hands. When he discovered it was balled into a fist, he unconsciously tried to smooth it out. "Even if he's not physically right for his part, perhaps he's a good actor," he said. "You shouldn't fret so. Duchess Newley wouldn't have recommended him with no reason."

"But that's the problem. He's to play Walter Weasel, and I'm afraid he will be *perfect* for the part."

Alexander frowned at this odd, contradictory statement. He was slightly familiar with the character. In the last scene, Horatio Hedgehog stresses the need for kindness to the weasel, whose change of heart ushers in the play's felicitous ending. It would, therefore, seem to make sense that whoever played the part was in some way slightly "weaselly." Alexander was conceited enough to think such traits would be much worse than being thought to be hedgehog-like. "If he's playing to type, I would think you should be relieved," he said.

She raised her eyes to him and gave him a wan smile. "I fear all my preconceptions will be confirmed."

His expression must have shown he continued to be perplexed since she leaned closer and said softly, "You see, he is my grandfather."

"Your—"

"Shhh."

"Sorry." Alexander realized his voice had risen to the command tone he used on the ship. "I was just surprised. Viscount Ambrose is your grandfather? And you don't know him?"

"I shouldn't have said anything." Miss Grant seemed to realize he was holding her hand and pulled it away. "I really don't want others here knowing I'm related to him. I've decided it would be best if everyone assumed we are strangers, since that is the fact. I doubt he will know who I am anyway."

Fortunately, Alexander managed to stop before he asked how this could happen—since the answer was blindingly obvious. Miss Grant was illegitimate. She'd never mentioned any family, only that she was a teacher at a girls' school. He could imagine a small version of Miss Grant, all knobby knees and elbows, unwanted and alone, being farmed out to the school as a child and continuing to stay there as an adult.

It was his turn to clench his fists. The morals of many of his class were sickening. He couldn't recall who Viscount Ambrose was, so he certainly didn't know if the man had a son, but Alexander thought it was a good bet this was the case. He couldn't decide whom he wanted to flatten more— father or son.

"My grandfather disowned my mother when she married my father, who was a poor curate with no connections at the time," Miss Grant explained. "It was a love match, and I was blessed to grow up in a happy home. But other than a brief outline of what transpired and hearing my grandfather's name, I know nothing about the man. Or my mother's side of the family, for that matter. I should have asked my parents more about it, but I waited too late. I lost them when influenza swept our village when I was nineteen."

"I'm sorry for your loss." The words came out automatically, but they were true. He was also relieved that he now knew who deserved a facer—the soon-to-be-identified Viscount Ambrose. Alexander turned so that he, too, could see the door.

"It was a long time ago," Miss Grant said. "The first piecing pain of loss has changed into a dull ache for what might have been. Getting a position at Claridge Academy has kept me from being alone in the world. I have made good friends there and hope I have made some difference in the lives of some of my students. I—"

Miss Grant's voice stopped and all the blood seemed to drain from her face. Alexander followed her gaze to see what had caused her distress.

A slender man who would nearly match Alexander for height stood by the door. His graying hair was slicked back from his face, accenting a rather prominent nose. With eyes that bounced around the room with the regularity of a nervous tic, Alexander was confident he was looking at Walter Weasel. Slightly to his left, a small woman trailed him. She would have disappeared into his shadow had she not been wearing a teeth-jarring pink dress with a matching fluffy pink feather waving above her head.

"The weasel, I presume," he said, leaning close to Miss Grant so he could keep his voice low.

She nodded her assent. "My mother had a similar nose."

Alexander knew very well what Miss Grant looked like, but he could not stop himself from giving her nose a quick glance. Her nose was exactly as he remembered—small and straight and altogether appealing. Appealing? Well, yes it was. But then, he had to admit he found *everything* about Miss Grant appealing.

She must have inherited her nose from her father. Some

people got lucky with the bits and pieces they picked up from their progenitors. Alexander loved his mother, but growing up he had often wished he and his brothers had been blessed with his father's boring, brown, straight hair. He had been teased mercilessly about his hair all his life. Fate had saved Miss Grant from being teased about her nose.

The duchess greeted the new arrivals with subdued grace and began moving among those assembled, making introductions. Alexander felt Miss Grant stiffen as the duchess, with her grandfather in tow, moved closer. Dinner was announced, however, before the group reached them, and the duchess diverted to organize the short promenade to the dining room.

Miss Grant let a small sigh escape. "Saved by lack of precedence." Then she looked at him with alarm. "I wasn't denigrating your social position," she hurriedly said.

Alexander smiled encouragement. "I didn't think you were. I suspect we are actually fortunate to be the people we are." That he was playing a role and not presenting his true self scraped on his conscience, but duty came first.

She smiled back at him. "And I suspect you are right. Your conversation is much more interesting than the usual dinner fare."

He almost asked if she were referring to dung beetles, but good sense intervened. "I hope you are not bored with African entomology," he said.

"Heavens, no. Although I do envy your adventures on the Dark Continent."

"I'm not sure if I've actually had adventures there." He uttered one of his truer statements since his acquaintance with Africa was limited to a very few ports and none of the interior. "I thought tonight you might be interested in hearing about my time in Madagascar," he said. "It's the home of the most amazing butterflies and moths."

"I look forward to hearing about them." She placed her hand on his arm to be led into the dining room. The moment felt ridiculously right. He just wished he had actually seen the beautiful insects he was about to describe and was thankful for the colored illustrations he'd found in the duke's library.

"I believe my favorites were the troidini," he said. "It's a group of swallowtail butterflies that contains nearly one hundred and fifty different species. All of them are brightly colored and feed on poisonous pipevine plants, which makes the butterflies themselves poisonous. But what makes the entire island truly fascinating is that it is now home to a number of unrelated butterflies that mimic the coloration of the troidini to make predators believe they are also poisonous."

"Oh, how interesting," she said.

Alexander wished he were leading Miss Grant into the deepest jungle instead of into a boringly normal dinner. He would love to show these wondrous creatures to Miss Grant—just as he'd like to view them himself.

He was well aware of the irony of his situation. He was planning to charm Miss Grant—and he very much wanted to charm her—with tales of benign creatures pretending to be dangerous while he sat there in his own false colors, pretending to be harmless.

Scene Three
Later, the same evening. The main salon of the Duke of

Newley's home stands empty. A group of well-dressed ladies enter together, stage right, talking, gesturing, and laughing.

Rachel leaned down so she didn't miss a bit of Emma Goodchild's description of her ideas for the characters' headdresses. She was amazed at the small woman's inventiveness and excited to see the finished products.

Due to their seating positions in the dining room, she and Emma trailed at the end of the line. When they entered the drawing room, most of the ladies had already found seats in a cluster around the duchess, and so they happily drifted to a bench at some distance from that group. Their location allowed them to continue their private conversation.

"I love your ideas for all the bird characters," Rachel said as they sat down, "but will you be able to find the appropriate feathers?"

Mrs. Goodchild, who had insisted she be called Emma, gave Rachel a saucy wink. "You obviously don't know the duchess well. She never saw an elaborate hat she didn't want... and what she wants, she buys. She has an entire unused bedroom stuffed with her purchases, many of which have never been worn, since, when she gets home, she realizes some are really too bizarre to wear. But, oh, what a wonderful source for ribbons and flowers and feathers. You've never seen the like."

"Excuse me," a haughty voice intruded. "Were you discussing my hair accessory?"

Rachel glanced up, surprised she hadn't noticed the approach of the lady wearing what looked like an ensemble made of a strawberry marzipan. "No. We're talking about costuming for the play that will be presented on Twelfth Night."

Rachel's tone was perhaps more strident and dismissive than she'd intended. The woman seemed to shrink into the confectioner's nightmare she wore, which made Rachel herself feel small. Emma had explained Lady Ambrose's less-than-stellar origins.

"Oh...," the pink lady said. "I'm sorry for my interruption." Her haughtiness now sounded more like chagrin.

"Please join us, Lady Ambrose," Emma said, lifting a hand that immediately had a footman's attention. Emma may be a plain Mrs., but she was recognized as a close friend of the duchess by the staff and carried with her that authority. "Your daring fashion sense indicates your input would be helpful."

Rachel was surprised by Emma's comment. She had seemed the soul of kindness, but her words could be interpreted as either sarcastic or toadying. Emma's look was, instead, sincere and welcoming. A chair appeared and a now rather flustered Lady Ambrose sat down.

"I'm Mrs. Goodchild," Emma said. "We were introduced when you arrived this evening. Please allow me to present Miss Grant, the author and director of the play we were discussing. Miss Grant, Lady Ambrose."

Rachel scrutinized the lady now sitting across from her. She was painfully young—considerably younger than Rachel herself. Her fingers were tightly knitted together in her lap, her smile shy and hesitant. Here was someone as unsure of her reception in the home of a duke as Rachel was. Lady Ambrose's initial imperious behavior was probably prompted by an expectation that she would be ridiculed, and it must have taken all her fortitude to go on the attack. Rachel suspected if she identified herself as the younger woman's step-granddaughter, Lady Ambrose would faint dead away.

"I've heard about the play," Lady Ambrose said. "I believe His Grace pressed Lord Ambrose into taking a part."

Emma laughed. "Yes, the duke can be very persuasive, especially when Her Grace is pushing him to do so."

Lady Ambrose laughed softly as well, which seemed to have a thawing effect. As they launched into a discussion of the overall plot of the play and the various characters, the young woman visibly relaxed. Rachel found herself treating Lady Ambrose as she would one of her brighter students, since the lady obviously had more intelligence than her poorly chosen dress would indicate. In the midst of costume discussions, Lady Ambrose asked if she could help Emma with the headpieces, and her offer was gladly accepted.

Rachel thought Lady Ambrose would be a good addition. When she wasn't overawed, she was a pleasant young lady. Unfortunately, as she became more comfortable, she seemed to forget some of the unwritten rules of polite society, particularly ones having to do with not asking personal questions. She pinned Rachel as neatly as an insect mounted in a collection when she asked, "Were you standing with your beau before dinner? When we entered, I noticed he was holding your hand."

Emma turned toward her with one eyebrow raised, and Rachel felt her face heat. "No, Mr. Kingston was just my dinner partner. He, ah, sometimes becomes very earnest. We were discussing butterflies he's seen in Africa."

"Is Mr. Kingston an explorer? I can't quite imagine him

tromping through a jungle." Emma's voice was laced with laughter and Rachel realized her friend was teasing her—and would now probably continue to tease her about Mr. Kingston for the rest of the house party. Rachel, nonetheless, found herself wanting to leap to Mr. Kingston defense.

Why could he not be an explorer? Yes, he was portly, but other than that first evening when he didn't seem to judge the size of his body correctly, he had quick reflexes and was really quite graceful. He had a keen and inquisitive mind. She was never bored in his company. But most of all, he made her feel he appreciated her for the person she was.

Over dinner he'd convinced her that she was fortunate in *not* knowing her grandfather, since his behavior toward her mother showed him to be cruel and controlling. Mr. Kingston had given her the confidence to tell Viscount Ambrose she wanted nothing to do with him—if he should recognize who she was. In this, she was luckier than his young wife who sat opposite her and kept looking nervously over her shoulder at the doorway.

As if Lady Ambrose's worried glance had foreshadowed the event, the gentlemen began arriving. The noise level rose as all the women became more animated, with perhaps the exception of Lady Ambrose, who seemed to shrink down into her chair. Rachel was facing the door, so she saw her grandfather scan the room, frown, and immediately head toward their group. He stopped to one side of his wife's chair.

Her voice changing to the haughty one she had used upon arrival, Lady Ambrose immediately introduced her husband to her two companions.

Lord Ambrose gave Emma and Rachel a curt nod, then said, "My dear, you should have joined the duchess's circle.

That is where you belong. Shall we go?" He held out his hand to help his wife rise and then escorted her across the room. Rachel couldn't decide if she were relieved or irritated that her grandfather hadn't realized who she was.

Emma smiled at their retreating figures. "I believe we have been snubbed," she said.

Rachel nodded her agreement. "It makes me wonder if we're important enough to get any cooperation from Lord Ambrose when the play goes into rehearsals."

"I'm sure he'll be very willing to follow your direction with the duke doing so, and from plays in former years, I know the duke will." Emma's face broke into a wide smile. "And here comes someone who, I'm sure, will be most attentive during practice."

Rachel looked up to see Mr. Kingston moving toward them. Her lips also curled into a smile and her heart did an odd little dance.

ACT THREE

Scene One
Two days later, mid-afternoon. The ballroom at the Duke of Newley's estate. Actors fill a temporary stage that has been erected at one end of the room. Other people stand nearby, watching the action on the stage.

"... and remember, it is in kindness and understanding that we find the Promise of Christmas." Alexander's commanding voice echoed in the large room, and he made a bow to where the audience would be in four days' time.

The final words of the play were met with a scattering of applause from those standing on the ballroom floor. This seemed to release everyone on stage from their assumed roles and there was a great deal of milling and laughing as people moved toward the door and their well-deserved tea.

"Wait!" Miss Grant called out. "We need to go over a few things before you all depart."

This brought everyone to quiet attention. Alexander thought if Miss Grant had been Mr. Grant, she would have made a good ship's captain. What she called her school teacher's voice was very like the one he used for command—and it had the same effect.

"Some of you are still relying too much on your scripts.

You know who you are, so I shan't belabor this, but by tomorrow morning, I'm asking that there be no paper in anyone's hands when you are onstage. I realize this is an amateur production, but the duchess and others have told me the Twelfth Night plays in past years have been quite professional. I would hate to think we are diverging from tradition. So, everyone needs to know his or her lines."

"And the cues," Mr. Goodchild, in his position as stage manager, added.

Miss Grant nodded. "Exactly. If you don't know where your lines fit into the play, memorizing them will do little good. And I also want to tell you that by tomorrow we will have scenery. Mr. Goodchild and his helpers have assembled a wonderful woodland scene and they will have placed bushes and trees in the areas we've marked on the stage. Consequently, if you've been ignoring the lines on the floor, tomorrow you could find yourself walking into a very solid tree. This is another reason all the scripts need to be off the stage."

Miss Grant paused to refer to a piece of paper she held. "That's all, but if you have any questions, please ask me as you leave. Have an enjoyable tea."

Alexander wove his way through the departing actors. He wanted to get to the duke before he left. Fortunately, Newley's escape was blocked by two of the ladies playing birds, who continued to flutter about as if still in their roles. "Your Grace, if I might have a moment of your time."

"Certainly, Mr. Kingston. But would you mind if we conversed in my study. I have a fine bottle of brandy there that appeals more than tea." He gave a self-deprecating shrug. "I had no idea standing around being a tree would be such hard work."

"But a fine tree you are, Your Grace. And Miss Grant has no cause to castigate you about not knowing your lines." Alexander managed to say this with a straight face. The duke only had three lines, and he delivered all of them as if they were the final reading of a Parliamentary law. The rest of the time, he did just stand around looking, well, like a duke pretending to be a tree.

"And you make an admirable hedgehog," the duke said as they walked down the hall.

"I suspect I got the part because of my appearance, although I do get the honor of having the last word." Alexander didn't add that having the last word when Miss Grant was in director mode was an accomplishment. He'd never guessed she would take so well to command until he saw her do it. The transformation was amazing. Confidence, which had not been immediately apparent, came shining through. She wasn't dictatorial, however. She listened to others' ideas on how their parts should be played, but once a decision was made, she made sure everyone followed through.

They entered the study and the duke motioned to one of the two chairs flanking a welcome fire. "Brandy?" he asked.

"Yes, please. Being a hedgehog is also thirsty business."

The duke returned, handed Alexander one of the two glasses he held, and stretched out in the other chair with a sigh. "The duchess's theatricals get more elaborate every year, but I must say using Miss Grant's play was one of her better impulses. I doubt, however, you're here to discuss drama, unless it has something to do with the high seas."

He looked at Alexander expectantly, his comment

seeming to answer the question of whether the duke knew Alexander's true identity and was familiar with his mission.

"I didn't think I could be a guest in your house and arrive in mufti without your knowing," Alexander said.

"I was the one who requested someone from the Admiralty to investigate my suspicions of one of my guests. I didn't say anything, however, since I didn't want to prejudice your findings. But even before your arrival, I knew you were not the buffoon your superiors wanted you to impersonate." He chuckled. "Although you have been quite convincing in that role. I hope you're here because you've discovered something solid."

Alexander shook his head. "Nothing concrete yet. But if I had to name the best candidate for smuggling cotton from the former American colonies, it would be Viscount Ambrose. Unfortunately, I can't be sure if this opinion is colored by my dislike for the man or if he is truly guilty of abetting the enemy."

"Yes, Ambrose's attitude toward those he deems his inferiors is off-putting. And, to be honest, he's the one I suspect of playing fast and loose with maritime regulations. At the beginning of the war, a couple of his ships were seized when they tried to run the blockade, but his excuse was his captains had sailed before they realized the Americans had declared war. I found this explanation hard to believe, especially when losing those ships was a crippling financial blow to him. It was when his money problems seemed to disappear, however, that my distrust of his business practices crystallized."

"I agree sudden wealth in times of financial adversity is suspicious," Alexander said, "but from the gossip I've gleaned, it would seem his new wife brought a very substantial dowry, which could explain his change of fortune."

"Ah, yes... I understand my wife and her coterie have been championing Lady Ambrose. They like her and feel she's the one who has been most wronged in this whole affair. Not only is Ambrose a difficult man to like, he's old enough be her father."

"Grandfather, actually. I believe Lady Ambrose is younger than his granddaughter."

The duke sat up straighter. "Granddaughter? I'm familiar with his three grandsons, all of whom are married with children of their own, but I didn't know he had a granddaughter."

Alexander cursed himself for not paying attention to what he was saying. His lack of discretion demonstrated he did not have the makings of a spy. Neither Miss Grant nor Lord Ambrose had admitted to their connection. Of course, it was possible Ambrose didn't know who she was, but he suspected Miss Grant, at least, would not like for her relationship to become common knowledge.

He could try to revert to his I'm-more-interested-in-insects-than-people persona, but the duke evidently knew quite a bit about him and would not be fooled. He was already uncomfortable with the lies and misconceptions he had strewn about him, particularly where they affected Miss Grant, and he didn't want to add any more.

"If I could rely on your discretion to not mention what I'm about to tell you..."

The duke nodded. "Of course."

"Well, Miss Grant is Lord Ambrose's granddaughter. Her

mother married a vicar, when Ambrose had a more impressive *parti* in mind, and he cut his daughter out of the family. Miss Grant had never met the man until he arrived here, something that came as a shock to her. And as far as I can tell, Ambrose has no idea who she is. His treatment of his own daughter and her family is one of the reasons I rather wish I could prove the man was guilty of something heinous."

"*Our* competent and clever Miss Grant, ignored by her grandsire, forced to work for a living... it's not to be borne." The duke came out of his chair like a jack-in-the-box and stalked to the sideboard. "Another tot?" he asked, raising the decanter.

"Please," Alexander said, regretting he couldn't ask for the entire bottle. He was afraid his stupidity could lead to difficulties. He was alarmed by the duke's reaction, particularly the emphasis on *our* Miss Grant, about whom the duke evidently felt paternalistic. Alexander doubted His Grace would be pleased to know that the shambling, counterfeit Mr. Kingston suspected he was developing a *tendre* for the clever and competent woman.

Scene Two
Two hours later. The Duke of Newley's ballroom. A forest made from wooden stakes with attached pine boughs and tubs of live evergreen shrubs have been added to the previously unadorned stage. A solitary woman paces among the foliage, stopping occasionally to look out at the empty room. A man enters from a side door.

"Are you playing all the parts by yourself?"

Rachel had been so absorbed in making sure the earlier blocking of the play still worked, she nearly tripped over a small juniper bush in surprise. She laughed when she saw Mr. Kingston smiling up at her. "I'm trying to determine if the placement of the trees and bushes will work when everyone is on stage. So far, I think we may have too many low bushes, especially holly, which can be lethal if it's bumped into."

"Lethal?" He gave her a teasing look she was coming to enjoy.

"Alright, that was an exaggeration. But I can attest that holly can definitely be prickly and painful. I'm also worried about the location of some of the pine boughs attached to these artificial trees. Since you're the tallest person who will be on stage, would you mind coming up to see if any of the tree branches interfere with your planned movements?"

"That I can do," he said, leaping onto the low stage with a grace that belied his size. He started mumbling under his breath, evidently coordinating his lines with his movements. He had to weave and duck under branches a couple of times.

"Do those areas need attention?" she asked.

"I don't know. Maybe this makes the trees look more natural. I seldom walk in the woods without having to dodge a limb here and there."

Still observing the trees, he moved backwards to get a different perspective and snagged the tails of his coat on one of the holly bushes. He continued to retreat, oblivious to the problem.

"Stop," she said. "You've hooked your coat and could tear the material." Perhaps because he was used to taking her direction while on stage, he immediately froze. She bent forward and began to slowly work the fabric free.

"You've saved me from a scolding from my valet," he said with laughter in his voice. "But I now see what you meant when you said these plants were lethal." He paused, then asked, "Was there any damage?"

Rachel looked up and realized he was watching her hands—hands that were, Dear Lord, patting the part of his coat that covered his ample fundament. She jerked her hands back as if she were scalded. She could feel an answering heat in her face. How had she not noticed what she was doing? He must think her a veritable hussy.

"I, eh, eh…"

"Why do you think Mr. Goodchild chose a plant that could cause so much trouble?" he quickly asked.

She straightened and looked him in the face. The dear man was pretending she hadn't done something mortifyingly embarrassing and was deftly changing the subject. "Mr. Goodchild is not at fault. I suggested the holly bushes. There were a number of them in containers along the edge of the terrace, and I thought they would be easy to retrieve and would add the appropriate Christmas ambience."

"What did you use for the woodland scene when you presented your play at your school?"

"Since at that point it was a harvest play," she said, "the action was set in a field, and we used wheat sheaves. Well, tied-up straw bundles, but the effect was the same. The woodland scene with evergreens was part of the 'seasonal adaptations' I agreed to."

Mr. Kingston hopped off the platform and went to the center of the ballroom. He surveyed the stage and then nodded. "If we banked a lot of the holly bushes to the front sides, they would still reinforce the Christmas theme and not interfere with any of the actors. Then we could use some less prickly bushes in the more central sections. I'm sure there are a number of tender plants that might work better in the glass house."

"Glass house? I hadn't realized the Newleys had one."

He nodded. "They have a substantial one behind the stable block. I've noticed it on my rambles about the property."

"Goodness, you're hardier than I am. With the skies constantly spitting rain and sleet, I've stayed indoors and substituted walking in the gardens with strolling in the long gallery with the other ladies."

"I'm used to being outside in all weather," he said.

Rachel nodded her understanding. She could have guessed this from the weathering of his face. Of course, that made sense since Mr. Kingston could hardly study insects if he stayed indoors.

"It's cold and windy today, but dry," he commented. "Would you consider making an expedition to the glass house to see if there is anything usable?"

The hopeful smile on his face did strange things to Rachel's breathing. She certainly wouldn't miss an *expedition* with Mr. Kingston. She'd already imagined trekking through Africa with him. "I'll need to get my outerwear, but I can meet you in the front hall in about fifteen minutes," she said.

"Good. I feel confident that we can find shrubs that will be much friendlier to the performers." He walked to the edge of the platform and held out a hand to help her down. To her shock, when she reached the edge, he grasped her around the waist and effortlessly swung her to the ground. His behavior couldn't be called inappropriate, although Rachel rather wished he'd held her longer, even if that would have been forward.

"Fifteen minutes then," he said, sending her on her way with fleet feet. As she hurried to her room, she mentally chose and discarded each of her two bonnets, finally deciding on fetching over warmth. She had a wonderfully warm cape from the Abandoned Closet that would make up for the impractical choice of hat. And by Heavens, she wanted to look fetching.

She made it back to the front hall within the agreed upon time to find Mr. Kingston already there, pacing the edges of the room and making his greatcoat furl around his legs. "Ready? Good." And he offered her his arm.

Existing inside a bubble of unreality, she floated next to him as they crossed the lawn, skirted the stable block, and arrived at the largest glass house Rachel had ever seen. She didn't feel the cold or the wind. What she felt was happy.

Inside, the glass house was warm and moist and smelled of damp earth and growing things. "Goodness," she said. "This seems to go on forever. It certainly explains where all the gorgeous flowers in the house have come from."

"The flowers and much more. If we don't find what we're looking for here, we will never find it. Oddly, this looks larger inside than it did from the outside."

"All I can think of is the huge amount of glass tax the duke is paying."

"Spoken like the daughter of a frugal vicar," he said, but his smile took any sting out of the words. The glass house brought home the difference in circumstances between herself and the rest of those in residence, however. Well, all those except, perhaps, for Mr. Kingston. He'd told her one of the reasons for his attendance was to meet with men who might help finance his next African trip. He had a small living from a distant relative, but it didn't cover extended travel. She wondered if one could raise butterflies among the tropical foliage in a glass house, then shook her head to chase away another impractical dream.

They wandered the paths between the containers and found a treasure trove of usable plants. When they finally reached the end and reversed their direction, Rachel said, "I think the boxwoods would be the best. And maybe a few of the acuba."

"And the acuba are...?"

"The ones you liked with the gold spots on the leaves," she said, giving him a slight nudge in the side. She was sure he remembered which plant was which. Mr. Kingston had a very quick mind. He'd memorized all his lines overnight.

"Ah, yes. The ones with freckles." He put a hand on her arm and stopped her forward motion. He then took the brim of her bonnet and turned her face toward him. "Have I told you that I am very fond of freckles?" His voice was lower than usual. Mesmerizing.

"No," she said, feeling breathless and peculiar.

"You have such an interesting sprinkle of them across your nose." He gently touched the area that Rachel had diligently scrubbed with honey and salt when she was younger. For the first time, she wished she hadn't bothered.

He moved his hand so it cradled the side of her head, and tilted her face more toward him. "I'm delighted with your freckles. I'm not so enthusiastic about your bonnet." Then he bent down and gently touched his lips to hers.

Rachel had been kissed twice. Both times by Stephen Langston. And neither of them had been anything like this. They had involved a great deal of pressure and wetness and embarrassment. Mr. Kingston, however, kissed like one of the butterflies he'd discussed—a soft enticing movement of lips as if a butterfly were sipping nectar from a flower. And like a flower, Rachel bloomed.

When Mr. Kingston started to draw back, she went up on her toes and followed his retreat. He chuckled and, slipping an arm around her waist, drew her close to him. She felt his soft, friendly-feeling stomach against her torso. But when her hands drifted to his shoulders, she was met with hard muscle.

Mr. Kingston was a man of disparate parts, but, Lordy, could he kiss. He nibbled at her bottom lip as if he wanted something more—but she had no idea what. She relaxed her lips and his tongue came sweeping in.

Rachel was so surprised, she jumped back. Mr. Kingston released his arm and let her go.

"I, eh, apologize for my behavior," he said, "but I was inspired by the kissing bough." He made a vague motion in the direction of the glass ceiling.

Rachel's eyes followed his motion. Hanging above them was an over-wintering potted fern. "A kissing bough?" Her tone indicated her skepticism.

He also looked up—and smiled. "Well, it looked like a kissing bough when I caught it from the corner of my eye. I'm sorry, Miss Grant. I felt that being under a kissing bough compelled me to kiss you."

"Since we've, eh, kissed, I think you should call me Rachel." She hoped she sounded confident. Never had she been more unsure. What she really wanted was the return gift of his name.

"Then you should call me Alexander," he said as he held out his arm. "We should go before we overstay the logical time needed to discover the shrubs we want."

She took his arm and walked back to the house, seemingly calm and normal. But with every step, she remembered she had just kissed Alexander Kingston—and it had been wonderful.

She thought he might be courting her. Not half-heartedly, at the behest of his family because she would make the logical wife, but because he found her appealing. Her. Rachel Grant. The choice of a kind and intelligent man. She felt almost giddy. During their long conversations they'd learned each other's histories and plumbed each other's hopes for the future. Although she hadn't known him long, she *knew* him.

As she dressed for dinner that evening, her hands shook with excitement. She wore her prettiest dress with the expectation of seeing appreciation in Alexander's eyes.

But he wasn't there.

Instead, her dinner partner was Mr. Warren, the twenty-year-old son of Viscount Warren. Rachel found him painfully young and banal. She was relieved when the ladies went through to the drawing room, where she immediately pleaded exhaustion and retired.

Once settled in her room and wearing her night robe, however, she sat by the fire for some time. Occasionally she would touch her lips with her fingers, smile, whisper, "Alexander," and wonder where he was.

Scene Three
Late that evening. A bedroom at the Duke of Newley's estate.
Two men relax before the fire.

Alexander suspected tomorrow he would regret substituting brandy for dinner, but right now it seemed like a very good idea. He'd had a day that he could only equate to piloting a ship through incredibly high seas for twelve hours straight. It had been exhausting. It had been exhilarating. But most of it was something he didn't want to do again.

Harris's chuckle broke a blessed stretch of silence. "I'm really sorry I didn't get to watch you sneak around all rigged out. I just keep imagining you looking under the bed, corset creaking." He chuckled again.

"If I had a better valet, I imagine my corset wouldn't creak." Alexander took another sip of his brandy, wishing the damned stuff would do its job and keep him from imagining anything. "And I couldn't take the chance of being seen as someone who had suddenly lost a third of his weight. If I'd been discovered in the hall, that would have been something I couldn't explain away."

"I still think you took a stupid chance," Harris said. "Checking Viscount Ambrose's room for damning information while he was at dinner was worth the risk, but to wait and confront him..." Harris shook his head.

Alexander regretted mentioning that last part to Harris, but what was done, was done. Ambrose had looked like he was the guilty party. Even the duke had suspected him. And Alexander had *wanted* him to be guilty, but this was primarily because of the man's disregard for his own granddaughter. Alexander felt his behavior was indicative of a lack of character. Unfortunately, Alexander couldn't prove anything that was illegal.

His marriage seemed to have solved Ambrose's financial problems. It must have galled a man who had such a high opinion of his own consequence to be forced to marry a mill owner's daughter for her money, but he'd done it rather than delve into blockade running, as had been suspected. He had taken a time-honored and legal way out of the financial mess the war in America had made for him.

So, when Alexander had found nothing incriminating in Ambrose's room, he'd made himself comfortable with a glass of the viscount's brandy and waited. The confrontation hadn't been pleasant, but Alexander had told the man just enough for him not to raise a hue and cry that he'd found a burglar in his suite. Even then, when those at the Admiralty learned of his behavior, they would probably not be pleased.

But what had driven him to the brandy decanter was the fear that Miss Grant... no, Rachel... would not be pleased. In his usual direct manner, he'd sailed into an area where he had no business being. He's asked Ambrose if he knew his granddaughter was in residence.

To his surprise, the viscount knew who Rachel was. He'd evidently followed the trajectory of her life from a distance. When Alexander had asked him why he had done nothing to make her way easier, he'd simply shrugged and said his interference would not be welcome. And then Alexander, obviously deluded that he had, indeed, become the wise hedgehog who could solve all the problems in the woodland glen, had suggested Ambrose at least ask.

Dear Lord, he was a foolish man. He had no idea if Rachel wanted to know her grandfather. But it had been a hole in her life that seemed to bother her, and Alexander wanted her happy, above all else. He wanted to tie up all the loose ends into a pretty bow and present it to her as a belated Christmas gift.

She just couldn't know the gift was from him.

Because he didn't exist—at least the Alexander Kingston she thought she knew didn't exist.

He'd been put in a position where he'd had to lie to her from the beginning. But with an honest explanation, she might have forgiven him for his subterfuge. *Might* have. At least until he'd kissed her. Or more accurately, the portly, bumbling version of himself had kissed her. The man who had trekked Africa studying insects had kissed her.

And this was the man she had kissed back—but that man was not the real Alexander.

Bloody hell, he'd leaped into unknown waters without determining if there were hidden rocks just beneath the surface. He wanted her to like the man he was, and not the man he pretended to be. Because he liked her... maybe more than liked.

After a lifetime of knowing who he was and what he wanted, Alexander was adrift. He feared he had botched a relationship with the only woman who had ever made him think living on dry land might not be so bad, if he could live there with her. And since he could think of no way to fix his conundrum, he'd tried to offer her a relationship with her grandfather as some sort of consolation prize. Of course, it was highly likely that when the facts were known, neither he nor her grandfather would be welcome.

"Are you looking forward to returning to the ship?" he asked Harris in an effort to put his mind on what had previously been pleasant thoughts.

But there was no answer. Harris, wise man that he was, had his head dropped to his chest and was blissfully asleep.

ACT FOUR

Scene One
Two days later, mid-morning. The stage in the Duke of
Newley's ballroom, now set as a woodland with trees and
bushes. The sides of the platform are festooned with red
ribbons and pine boughs. A rehearsal is in process.

"... and remember, it is in kindness and understanding that we find the Promise of Christmas." Alexander spoke the closing lines, and Rachel, in her role as the audience, clapped enthusiastically. Alexander really was most endearing. The entire cast on stage waited for the count of five as they'd practiced and then bowed as one.

"Nicely done, all." Rachel said. "I think we're ready for the dress rehearsal tomorrow. I know you all have already discussed what you'll be wearing with Mrs. Goodchild, and your special headpieces will be delivered to you today. Be sure these fit correctly and are secure. We don't want you to lose your heads at an inappropriate time."

The group either smiled or chuckled as she'd expected.

"Now, do any of you have any questions?"

No one indicated any problems, so she released the cast with a happy sigh. The play had come together better than she'd anticipated. No one had tripped over a shrub container, no one had knocked down a tree, and everyone had remembered their lines and cues. A few of the participants were guilty of overacting, but she thought that was part of the fun and simply showed enthusiasm for their roles.

To her surprise, the three main actors had risen to the occasion and were excellent. The duchess as the Christmas Fairy—the Christmas Sprite renamed to more closely fit the persona of the lady playing the role—was both engaging and dignified. Alexander managed to deliver his lines with a pomposity that might be wisdom but was surely comical. And Viscount Ambrose was the most weaselly weasel that had ever lived, although she wasn't sure if this as a product of acting or personality.

"Excuse me. Miss Grant." She turned to see the weasel himself.

"Yes, Lord Ambrose. Is there something you need?"

His eyes shifted around the room in a furtive manner. If she'd needed confirmation that he'd been playing himself, there it was. "May I speak with you, eh, privately?"

She looked around at the clusters of people slowly drifting out the door. "If you wait for a few minutes, we will probably be quite alone here. Or we can walk around to the rear of the stage now."

"Perhaps at the rear?" He sounded tentative, quite unlike the imperious person she had come to expect.

"Certainly." She led the way, intrigued and suspicious at the same time.

When they had reached a spot where they were hidden from the rest of the ballroom by the grove of artificial trees that formed the back of the stage, she stopped and turned toward him. "How may I help you, my lord?"

"I know."

Rachel's breath froze and she felt her back stiffen. "Know what?"

"That you're my granddaughter. I've always known."

Anger flooded through her like boiling water poured into her veins. "You've *always* known? You knew my parents had died and that I could no longer stay in the home I'd always lived in because it would be needed by the new vicar?"

He nodded.

"And then you knew I was homeless and without funds and you did nothing? Why would you tell me this when it can only make me despise you?"

"I assumed you had been *raised* to despise me, but I would have intervened if your position had worsened. As it was, you were able to get a position fit for a gentleman's daughter at an excellent school." He looked defiant rather than penitent.

"I wasn't *raised* to consider you at all," she said. "I knew nothing of you except your name and the fact that you'd disowned my mother. At least, until you walked in the door here."

Surprise flickered across his face. "Your parents never…"

"What? Mentioned you? Cursed you? No, none of that. My mother just said you had closed the door on her when she married my father—and then wanted nothing to do with our family after that."

"The first part of that is an approximation of the truth, but it is not the whole truth. I did, indeed, close the door on your parents when they eloped. I disapproved of your father. He was a ne'er-do-well who had been given a good education and a decent legacy, but before he met your mother, he'd run through all his money and had no choice but become a curate unless he wanted to be on the street. He was lazy and irresponsible. He used people. And with your mother having a substantial dowry, he was hoping to use her. Your mother, however, was a headstrong young woman and wouldn't listen to reason."

He shrugged as if his coat were binding him. "I admit to closing the door. I didn't want your father to have access to the dowry. But it was your parents who dropped the bar on the other side of that door and wouldn't let *me* in. I came to them after your birth, offering to give you a season and a dowry when you were of age. But I was soundly rejected. If your parents made no plans for you if they died, it is not my doing."

Could any of this be true, or was it self-serving drivel? Had her father been lazy and irresponsible? To her, he had always just been her father—a loving but perpetually disorganized man who relied on her mother, and later her, to help with duties in the parish. Her mother would not have contracted influenza had she not been tasked with visiting the sick. Ironically, she brought influenza home with her and gave it to her husband.

Rachel had always blamed her grandfather's influence for keeping her father in a small parish where the living was poorly paid. It hurt her to consider the possibility, but what the viscount had said made her wonder if her father had not risen in the church hierarchy because of his own slip-shod ways. Not every vicar had a calling or was competent to do his duty. Stephen Langston's face popped into her mind. She now knew without a doubt that she'd had a lucky escape when he'd married another.

When she didn't immediately respond, Lord Ambrose pulled his importance around him like a cloak. "Evidently you have nothing further to say, so I'll leave. But know that if that fat man who accosted me in my room asks you to marry him—reconsider. I'll give you a dowry of ten thousand pounds, but only if it is to someone who is worthy of your heritage."

He turned to walk away while Rachel stood dumbfounded. Her grandfather thought Alexander wanted to marry her? Oh, the idea had sneaked into her dreams and made her heart beat faster. Why would it not? He was clever and interesting and certainly knew how to kiss.

But by late last night, the dream had dissolved into tears and heartache. Ever since they'd kissed, Alexander had been remote. The only reason she could find for this behavior was that she'd disgusted him with her forwardness. She remembered clutching his shoulders and leaning her body against his. She'd held him tight when he initially wanted to step back and only released him when he surprised her. She'd evidently given him the impression she had more carnal knowledge than she did.

With a second shock, she realized Viscount Ambrose was offering her an amazing fortune to marry someone "worthy."

She chased after her grandfather. "Wait! Was the money you're offering me my mother's dowry? And did you insist that you were the only one who could decide if her prospective spouse met your specific criteria?"

"Of course not! Your mother's dowry was half as much, and it took me most of her life to build the income from the estate to the point I could afford that. But yes, I reserved the right to determine the worthiness of the man she would marry. I know you think I was cruel and uncaring, but I wanted the best for her. I wanted her to be able to move in society with greater ease than I ever had."

He shifted from foot to foot, all haughtiness gone. "You probably don't know that I was a second cousin when I inherited the title. My father was just barely holding on to being gentry. In reality, he was a farmer. I didn't have a fine education. As soon as I was old enough, I helped on the farm. When my father died, I was still not much more than a boy, but I managed to make the farm profitable. I supported my mother and siblings.

"And then, unexpectedly, I was a viscount and inherited a bankrupt property. But I already knew how to farm. I knew how to stretch the money I had through frugal living. But what I didn't know was how to move in society—and the cruelty of those who did. They found me a figure of fun. And so, yes. I wanted to have a say about the man my daughter married. I didn't want her to suffer as I had."

Then he seemed to run down like a watch that needed to be wound. Odd, without his armor of arrogance and high-handedness, Viscount Ambrose did remind her of a tall, thin, rather stooped farmer.

"Thank you for telling me this," she said, at a loss of what else to say.

He nodded. "If you have need, contact me."

Then he walked around the corner of the stage and left Rachel to ponder what he'd said in the shade of a forest of counterfeit trees.

Scene Two

Afternoon of the same day. The Duke of Newley's study. A gray-haired man sits at a desk decorated with what looks like a strange sculpture made from pine branches. He looks up from his writing as a large man is announced.

"Mr. Kingston, Your Grace."

The butler discretely closed the door, and Alexander was left wondering why he'd been summoned. Had Ambrose complained about his late-night visit? If this were the case, it was possible the letter the duke was currently writing was to the Admiralty.

Alexander was surprised he didn't feel more alarmed at the prospect. What could those idiots in London have expected? He was a deep-water sailor and not adept at subterfuge.

"Ah, good, Captain. Please come in and have a seat." The duke had risen from his chair and indicated another directly across the desk from him.

Alexander crossed the heavy carpet on silent feet and took his place. His eyes were immediately drawn to the collection of branches gracing one corner of the desk and he smiled. "I see your headpiece for the play has been delivered."

The duke laughed. "Yes. And I see the fine hand of my daughter Margaret in its rather ridiculously large design. She's angry with me because she has not been allowed to join the festivities. At fourteen she imagines herself ready for adult company. Her mother and I didn't agree, and she has been prowling the nursery like a caged animal and tormenting her younger brothers. The duchess decided to harness this energy to help make the headpieces." He surveyed the costume piece. "I must say, however, that it is amazingly balanced, even if I did use the lack of balance as an excuse to remove a large and untidy bird's nest that had been tucked into the highest branch. The nest made me feel too foolish."

Since the bird characters all hovered around the tree, the nest made sense, but Alexander decided to keep this observation to himself. "I've not received mine yet," he said.

The duke moved his gaze away from the branch collection. "Since no one on the costume committee is irritated with you, your headpiece will probably be less bizarre. But I didn't ask you here to discuss the play. I wanted to let you know that I've written to the Admiralty and wanted to appraise you of the letter's contents."

Alexander kept his body visibly relaxed, but his mind had gone on alert. That damned Ambrose with his overweening opinion of himself must have complained. "I appreciate your letting me know what you've written, Your Grace."

The duke nodded. "I thought the Admiralty needed to know as soon as possible that Viscount Ambrose should no longer be under suspicion. If there have been problems with American cotton finding its way to English mills, the Navy needs to look elsewhere. I included both of our assessments. Although, I did not include the most recent information about the man I received from my wife."

"From the duchess?" Alexander couldn't imagine that she too had been pressed into this investigation.

"Yes. It's amazing what the ladies discuss when we are

not around. It turns out Ambrose was not as financially rolled up as was rumored. Evidently, he was the one who began that rumor to make his marriage seem one of financial necessity."

"And it wasn't?"

"No, it seems the man has a *tendre* for his young wife and, due to the age discrepancy, feared he would be the butt of jokes if this were known. He was willing to have everyone believe he was in financial difficulties more than their knowing he had married for love. People assign their dignity to the oddest things, but there it is."

"Affairs of the heart are often the most privately held secrets of people's lives," Alexander observed. He was thinking of his own feelings toward Rachel Grant—and was trying to determine if they could be categorized as an affair of the heart. He could see where it would be embarrassing to talk about his feelings.

"Very true. But the information my wife discovered neatly backs up our conclusion that Ambrose has done nothing criminal, although I must admit that I still don't much like the man."

"Neither do I," Alexander said, but the fact that Ambrose cared for his gauche little wife made him more sympathetic.

The duke leaned forward and traced the edge of his blotter with his finger. "But I also asked you here for a more serious purpose. What is your impression of the Admiralty?"

"Do you want a polite answer or an honest one?" Alexander was conscious that he might be stepping into an ambush.

"Oh, honest, to be sure. I'm on an unofficial advisory council with the First Lord, and I know Melville is looking for a truthful assessment. Particularly from his front-line officers."

Alexander ran his fingers through his curly mop of hair. Honest? If he were too honest, he could get himself court-martialed. But he and his fellow commanders had a number of complaints about how the navy was being run, and this seemed an unexpected opportunity to give his opinions to someone who was in a position to effect change. And so, he leaned forward, elbows on knees, and began to talk, his voice accompanied by the soft sound of waves lapping a shale beach that was made by the Duke of Newley's quill as he took notes like a schoolboy.

After nearly an hour, Alexander finally sat back in the chair, finished. His recitation had left him exhausted—and he had no idea if it had done any good. The duke had nodded several times, but Alexander didn't know what that meant.

The duke looked at him with another of those indecipherable nods. "Organized, concise, insightful. Everything I'd hoped for. I can't tell you how helpful this will be. I especially liked the phrase 'dry-foot sailors.' I assume you think planning would be improved if there was input from the 'wet-foot' variety."

"I think a better term would be deep-water sailors, Your Grace."

"Right." The duke made a notation, blew on the ink, and began stacking and straightening all the pages he'd written. Since he'd not been excused, Alexander sat in silence and watched.

"Now, I have an offer for you," the duke said. "How would you like to join the staff at the Admiralty and oversee some of the changes you've suggested?"

Alexander's alarm was so great he unthinkingly came to his feet. He felt his breakfast rise in his throat as if he were suffering from *mal de mer*. He saw the *Wheatley* and her lovely eighty-four guns sailing away without him. "Oh, no, sir... eh, Your Grace. My place is on my ship. That's what I was trained for and where I can do the most good."

"But what if I told you that I think you could do the most good at the Admiralty. I'm offering you a choice. Under different circumstance, you could simply be assigned there and would have to follow orders."

All the starch deserted his legs and Alexander sat back down. "That is true. But it would not make me happy."

"Well, would it make you happy to have command of the *Caledonia*? I happen to know Captain Sheridan is retiring in about a year. That would give you time to make some of your suggested changes, and you would probably still have plenty of opportunity to fight the French. Unfortunately, the Little Corporal is proving more resilient than we'd hoped. Would knowing you would have this command make duty at the Admiralty more palatable?"

Alexander wondered if his bushy hair was standing straight out from his head. The hairs on the back of his neck were definitely at attention. Bloody hell. The *Caledonia* with her amazing three decks and the firepower of one hundred and twenty guns... If the Duke of Newley really were a tree, he was handing Alexander the biggest, shiniest apple from the top-most branch.

"As bribes go, Your Grace, you've certainly chosen one that can't be beat."

Newley smiled like a man who knew he had a winning hand. "Dukes don't offer bribes. I prefer to think of the

Caledonia as a reward. And if it makes you feel better, the offer would be in writing, signed by both myself and Melville."

Alexander's mouth was so dry he wasn't sure he could answer. This was a once in a lifetime opportunity. And a year ashore after a life at sea had its appeal, especially when he'd found someone with whom he'd like to spend that year—and all the years beyond. Of course, it was a gamble, but if he could be honest with the duke and receive such a prize, he hoped being honest with Rachel would bring him an even more wonderful reward.

"Yes," he managed to get out.

The duke stood and extended his hand. "The deal is then struck," he said. "And now we need to get to the billiard room. The tournament is about to start."

"I'll have to miss it," Alexander said. "This," he touched his stomach, "gets in the way of my play."

"Oh, right. The padding. Now that was an example of the Admiralty making things ridiculously complicated when it was not needed. But once you're in London, perhaps you can discover who came up with such a cockamamie idea and plant the man a facer."

As far as bribes went, that was almost as good as command of the British Navy's premiere ship. Well, almost…

Scene Three
The central corridor of the Bachelors' Wing at the Duke of Newley's estate. A young woman enters, looks both ways as if to determine she's alone, then dashes forward.

Rachel hurried down the hall carrying the hedgehog's headdress. Even though Emma Goodchild had created it, Rachel was inordinately proud of how it had turned out. A cap that could be tied under the chin had been adorned with white "spikes" made from tightly rolled paper. The cap itself came down to a v-shaped widow's peak on the forehead, reinforcing the hedgehog impression.

Emma had made it to fit Alexander's head, or at least that was the intention, and Rachel was anxious to make sure the headdress was correctly sized. Her need to know if any changes were necessary was the only reason—well, *one* of the reasons—she was planning to knock on the bedchamber door of a single man. She never would have dared do so if she'd not overheard that all the men would be in the billiard room. Evidently, quite a bit of money was being wagered on a hotly contested match currently taking place.

All she had to do was hand the headdress to Alexander's valet, and when they gathered for dinner, she could legitimately seek Alexander out to be sure that it fit. Even if she'd given him a disgust of her actions, he would never snub her in public. He was too kind for that. She also hoped this would mean he'd be standing next to her when the dinner gong sounded and thus, could possibly be her dinner partner. Her need to see him and talk to him was like a persistent ache.

Her grandfather had planted the seeds that Alexander cared for her, and the house party couldn't end without her determining if this was the case.

She took a steadying breath and rapped on the door. She stepped back from the door to hold the headdress in both hands. In short order, the door opened the width of a man's face. This particular face was narrow and topped with sandy colored hair. "Yes?" the man said.

She held the spiky headdress before her like a gift. "I'm Miss Grant," she said, "and Mr. Kingston's head covering for the play has been completed. Since our time is limited, and we have a number of other costumes yet to complete, I'd be grateful if he would try this on and make sure it will do."

The man peering through the door looked dubiously at the proffered headdress, and then he grinned. "I, too, am anxious to see the c... eh, Mr. Kingston wearing this."

In retrospect, what happened next seemed as choreographed as instructions for blocking the action in a play:

The valet swings the door wide to admit the headdress's paper spikes without damage.

"Harris, where did you put my damned hairbrush?" Mr. Kingston asks as he walks around the side of a privacy screen.

Miss Grant looks at Mr. Kingston, her body tensing in shock.

Mr. Kingston looks at Miss Grant in horror. He utters an extremely vile word.

The door slams shut in Miss Grant's face.

The authentic Rachel Grant, school teacher and vicar's daughter, stood frozen, facing the door. The lines and stage directions life had taught her had been wiped from her mind. If she heard the cue to run, her legs did not obey.

What had just happened? She was unable to process the scene. The man who had walked around the privacy screen had been naked. Well, mostly naked. He'd worn a length of

184 • Hannah Meredith

sheeting wrapped around his waist. But his chest, shoulders, lower legs, and feet had been without cover. She'd never seen so much of the male anatomy in her entire life.

It was shocking... It was also magnificent... But it was *not* the Alexander Kingston she knew. Gone was the portly, corseted, shambling giant. No, what she'd viewed was a Greek god come to tempt all the females on Earth.

What she'd seen had to be a trick of the light or a hallucination brought on by a sleepless night—or perhaps she was starting to run mad.

She jerked back as the door suddenly opened. The valet from earlier stood there. "Won't you come in?" he asked with a bow, as if the part he played had been changed from valet to footman.

"I could never enter an unmarried man's bedchamber," she said. It was as if the words had returned her to the script, even if it was a script she'd never read. She could now hear the whispered prompt to run. She swiveled on reanimated legs to do so—and was grabbed about the waist.

In a flash, the valet-cum-footman-now-ruffian deposited her inside the room and closed the door. "Got her," he said loudly, and then placed his back to the door to bar her exit.

Rachel didn't know if she was frightened or angry. Anger seemed a better option than fear, and she knew exactly where her ire should be directed. She marched toward the privacy screen and felt a slight sliver of disappointment when Alexander appeared—completely covered. She couldn't call him dressed, since he wore only an oversized shirt and loose trousers. She realized the clothing would have fit him in his earlier incarnation.

"What is the meaning of this?" She stalked toward him.

"You've obviously lied to me since we met, and now you've forced me into a situation where my reputation is at risk. What type of man are you?"

"It will take a while for a thorough explanation. And if you'll be seated, I'll give it to you." Alexander spoke in the calm tones one used on an overwrought six-year-old, which Rachel found even more infuriating.

"I think much better when I'm moving," she said, beginning to pace. "You can sit if you so desire. I'll walk around the room while you tell me the truth. You *are* familiar with the novel concept of telling the truth, aren't you? Since you haven't been honest about your appearance, even after you kissed me, I'm withholding judgment on your veracity until I hear everything."

"You kissed her?" The valet by the door sounded incredulous, but when she looked at him, he was grinning like a loon.

"There was a kissing bough," Alexander said, as if that described his only reason for kissing her, when they both knew there had been no such thing. Her only satisfaction was he looked very uncomfortable with his pronouncement.

"Oh," said the valet, "you *had* to act due to a kissing bough." If anything, the man's smile broadened.

Alexander was now scowling. "You," he pointed at the man guarding the door, "go below stairs and iron some cravats or something. And you," he now transferred his glare and pointed finger to Rachel, "sit down. I cannot have a serious conversation with someone who is flitting about like a demented fairy."

Rachel's first impulse was to argue, but the surprise at his comparing her to a fairy took away her power of speech.

No one had ever looked at her and seen a magical creature, demented or otherwise. She'd asked Alexander for the truth, and becoming stationary seemed the only way she was going to hear it. She took a seat in one of the high-backed chairs before the fireplace.

Alexander continued to glower at his valet until Rachel heard the door open and close behind her. Then he sat down in the matching chair on the other side of the hearth, his loose shirt billowing around him as if it were trying to reproduce his earlier form.

He leaned forward and looked her directly in the face. "I'm sorry for all this, this... subterfuge. It was a necessary consequence of an assignment from the government. And I *am* working for the government, specifically the Admiralty. Normally, I'm not quite such a buffoon and am, instead, Captain Lord Alexander Kingston, Captain of the *HMS Wheatley*."

His pronouncement froze her into complete immobility. It was an effort to draw breath. Meanwhile her mind screamed *No!* in the three languages in which she was conversant as well as in a number of strange tongues not yet known to man. First of all, the perfectly charming and affable Mr. Kingston had metamorphosed into a flame haired Adonis, and then he'd identified himself as the captain of a naval vessel—and a lord to boot.

Each of these changes rang the death knell to her stupidly burgeoning hope that he was as attracted to her as she was to him. Heavens, she had thought she might be in love with the man. She'd been ensnared by his quick mind and easy-going nature. And she thought she might be an adequate *parti* for the slightly awkward man.

But Mr. Kingston, *her* Alexander, had not existed at all. Instead, he was a man so far beyond her reach that she was surprised he'd ever spoken to her.

No wonder he'd withdrawn when she had so enthusiastically thrown herself into what was probably intended as a quick peck from a man who honestly thought a hanging fern was a kissing bough. He was trying to defuse her expectations and let her down softly. All along he'd just been being kind to a spinster school teacher who was out of her depth.

Rachel had long ago tallied up her strengths and weaknesses, and she was realistic enough to know when she did not fit in. She'd been unable to secure the affections of a balding, boring, ineffectual vicar. The idea that there could be anything between someone like the real Captain Lord Alexander Kingston and herself was laughable.

So why did she feel more like crying than laughing?

She shot to her feet. "I will keep your secret," she said, even if she was unclear about what his secret comprised. "And now I must..." Run? Escape? Scream? All true, but poor explanations. "I must... leave before I'm discovered, and we are compromised."

He had reached for her, but his hand dropped on that statement. If there was one thing of which she was sure, Captain Lord Handsome would not desire being caught up in a scandal involving someone like her.

She threw herself at the door, grabbed the handle, and was down the hall within a single heartbeat. It was not until she'd reached the safety of her room that she allowed herself to cry.

ACT FIVE

Scene One
The next morning, the day before the Twelfth Night
performance of the play. At the Newley estate, a lone man
enters a hallway with many doors. He stops to speak to a
footman and then hurries on, opening doors and looking into
rooms as he passes.

Where in the bloody hell had Rachel Grant gone to ground? Wherever it was, Alexander would not rest until he found her. Her avoidance tactics had gone on for far too long.

Yesterday afternoon, he'd been unable to immediately pursue her when she'd fled his bedchamber as if chased by banshees. He could only appear as his altered self in front of the other guests and so was stuck in his room until he could don his disguise. He quickly discovered this was an impossibility on his own, although he nearly bent himself double trying to do so. He'd stupidly sent Harris away, and while he rang his designated bell with the impatience of a dowager needing a chamber pot, it seemed to take forever for the man to return and kit him out in his ridiculous rig.

When he was once again the portly Mr. Kingston, Rachel had pulled a disappearing act. He consoled himself by reasoning he would see her at dinner.

He was at dinner. Rachel was not.

She had sent the excuse of a megrim brought on by stress over the play and said she would take a tray in her room. Stress, his arse! She was avoiding him with the confidence that he could not appear in the wing that housed the ladies, much less in her chamber, without courting scandal. Alexander was quickly learning the rules of Society chafed more than the straps holding on his idiot buttocks.

Undaunted, Alexander planned to waylay her at breakfast. Much to the consternation of the staff, he arrived before the buffet had been set out and stayed through the comings and goings of most of the guests. Rachel, however, again did not make an appearance. Pushing his pride to the side, he sent a note to her room begging to see her, only to have it returned along with the information she was not in her chamber. Which meant she was anchored in some unlikely harbor she deemed safe.

He was determined to track her down. Since persistent sleet made her choice of any place outdoors unlikely, he armed himself with coin and sought information among the staff. Three likely hiding places had been suggested, but two had already proved to be empty, and so he was now looking for the bedroom in an old wing of the house that was used by the duchess for storage.

He'd had to open four doors before he found her, sitting on a bed surrounded by a rainbow of feathers and flowers and lady's bonnets. A feeling of tenderness well up inside him. She looked like a girl playing dress up.

Her initial look of surprise changed to one of alarm. "What do you want?"

He walked into the room, but left the door ajar and

didn't approach her. In the restless, dark hours of night when sleep eluded him, he'd mulled over her behavior and decided one of the many possible reasons for her abrupt departure was that she had felt trapped. He wanted Rachel to know she was free to leave.

"You left yesterday before I had the opportunity to complete the explanation for my... eh, transformation."

"I thought I'd seen and heard quite enough," she said. "Your explanation was clear. You are not the man you presented yourself to be. You are, in fact, *not* a rather endearing man fascinated by unusual insects. Instead, you are some sort of spy who is both a lord and a ship's captain and has a much different..."

She waved her hand up and down in some sort of signal he didn't understand—perhaps because he'd become fixed on the word *endearing*. Well, she had included *rather*, but he was pleased, even with the qualifier.

"... form," she finally said.

Alexander nodded agreement. He wanted to be agreeable until he could learn why she was so upset. Well, other than his being a lying clodpate. But that was something he would prefer to ignore. "All true. But, except for the superficial things you've pointed out, changes that were necessitated by my orders, I have been honest with you."

"Superficial? Come now. You changed your appearance and your social position. You made me believe I had your regard, and you were only using me to further your deception. I doubt an honest word has fallen from your mouth. Are you even interested in insects? Are there really such things as troidini butterflies? My heavens, have you ever been to Africa?"

During her recitation, Rachel had come to her feet. He could almost feel the anger simmering around her—and it seemed to spark a similar emotion in him. This reaction might have been caused by the realization he was losing the battle before he'd had an opportunity to bring his guns to bear.

"I have been truthful wherever I could," he said. "I may have exaggerated on occasion, but I have never told you an unnecessary falsehood." He paused, his conscience pricking him like a burr in a stocking, since his exaggerations had been prolific.

"Well, perhaps that is not totally true," he continued. "I damned well knew there was no kissing bough above us when I kissed you. I did that because I *do* have a regard for you. Probably more than simple regard. You haunt both my waking and sleeping hours. I look forward to hearing your laughter. I want to bask in your kindness—for you have shown your character in your kindness to a fat, bumbling man. You are the first woman I've met who makes me think life on dry land would be worth it if you were at my side. In short, I would like to make you my wife."

He felt short of breath, as if he'd run a long distance. And maybe he had. He was very far from where he thought he would ever be. And Rachel had brought him there. But instead of the beatific smile he'd hoped for, she was shaking her head as if in denial.

"I don't see what this pretense is in aid of. You know we would not suit. I'm well acquainted with what I am, or perhaps more specifically, who I am." She held up one finger. "First of all, I'm a school teacher who is past her first flush of youth."

"You're hardly old," he rebutted. "You've simply outgrown the unappealing, flighty stage of the very young."

She ignored him, holding up a second finger. "I have only the slightest claim to being a member of the aristocracy, and you are a lord."

"Courtesy only."

"Oh, that makes things so much better. Your father is what? A duke?"

"Sarcasm does not become you," Alexander said. "My father is a marquess. And your grandfather is a viscount. I don't see much difference."

"And lastly," she held up a third finger, "I'm realistic enough to know I lack the beauty to ensnare a man who looks like you really do. I couldn't even hold the affections of a slow-witted vicar. Pairing me with an intelligent man who looks like a Greek statue..." She opened her hand completely. "... impossible!"

She reached back and picked up two of the elaborate bonnets that were close at hand, turned, and flounced by him.

Before she reached the door, he asked, "What are the bonnets for?" Stupid question, but it was the only one that came to mind, and he didn't want her to leave.

"The Duchess of Newley has decided to change her gown so she looks *more queenly*. At the last minute, she's decided she should be the Queen of the Fairies rather than a run-of-the-mill fairy, and so her headpiece needed to include the color of her more elaborate gown." She shook the flower-bedecked bonnets at him. "Needless to say, I have had all the aristocratic capriciousness I can handle. I don't need any more from you."

"I'll be at the dress rehearsal," he said, trying to hold her in place.

"Good," she said as she breezed out the door.

"Well, that didn't go quite as I'd anticipated," he said to the now empty room.

But he did not feel discouraged. In the midst of listing all the reasons they would not suit, Rachel had actually given him compliments that, at least to his mind, showed she was interested. And if she were, he still had time to play on this interest.

It would take some doing, but he had a plan. To make it work, however, he needed to convince the duke to help him, which meant he had to find the duchess. He might have spent most of his life on a ship, but he understood where power lay when he saw it.

Scene Two

Afternoon of the same day. In the ballroom at the Newley estate, a play is in progress. The set is in place and all the characters are now crowned with headpieces. The rear of the seating area is filled with liveried servants. In the front row is a lone woman, watching with great intensity.

Rachel frowned at the stage and waited for something—anything, really—to go wrong. If, as universally believed, a poor dress rehearsal led to a perfect final production, the reverse must also be true, in which case, the play tomorrow night would be a disaster. So far, everything had been disgustingly perfect. Even Lady Anne Pierce, who regularly

194 • Hannah Meredith

muffed at least half of Rebecca Wren's lines, had not missed a single cue.

And now all that was left was Horatio Hedgehog's final soliloquy. For reasons she chose not to examine, Rachel didn't want Alexander to make mistakes that would embarrass him. But if he spoke his lines exactly right, then tomorrow, when those in attendance at the house party and all the near neighbors would be in the audience, the play would be doomed.

She held her breath as he approached the final line, and then, to her shock, she realized everyone on stage was saying the line *with* Alexander. No, the words were coming from behind her as well. The staff in the audience also happily reciting, "... and remember, it is in kindness and understanding that we find the Promise of Christmas."

Mr. Goodchild, standing in the wings in his role as stage manager, seemed to take this deviation in stride. He simply nodded at the words and turned to the next page of the script. *Wait!* What next page? These were the final words. Everyone was to count to five and then bow together.

Instead, The Tree stepped forward. Totally wrong, her mind screamed. The Tree was to stay stationary. He was a *tree,* for Heaven's sake. This movement seemed to excite the birds, however, since Lady Anne Pierce and Lady Elwin both started running around, flapping their arms like wings.

Had she been hoping that something would go wrong? What was she thinking?

"As wise Horatio tells us," the duke said in sonorous tones, "the Promise of Christmas is made up of two parts, kindness and understanding. But the two march hand in hand. We thank Horatio for this reminder." He gestured to

Alexander who bowed and backed off the stage, the rest of the actors making a path so he could disappear behind a forward stand of trees. Disappear? Normally he could be seen, but someone had added a swath of lower branches, which obscured everything behind it.

Rachel couldn't understand how she had lost control of her own play. Everyone but her seemed to have studied a different script and was having no problem with it.

"We need to cultivate kindness to accept the mistakes that others make. And we should show understanding when others do something hurtful," The Tree continued. "Most of us will occasionally stumble and are fortunate if our errors are met with compassion and good will."

"I, for one, appreciate the understanding of all those here in the woodland glen," Walter Weasel said. "I sometimes forget how being a weasel can injure others, since it is the nature of my kind to think only of myself. But the kindness around me has made me look for the kindness in myself." He looked directly at Rachel. "Doors that have been closed for years can now be opened, if there is tolerance on both sides."

Rachel was uncomfortable that part of a story she'd written was being used by her grandfather to pressure her to reassess what she had always believed. But she found herself suddenly hopeful that the two of them might come to some sort of compromise. It would be nice to have family again. She nodded at the viscount, who smiled back in a very unweasel-like way.

"Well said, Walter." Alexander's voice brought Rachel's eyes away from those of her grandfather. "But he is not the only person in the woodland glen who needs another's good will. Horatio Hedgehog had stepped out from behind the artificial trees—but it was not Horatio. In the character's place stood what could only be the genuine Captain Lord Alexander Kingston, resplendent in his dark blue uniform, gold epaulets shining.

Those on stage seemed unsurprised by the transformation. They had obviously been forewarned. Behind her, however, Rachel heard shuffling, intakes of breath, and more than one "Oh, my." The staff that now made up the audience had been taken by surprise, even if they had dutifully learned what had originally been the last line of the play.

Rachel was equally surprised. She had seen Alexander without his padding—actually, much more of him than was now displayed. But even she was tempted to say "Oh, my" as he stood in all his glory on the stage. He was one of the most handsome men she had ever seen. But, oddly, what she most noticed was the same, fond smile she had come to know.

"I would like to say I come before you without artifice," Alexander said. "But like most creatures, I often wear disguises that hide my inner self from scrutiny. The hedgehog will roll into a ball to protect his vulnerable areas. People are not so different."

"My coat changes color in the winter so I blend with my surroundings," the weasel said.

"I shed my leaves before the coming of the winter storms so my branches will not break," said The Tree.

"And these are just some of the strategies I've given to the inhabitants of the forest glen that allow them to protect themselves." The Fairy Queen made a gracious bow.

Rachel was shocked by this new participant. Somehow Alexander—and he had to be the instigator—had suborned even the duchess to plead his case. The play didn't need to reach its new conclusion for this purpose to be obvious.

Alexander took two steps forward, drawing all eyes back to him. "And so I ask... when we pretend to be someone other than who we are, are we attempting to maliciously deceive, or are we, like some butterflies, taking on protective coloration?"

He paused and looked directly at her. "This coloration doesn't necessarily change our essential nature. The portly man you all took me for is no different than the man who now stands before you. I may have presented my hopes and fears and dreams in different guises, but they are basically the same. Deep inside I am the man who wants to trek through Africa looking for fascinating insects, but I must currently do my duty to my country, so this is a dream that must wait."

Rachel was amazed at how the original purpose of her play could be so changed—and yet, still somehow managed to seem logical. Or perhaps she just wanted it to make sense. She knew people were often willfully blind when it meant the secret wishes of their heart might come true.

Alexander walked to the very edge of the stage. "And so I can only hope that the Lady of the Words, who has converted the creatures of the woods into sentient beings for the purpose of this play, would have the kindness and understanding to recognize this true heart that stands before her. Although some of my actions might appear misleading, they were without malice."

He suddenly dropped to one knee, and Rachel realized this new play would finish on a question. It would still be up to her to write the ending. And this ending would depend on whether she listened to her head or to her heart.

"Miss Grant," Alexander said in a voice that reached the far corner of the ballroom, "would you do me the great honor of becoming my wife. I cannot promise a lifetime of smooth sailing, but I can promise I will always be your safe harbor in any storm. I will try to complete you as you already complete me. Take the chance on a lonely sailor and say yes."

"Say yes," someone prompted from the audience behind her.

Mr. Goodchild looked at her and said matter-of-factly, "The script indicates your line is 'yes.'"

Rachel didn't believe she was susceptible to pressure, but she *did* want to say yes. She remembered Alexander's thoughtfulness, his quick smile, the soft feeling of his lips on hers. A lifetime of that would be a dream, and it was a dream Alexander was offering her.

"Will you love me as I love you?" she asked, exposing her deepest wish not just to Alexander, but to all present.

He swung down from the stage in one smooth movement and was suddenly standing in front of her. "I will always love you."

"Then yes," she said, confident that this was the right answer and the only one that could be given.

Those on stage joined the audience in applauding and loudly cheering. It should have been beyond embarrassing but was instead exhilarating. She had followed her own advice and used kindness and understanding to see into the heart of this wonderful man who stood before her and had received a Christmas Promise she had never anticipated.

Then ignoring all propriety, he pulled her to him and kissed her. Without the padding she'd come to expect, he was hard and warm and altogether incredible. Her arms crept around his neck and she kissed him back for all she was worth.

"I believe our play has ended," came the voice of the duke from the stage. But Rachel knew he was wrong. The play was just beginning.

About Hannah

Hannah Meredith has always wanted to know what is on the other side of the hill. She and her husband promised themselves that when they retired from their "day jobs," they would travel as much as was physically and financially possible. There are just so many hills out there with mysterious other sides.

And so, over ten years ago, they began their rambles. They have now visited all fifty states and over fifty foreign counties on all the continents except Antarctica, which just seems too cold. In the process, Hannah has become very good at finding "deals," since money saved on one trip means that another can be taken. She has become enthusiastic about air miles and mom-and-pop motels in very small towns. During the same period, her husband has become adept at driving where he can't read the road signs or is on the "wrong" side. Yes, they get lost a lot, but even then, there are all those intriguing hills…

Hannah admits she could get more books finished if she didn't gallivant around so much—or continue to tweak what is already on paper. But she knows some of the most interesting journeys are those of the mind and wants those trips into other times and places to be as compelling as she can make them. Hannah currently has five standalone books available, *Kestrel*, *Indentured Hearts*, *Kaleidoscope*, *A Dangerous Indiscretion*, and *Song of the Nightpiper*, which was a 2018 RITA finalist. Her novellas have appeared in all the *Christmas Revels* anthologies.

If you'd like to keep up with Hannah, you can find her at her website, http://hannahmeredith.com or at her Facebook page, http://www.facebook.com/HannahMeredithAuthor. With the rest of social media, she is, alas, a dud.

Yuletide
Treachery

by

Kate Parker

Chapter One

Miss Frances Smith-Pressley opened the door that had been pointed out to her and slipped inside. The others were dressing for dinner; she didn't have much time to start exploring the Wolfbrook library.

The light filtering in through the shutters showed a high, ornate ceiling over two levels of filled bookcases, the second of which rose upward from a wrought iron balcony that encircled the room. She twirled around in the center of the space, her soft slippers skimming over the thick Aubusson carpet as she drank in the smells of old leather and dry parchment.

The library was every bit as thrilling as she'd heard. It would take her the whole Christmas holiday to study even a fraction of the works assembled here.

She started to skim the stacks. Astronomy. No. Natural sciences. Not today. And then... Was it even possible? Illuminated texts written in Latin. She'd only seen them in museums under glass. Here she could touch them. Study them. Read them.

Taking out the white cotton gloves she always carried hidden in the pocket of her skirt, she slipped them on before taking one of the medieval manuscripts from its place. She carried it over to a desk and sat down to open its vellum pages.

She could almost believe lightning sprang from the book and energized her fingers, her heart, her mind. Her Latin was equal to the task, and she was soon immersed in the Gospel of St. Matthew. There before her was the Christmas story, written out by monks centuries before.

"Who gave you permission to invade the library?"

The baritone voice broke through her concentration. She looked up at an apparition. Her breath caught in her throat before she realized this was a normal man. He wore a normal man's evening wear, displaying broad shoulders, a flat stomach, and long legs. But where his face should be, piercing blue eyes stared at her out of a brown leather mask.

She took a deep breath, closed the gospel with a dejected sigh, and rose to face the figure. "I was led to believe it was allowed."

As the masked man strode toward her, every muscle tensed. It was all she could do not to step back or fall into the chair.

"By whom?" His voice was quieter. Menacing.

"Walter Ogilvy, the earl's brother, told my father." She wondered if this strange man could hear her knees knocking.

"Who is your father, child?"

Child? Child? "I'm not a child. I'm the elder daughter of Sir Edmund Smith-Pressley, and you should speak to me with the respect due a well-born young lady." She might be a bit on the short side, especially compared to her willowy younger sister or this strange man, but she was twenty-four, nearly old enough to be put on the shelf by society.

"My apologies, Miss Smith-Pressley, but watching you dance around the center of the library, I mistook you for some chit not yet out of the schoolroom." His tone hinted that he was laughing at her, but the hole where his mouth should be was too narrow to tell. The leather gave him a permanently blank expression.

Society laughed at her auburn hair, her average stature, her love of reading, her lack of a swain. And now this…thing who would not show his face was laughing at her, too. "I apologize, good sir, if I've offended your sensibilities. I shall talk to whoever is in charge of this library and get their permission. You needn't worry about it any longer." Frances used a tone of dismissal and sat down to study the handwritten book again.

She thought he'd left the room until she realized he was reading over her shoulder. Drat the thick carpet that muffled footsteps. Keeping her head down, she tried to study the manuscript, but all she could focus on was this enigmatic man.

"Can you read Latin?"

"Of course." Now he was doubting her abilities. She glared at him over her shoulder.

"It's unusual for a well-born young lady to read Latin."

"I'm an unusual young woman."

There was a slight pause before he said, "You have my permission to use the library whenever you wish."

"Your permission?" Then he must be… Frances turned and looked fully at the masked figure.

"Yes, I'm the reclusive Earl of Wolfbrook." There was a mocking note to his voice.

As she was a guest in his home, he was probably already aware of who she was. Again, he was making fun of her. "And this is your library. You might have introduced yourself without adding ridicule."

"You complain of being ridiculed, but you wander into private areas of a private house and expect to be warmly received."

Wonderful. Now he was being haughty. "You didn't post any signs or have your brother warn me. Perhaps you will inform me of when I can make use of your library so I will no longer impose on your—courtesy."

"Don't be rude."

Frances rose from her seat. "Then don't make fun of me." She found herself toe to toe with the earl, looking up into his blue eyes and trembling with fury. She'd been denied entry into too many libraries by men using a similar patronizing tone.

"I wasn't making fun of you. And are you cold? Frightened? You're shaking."

"I'm angry. I'm a follower of Mary Wollstonecraft and a believer in her arguments in A Vindication of the Rights of Woman. I read Latin and a smattering of Greek. I've written scholarly papers for two prestigious periodicals—"

"In your own name?" he asked, sounding amazed.

She deflated. "No, I used my cousin's name."

"Life is unfair. I, of all people, don't want to add to that. Use the library whenever you want. I would never dream of preventing a student of Wollstonecraft the use of my library." He walked across the room and picked up a book. Then he strode to a door she hadn't noticed before, blending as it did with the bookcases around it. As he disappeared through the doorway, he added, "Thank you for using white cotton gloves when looking at the old manuscripts."

Frances stared as he closed the door. Now that he was gone, she had more questions. Questions about the library.

Questions about him. She often had to defend her interests, but as she studied their conversation, she realized she hadn't needed to defend herself to him.

Well, not her knowledge of Latin and Greek.

He hadn't questioned a woman's right to use the library. He'd objected to her entering without his knowledge or permission. Didn't he speak to his brother? And he'd thanked her for her use of white cotton gloves on his precious works.

She should thank him for granting her free access to his library and for not being a pompous ass like so many of his kind, but now she doubted she'd get a chance.

♠♣

John Ogilvy, Earl of Wolfbrook, carried the book to his study and joined his guests. "This is the book I mentioned, Crawford," he said to the man by the window. "By the way, I just met your daughter in my library, Sir Edmund."

"I hardly need to ask which one," Sir Edmund said into his whiskey glass where he sat by the fire.

"It's unusual for a young woman to read Latin," John said. "You must have seen that she received a good education."

"And my wife has never forgiven me. She wants both of her daughters married and settled. I am frequently accused of encouraging Frances's immodest pursuits and ruining Georgina's chances as a result."

"Immodest pursuits? Really, Sir Edmund, I hope it's nothing that could compromise our efforts," Lord Crawford said.

"I doubt Sir Edmund could be blackmailed because his daughter reads Latin." John smiled behind his mask. "What else has she learned?"

"She is quite good with cyphers and codes, with map reading, with history and geography, and with political thought." Sir Edmund shook his head. "She'd have made a great son."

John nodded. "She takes after her father."

"I've worked at these fields for years. She is a natural."

Interesting. Well-educated and talented. Miss Smith-Pressley could be valuable for tracking down the traitor. He would assume, as an Englishwoman and his friend's daughter, that she would support their cause against Napoleon. At least, until he had evidence otherwise.

"Can we get back to the topic at hand?" Crawford asked with a testy note to his voice. "We have a traitor in our midst, and we need to figure out who it is before any other secrets are sent back to France. Napoleon is still a threat."

"And before anyone else is caught in the traitor's trap," John murmured and touched his mask. He was lucky he hadn't lost his sight. He was lucky he could still eat, if only soft foods. He could still hear.

He was aware of how dangerous the traitor was. He needed to be stopped before anyone else was injured or killed. And whoever the devil was, he was at Wolfbrook Manor for this Christmas house party. They'd made sure of that.

"I wish we knew who we're dealing with," Sir Edmund said. "The clues have narrowed down the field to a few, and every possibility has been invited and arrived. Every one of them is a government official or soldier with the knowledge of the contents of certain papers that have been passed on to the French."

"All dangerous men," Crawford said.

"But only one of them is a traitor," John reminded them. He didn't feel the need to remind them just how dangerous this traitor was. "Now that you have the candidates here, what is the plan to root out the danger?"

Crawford looked at Sir Edmund. "That's your field. You're our Foreign Office expert."

Sir Edmund roused himself half out of the well-padded chair. "But I'm not the expert in catching traitors, Lord Crawford. That would be you and Lord Wolfbrook. I've given you the list. Now it's up to you to weed out the man we've been searching for."

"What would I know of such things?" Crawford said. Wolfbrook heard a hint of whininess in his voice. The same sniveling tone the military hero used when he didn't know which way to turn his troops. "Espionage is Wolfbrook's area, not mine."

There was no help for it. Wolfbrook studied his brandy glass as the beginning of a plan formed in his mind. "You claimed your daughter has some talents that might prove useful. May I bring her in for consultations, Sir Edmund?"

"Of course. It will keep Frances happy and feeling useful, and out of her mother's way."

"Really, Wolfbrook, using a young woman for such a dangerous mission." Crawford was whining more than before.

"I assure you, Sir Edmund," John bowed, "I have no intention of endangering your daughter. I plan to use her education to help me draw up plans." He smiled. "After all, she can't be involved. She's a woman."

"Do keep her safe," Sir Edmund said, sinking back into his chair. "I'm rather fond of my elder girl, even if she is a disappointment to her mother."

John knew he'd never have a child. No woman would marry anyone, not even an earl, with a face and body as battered and disfigured as his. But it would be a pleasure to work with a lady who read Latin and maps and understood geography as well as Sir Edmund's elder daughter was reported to.

If she could be taught to avoid that terrible tendency of women to say everything that slid through their minds, she would make a helpful ally in the search for the man who disfigured him.

Chapter Two

The Christmas house party at Wolfbrook Hall was a large one, and Frances hated large parties. She was always made to feel clumsy and unattractive and, according to her mother when Frances tore herself away from the Gospel of St. Matthew to get dressed for dinner, unfashionably late.

"You're wearing that?" her mother asked, followed by a long sigh. "I suppose you don't have much choice in color with your auburn hair. It comes from your father's side, you know."

Frances knew. She'd heard it often enough. With a sigh, she said, "What's wrong with lilac?"

"It's a spring color, not a Christmas color." Georgina smirked at her sister. Georgina was dressed in red velvet, so of course, with her blonde hair, blue eyes, and svelte figure, she looked lovely.

Frances stepped to the other side of her mother so not to be too close to the color that made her skin turn ruddy and her hair turn muddy. Once Georgina had realized how Frances looked around red, she had worn it at every opportunity. Tonight was no exception.

"I'm walking in with your father. Go stand next to your sister, Frances," her mother ordered.

Georgina smirked. Walking next to Frances would guarantee Georgina would look especially beautiful, and

Frances knew it. She suspected their mother planned their entrance for the first dinner this way, being determined to find her younger daughter a suitable spouse.

Their mother had given up on Frances years ago.

Their father joined them, gave them all equal smiles followed by a wink to Frances, and they paraded downstairs to the hall outside the dining room.

"How unfortunate, that lilac," Lady Crawford whispered to her son, Henry, as she glanced at Frances, who couldn't help but overhear. Lady Crawford whispered as if she wanted the entire room to hear her every thought.

"Sorry. I was looking elsewhere," Henry said and gave Georgina a wide smile. His eyes never wavered toward Frances.

Hurt and shame tightened the muscles in Frances's face and throat until she was certain her expression must be a frightening grimace. She breathed a sigh of relief when the doors to the dining room opened and the group strolled inside.

The table was huge, easily accommodating the guests. Gleaming silverware and sparkling glassware were spread on white linen at every place. Candles burned from candelabras placed around the table and along the edges of the room. Frances barely had time to appreciate the elegance before she found herself seated between Colonel Sir Robert Willard of the British Army and Lord Ramsey of the Foreign Office.

Both men were over forty and married, unlike her sister's dinner partners, the youthful and unmarried Henry Crawford and the young and eligible Lord Wethers. Frances wondered if this was at the request of the wives of her dinner partners who weren't worried about their husbands straying with her, or her sister's dinner partners who wanted a potential parti to dine with.

Frances glanced at the head of the table where Walter Ogilvy sat. She didn't see the masked earl she'd met earlier. She turned to Colonel Sir Robert Willard. "Where is the earl? Isn't he eating with us?"

"Wolfbrook never eats in company. His mouth was damaged in the attack. He can only eat soft food. Doesn't want to be stared at. Doesn't want people feeling sorry for him."

"Have you met him?"

"Yes. We served in France together. Espionage, you know. I doubt you'll meet him during this house party. I only get to meet him in his rooms by invitation. But Walter and Susanna Ogilvy will have plenty of entertainment for you youngsters. You'll have a good time."

Don't count on it. Frances gave him a smile and asked how he and his men were adjusting to life in England after their part in the war. She learned many of his soldiers were Welsh who were glad to leave the continent and return to their villages in time for Christmas.

Then the next course arrived, served by liveried servants, and Frances turned to Lord Ramsey. "Are you friends with the earl or with Walter Ogilvy?"

"Both, actually. They were both involved with the Foreign Office during the fighting. Shame about poor John. He suffered a brutal attack. Disfigured him. He turned into a recluse. Would you pass me the rolls?"

Frances discovered Lord Ramsey had been at Wolfbrook Hall before, and they began a discussion of the building's architecture. Lord Ramsey looked shocked when she mentioned the mathematics behind the spacing of the windows.

Silence fell between them. Frances, practicing her never too steady social skills, said into the break, "Who would do such a terrible thing to the earl?"

"The French, of course. Dirty scoundrels. Pardon my language, young lady."

Frances nodded at his apology. "Was this during a battle?"

"No. Before. He was caught spying."

Her father had mentioned how nasty the French were to spies. Frances shuddered as a servant brought the next course.

Eventually, dinner was over, and the ladies adjourned to the drawing room, allowing the men to have their brandy and cigars in peace. Frances walked along, wishing she could become invisible. All they would discuss was courtship and marriage and children, while her mother would glance at her with fury in her eyes. Georgina would simper, and their mother would be congratulated on her beautiful, talented daughter. Other women, married, settled, secure, would look on Frances with pity.

How she hated their pity.

There were two eligible young ladies, Frances didn't count herself, and the next half hour was spent suggesting matches for each. The girls themselves commented favorably on the matches for each other and showed none of their true hostility for their rival.

Frances could bear it no longer. "Is the earl married? I've not heard mention of a countess."

A few of the women laughed. Lady Crawford said, "Haven't you heard? He's a monster. Disfigured by the French during the war. And he was so handsome before. A shame really. Not for Susanna, his brother's wife, though. Her husband or her son will inherit once the earl dies."

"Which shouldn't be long now," another matron said. "I've heard he's bedridden from his injuries."

"And he wasn't married before the war?" Frances asked.

"No. He never married."

"Poor man," Georgina's rival said.

The men joined them and all talk of marriage and the earl stopped. A footman came in and headed straight for Frances. She glanced around, wondering who he was really looking for when her father joined the footman. "Frances, the earl would like a word with you."

She was in trouble for wandering into the library. That had to be it. She rose and said, "Yes, Papa."

Aware that every eye in the room was on her, Frances linked arms with her father and kept her head held high as she followed the footman out of the room.

ജ‍ന

John looked up from his desk as a soft scratch was followed by the opening of the door to his study. He started to reach up for his mask to make sure it was in place before he consciously stopped his hand. He knew the blasted leather device was where it should be, hiding the scars and crushed bones that made up his face.

The brilliant beauty that was Miss Smith-Pressley came into the room in a lovely pale purple frock, walked up to his desk, and gave him a graceful curtsey. Unlike other young ladies, including his brother's wife, she displayed no fear despite what she must think of meeting a masked man.

"You wanted to see me, my lord?"

"Yes. Thank you, Isaiah."

The footman left, shutting Sir Edmund and his daughter in with John.

He leaned forward slightly and said, "Please, sit down. This may take a while. I'm sorry to take you away from the company."

She walked over and sat in a straight-backed arm chair, and he found himself walking over to sit across from her before he realized he was being drawn from behind his desk.

"I have no desire to spend the evening listening to others bemoan my fate as a bluestocking. And your fire is quite pleasant," she told him.

"I find the warmth helps with my—affliction." Blast. Why did he mention his scars?

She gave a small nod as if filing the information away and then said, "How may I assist you?"

"We have a traitor in our midst. I tell you in the upmost secrecy that this party has been carefully planned to bring together all the possible candidates for traitor to our king and country."

"You want my help in ferreting out the culprit? Why do you think I could be of use?" Frances looked genuinely puzzled. What she didn't appear was frightened, or even mindful, of his appearance.

"Because you're a wonder at math and cyphers and have the best mind in this entire assembly," Sir Edmund said.

John flinched. He had forgotten Sir Edmund entirely. He was finding he forgot everything else when Miss Smith-Pressley was in front of him. And that could put him in danger from his old enemy.

"Do you need some writing deciphered?" she asked him.

John reached into his pocket and pulled out the twice folded piece of writing paper. He held it out and brushed her fingertips as he handed it to her.

He felt as if his hand was on fire. She seemed unaffected as she opened the note and read.

"This appears to be a request for an assignation. Are you sure it isn't exactly as it appears?" Her clear hazel eyes stared straight into his. Thank goodness the holes for his eyes could be large enough to link gazes with her without showing any of his facial damage.

"We would think so except it was found inside a pound note in the servants' quarters. When questioned, the servant admitted being asked to take it to the coaching inn to be sent to London." John smiled ruefully. "It was the pound note, not the message or the chore, that caused the jealousy among the servants and brought the paper to our attention."

Frances nodded. "I imagine if you are to catch this traitor, it will be because of a minor slip such as this. So, who are our choices?"

"Your father, Lord Crawford, his son the honorable Henry Crawford, Sir Desmond Montague, the honorable Percy Jones, Colonel Sir Robert Willard, Lord Ramsey, and Lord Wethers."

"And you and your brother?" Her unblinking stare hardened.

"Neither of us was in a position to learn certain information we believe was passed to the French."

"Are the eight men you named the only people who could have learned this information? Not a clerk in the

Foreign Office or an aide in the army?"

"Yes. That's why they've all been asked to spend Christmas here. They are our only choices." John's hands fisted. And one of these men was the only one who could have been behind the attack that disfigured him.

"You're certain?"

"We both are," her father told her.

"Then I need some large sheets of paper, pen and ink, and a table to work at." She looked from him to her father. "We might as well make a start tonight."

"People will talk," her father said.

"You're here as our chaperone. Tell people the earl and I had an agreeable conversation about old manuscripts." Frances smiled at her father and rose. John nearly leaped to his feet. "Now, where shall I work?"

John supplied her with everything she needed to use and offered his map table as a workspace. She sat, and in a plain print, copied the message with each word in its own box.

"You're starting with word placement and substitution?"

"It seems the most obvious," she told him, not looking up. "You don't need to watch over my shoulder. I know what I'm doing."

He'd been staring at the way her auburn hair gleamed in the candlelight, but it would be useless to tell her so. She was beautiful. He was disfigured. "It might be possible that I could help. My brains weren't injured. Only my appearance."

Oh, why did he snap at her? She was only trying to help. Willingly helping. His manners, never good since his injuries, were failing him.

Chapter Three

Frances shot him a glare over her shoulder. "Then sit down here next to me and stop lurking like a vulture. You, too, Papa."

Both men sat, and John breathed in the heady smell of wildflowers. He was able to smell few things, and none of them as delicate as her scent.

She paid no attention to him, allowing him to stare at her as much as he dared in her father's presence. He liked Sir Edmund and didn't want to annoy him, but the man's daughter was a fascinating blend of clever and lovely.

"I think we can rule out word transposition," she finally said, handing John the notes she had made. "Do you agree?"

John looked it over. Her work was faultless. "Yes, I do. Your work is very clear."

"Father?"

Sir Edmund hid a huge yawn behind his hand. "I'm sure you did well."

She rose. "Perhaps we should continue this tomorrow? I'm certain no one will miss me until luncheon. What does your schedule look like tomorrow, my lord?"

John stood quickly and waited for Sir Edmund to rise to his feet. "I'm sure I can schedule some time in the morning to meet with you. Sir Edmund?"

"I'm at your disposal." He tried to hide another yawn.

"Ten o'clock should be good. We'll meet back here then. Remember, this is a secret endeavor necessary to the wellbeing of our country. Tell no one." John turned away to return to his rooms to take off his hot, hated mask.

"You're welcome," Frances said behind him.

He swung around. "Excuse me?"

"When someone does you a favor, it is customary to say thank you. I was simply replying."

Before she could turn around and flounce out, John crossed the room to her side. "You should thank me for inviting you to assist your country. Assist in a way, I might add, that uses your...surprising talents."

Once again, he was the recipient of her scowl. "No more surprising than learning you were a spy. Stealing secrets."

"I was working for my country," he growled in a tone he once used on incompetent soldiers.

"So am I, apparently." She turned and marched out of his study, a study in violet sternness.

Her father made a helpless gesture and followed her.

John Ogilvy, Earl of Wolfbrook, looked at the papers in his hand. The top sheet was the grid Miss Smith-Pressley used to come to her first conclusion about the message. Her neat penmanship danced before his eyes.

Furious, he threw the papers on his desk and stormed out to his room, untying his mask as he went.

෨෬

Her father caught up to Frances as she reached the main staircase. "Really, my dear, we should—"

"No, Papa, we really shouldn't. If you're going in to visit with Mama and the company, please tell them I have a headache and beg to be excused. However, I doubt anyone will ask."

Before she could flee up the stairs, her father reached out for her arm. "You need to develop an understanding of these people to guide you in finding our traitor."

"I can't talk to these men." Their wives, sweethearts, or mothers wouldn't allow it.

"Then talk to the ladies in their lives. Get an understanding of their home lives. Who needs money. Who wants power."

Frances hung her head. "Mama or Georgina would handle this much better than I ever could. I don't know how to talk to women."

When she looked up, her father was smiling broadly. "Then it's about time you learned. Think of this as a practical lesson in the study of human nature."

"You believe it will help catch the traitor?"

"Yes. None of us have had any luck talking to the men. Perhaps you'll find a clue talking to the women."

Frances pasted on a smile, held out her arm to her father, and the two of them advanced on the drawing room.

When they entered the room, she felt every pair of eyes focus on her. Her father escorted her to where her mother, sister, Lady Crawford, and another young lady were sitting.

"Oh, there you are," her mother said. "Whatever took you so long?"

"The earl learned I read Latin and wanted an outside opinion on a manuscript he is considering purchasing." As lies go, it wasn't brilliant, but Frances doubted anyone would care enough to question her story.

"Why would he ask you?" Lady Crawford demanded.

Frances realized she'd have to be careful around this

older woman, who appeared to be equal parts sharp and outspoken. "My cousin is an expert on the subject, and he has given me more than my share of credit for help in researching his scholarly papers."

"Hmpf. Not very ladylike."

Lady Smith-Pressley glared at Lady Crawford and said, "Miss Ramsey, I don't believe you've met my elder daughter, Miss Frances Smith-Pressley. Frances, this is Miss Jane Ramsey."

Frances curtsied and sat. Her father bowed to the group and made his escape to the card room.

"You've met the earl?" Miss Ramsey asked. "Is he as dreadfully sick as they say?"

"Not at all. He appears to be physically and mentally well."

"But he won't meet his guests. Well, most of them," Lady Crawford said with a glance down her nose at Frances.

"He was left with certain signs of affliction that might be off-putting at the dinner table," Frances said. She needed to question these women, not the other way around. "How, exactly, was he wounded? I'm sure you've heard more than I have."

"He was caught by the French behind their lines near Napoleon's tent. He passed as a French soldier until he was recognized and betrayed by a British traitor who was visiting behind the French lines. They beat the earl savagely and left him for dead." Lady Crawford gave a sigh. "He was such a handsome, vibrant man before."

Frances found him still to be vibrant and domineering, which she knew better than to tell these ladies. They would demand all the particulars.

Miss Ramsey asked what was probably on all their minds, since they had little to entertain them. "What does he look like now?"

"I don't know." It was a truthful answer.

It also didn't satisfy Georgina. "Come now, Frances. You were in the same room with him tonight. I know it. So, tell us everything."

"He was fully dressed and wore a leather mask over his face, so I saw nothing of his wounds. I know nothing of his appearance." And she was determined not to satisfy their curiosity. "Where was he when he was injured?"

Lady Crawford spoke first. "He was attacked near the French camp before the Battle of Tres Fleures."

"But they didn't find him until late the next day, after we routed the French," Lady Susanna Ogilvy said as she joined the group. Her scowl shifted to a gentle smile. "I wanted to tell you we plan to have skating and sledding tomorrow after luncheon, if you'd care to join the party."

Lady Crawford and Frances's mother declined, but Miss Ramsey and Georgina immediately agreed.

"What about you, Frances?" her sister asked with a smirk.

"We'll see. I have the earl's permission to visit the library again."

"You are so dull," Georgina replied with a sniff.

Miss Ramsey said, "I heard that you read Latin."

"And Greek." Frances said. Immediately, she knew from her mother's scowl that she hadn't kept her pride out of her voice. Her mother would chastise her later for her bad manners.

"Her father indulges her too much," Frances's mother

said. She didn't sound happy about her husband's quirks.

"Goodness." Miss Ramsey gave a little giggle. "I wouldn't know where to start. My father says it's a good thing I wasn't born a boy."

With her blond curls and delicate features, Frances thought Miss Ramsey would make a terrible boy. Fortunately, she stopped the thought from crossing her lips.

Frances asked her mother, "Would you rather I went sledding tomorrow?" She bit back a sigh as her mother looked from one daughter to the other and considered. Frances was more athletic than Georgina and delighted in keeping up with the boys. She had won a few admirers with her skill and might have made a fair match if she'd shown any interest in any of them.

"No, you'd probably better stick to the library. You'd be happier there."

Frances could taste bitterness as she heard her mother favor her sister. Again. She wasn't here to fight with her mother. She needed to learn what others knew about the traitor. "Did they catch the traitor responsible for the earl's injuries?"

"No, and please don't ask about it. The episode is still upsetting to the whole family," Susanna Ogilvy said as she walked out of the room.

"Frances, what have I told you about asking impertinent questions?" her mother snapped. "Now you've insulted our hostess."

"I didn't mean to. I'm sorry. And I'm very sorry that a traitor could get away with inflicting such harm to a British officer and get away with it."

"The traitor never laid a hand on the earl. He had his

French minions do the damage," Lady Crawford said.

"While the traitor escaped? How terrible." Frances felt free to express her anger at the man who sold out his king and country. Worse, he was responsible for disfiguring the man just as much as if he had inflicted the damage himself.

"But why? How could a man turn his back on his homeland?" she asked of no one in particular.

"Disappointment. He'd expected royal favor and had been rejected by the government," Lady Crawford said.

"He'd been turned down by his lady love in favor of another," Miss Ramsey said. Frances recognized a silly mind similar to her sister's.

"Money," her mother said flatly.

"Lady Smith-Pressley," Lady Crawford sounded scandalized. "How can you say that?"

"That's what most of these young men want, isn't it? Money to buy an estate. Money to claim a well-born bride."

Frances looked at her mother, impressed at her clarity of thought and outspokenness. She suspected she was seeing an inkling of the woman her father had found worthy to marry.

If her mother was right, then the only people currently suspected by the earl of being a traitor would be Sir Desmond Montague or Percy Jones. Lord Wethers had very recently inherited a title and an estate, and Henry Crawford was his father's heir. Could it be so easy as to narrow the field down to Sir Desmond Montague and Percy Jones?

While Sir Desmond had been knighted for bravery, the title hadn't come with lands. Percy Jones was a younger son with neither title, lands, nor riches. Money could come in handy for both of them.

Frances would have to keep an eye on both men. Better

228 • Kate Parker

yet, she'd tell the earl about her reasoning and he could have his servants watch them. Meanwhile, she would be free to read in the library.

Yes, this could be a very pleasant Christmas.

Chapter Four

John always rose before the sun, a gift from his painful scars and broken bones. He washed and dressed and then ate the breakfast of oatmeal and soft-boiled eggs his valet brought to his desk in his study while he read his correspondence. Once he'd finished his meal with a cup of coffee and whiskey to numb the pain, he put on his mask and called for his secretary so he could dictate replies to all the messages that had come in the previous day.

Rifle butts had stiffened his fingers, making legible writing impossible. Just one more indignity piled on top of many others, cutting off his contact with his fellow man, and making his capture of the traitor that much more difficult.

When his secretary left to post letters and deliver his orders for running the estate, John allowed himself to look at the clock one more time. Would Miss Smith-Pressley and her father have risen? Had they given any thought to catching the traitor?

How long would he have to wait until he saw her again? Saw them, he mentally corrected himself. He needed to stop thinking of himself as the man he used to be. He had nothing to offer her.

A smile crossed John's ravaged face beneath his mask. He had his library. He had estates with a sawmill, a grain mill, forests, farms, and a quarry, making him a wealthy man. No

230 • Kate Parker

other woman would consider this recompense for living with a recluse, but Frances, Miss Smith-Pressley, was an unusual lady. She might consider him a good deal if he threw his library into the bargain.

And she was the only woman he'd ever met who was worth bargaining for.

Restless with his thoughts, John wandered out of the study and into the library. He froze as his gaze fell on Frances, her white cotton gloves covering her slender fingers, her head bent over a Shakespeare First Folio. He continued to study her as his feet carried him toward her without conscious thought.

He was about four feet from her when she glanced up at him, startled. One hand went to her throat as her eyes widened. "I didn't hear you, my lord."

"Excuse me for startling you, Miss Smith-Pressley. I must appear like something out of a nightmare."

She leaned back to look up at him squarely in the eye. "Why would you think that?"

"I'm wearing a mask."

She waved his concern away with an elegant sweep of one hand as she turned back to the folio. "We all wear masks. Yours just happens to be visible."

"My appearance doesn't frighten you?"

"No. Why should it? I don't see what you're hiding. Only a leather mask, and there's nothing frightening about a piece of cow's hide similar to the shoes I wear."

Thank goodness for that. Susanna and Walter couldn't bear to look him in the eye, with or without his mask. Of course, they knew what he had looked like before. "Have you had any more thoughts on the problem at hand?"

"You're positive your servant doesn't know the identity of the man who gave him the coded message?" she asked him, her gaze still on the folio.

"Positive. His eyesight is poor and the traitor surprised him in a darkened servants' staircase where the lamp had been extinguished. The traitor used a falsely high tone so his voice couldn't be recognized. The servant didn't touch him or smell anything unusual." He sat in a chair near the table where she worked and leaned forward, breathing in her scent of wildflowers.

"The traitor must be familiar with your servants, since he found one who couldn't identify him. Does that fit either Sir Desmond Montague or Mr. Percy Jones?"

"The traitor is a master at discovering information. It could describe either of those men or the others who have been invited here. Why are you focused on those two?"

"I wondered aloud last night why anyone would turn traitor." She looked up at him. "My mother, usually a silly woman, said money. Money to buy a title and an estate to attract a bride of high birth. I imagine that is the size of the bribe offered to buy a man's loyalty to a hostile government."

He nodded. "Jones is a younger son without hope of title or inheritance. Montague holds no property and he has only recently been knighted. But what about your father? He is a baronet with two daughters who will need dowries to make advantageous matches, no matter how delightful they are, and no son to support and protect his sisters and mother when Sir Edmund dies. Lord Crawford's wife and son spend as if he had the income of a duke, not a baron. Wether's father left him with little but debts when he inherited his sad little estate."

She nodded her head to acknowledge his reasoning before she said, "And there is your brother Walter who has nothing should you survive and produce an heir, and everything if you die."

"It's not Walter."

"The same reasoning that applies to these other men also describes your brother."

"It's not Walter." He looked down and found his wounded fingers had turned to claws. As close as he could come to making a fist.

"Your hands were injured, too." She made it a statement, not a question.

"Are you always this brazen?" He snapped at her without thinking. First Walter and now this. Did she have to notice everything so clearly?

"Yes, to the shame of my parents."

Her contrite tone softened his anger. "Your clarity of sight is why you should be able to help me catch a traitor."

"And then? After you catch him?"

"The penalty for treason is death."

"But not at your hand." She reached out and touched his sleeve. Not his crippled hand, but his pristine sleeve. Still, she touched him. The first person to touch him who wasn't a physician or a servant.

"I'll have the sheriff lock him up until the next assizes. He won't die at my hand. At least not at Christmas."

She gave him a bright, genuine smile. "When shall we work on the coded message again?"

Beneath his mask, he smiled. "Now would be fine with me."

ഇരുജ

Frances rose and allowed herself to be escorted through the disguised doorway that led to the earl's study. "Perhaps you could send a servant to fetch my father? He is skilled at cracking codes."

And she felt the need for a chaperone. She wasn't sure if she wanted a guardian against this virile man or against her own curiosity.

"Of course." He rang the bell and a servant immediately appeared. "Could you bring Sir Edmund Smith-Pressley here?"

The servant disappeared.

Once again, he brought the note and her supplies to the map table. This time, she noticed how he balanced the paper, pen, and ink on his hands rather than hold it as most people did naturally.

She guessed he wouldn't appreciate her commenting on the skill he'd developed even though she was impressed. "Thank you," she said and sat at the table. "Shall we try letter substitution first?"

Setting up various graphs, she printed the message, one letter to a square, on each. Then she began trying reversed alphabets and shifted alphabets, any pattern she knew was common. When she looked up, she was surprised to see her father sitting across the large table from her and the earl at her side, watching her work.

"None of the usual letter substitutions work," she said, handing the earl her work. "What time is it?"

"Nearly time for luncheon, and your mother and I expect you to go sledding with the young people afterward," her father said.

Frances turned to look at the earl. "This will wait," he

told her. "You've made good progress this morning, and we have two days until Christmas. Plenty of time to solve this and catch a traitor."

She turned back to her father. "I thought Mother didn't want me to go out with the others. I might show up Georgina."

"I have no desire to look for a husband for her among a group of suspected traitors," her father said, rising.

"Then it's safe for me to go out with the sledding group," Frances murmured. She glanced over at the earl as she rose and saw something change in his eyes. He must have heard her. How embarrassing to have her private thoughts overheard.

As her father reached the door, the earl said, "I look forward to working on this note tomorrow morning." Then quieter, for only Frances to hear, he added, "Meet me in the library tonight after dinner. Whenever you can get away."

Her heart beat faster. A secret candlelight assignation with an earl. A virile, enigmatic earl. She nodded, a small smile lighting her features. She could hardly wait.

Catching up with her father, they reached the rest of the house party as they entered the dining room for luncheon. All talk was about sledding and the few brave souls who planned to skate on the pond. Frances watched the suspected traitors, but no one gave themselves away. They all appeared to be merry and bright, looking forward to the Christmas activities.

After they ate, everyone who planned to go outdoors went to their rooms to collect hats and coats and gloves and then met by the terrace overlooking the sledding hill with the pond at the bottom. Servants had already left sleds there for the young people to use. Henry Crawford and Lord Wethers brought their skate blades.

The older group planned to spend the afternoon playing whist and *Vingt-et-un*.

Frances was surprised to find children in their party. This was the first time she had seen Walter and Susanna's son Ethan, the two younger Ramsey children, and the pair of Willard offspring. The nursery had to be some distance from the rooms of the mansion Frances had been in, since she hadn't heard a single childish voice.

The cheering children and their happy parents led the first charge down the hill. Henry and Lord Wethers raced down the slope, shouting and laughing, to tie on their skates at the edge of the pond.

Sir Desmond took Georgina on the second run on a sled. It appeared to be one of the fastest available, and Frances hoped to try it out. Georgina screamed the whole way down the long, rolling hill before stopping when they reached the pond.

Frances was paired with the Willard's fourteen-year-old daughter, and they were given a slow, boxy sled to take down on the third run. Frances steered them down the steepest part of the slope, giving them a somewhat faster ride and leaving them nearer the pond than the others.

As they started to walk up, Frances pulling the sled, the girl, Lucy Willard, said, "My mother is going to have words with you about taking me down a faster, steeper route." She sounded wistful.

Frances shrugged. "Then I suppose she won't allow you to ride with me again."

"You're going to slide down the same path again?"

"Of course. Why go sledding if you're not going to go

fast?"

"That's what the boys do."

"Why let the boys have all the fun?" Frances smiled, her mouth showing just above her knitted scarf.

Lucy thought for a moment. "We shouldn't, should we? Let them have all the fun, I mean." She returned the smile and sped her walk up the hill. "I'll tell her my father said it was all right. Far be it for her to contradict Father."

This was a new perspective on Colonel Sir Robert Willard, one of the possible traitors. "Your mother never contradicts your father?"

"Never. She never asks for an extra penny, she doesn't ask him where he's been, and she never disagrees with him. He has a terrible temper. It's dangerous to disagree in our house."

Could it be that the earl was badly beaten because of a disagreement and not because the traitor was after a fortune?

Frances was contemplating this new possibility as she approached the top of the hill. There, standing to the side, his face wrapped in a knitted scarf under a knit cap with only his blue eyes showing, was a figure who could only be the earl.

Chapter Five

Frances waved at the thickly covered figure as she reached the top of the hill. She saw heads turn as conversations ceased and members of the sledding party looked to see who she waved to. The earl's sister-in-law, Susanna Ogilvy, looked as if the cream had turned rancid. Fear crossed the features of several people.

The earl didn't appear to notice. He raised one hand in greeting to Frances and walked in her direction.

When Frances reached him, having handed off the sled for someone else to use, she greeted the earl with, "I didn't expect to see you out here today. Will you be sledding with us?"

"I should hope not." Susanna joined them, ignoring Frances as she said to the earl, "Should you be outside in this bitter weather? You're not ready for the strain. You might get pneumonia from the cold."

"Susanna, you worry too much."

She must have heard the smile in his voice, because she answered with a smile of her own. "Don't stay out too long. Please?"

"I won't." The earl turned to Frances then. "I'm afraid I can't handle a sled yet, but I thought I'd come out to watch. You handled that drop along the edge of the terrace very well."

"Thank you. It was fun." She blew out and said, "It's definitely getting colder. When we first came out, it was sunny and I couldn't see my breath. Now the sun has gone behind dark clouds."

"Then you'd better get in any more sledding you want today. It looks like we'll get more snow soon." Frances could see a twinkle in the eyes peeking out from the knitted cocoon around his face.

"Uncle John, watch me do snow angels," a tot said, running up to the earl.

"Lead on," the earl said and was half-dragged by the little boy clutching his sleeve. They headed toward the outside of the ruins of a castle that seemed to be attached to the house. Frances wanted to ask him about the ruins, but the earl had already moved on.

"Come on," Lucy Willard said. "I've found us a different sled."

Frances helped her get the sled runners aimed properly and then they both climbed on. Just as they pushed off from the top of the snowy incline, Frances heard a recognizable scream. Why was Georgina screaming?

Frances tried to look around her but the sled was going too fast. Lucy let out a shriek. If she didn't change their path, she and Lucy would end up on the frozen pond.

Out where Georgina and some man had just ended their run.

The ice looked safe enough. Frances aimed the sled to stop near her sister and prayed for a safe landing.

Faster they flew, the wind stinging her face and threatening to knock her hat off her head. They bounced over a bump, flying through the air for a moment before hitting the snow hard enough to force the air from her chest, and then traveling at ever greater speeds.

Lucy gave a shriek and then laughed. She gave another shriek as they flew off the bank and slid across the pond.

When they finally came to rest, Frances was pleased to see her sled had traveled a few feet beyond her sister's.

As they clambered up, Frances heard a male voice say, "Goodness. Two girls hold the distance record now." Henry Crawford and then Lord Wethers bowed over her hand and then did the same to Lucy.

Lucy beamed from ear to ear.

Georgina walked up to them, Sir Desmond Montague at her side. He moved from too close to Georgina's side to too close to Frances's. Georgina shot daggers at her sister as Sir Desmond said, "We should race together on the same sled. We'd beat everyone else, hands down."

"Oh, no. Lucy's the one with the talent. You should take her down on your sled." If Sir Desmond sat this close on the sled with Lucy, he would cause an argument with Colonel Sir Robert Willard. It would be the fastest way to get two of the treason suspects into a fight and get tongues wagging.

Sir Desmond smiled rakishly. "But you're the interesting one. What do you look like when you're not all bundled up?"

Frances sniffed as she glared at the man. Georgina was welcome to this rogue. "When you see me at dinner, you'll be unimpressed. My sister received all the grace and beauty."

He was still too close and smiling too much. "I can't believe that. Anyone who could charm the Earl of Wolfbrook has many talents."

"Why do you say that?"

"The entire house party is wondering what you and the

earl are doing. Surely you've entranced him."

"I don't think so." Frances glanced around to find the skaters, Lucy, and her sister were off the pond and heading toward the house, talking animatedly together. She was alone with this plague of a man. Alone with him as it began to snow.

She moved toward the house, but he grabbed her sleeve. "What is your hold over the earl?"

"I don't have one." She jerked her arm away from him, but he kept his tight hold on her coat.

"Can you get me in to see him?"

"No. And let go of my sleeve or I'll scream." If she didn't call for help soon, no one would hear her. Everyone was at least half-way up the hill and most of the people who'd been on the terrace had gone inside.

"I suggest you release her," a male voice said from behind them.

Frances spun around, forcing Sir Desmond to loosen his grip. "My lord." She gave him a curtsy and a smile. The earl looked even bigger in the heavy padding of his warm clothing, and Sir Desmond shrank back.

"Did you want to see me for some reason, Montague?" came out of the knitted scarf wound round his head.

"To thank you for your kind invitation to this delightful Christmas celebration. To learn how you are faring, now that you're back on your estate. I'm glad to find you are up and about. To gain your advice on how I can obtain a position in the Foreign Office." Sir Desmond had recovered from his temporary embarrassment and now sounded charming and at ease.

"We're happy to have you at Wolfbrook Manor, and as

you can see, I am faring well these days." The earl then turned to Frances. "If I may escort you to the house, I believe Susanna and Walter have something planned for the entire party."

"But my lord. I need…" Sir Desmond began before giving up.

"Thank you, my lord." Frances put her arm through the earl's and walked slowly up the hill, leaving Sir Desmond to bring both sleds as the snow fell harder.

ℬℭ

As the snow blew in their faces, John found it harder to climb the hill with each step. He kept on, refusing to show weakness to either Sir Desmond, the brash social climber, or the beautiful Frances Smith-Pressley.

Halfway up, he couldn't take another step. He gasped for air, wishing he could sit and rest. He hadn't had this much exercise since he'd fallen victim to the savage attack. The cold was stiffening his mended bones. He was aware Sir Desmond was coming up behind them, but he didn't have the energy to move.

Frances glanced at him and said, "Thank you, my lord, for waiting for me. I find climbing this hill in the snow exhausting."

All John could do was nod in answer.

"Thank you, Sir Desmond, for taking my sled back," she said as the other man reached them. "We'll catch up when I'm rested. The earl will help me get back to the house."

"Yes. Go on. No sense missing the fun inside." It took all of John's strength to get out those few words.

"I'll see you up there." Sir Desmond glared at him before he continued his climb and was soon at the top of the hill, leaving the sleds on the terrace.

"You're quite a convincing liar," John breathed out in a gasp.

Her stare should have melted his scarf, but John stood looking at her, silently daring her to say what she thought of his weakness. She was helping him up the hill, not the other way around.

"Would you rather Sir Desmond stopped to help you up the hill," she asked, "or would you rather climb up it with me?"

"With you. Every time."

"Then don't call me a liar. I was merely—assisting you." She gave him a smug smile. "Now, shall we try to make it the rest of the way before we turn into snow people?"

Her clothes were covered in snow. It was coming down heavier with each passing minute, and flakes were melting on her eyelashes. He was freezing. "Let's give it a try."

Linking arms again, they trudged step after step up the hill. They were nearly to the top when Frances said, "Thank you for coming to my rescue. Sir Desmond was preventing me from returning to the house with the rest of the group."

"What would...you have done...if I hadn't...arrived?" he gasped out.

"I was getting ready to give him my loudest scream directly into his ear."

John couldn't help it. He laughed at the image of Frances Smith-Pressley deafening Sir Desmond and bringing the entire house party down to the pond. By the time he finished laughing, he found himself halfway across the terrace.

Frances was guiding him to the door where she and the party had come out onto the terrace. He steered her instead to the door that led directly to his rooms.

She raised a snow-covered eyebrow, but she followed his lead.

He pulled open the door and leaned on the handle as she walked in. By the time he set a foot indoors, the footman Isaiah was there to assist him.

Watkins, his valet, rushed up and put an arm around him to help him to his room. "Isaiah, take the young lady's outerwear and guide her to the dining room for a hot cup of tea. Come along, my lord."

Exhaustion made his feet heavy and stole his breath away. It seemed forever before he was seated in his bedchamber. By then Miss Smith-Pressley was gone.

John couldn't thank her for her help in climbing the hill. He couldn't warn her of Sir Desmond's terrible reputation with women. He couldn't make sure she was going to be in the library some time that evening.

Somewhere on the edge of his consciousness he heard someone call for more wood on the fire and felt his boots removed and replaced with his slippers. His scarf was replaced with his mask, and a blanket encircled his shoulders.

His last thought before he fell asleep was a hope that Miss Frances Smith-Pressley was all right.

ᔕᄋᔓ

"Frances, we were worried about you," her father said as she entered the dining room, rubbing her sleeves in an effort to fight the chill from her outdoor adventure.

"I'm sorry. I was delayed." She took a proffered cup of tea from a servant and sat, holding the cup on the table between her chilled hands. She leaned over the steaming liquid, feeling the warmth on her face and fingers.

Her father sat down beside her. "It's grown windier, and the snow is coming down hard now. There will be no more sledding today."

"The children certainly had fun outside." She gave her father a smile, wondering when it would be safe to ask about working on the note that needed deciphering.

"I think you did, too," Lord Wethers said, sitting on her other side. "I watched you come down the hill. You flew over those bumps. You looked so happy."

"Not as happy as Lucy Willard. She enjoyed speeding down the hill."

"That girl will lead her parents on a merry chase in a few years," Lord Wethers said before taking a sip of his tea.

"As well as her suitors," Frances replied. She needed to bring the conversation around to the search for a traitor. "It was good to see the earl out for a little while."

"It's nice to know his failure hasn't put him out of commission as we were led to believe," Lord Wethers said, glaring into his tea.

Failure? Led to believe? "What do you mean?"

Lord Wethers glowered at her as he rose. "You should ask your friend the earl about Noiuelle. About the battle before Tres Fleures and how the earl failed his king and country."

Chapter Six

Lord Wethers bowed to Frances and her father and stalked off.

"Well," her father murmured.

"What do you know about Noiuelle?" Frances asked him.

"I know that Wolfbrook brought back good intelligence. I also know that the generals had been fed information that made him look incompetent. Sloppy. They didn't listen to the earl and as a result, a lot of our brave soldiers died."

"So the generals trusted him at Tres Fleures?" The tea went down welcomingly warm.

"They needed a piece of information that could only be gained from Napoleon's headquarters. Wolfbrook agreed to take on the dangerous mission to prove he was reliable."

Frances looked around her before she whispered, "Even though there was a traitor in the British camp?"

"They didn't know until they recovered Wolfbrook's battered body and brought him back to our camp half dead. When he regained consciousness, he told us. And then certain things, little things that didn't mean anything at the time, added up. We knew we had trouble in our midst." Her father stretched out his legs. "Now, I'm going into the card room to see what I can hear. You need to talk to the ladies."

"Yes, Papa." They rose at the same time and went their separate ways.

Frances walked into the drawing room and joined her mother, Lady Crawford, and another matron who said, "My daughter can't stop talking about how much fun she had sledding with you."

"I'm glad she enjoyed it, Lady Willard. Everyone seemed to have a good time, including the earl." She hoped the ladies would start talking about the war and what they had heard.

"Susanna Ogilvy was worried at first," Lady Crawford said, "but she doesn't seem to think the earl is any the worse for his adventure today."

"From what Sir Robert said, I didn't think the earl could get out of his sickbed," Lady Willard replied, her eyebrows raised.

"Sir Robert must be pleased for his old friend. Lord Crawford, too," Frances said.

"Of course he is. Why wouldn't he be?" Lady Willard snapped.

The other two ladies stared at her.

"They had their differences in military strategy," Lady Willard said with a wave of one hand. "The earl had some strange and dangerous ideas, Robert said, but no one deserves a beating like the earl received. Especially from those rotten French soldiers."

Lady Crawford nodded her agreement. "When they brought the earl into camp, my husband's first thought was he was dead. His heart sank. The earl was a very brave and very good spy."

"Who found the earl?" Frances had no idea, but it might prove important in their hunt for the traitor.

"His brother, Walter, Percy Jones, and my son, Henry," Lady Crawford said. "They were worried when he didn't show up during the battle and immediately afterward went looking for him."

"Where did they find him?"

"Among the trash left behind where Napoleon's camp had been. They found enough to make a litter to bring him back to the English camp. They feared they were bringing him back to bury." Lady Crawford appeared well-versed in the story.

"His brother, Walter, is a little older, but both Percy and Henry are young men. They must have been shocked to see such injuries. To see such suffering," Frances's mother said. Once again, Frances was impressed at her mother's clear-sightedness.

"His brother was the one who was hysterical. Such a weakling, but the earl and his brother are very close. Henry and Percy were the ones who tended to the earl and built the litter," Lady Crawford said.

"It's a good thing they were there," Frances said. "If they hadn't gone out to find him, he might have died and never been found."

"Walter was most insistent that they look for him. He sent parties out in all directions toward the French lines in the search. It was unfortunate that Walter was with the team that found his brother. He's always been a bit of an infant," Lady Willard said.

"Oh, Lady Willard," Frances's mother said.

"It's the truth," Lady Crawford said. "He's always depended on the earl, even as boys. And he admits it. Walter would be nothing without Wolfbrook and Susanna. She's a strong woman."

Could Walter have grown tired of being in his brother's

shadow? Had either Percy Jones or Henry Crawford built the litter hoping it returned a dead man to camp? Was a difference of opinion about strategy enough for Sir Robert to direct the attack on the earl? And what happened at Noiuelle? Frances excused herself and went in search of more ladies to question.

She passed her sister being flattered by Sir Desmond. He certainly wanted the earl's help in finding a lucrative post. Would he try to kill a man he wanted aid from?

Sitting next to Lady Ramsey and Susanna Ogilvy, Frances let her eyes roam the room. In an effort to learn about something that wouldn't upset her hostess, she said, "Lord Wethers is certainly a skilled skater. I wonder where he learned."

"The Low Countries," Lady Ramsey said.

"Really. I've heard about the residents skating on the canals in winter to get around the countryside. He never mentioned living there," Frances said, trying to sound like she'd spoken more than a dozen words to the man.

"His mother's family is from somewhere near Amsterdam," Susanna said.

"I hope they haven't suffered damage from the fighting over there," Frances said. "Napoleon's armies haven't been kind to their neighbors."

"No, they haven't," Lady Ramsey said.

"What exactly is your point?" Susanna said, scowling at Frances.

"I don't have a point. I'm just interested in people." She gave her hostess a smile. "I haven't worked up the nerve to ask where you met your husband."

"I met him at a ball given by my cousin. He was in

uniform and he stole my breath away." For the first time, Susanna appeared to relax. She smiled. Her normally sharp tone softened.

"He seemed to enjoy himself in the snow this afternoon," Frances said.

"So did the earl. I never expected him to spend so much time outside. I admit to being worried, but he returned to his rooms without mishap." Susanna held Frances's gaze. "I suppose we have you to thank for his improvement today."

"I think you can credit your son, Ethan, for his time outdoors."

"He wouldn't have walked outside for anyone but you, Miss Smith-Pressley."

Frances was aware of Lady Ramsey watching them closely. She smiled and said, "I'm a nine day's wonder. A woman who reads Latin." Still, she felt heat rise on her cheeks and feared it would give away to the two ladies how much she thought of the earl. The sad, unattainable earl.

☙❧

John finished his dinner of soft, overcooked fish and smooshed vegetables and put his mask back on. He hoped, despite his poor showing in the snow that afternoon, that Miss Smith-Pressley—that Frances—would come to the library that evening.

He looked forward to seeing her. Not that she would give him a thought once the Christmas house party was over, but he dreaded the idea of her leaving.

Was this love? He'd certainly never felt anything like this when he was whole and healthy. Never before had he feared a woman leaving his side.

Isaiah led the way into the library with a single lighted

candle and then lit two more on a desk next to his master's favorite reading chair before the cheery fire. John picked up a volume of Shakespeare's sonnets and sat, planning to read until Frances, until Miss Smith-Pressley, arrived. Or didn't.

His mind wouldn't stay with the beauty of Shakespeare's words. Instead, it traveled, once again, to that encampment in the countryside where French villains beat him unmercifully after an Englishman pointed him out as a spy. He'd heard the Englishman's voice and his weak French accent and word choice, but he'd never seen the man. The traitor was inside the tent, giving away English battle secrets. And giving away the spy in their midst. Him.

Why couldn't he remember that voice? He'd listened outside doors, but none of the suspects sounded like the voice in his memory. The voice had faded until it sounded like everybody. Even his brother.

It couldn't be Walter. It couldn't.

Light flickered in from the hallway and then Frances stood before him. "They're singing Christmas carols around the piano. Would you care to join them?"

He leaped to his feet. "And shock them with my mask?"

"It's not as shocking as you might imagine."

"What do you think of my mask?"

"Nothing. I don't think of it at all." She glanced around her. "Shall we sit?"

They sat facing each other across the hearth, the fire giving off ample warmth. "Do you think of me at all?" he asked after a long pause.

"Yes."

"I have nothing to offer you."

"You value yourself too little."

"I don't travel from this manor house."

"Why would you? Everything you want comes to you." She paused as she stared at him. "We came, along with all your other guests."

He smiled in spite of himself. "You don't like me, do you?"

"You developed the habit of ordering everyone around from your sickbed. You like having everyone around so you can snap your fingers and we will do your bidding."

"You don't think I should find the traitor?"

"I think you should. But while you're about it, you might be more polite."

"I've tried being polite, and people died." So many good English soldiers.

"At Noiuelle?"

He stared at her, only the ticking of the clock and the sparks in the fire showing signs of life. "Where did you hear that name?"

She held his gaze. "Someone mentioned that your failure at that battle cost lives."

"I didn't fail. Someone, the traitor, convinced the generals that my information was incomplete. Inaccurate. Wrong. The battle proved my information was correct, if only the generals had acted on it. If only they had admitted that they were wrong to mistrust me." He heard the bitterness in his tone and couldn't hide it. Not from her.

"Does anyone blame you?"

"Probably those who lost family in that battle. Wethers lost his younger brother. I know he's never forgiven me."

She kept looking into his eyes. Hers were a brilliant hazel that he wanted to study all night. "Does he blame you enough to have turned you in to the French on your next mission?"

"I hope not." He'd regret being hated that much for something that wasn't his fault.

"Why did he come here if he blames you for his brother's death?"

"He has no family left. No one to celebrate Christmas with."

He could see tears shimmer in her eyes. "That is so sad. What happened to them?"

"His mother died years ago, his father shortly after his brother. There were no other children. And he has never married."

"Like you."

"I have my brother and his family."

She gave him a look that told him she found him wanting. "Then you are much more fortunate than he is."

Anger poured through every inch of his body. "How can you say that? My body is ruined."

"Despite that, you have people who love you. You have a houseful of guests to celebrate Christ's birth with. You just choose to turn your back on all the joys in your life."

"I choose? Do you want to see what I have no choice facing every day?"

She nodded, holding his gaze with her eyes. "I do."

"Even my family choose not to gaze on this." John slipped his mask from his face and faced Miss Smith-Pressley. Faced Frances. "Do you see why I hide behind a mask? Am I really so fortunate?"

He stared at her, expecting her to run from the library. To run from him.

Chapter Seven

Even in the flickering candlelight, Frances could see his face was scared, lopsided, and crushed. By day, she knew it wouldn't look so demonic, but the damage would be more evident.

She could also see how he was so much more than his wounds. A sharp mind, a clever wit, a body that appeared to be well on the mend. A person so many counted on and loved.

"I'm sorry," she finally whispered as she reached out a hand and touched his cheek. "It must be painful."

"It is. And except for the footman Isaiah, Watkins my valet, my brother, and Susanna, you are the only one who has seen my shame."

"Shame? Is that how you see it? You are not to blame for your face any more than I am to blame for mine. Or my sister to be credited for hers." She didn't stop to consider her next words before she blurted out, "I suppose as long as all you think about is your face, and your misery, all you will focus on is your hunt for the traitor. You won't see the possibility of enjoying your guests this holiday season, or the joy your library can bring, or the wonder of being alive."

She rose, forcing him to his feet also, and said, "You are crippled, but it is not your face. It's your heart."

"And you claim I am rude. I asked you to help decode the

note and find the traitor, not sit in judgment on me."

She noticed his mouth didn't open as far when he spoke as most people. A scar from the corner of his mouth almost to his eye, and another scar from his upper lip to near his nose seemed to hold his mouth closed. "I'm not sitting in judgment on you. I only hope you will find a way to enjoy life more."

"I will wait to enjoy life, as you put it, until we find the traitor who did this to me."

"Until you find him, he controls your life. Do you really want him to be so powerful? Do you mean to make him so powerful?"

She watched as the earl picked up his mask and stomped back into his rooms, leaving her with the candles. She blew out the ones on the desk and walked out of the library carrying her candle with her.

ဆာ∝

Rather than hide in her room, Frances decided to take her own advice and followed the sounds of music to the ballroom where some of the guests, led by Walter and Susanna, were vigorously performing country dances. Others were sitting in chairs lining the walls and listening to the piano played by Miss Ramsey, who was accompanied on the violin by Lord Wethers.

Frances sat next to her father and listened to the spirited tune, tapping her foot and nodding her head in time to the music as she watched the dancing.

Then she heard a man's voice say, "You were like this at school."

Suddenly, she was focused on the conversation behind her and so ignored everything else.

A slightly deeper man's voice said, "I had no choice. I

don't like living my life at the pleasure of others. At the pleasure of the rich." His tone was sour.

Frances faced forward as she listened to them move away from her. When she could hazard a glance, there were four men talking at a distance. Henry Crawford, Sir Desmond Montague, Percy Jones, and Colonel Sir Robert Willard. Four men who could have said those bitter words.

But were they aimed at the earl? How could she find out?

Walter Ogilvy came over and asked her to partner him in the next dance, and all thought of hunting a possible traitor slipped from her mind. They whirled around, a quarter hour of breathless back and forth, up and down the line. She couldn't have stopped smiling if she tried.

When the music stopped, the dancers slowly made their way to the sides of the room, panting and laughing. Frances felt a tap on her shoulder and turned to find the earl, formally dressed and wearing his mask, standing before her. Wordlessly, he bowed and then held out his arm.

A buzz of whispered voices rose around them. He wanted to dance with her.

Frances curtsied and took his arm to walk back onto the dance floor, her head held high. All around them, partners were chosen and joined them as the musicians began a rollicking tune.

As the head couple, Frances and the earl went down the line of revelers first, holding hands. She felt his rough, scarred skin against hers and was moved by his gentle touch. Then they stood across from each other as the other couples passed between them. There was no time to talk.

For some reason, despite her harsh words to him, the

earl wanted to dance with her. In public. A place he felt uncomfortable.

Twice in one day he'd gone out among his guests. Was he showing himself to the traitor, or was he taking her advice and beginning to live his life without thought of revenge?

She glanced across the room and saw Lord Wethers staring at the earl from over his violin. His expression glowed with fury. He was no doubt angry about his brother's death, but was he angry enough to commit treason?

No, wait. His brother died at Noiuelle. The traitor was thought to be working against the British before then, making the generals discount the earl's information before that battle. Before his brother died. It couldn't be Lord Wethers.

She gave the earl a smile and continued with the next steps of the dance.

As the music stopped to wild applause, Lord Wethers bowed to Miss Ramsey and then put his violin away. Miss Ramsey curtsied to Lord Wethers and joined her parents in the march to the dining room and a late supper.

Frances asked the earl, "Will you join us for a bite of supper?"

"I would, but I cannot eat in front of others. My mouth cannot be trusted."

"A glass of wine, perhaps, or a cup of tea. The dance was exhausting. You must be as parched as I am."

"I am, but I'm afraid there is no tea on offer in the dining room. However, I know where we can procure some." He held out his arm.

Frances took it with a smile, aware that they were the only two people left in the ballroom. He led them down a side corridor and into his study where he let go of her arm and rang the bell.

Isaiah and the valet, Watkins, came in from two different doorways. The earl gave his order, and Isaiah bowed before leaving. The valet said, "I'll wait until you ring, Milord," and disappeared the way he arrived.

"Did you enjoy the dancing, my lord?" Frances asked.

"Yes. Very much." More than he had in ages. And it was thanks to his partner. "I'm looking forward to the tea."

"So am I." She gave him a tentative smile. "I think I can rule out Lord Wethers."

"Why?" He didn't mean to bark the question at her, but Wethers hated him.

"He had nothing against you until his brother died at Noiuelle and he chose to blame you. I have been led to believe the traitor was destroying your reputation before then."

He nodded. Now that he had stopped dancing, his time in the snow and on the dance floor was causing the healed breaks in his arms and legs to ache. He closed his eyes against the pain.

When he opened them, Frances was staring at him intently. "Are you all right, my lord?"

"John. Please."

"My name is Frances." He nodded, and she continued, "Are you all right, John?"

"I haven't been this active since before Tres Fleures. I'm a little—sore." He knew when she left, his servants would hear a great deal of cursing. He was near agony.

"Perhaps what you want isn't tea."

He smiled beneath his mask. "I plan to add something to

my tea. Would you care for any?"

"No. I'll be happy with tea, but if you'd like me to leave—"

"No." He realized how blunt that sounded. "No. I'm enjoying your company. I'm enjoying the company of someone who was willing to touch my wounded cheek without being forced."

Then the tea arrived and Frances poured, her cheeks a pretty pink from dancing and blushing.

"Are you looking forward to Christmas?" Frances asked.

"I haven't felt very much like celebrating Christmas this year." John added whiskey from a flask to his tea. "I spent the summer flat on my back. It wasn't until harvest that I could put weight on both legs and walk around the house. Today was only the third or fourth time I've gone outdoors. I haven't been on horseback since before Tres Fleures."

John gritted his teeth against a wave of fire. "I spend every day in pain. I want the traitor turned over for justice. Then I can enjoy greenery and ribbons."

"Perhaps you can have both justice and greenery."

"Not this Christmas."

He could tell he had snapped at her by the widening of her eyes.

"Very well," she told him. "We'll hunt for a traitor to wrap up in a bow for your present this Christmas. It's not Lord Wethers. It's not my father. I don't think it's Lord Crawford or Lord Ramsey because they both have too much to lose if they're caught. A traitor is someone with nothing to lose, and I don't see those men risking all they have. That leaves us with Colonel Willard, Sir Desmond, Percy Jones, and Henry Crawford. And from something I heard tonight, I think he went to school with one of your other guests."

He took a sip of tea to moisten his mouth by pressing the fragile cup against the narrow hole on one side of the leather and his lips against the other. It wasn't efficient, but he could get a little without spilling. "Montague, Jones, and Crawford went to school together, and none have anything at present to lose. Willard does, if only his family and his commission, but he sets high store by them, and he is older than the others. Let's focus on the three young men."

"Where do you want to start?"

Where did he want to start? He ached too badly to think. "It's been a long day. Let's meet tomorrow after breakfast, and bring your father. Between the three of us, we should think of something."

She finished her tea and rose. "Get some rest. I'll see you in the morning. Good night."

John managed to say, "Good night," before she was gone, with the door shut behind her. Then every bit of restraint slipped away as he shouted for Isaiah and Watkins.

ഌരു

Frances helped herself to tea, eggs, and toasted bread and sat next to her father at breakfast the next morning. They were apparently the first two of the house party downstairs. He smiled at her over his cup and said, "You had fun on the dance floor last night."

"I did. I also overheard something last night, and the earl wants us to meet with him in his study after breakfast."

"Then eat up, child. You don't want to keep the earl waiting." Then he added quietly, "We need to talk first. For only your ears. Finish your breakfast and we'll walk in the castle."

Frances hurried her breakfast and then followed her father down one hall and then another to a stout door. Her father pulled it open and said, "The castle."

Frances found herself where the manor butted up to the original castle. The ancient stone walls were open to the sky except for one roofed area shut off by a thick door. She walked forward through a thin dusting of snow and stepped through the doorway into the armory.

Despite the thick, medieval stone walls and wooden beamed roof, the room was surprisingly well lighted by the reflection off the snow through the plain glass windows set into the many arrow slits. Light reflected off the gleaming suits of armor, swords, pikes, and spears. Long bows and crossbows lined the walls.

"Someone took great care in building this room," Frances said, glancing back at her father.

"The current earl built this. He hated to see the entire castle unused."

Frances moved forward around a pillar surrounded by suits of armor and found a figure reclining on his back, a pike sticking out of his chest. "What an unusual display."

"What display?" her father asked behind her.

She moved forward and saw the stain on the man's shirt, and smelled the blood in the cold air. "Oh, dear heavens, it's Lord Wethers."

Chapter Eight

Her father took one look at the bloody figure and bolted from the armory. Frances stared at Lord Wethers reclining on his back. The pike blade held his shoulders up. His chest was bloody where the pike impaled him while the staff remained angled to a height above her head.

She looked away as her stomach clenched. All around the stone walls, pikes and swords were hanging in decorative patterns, terrifying her. Suits of armor ominously stood ready for battle. The air was cold as death.

She stared at the pitiful body as she shrank inside her clothes. It was horrid. Obscene. How soon until her father returned with help?

"Why?" She jerked her head away and felt herself frown as she stared at the glass in the arrow slits. His death made no sense.

"I don't know. Perhaps there is something going on here that has nothing to do with the traitor."

Frances looked up to find herself gazing into the puzzled blue eyes of the earl. She lay a hand on his sleeve, wanting contact with his warm and sensible self, and said, "Do you believe that is possible?"

"No." He gazed at the ceiling and out the window before he fixed her with his stare. "But as you keep reminding me, there is more to life than my hunt for the traitor."

"Before, this was an academic search for the meaning of a coded message. Now, we're hunting for a killer." Frances shivered, more from the thought than the cold.

"The day before Christmas a peer of the realm is murdered at a gathering of suspected traitors. He went to school with three of our most likely choices. I doubt anyone here had a reason to murder other than to stop the traitor— or to silence accusations that would point to the traitor," the earl murmured.

"You think someone found out Wethers was the traitor and acted to stop him?" her father asked. He looked pale as he held his handkerchief against his nose to block any smell of death.

Frances answered before the earl could. "No. I think he found out or remembered something that pointed to the traitor, and the traitor eliminated the threat. Lord Wethers had a title, and if he worked hard, he possessed the means to amass wealth. He didn't need French gold." She shook her head. "Not like the others."

"Nor Henry Crawford. He's in the same position Wethers was in a few months ago. He's heir to a title and estate that needs good management," her father said.

"Then we're agreed it's either Percy Jones, a younger son, or Sir Desmond, raised as the ward of a wealthy nobleman whose children, not him, received an inheritance." The earl raised his brows as he glanced at her father, who nodded his head.

"I think it's Sir Desmond. Percy didn't know if his older brother would survive the battles when the traitor began his work. He might have inherited. Besides, he's likeable. Sir Desmond has been spending time with both Georgina and me, and I know in my case, all he wants is access to the earl." Frances looked up at him. "Stay away from him, my lord. He wants something from you, and he doesn't accept no as an answer."

"What did he want from you after you were sledding?" the earl asked.

"He wanted me to get him in to see you. To get him an offer of employment from the Foreign Office."

"He's asked me for the same thing. If he was searching for employment," her father said, "he isn't the traitor. The traitor is rich."

The earl nodded.

"How do we know that?" Frances asked. "Did the French tell you they paid him riches? Or do you just imagine that? Did the French pay the traitor what they promised? They still lost Tres Fleures and the later battles. Would they be willing to pay a traitor they no longer trusted?"

"Your daughter is very wise," the earl said, "but I suggest we keep a watch on both men."

"Good idea," Sir Edmund said. "Come along, Frances. It's cold and it stinks in here."

Frances gave the earl a curtsy. "I'll talk to you later, my lord?"

"I need to make arrangements for this poor man's body, and to contact the sheriff and the magistrate about the death of a peer. I'll speak to you later."

As his last words put a smile on her face, Frances left the armory.

She followed her father back to the main part of the manor house, wondering who she would find first, Percy Jones or Sir Desmond Montague. As it was, she found them together with the other young people planning a trip into the woods to collect greenery to decorate the house.

"Do you want to join us, Miss Smith-Pressley?" Lucy Willard asked.

"Yes. I could use some outdoor exercise, and I love the smell of fresh cut pine. May I, Papa?" As Frances turned toward her father, she caught a glimpse of Georgina standing next to Sir Desmond. Both of them seemed to be glaring at her.

Why? Georgina considered her a threat whenever eligible men were around, but why did Sir Desmond dislike her? He didn't need her to obtain an invitation to speak to the earl directly. Or did he?

Plans were made to bring a couple of footmen for help and to bring tools as well as sleds to carry the greenery. In a quarter hour, they would meet dressed in their outdoor wear, ready to battle the woods and the new layer of snow.

Frances reached the room she shared with Georgina first and walked in. A folded piece of paper lay on the floor. She had just picked it up and was beginning to open the note when Georgina came in and snatched it from her hand. "Don't snoop."

Turning to face her sister, Frances asked, "It was on the floor. How do you know it's yours?"

"Because I'm the one who always has secret admirers." Georgina turned her golden head toward the note as the pleased expression fell off her face. "How disgusting. It must be for you."

Frances took it out of her hand and looked at the printed words. Printed in a similar hand to the note the servant was supposed to deliver to the coach going to London. This time the note read, "MIND YOUR OWN BUSINESS OR DIE."

It would do no good to give the note to their parents. They would only refuse to let Frances work with the earl. There was no time to give the note to the earl in person.

She rang the bell and then set about wrapping up for the trek through the woods.

When a maid arrived, Frances gave her the note with instructions to take this to the earl and to say it was found in Frances and Georgina Smith-Pressley's room.

Georgina left almost immediately after the maid, leaving Frances alone to finish dressing. Ordinarily, she loved solitude, but after that note and the body she'd seen, she wanted to stay in the security of a large group.

She hurriedly finished with her boots and scarves and ran downstairs to find herself at the end of the group with Percy Jones and Lucy Willard. The rest were making their way in small groups spread out between the house and the woods.

"You haven't seen Wethers, have you?" Jones asked. "I know he'd hate to miss this."

"No," Frances replied. Did he not know, or was he testing her to find out what she knew? She hated being so suspicious. So dishonest. "He'll catch up if he's coming. Are you ready?"

They set off after the others over the churned path in the snow. Lucy made a snowball and threw it at Percy, hitting him squarely in the back.

Laughing, he attacked, quickly pelting both Lucy and Frances. By the time they reached the others just inside the woods, all three were covered in snow.

Georgina, standing next to Sir Desmond, frowned when

she saw her sister. In response, Frances brushed the snow off herself and Lucy and settled her laughter into a pleasant smile. Sir Desmond winked at her.

The group scattered around the woods, cutting fir and holly branches and loading up the sleds. Frances didn't realize she was alone until Sir Desmond tapped her on the shoulder. "Have you spoken to the earl yet about giving me a good recommendation at the Foreign Office?"

"He wouldn't listen to me." She glanced around. No one was in sight. Their laughter sounded miles away.

"I can't believe that. You have him following you around like a lapdog." There was scorn in his tone.

"Not at all." She tried to sound indignant, but her curiosity about the earl's intensions rang through.

"A sweet thing like you? You can make him, can't you? Or perhaps your father would be willing to help me find a position for your sister's sake. To protect her reputation. See you at the house." He smiled at her, kissed her on the forehead, and walked off whistling.

To protect your sister's reputation. What had Georgina done? Or what had she done that could be construed to be wanton? Frances found her way back to the group while she wondered what to tell her father. And what to tell the earl. If she should tell the earl.

"Miss Smith-Pressley, what's wrong?" Lucy asked, running up to her, kicking snow with every step.

"Nothing now. I got lost and realized I had no idea how to get back to the house." Frances gave the girl a smile and then looked at the sleds piled high with their choices for decoration. "You've been busy."

"We've finished. We're heading back to the house now."

"Good. I'm freezing." Frances fell into step with the girl. "Think they'll have some hot chocolate for us?"

"I hope so."

They followed the sleds back to the house and handed off cloaks and gloves and hats to waiting servants before entering the dining room where hot drinks were being served. Sir Desmond was in close conversation with Georgina who looked eager but was blushing furiously.

Once she had her chocolate, Frances said, "Lucy, I need to break up a conversation. If you'll excuse me?"

"May I help?" She took a step to follow her.

"Not this time." With a smile, Frances walked to the corner where Sir Desmond was leaning over Georgina, his mouth practically on her ear. As she reached the couple, she felt Lucy bump her arm. Too late to do anything about the girl listening in now. "We certainly have a great choice of branches for decorating this afternoon. I've heard Susanna has chosen you to lead the ribbon tying."

Georgina stopped mid-giggle and smirked at her sister. "You didn't think she'd pick you, did you?"

Frances felt Lucy bristle beside her and laid a hand on the girl's shoulder as she said, "You don't think anyone is going to pick you for anything if your behavior is not acceptable, do you?"

"Jealousy doesn't become you, sister."

"Already the gossip has started."

"You—." Georgina reddened as she looked for a proper threat.

"Sir Desmond kindly shared it with me." Frances dipped him a small curtsy as she added, "He wanted your family to be warned about what others are saying."

Georgina turned to Sir Desmond, a horrified expression on her face. "Really?"

"I don't want any misfortune to befall your precious character." He held her hand like a supplicant.

Georgina looked from Sir Desmond to her sister, gave a small high-pitched growl, and hurried away, meeting her parents in the doorway. Sir Desmond gave Frances a murderous look and stormed off in another direction.

Lucy beamed at Frances. "It's always fun to be around you. It's like watching Shakespeare."

Frances shook her head and sighed. The room was becoming crowded as if the entire party was assembling in this room. "You are never to repeat what you heard to a living soul."

"I know that." Her tone was defiant.

Staring at the girl, Frances continued to shake her head as she murmured. "If you say a word, you could ruin my sister and destroy my family. A shame, since there's no truth to the rumor. Sir Desmond made it up to forward his own interests." She smiled grimly and continued. "When you're older, you'll have to watch out for young men trying to advance themselves as well as people whose tongues flap out of boredom."

Before Lucy could say a word, the earl came into the room followed by a stranger. Every head turned toward their masked host as he said, "I'm afraid I have bad news."

Chapter Nine

John paused to make sure he had everyone's attention. Many of them looked away from the mask, but they were all listening to him.

"Lord Wethers was found murdered this morning."

Gasps and murmurs could be heard around the room.

"We've found no hint that the murderer came and went during the small hours of the morning, so we believe the killer is still here. The sheriff will want to speak to each of you in turn to discover if you have any information about this wretched business. Please show him the same consideration you have always shown me."

He looked around, but everyone appeared surprised. Someone was acting, and he was doing a good job. He stepped aside and let the sheriff address the party.

John glanced around before he finally spotted Frances. He couldn't think of her as Miss Smith-Pressley any longer. He nodded to her, hoping she would come over to speak to him, but she merely nodded in reply.

Drat. He'd have to send a servant with a note. He couldn't just walk over and speak to her. Not with this absurd mask making his every move obvious.

He needed to speak to her. To find out if she was all right after the shock of finding the body. To discover if she had learned anything while out hunting branches for Christmas decorations. If the note in her room had frightened her. For the pleasure of her company.

"My lord, may I use one of your parlors to conduct my interviews?" the sheriff said, breaking into his thoughts.

"Of course. Susanna, is it all right if he uses the blue drawing room?" It was small, and the interviews couldn't be overheard by servants or the killer.

"I'll have a fire started immediately to warm the room and have a footman summon people and bring you anything you may need." She left, signaling to a footman to follow her.

"Thank you, my lord." The sheriff bowed to him. "Now, everyone, please come only when you are summoned." The sheriff followed Susanna while some of his men took up positions at the doors.

Not waiting to see if he could, John left the room and went back to his study. "Isaiah, bring Sir Edmund and his daughter, please. They were in the dining room a minute ago."

"Yes, milord," he said, disappearing through the doorway.

What excuse could he use this time? She was magnificent, and he wanted to spend time with her without causing talk. And he needed her help to find the traitor.

The only new clue he had was the anonymous note left in her room.

He sat and stared into the fire looking for answers to the identity of the killer. None came to him by the time he heard a scratch on the door and he rose to greet Sir Edmund and Frances.

"I hope you have both recovered from your shock this morning." John went straight to her and took both her soft, capable hands in his mangled ones. He stared into her hazel eyes while he tried to hide the longing and devotion in his.

"Yes. You've seen the note?" A small smile played across her face.

"I have, and I hope you stay in the presence of at least one other person until we find the killer. If necessary, I'll be your bodyguard."

"That would be one more task for you to perform." She gave his hands a squeeze. "Are you all right, my lord? You've had to deal with all the details as well as having to see the body of your friend."

He'd been an earl a long time, and no one had ever before worried about how he coped with the burdens of being in charge. She was special. "The war with Napoleon has made seeing dead bodies an all too common occurrence."

"Then you have my sympathies."

"Thank you, Frances."

She blushed and looked down for a moment before she gazed at him and said, "You're welcome, John."

Glancing over at Sir Edmund, he saw rising speculation and awareness on her father's face. "Please, Sir Edmund, don't say a word about this to anyone. Not even your lady wife. To do so might make Frances a target of the traitor, and I won't have that."

"Have you come to an agreement?" Sir Edmund asked.

Was he that obvious? "I'm not sure I have a right to. Not with a face I must keep covered and hands unable to hold a pen."

"Shouldn't that be my decision?" Frances said. She was no longer smiling.

Beneath his mask, he raised his brows. "You are a most

remarkable lady, not willing to let your father make that decision for you."

"It may be bad manners, but it does lead to happier marriages." She pulled her hands away and set them on her hips.

"Perhaps you want to ask for my hand in marriage instead of the other way around." He was practically laughing now.

"Then you will have to convince me that you are worth marrying if you expect me to ask you." She held his gaze, and he found he glanced away first.

He had been toying with the idea of speaking to Sir Edmund about her marriage. Sir Edmund was older, a man, settled, with no idea of romantic love. John might be able to convince Sir Edmund. To convince a woman as beautiful and brilliant as Frances, he'd have to go back in time to before Tres Fleures. Before the traitor destroyed his face.

"I can't do that."

"Why not?" There was a challenge in her tone.

"Do you think I wear this mask for fun?" He did more than disagree with her. He yelled at her. Immediately, he was embarrassed, and that made him even angrier.

"Even with a mask, you could try to remember your manners." She sighed, paced the study and returned to face him. "You are more than your mask. More than your injuries. I'm sure it's not fun, but you can have a full life with a mask every bit as much as you can without one."

"I see the way people look at me out of the corners of their eyes. I see shock when they come face to face with my mask the first time. Even you, my dear."

She blushed, and he found himself admiring the delicate

pink of her face. "In some ways, my lord, the mask is more shocking than your face."

"My face is pitiful, and I have no desire to be pitied."

"I've seen your face, and I don't pity you for it. I pity you for your scarred spirit. For thinking all anyone can find to love about you is your face. For believing—" She stopped at the sound of scratching at the door.

The footman came in and said, "The sheriff wants to speak to Sir Edmund."

"Of course, he wouldn't want to talk to me," Frances murmured and followed her father out of the room, her head down.

For believing—what? He'd give anything to learn what Frances was going to say.

ഇരു

When her father was ushered into the blue drawing room, Frances was directed by the footman to the green drawing room. She found it had already been decorated in greenery held together with red ribbon.

All of the older people were seated there. Her mother was deep in conversation with Lady Crawford, but beckoned to Frances the instant she saw her. When Frances reached her, her mother said, "Where have you been?"

"The earl summoned Father and I."

"You're spending a lot of time with the earl," Lady Crawford said, curiosity naked on her face.

"Not so much as all that," Frances said, putting on her most demure tone.

"Should your mother be ordering your trousseau?"

"I don't know why." It was up to her father and the earl to make the final decision and the announcement. Lady

Crawford was trying to trip her up for the sake of a piece of gossip, and Frances wanted no part of this. "Who did the decorating? It's quite clever."

"The young people, of course." Her mother gave her a sharp look. "Why don't you check the music room or the ballroom? I believe that's where they are working now."

Frances gave the older ladies a curtsy and went back out into the hall. The children were working on the stairway, giving contradictory orders to amused staff and getting in each other's way. From the direction of the music room, she heard a carol on the piano and some feeble singing.

When she opened the door, she found Miss Ramsey playing and Percy Jones and Lucy singing while they hung greenery.

"Oh, good. Come help us. Mr. Jones is hopeless," Lucy said.

Percy came down the ladder. "I need someone to give me good directions." He made a face at Lucy that she returned.

Frances couldn't resist giving orders. They were nearly finished when the footman came to request that Percy speak to the sheriff. He finished putting up the last bough over the curtains, came down the ladder to give the ladies a theatrical bow, and followed the footman.

"Do you think we could put the rest of the greenery over the mantelpiece?" Lucy asked.

"Why not?" Frances picked up some holly and put it next to a clock.

"I must get back to Mama," Miss Ramsey said and hurried away.

"She's what my father describes as decorative," Lucy

said as the door closed.

"That's a good word for her," Frances agreed and helped Lucy with the greenery for the rest of the mantelpiece. "Do you think we should put some on top of the piano?"

"How about prickly holly leaves on the piano bench?" Lucy asked with an eager smile.

Frances raised her eyebrows and pursed her lips so she wouldn't laugh. In a number of years, Lucy would be in the same position Frances was now. Admired for her good works, liked for her personality, and unloved by any suitors. "I think we'd better stick to the top of the piano."

Lucy shrugged but then willingly helped. When they finished, they went into the hall where the children were still working on the staircase.

"Do you think we should help?" Lucy asked.

"Susanna looks like she could use some assistance in organizing her helpers."

Lucy led the way into the crowd of youngsters to where Susanna stood, her hair mussed and her gown covered with pine needles. Frances followed. "What can we do to help?"

"Can you each take a child and help them?" There was a begging note to Susanna's voice.

"Of course." Lucy took her younger brother and Frances took the Ramsey lad. Within a few minutes, chaos had been defeated and the hall was looking festive. After pleas to the footmen to reach the higher places by ladder, it wasn't long before the hall and stairs were decorated.

"The music room and green drawing room are finished. Is there anything else that needs to be done?" Frances asked.

"Your sister and some others went to decorate the ballroom. That is the only area left, I believe."

Frances curtsied to Susanna and strolled to the ballroom. Entering the wide double doors, she was glad to see the task was done and everyone had left. Then, in the center of the polished floor, she spotted a piece of paper.

Walking over, she discovered it was addressed to her. Unfolding the paper, she read, "Either convince the earl to get me a position at the Foreign Office, or your sister will be destroyed."

It wasn't signed. It didn't have to be.

Chapter Ten

Taking the paper with her, Frances left the ballroom and headed, uninvited, to the earl's personal quarters.

When she tapped on the study door, the footman Isaiah answered. "I need to see the earl," Frances told him.

"He's not available at the moment."

"It's important. My sister is in trouble. Tell him." She was shrieking, but she didn't care.

The earl, Lord Crawford, and her father appeared behind Isaiah. "It's all right," the earl said. "Where's your sister?"

"I don't know. I found this in the ballroom where she was supposed to be decorating earlier." She held out the note. "It's from Sir Desmond."

"It's unsigned," Lord Crawford pointed out.

"Sir Desmond has said this to me before. I—I refused to help him. I believe him to be the traitor. He told me Georgina would be ruined if I didn't help him, but I didn't believe him. What could he do in a houseful of people?"

"Georgina is missing. We found out shortly after the sheriff left. That's why I'm here," her father said quietly. "Do you have any idea where she might be?"

"Isaiah," the earl said, "have the servants check all the outbuildings for Miss Georgina Smith-Pressley. Let the three of us begin with the attics and work our way down."

"I'm coming, too."

"Frances, go comfort your mother," Sir Edmund said.

"You comfort her. I'm searching for my sister. This diabolical creature sent me the note." Frances folded her arms over her chest and stared at her father.

"I'll keep her safe, Sir Edmund," John said. "Come along, Frances." He held out his arm, thrilled when she placed her hand on his sleeve.

Grumbling, Sir Edmund followed the others up flight after flight of stairs to the attics. They went from one space to another without luck. As they started back down the stairs, Frances said, "Is anyone checking the castle ruins? Lord Wethers's body was found there."

"If Sir Desmond killed Wethers, it would make sense he'd use the same location again. Come on." John hurried downstairs to the entrance to the castle, Frances scurrying behind him, trying to keep up.

When John reached the heavy door keeping out the cold, he stopped and held up his hand. "We need to be quiet from here. If Sir Desmond's in there, we want to surprise him."

Three heads bobbed agreement. The only one he paid attention to was Frances's, and he gave her hand a squeeze with stiff fingers.

She smiled at him, and he opened the door and strode in. The absence of a roof and the churned-up snow on the stone floor gave enough reflected light that no candles were needed in this area during daylight. They spread out around the main level of the castle, checking behind broken walls and peering into the cellars where the floor had given way.

John saw the snow on the path ahead of him was undisturbed. He headed back the way he had come until he found Frances starting up a narrow stone stairwell.

"You can still see footprints on these stairs. They are too large to be Georgina's," she told him as she continued to climb.

"Come back down. It's dangerous. Let me go up first," he told her.

She ignored him as she continued her climb. "I'll be— Georgina. I've found her. She's bleeding." He could hear Frances's voice echo off the stones.

He hurried up after her. Behind him, he heard Crawford and Sir Edmund's voices as they made their way to where he was.

When he reached the top, he saw Frances carefully step around the narrow ledge and then kneel on the ice next to her sister's prone body. Between the sisters and him was a chasm going down past the main level into the snow-covered stone floor of the cellar. The ledge Frances was on was barely two feet wide in places where it stuck out from the ancient walls.

"Get ropes and some able-bodied young men," John called to the two men behind him. "And if anyone sees Sir Desmond, they are to hold him until I have time to deal with him."

"Yes, Wolfbrook," Crawford shouted and hurried away.

"Frances, be careful." Sir Edmund said from where he stood behind John. "If you slip, you and Georgina could both fall."

"I am aware of that, Father." Her voice showed her annoyance.

"How sturdy does the ledge feel?" John asked.

"The mortar between the stones crumbles every time I move. I don't know if it will hold any more weight." Her voice wobbled.

"Don't be frightened, Frances. We'll get you both out of there safely." He tried to sound comforting. He was terrified he'd fail.

"I'm not frightened. I'm cold. My face and fingers are getting numb." She looked down into the abyss and then across at him. "That's quite a drop. Too bad there's not more snow down there to break our fall."

"It's only Christmas Eve. We don't get our deepest snows until March." Christmas. Christmas. The plan formed in his mind. "Sir Edmund. Go into the house and tell my servants I need four thick fir trees, at least twenty feet tall, brought to the main level of the castle."

"What?" The man gazed across at his daughters, obviously in shock.

"Four fir trees, twenty feet tall, brought here now." He snapped out his words.

Sir Edmund went to do his bidding, John hoped. "Frances, can you hang on for a while? We'll get you both to safety, but it will take time."

She nodded her head. "I'm worried about Georgina. Her skin is cold and she's not moving."

"Is she breathing?"

"Yes."

John slumped. That was good. Now to get them both safely into the house.

He heard Crawford come up the stairs. "Percy Jones is bringing some rope."

John looked around Crawford to the wiry Jones. "Do you think you can take two ropes out to Frances? We'll hold on to one end here."

Jones nodded. "I can do it, but I only have enough rope for one here."

John looked around, aware everyone was looking to him for answers. He was the earl. "Are there any of the strongest servants here?"

"They've gone out to bring back the twenty-foot evergreens."

John glanced back and said, "Let's tie one end of the rope to the top of the steps coming up here, and then a large noose to the other end."

"A noose, my lord?" Jones looked puzzled.

"It's a good strong loop. I want you to take it out to Frances, have her put it around her waist, and then both of you come back here. Are you willing to make the trip out there and back?"

Jones straightened his spine and nodded once. "Yes."

"Good man."

John found he trembled from the cold and fear as Jones made his way along the icy shelf. He gave Frances the noose end of the rope while a servant tied off the other end behind John and Crawford.

He saw Frances shake her head and then slip the rope around her sister. Brave, foolish Frances.

The movement must have awakened Georgina, because she stirred and nearly rolled off the ledge before Frances and Jones stopped her. All three slipped and stone dust rained down on the main level.

"The rope is secure, my lord."

John nodded, unable to speak. His first idea might save Georgina, but it wouldn't help Frances or Jones. He could see Frances speaking to Jones and her sister, but she kept her voice low so he couldn't hear her. Jones nodded. What had he agreed to?

Then Jones returned along the ledge, picking his way carefully as more stone dust fell. When he made it to John he said, "The two Miss Smith-Pressleys are staying out there until the younger feels strong enough to walk back."

"Idiot woman."

"My lord?"

"Sorry, Jones, that wasn't a criticism of your bravery. How is the ledge holding up?"

"Steady enough where the women are, but that section midway around feels like it will let go at any time."

"Blast. Where are those trees?"

As if to answer his question, some of his servants came into the far side of the castle lugging a tall, thick evergreen tree.

"Bring the tree to the side of the tower on your level and lay it down. Then get on either end and pull it across the gap in the floor," John directed.

When they finished, John could see his idea would protect the two women. If the other trees arrived in time.

"Good idea, John," Frances called to him. "It should break our fall."

"I don't want to fall. I want out of this freezing, dirty castle now," her sister complained.

"Wait until we get the other trees in place. How is that going?" John called to his servants.

"The second tree is almost here. Then we'll have to go find the other two to chop them down."

John looked at the two women. Both were pale and visibly shivering. It would soon be dark, and lighting both levels of the drafty ruins would be impossible. "Let's get this second tree in place and then we'll see. Put the base of the tree by the top of the first tree on the side of the hole where the two ladies are."

While the other servants did as he commanded, John called Isaiah to him and gave him one more instruction.

When they were done, John wouldn't have wanted to walk on the trees and trust them to carry him to safety, but it would keep the two women from falling straight down to the stone cellar floor. A fall that would surely kill them.

"All right, Frances. I want you and your sister to walk around the ledge to us." He tried to make his voice calm and commanding. To his own ears, he sounded timid and weak.

"I'm going first. I'm cold and injured and I want to go inside and sit by a fire," Georgina said, rising unsteadily.

"This isn't how I planned to spend Christmas Eve, either." Frances pressed back against the stones and helped her sister get in front of her. "Of course, I wasn't foolish enough to listen to Sir Desmond."

"Must you criticize everyone I talk to? Everything I do?"

"How did you end up on this ledge having to be rescued?" Frances sounded annoyed. With the steel in that tone, John decided he never wanted to get on her bad side.

"He said he found something miraculous to show me, but we'd have to climb out here. I don't remember anything else."

"How can you be so foolish?"

Georgina turned her back on her sister and hurried along the ledge until she hit a slippery spot. Then her feet started to go out from under her. She clung to a rock protruding from the ancient wall as her feet slid and shifted, trying not to fall off the narrow, icy stones.

John heard himself gasp as rock began to fall away from the perch where the two young ladies stood. Georgina screamed and grabbed the rope tied around her middle as well as the protruding stone. Frances's face was bloodless as she pressed her body against the rough wall and hung on by her fingernails.

Chapter Eleven

Georgina jumped and landed on a drier, stable patch of stone as the ledge under her fell in pieces through the trees and crashed on the cellar floor. Then she stormed the last few paces and reached the men, pushing off the rope as she sobbed on her father's shoulder. Percy put his jacket over her shoulders and she leaned on her father, using him for support as they turned their backs on Frances and climbed down the stairs.

"I'll get Georgina inside to her mother and return immediately," Sir Edmund called over his shoulder. "Be careful, Frances."

And so Frances was left to her fate on the weakened ledge.

She stood there, watching as her father and sister left her clinging to the cold, snowy rocks as darkness began to claim the castle.

John couldn't leave her to her fate. She was brave. Magnificent. "Frances, can you make it over here on the ledge?"

She looked at him, anguish on her face. "So much of the ledge is missing. I'm afraid."

"You have every reason to be frightened. But if anyone could move along that ledge and get to here and safety, it would be you."

When she didn't move, he held out his arms to her and said, "Please, Frances. Come to me. I need you."

She nodded and inched her way along the curve of the ledge, hugging the wall. Someone called his name from behind him, but he ignored them. Every fiber of his being was focused on Frances. He was moving his muscles, trying to coax her toward him.

She slid one dainty shoe forward and then the other. When she reached the section that her sister had broken off, she stopped and gazed at him. He was as close to her as he dared, but there was at least five feet between them. "Can you jump?"

"It's too far. I'm trapped."

"I'm going to throw the rope that was around Georgina to you. I want you to put the loop around your waist." He waved his hand and a servant brought him the looped end of the rope in a coil. "Here it comes."

He threw the rope to her. She reached out and caught it, but her foot slipped on the slick stones. She leaned back against the ancient wall just as the ledge gave way.

And then she was falling, screaming, into the abyss.

Not stopping to look, John turned and ran down the stairs. He reached the bottom of the curving steps, panting, and saw motion to the side. Percy was standing on the rim of the main floor in a mess of fir needles, beckoning to Frances.

John raced over and said, "Frances, are you all right?"

"The trees broke my fall." She let loose a long sigh. "Your wonderful trees broke my fall."

"Can you crawl over to us?"

"I'm trying." She moved forward a few inches before one knee slid between branches. Hanging on to the trunk, she moved forward a few more inches. Then a foot. Then two feet.

"You're almost here, Frances. Please, come to me, my darling." Under the mask, he was smiling.

His smile grew as she smiled back and quickly clambered another foot. She was almost in reach.

And then the tree began to shake. Frances paled and gripped the little branches.

Across the abyss, Sir Desmond stood, one foot on the base of the tree Frances clung to. "It would be a shame if after all this, Miss Smith-Pressley were to fall."

"What do you want, Montague?"

"Safe passage out of here and a position in the Foreign Office."

John's temper flared for an instant before he remembered Frances didn't deserve to spend her life in pain from a fall into the stone cellar because he wanted revenge. Forcing his voice into a conversational tone, he said, "You can have safe passage and gold. A position in the Foreign Office isn't mine to give. Don't you want to go home to France?"

Out of the corner of his eye, he saw Frances inch her way closer to the edge. She was almost within reach.

Sir Desmond saw it as well. He began to shake the base of the tree again and Frances clung to the branches.

"If she falls, the deal is off."

Sir Desmond stopped shaking the tree. "Do we have a deal?"

"I told you what I can give you. Are you content?"

"If your word is good. Is it, my lord?" His tone was sarcastic.

John had been brought up to believe his word was his

mark as a gentleman. To give in to Sir Desmond was the last thing he wanted to do. Give a traitor safe passage off his lands? Reward him with gold? Pay the man who disfigured him? Never.

He was about to tell his servants to seize him when he looked at Frances. She was freezing, vulnerable, terrified. Was he willing to give a traitor what he wanted in exchange for Frances's safety?

He knew the answer before the words were out of his mouth. "I would suggest you head straight to France after we finish our dealings. I will report Wether's death and your involvement as well as your role as a traitor. I will not try to delay you, but I will not hinder the sheriff. Are my terms acceptable?"

Sir Desmond took his foot off the tree. "Let's see this gold."

John squatted down. "You're safe now, Frances. Climb over here and then get warmed up in the house. Jones, assist her, please. I'll talk to you as soon as I see Sir Desmond off." Anything to keep the traitor's foot away from the trees keeping Frances safe.

He rose then and told Sir Desmond, "Come."

The rogue followed him toward his study. "Why did you have me beaten by the French?"

"You were too close to catching me, and you'd learned too much about our plans. Nothing personal. I didn't realize how the French would respond. The French saw you as a representative of everything aristocratic. And still we lost Tres Fleures."

"Why throw in your lot with the French?"

"You wouldn't understand," he sneered.

John turned his head to glance at the traitor so the mask wouldn't block his view. "Try me."

"They promised me gold and land. So did my guardian who held my inheritance from my parents, but instead, he gave what was mine to his children." He followed John into the study. "There is nothing for me here in Britain. Why not go to the side which would give me what I want."

"Why did you put Miss Georgina out on that freezing ledge? You could have escaped more easily without causing a ruckus."

"To get gold coins from you." Sir Desmond nodded toward the safe.

"If she'd fallen, you would have gained nothing."

"Georgina wouldn't fall. She might pull a few people into that pit beneath her, and she almost knocked her sister off the ledge, but Georgina will always turn out just fine."

John stood next to the safe shaking his head. "I still don't understand."

"I tricked Georgina into going out there with me and then knocked her out, knowing her sister would go out after her. And I knew you'd move heaven and earth to save the lovely Frances. The evergreens covering the hole into the pit was a stroke of genius, my lord. Receiving gold to go away was my goal, not hurting Miss Frances." He smiled. "And it worked."

"Why did you kill Wethers?" John asked as he opened his safe and pulled out a small bag marked with the Wolfbrook crest loaded with gold coins.

Sir Desmond held out his hand.

John stared at the hand for a moment before he looked the traitor in the eye and said, "Why Wethers?"

"He told me he figured out I was the traitor. He attacked me because of his brother's death at Noiuelle. I killed him in self-defense."

Complete rot. Still, John dropped the bag of coins into Sir Desmond's palm.

Montague checked the shiny coins, said, "Nice doing business with you," bowed deeply, and left the study.

John rang the bell and Isaiah appeared. "When did the sheriff say he would return and where is Miss Smith-Pressley?"

Isaiah didn't hesitate long enough to ask which Miss Smith-Pressley he meant. "She is in the yellow drawing room with her parents and sister. The sheriff should return with some men within the hour. The snow has been packed down along the main road, speeding their travels."

John let out a long breath. Treason, murder, everything was out of his hands now. The sheriff would start the hue and cry after Sir Desmond that would spread down England to the channel.

He felt a great weight lift from his shoulders. His anger and revenge were gone, thanks to Frances, and life was beginning to open up for him again.

Striding through the ground floor, he came to the yellow drawing room and pushed open the door. Frances sat on a sofa next to her father, while her sister continued her litany of complaints on another sofa seated with her mother. Jones and young Crawford sat nearby, providing Georgina with an audience.

At least Frances's color had improved and her hands no longer trembled while wrapped around a cup of steaming tea. He pulled up a chair and set it directly in front of Frances.

Meanwhile, he heard Georgina say, "...a relic from the Middle Ages. Sir Desmond said only the bravest get to see it. We climbed around that dangerous ledge..."

"Frances, are you recovered?" He was so glad to see her on firm ground that he could barely resist hugging her.

She gave him a shaky smile. "I'm working on it."

"You're very brave. And very loving, going out to save your sister. Could you spare some of that loving for me?"

For once, she didn't have a ready reply, but her face turned crimson.

"Sir Edmund, may I have the hand of your daughter Frances in marriage?"

Sir Edmund sat bolt upright with shock on his features. And then his expression shifted to joy. "Young man, if Frances is content to become your wife, I will happily welcome you into the family."

John gazed at her. She kept her face tilted down.

"Frances, say something to his lordship," her mother demanded.

She stared at him for a moment before saying, "Are you going to live in the past or the present?"

"The traitor is gone. Whether he is captured is up to the sheriff, who will chase him for the murder of Lord Wethers. I have nothing more to do with his hunt, his capture, or his punishment. While I still wear the scars and bear the pains of the past, I will endeavor to live every day in the present."

"Will that be enough for you?" she asked, reaching out for one of his hands.

"Will I be enough for you?" he replied, taking her hand in his.

She smiled then. "May I visit the library any time I

desire?"

"It will be as much your library as mine."

"Kiss me, John."

"Through my mask?"

She shook her head.

Slowly, he slipped it off. Around him, there were gasps, but Frances looked at him steadily. He leaned toward her as she leaned forward. Her eyes closed as he pressed lips that felt misshapen to hers. Somehow, her lips fit against his perfectly.

It was a wonder.

When he regretfully pulled away, she opened her eyes and smiled. "Will you marry me, Frances?"

"Yes, John."

With those words, he felt the same jubilation that poured from every ounce of his being as when he was found and rescued after the Battle of Tres Fleures. The hope of life. The most immeasurable happiness.

"My dear girl," her father said.

"Oh, Frances, you make me proud," her mother said.

"You're marrying an earl?" her sister said in a tone of disbelief.

"Well done," Jones said as Henry Crawford clapped him on the back. "When is the wedding?"

"In the spring," her mother said.

"In the summer. Here," Frances said, "on the anniversary of Tres Fleures. To mark how far you've come in a year. And how much you love Wolfbrook Hall."

"And how lucky I am. Now, if you've recovered from your ordeal in the castle, we need to find my brother and Susanna and tell them what will occur." John slipped on his mask again.

"Is that necessary?" Frances asked, staring at his covered face.

"It is for Susanna, and I have no desire to upset her. It's Christmas, and she has done all the planning while I've felt sorry for myself."

"She's done well." Frances was still smiling. "Shall we find them before everyone scatters to get ready for dinner and then the dancing? Will you lead the first dance, my lord?"

"Yes, and the procession to the church in the morning. You are the best Christmas blessing any man could hope for."

"I can't believe my bad manners in the library led to all of this." She turned a lovely rose.

"I was equally rude. I never imagined such good fortune could come from so woeful a beginning."

A commotion at the door dragged John's attention away from Frances. The sheriff stood twisting his hat in his hands. "I have bad news, my lord. As we were approaching from the main road, a horseman saw us and veered off to go across the fields. The horse stumbled and threw the rider. He broke his neck. It was one of your guests. Sir Desmond Montague."

John shook his head. "He killed Lord Wethers when he discovered Sir Desmond was a traitor aiding the French."

"And must have stolen this from you." The sheriff handed back the bag of gold coins. "At least he saved us a trial."

"That terrible business is finished." John gave a long exhale. "And the body?"

"My men are putting him with Lord Wethers until the weather breaks."

"Thank you."

The sheriff nodded and left, freeing John to focus on the beautiful, brave Frances again. And then they hurried away, hand in hand, to tell everyone about their upcoming wedding.

ঙ৹ওে

When the bells rang out Christmas morning from the church across the countryside, John was already fed, washed, and dressed, and ready to face a new day. He walked into the library where Frances was studying a reprint of a book in Latin.

"Happy Christmas," she said, glancing up at him.

"Happy Christmas, my love."

She gave him a smile. "Are you content with how life is unfolding?"

"I feel reborn this Christmas morning," came out before he considered his words. And then decided they fit his mood perfectly.

She rose and walked over to put her arms around him. "Then all is well. May this be the first of many happy Christmases in our future."

The Earl of Wolfbrook couldn't think of anything better as he slipped off his mask to kiss Frances. His love. His mate.

About Kate

KATE PARKER grew up in the Washington D.C. area where her mother and sister still live. But somewhere over the years, Kate caught the travel bug. She left the city of her birth and moved to a small Southern town followed by a college town on the Front Range of the Rockies. When she's not writing, she's traveling the world to research the places and people who populate her stories.

Coming next from her fertile and murderous imagination is the second Milliner Mystery, *The Murder at the Marlowe Club*, where Emily is again involved in helping Lady Kaldaire solve a murder and finds herself allied with her father's criminal family while disobeying the orders of a handsome Scotland Yard detective. Then Kate will leave the Edwardian era with the first automobiles and fabulous hats to enter London in the anxious days before WWII in the newest in the Deadly Series, *Deadly Travels*. The British spymaster Sir Malcolm, with the approval of her employer, newspaper publisher Sir Henry, assigns Olivia the job of finding the killer of a Quaker debutante, but both men have secret agendas that send her back to Nazi Germany. One wrong move could make Olivia the victim of an unknown killer or the Gestapo, and diplomatic credentials may not help in increasingly enemy territory.

Read more about Kate at www.Kateparkerbooks.com and at www.Facebook.com/Author.Kate.Parker/

A Perfectly Unexpected Christmas

by

Louisa Cornell

Chapter One

Bemerton Hall, Wiltshire
November, 1816

Dammit!
That's what comes of wandering around a strange house in the middle of the night before your wedding.

The Chinese lacquered table rocked furiously in the dark. Portia reached out blindly and managed to save the imitation Ming dynasty urn before it rolled onto the floor. She steadied the table, when what she really wanted to do was fling it down the stairs. Who put a hall table in the middle of the corridor, for pity's sake? Once the urn was safely settled on its little carved mahogany stand, she sat down on the thin Turkish carpet runner and fished around for the mule she'd kicked off her foot when she ran into the table.

Father would be mortified. Which was as good a reason as any to continue this little excursion to the kitchens. Under the watchful eye of the Countess of Bemerton, her future mother-in-law, Portia had participated in a reducing regimen guaranteed to ensure she fit into the wedding gown the countess had brought up from London. She had no idea if the gown would indeed fit, but at this point she did not much care. It did a lady little good to wrestle herself into a gown if she perished from hunger the night before she was to wear it.

In the foyer, the case clock, ancient and leaning to one side, struck midnight. If this were one of Mrs. Radcliffe's gothic novels, a villain would slink out of the shadows and spirit Portia away. At the moment, only one villain had her palms sweating and her stomach in knots. Her brother, Alexander, Marquess of Winterbourne. He'd arrived three days ago and had spent the better part of those three days trying to talk Portia out of going through with the marriage. He and Lord Thornley traveled in the same circles. Notorious ones. They'd gone to school together. The viscount was the last person Alexander wanted her to marry.

When she flatly refused to change her mind, her brother had insisted upon drawing up completely new marriage settlements himself. He'd forced Lord Thornley to sign them in the presence of witnesses and had sent them on to his own solicitor by way of one of his outriders. Portia had refused to speak to her brother for the rest of the day. She would not put it past Alexander to bundle her into a carriage at dawn and not spare the horses until they reached Suffolk.

"And he calls Father a bully," she muttered as she made her way down the stairs. Their father, the Duke of Wharram, was a bully and worse. She'd not let his hand in arranging this marriage put her off. In ten hours, Lady Portia Edwina Chastleton would become Lady Portia Traherne, Viscountess Thornley, and nothing and no one had the power to prevent it. For once in her life she'd made her own decision, and for reasons her family might never understand, she intended to hold fast. Lord St John Traherne, Viscount Thornley, might be the only decent gift her father had ever given her—a chance to escape the burden of who her family believed her to be.

The footman in the foyer had nodded off on the bench beside the front door. Thank goodness the lamp on the dainty stand across the foyer shed enough light for Portia to see down the narrow hallway that led to the door to the kitchens. She'd eschewed a candle in the hope of sneaking down to gather a few apple tarts and a glass of milk and arrive back in her bedchamber undetected. The countess frightened her enough in daylight. She shuddered to think of running into her in darkness.

A burst of masculine laughter drew her attention to the billiard room. The lair to which her bridegroom and his friends had withdrawn, almost from the moment of her arrival two weeks ago, lay between her and her destination. *Drat!* Portia chewed her fingernail and rubbed one foot against the back of her leg. Against the cold, she'd thrown her brown flannel dressing gown over her white muslin night gown. In spite of the light of the full moon pouring through the windows, the dark color of the garment also allowed her to slip past two sleeping footmen completely unnoticed. Not that she had any trouble going unnoticed. When it came to making herself invisible, Portia had the skill of a Rembrandt, perhaps even a DaVinci.

More laughter and snatches of loud conversation forced her feet to carry her closer. Someone had said her name. The billiard room was entered by way of a set of double doors. One of the doors stood slightly ajar, allowing light and noise to creep out into the hallway. Portia edged closer. She'd fully intended to make her way past the billiard room with as much stealth as she could muster. Stealth was something each of the Duke of Wharram's six children had learned early in life. Once she reached the kitchens, she'd planned to use the servants' staircase to return to her chambers on the second floor. Falling up a staircase in the dark was far less painful and deadly than falling down. A shiver went through her. She rubbed her arms and took one more step towards the crack in the doors.

"Come now, Thornley. You cannot mean that." Lord Rupert Pearce had a voice like a braying ass. His character and demeanor were not much better. Which might be an insult to asses all over England.

"I do," her soon-to-be-husband replied. "I rather like a woman with some meat on her bones. A cushion in bedplay and a source of heat on a cold winter's night."

Portia flinched. She did not really expect a man like Viscount Thornley to fall madly in love with her on a mere few months acquaintance. He was ridiculously handsome with sharp features, thick, dark brown, wavy hair and eyes the blue of a summer sky. Tall and lean with a horseman's physique, he had to be aware how incongruous a couple they made. Still, a woman preferred not to be likened to a mattress and bedclothes. Especially the night before her wedding. She should go before she heard more.

"All well and good if a man intended to bed the lady more than once," Lord Beeton, another of Thornley's friends, said. "With a face like hers once is all I could stomach."

The room erupted with raucous laughter and the clinking of glasses.

"Unfair, gentlemen," Thornley announced over the laughter. "Quite unfair. Lady Portia has very fine eyes and a nice smile."

"Not to mention the largest dowry in England," Lord Pearce added. "For that amount of money, close your eyes, wed and bed *Lady Porka*, and make for London with all due haste and as much of her money as you can muster."

"My plan exactly, Pearce," Thornley assured him. "Close my eyes and think of England. To *Lady Porka,* gentlemen. To her fine eyes and her even finer dowry. Which I intend to put to good use far away from my future viscountess."

Her eyes burned. She took a step back, then two more before she turned and fled back the way she came. Portia raced down the corridor and into the foyer, tripping as she started up the main stairs.

"My lady?" The footman emerged from his seat on the bench in the corner. He took her elbow and helped her to her feet. "Are you hurt?" The concern in his face and voice nearly undid her. A stranger, a footman, cared more for her feelings than the man she was about to marry.

"No. Georgie, isn't it? I am not hurt." She straightened to her full, though negligible height. "Good night."

"Yes, my lady. We are all very happy you have come to Bemerton, my lady."

The air burned as she drew it in through her nose, like water when she plunged into the lake at Wharram Place to swim with her sisters. She offered him a smile and fought to still the tremble of her lips. "Thank you," she murmured and forced herself to climb the long staircase one step at the time. She made it the second-floor landing by sheer force of will. Only then did she break into the run her body demanded.

Only then did the tears burning in her eyes flood down her face. Only when she'd fumbled her way into the pretty chamber she'd been assigned and flung herself across the bed did she allow herself to sob into the counterpane. She clasped handfuls of the bedclothes and tore and scratched at them. When her body shook so she could no longer breathe she rolled over and swiped at her stinging cheeks with her fists.

Stupid, stupid, girl! Your first try at independence and look at the muck you've made of it!

She sat up, still hiccupping sobs and wiping away tears that refused to heed her demands to cease. She glanced at the door to the dressing room where her chaperone, Nanny Rose, lay sleeping. It would not do to wake the old woman as she would run straight to Alexander. He'd call off the wedding without asking Portia a thing. She'd be under the thumb of her family once more. Which was only a little more palatable than being under the thumb of a husband who had to close his eyes to bed her. And assumed she'd close her eyes when he made off with her dowry.

Portia stared at the flame of the candle flickering on her bedside table. A splotch of deep red caught her eye. A haphazardly tied ribbon encircled a thick bundle of papers. She plucked them from the table and slid them free of their red binding. A tear dropped onto the first page. She blotted it quickly with her nightgown. She dragged her sleeve across her face and shook her head to clear it. Once she'd read through every page, she started with the first once more. Over and over she read the pages of her marriage settlements.

When the sun's first rays attempted to break through the gaps in the drapes Portia tied the ribbon around those papers and tucked them beneath her pillow. Dry eyed, she lay her head onto her pillow and stared at the new gown, her wedding clothes, hanging on the corner of the wardrobe. And planned exactly what sort of marriage she intended to have.

Chapter Two

Hindon Abbey, Wiltshire
November, 1817

Some fool had hung a settee on the ceiling. Whose ceiling? Lord St John Traherne, lately Earl of Bemerton, turned his head in order to assess his surroundings. And immediately regretted it. The room shifted in an ever-increasing circle around him. He fought the urgent desire to cast up his accounts, but only in deference to the sudden sight of a table held up by four elephant's feet. Followed by a patch of horrid lavender Aubusson, followed by Pearce's crumpled form on top of the aforementioned Aubusson.

Pearce.

Elephant's feet.

Hindon Abbey. He was at Hindon Abbey, Pearce's ancestral pile in Wiltshire.

St John closed his eyes and drew in a deep breath. Another mistake as the air smelled and even tasted of stale cigar smoke, rancid food, bad ale, sweat, and a bit more distant—an unemptied chamber pot. As slowly as his long frame allowed, he shifted his body to the edge of the prickly horsehair sofa and raised his head from its precarious position hanging over the side of it. He levered himself into a sitting position, which resulted in the previously dangling settee suddenly appearing in its proper position before the fireplace. Good thing too. The Countess of Raddock, Pearce's mother, would not be amused by a hanging settee. Unless Lady Jersey had one first, in which case the countess would have three.

He kicked at his recumbent friend. "Pearce." St John suppressed a groan. Even the simple task of rousing the architect of his current state hurt his head. "Pearce, wake up. We're supposed to be somewhere. Wake. Up." He punctuated his last two words with painful kicks to his friend's buttocks. Painful for St John. Pearce only grunted once and rolled over, out of his reach.

They *were* supposed to be somewhere. Weren't they? He remembered a long carriage ride from London over a week ago. Or was it two? They'd made the journey for a very specific reason. What was it? A blurred visual search finally revealed an open tantalus before a broad, tall set of mullioned windows at the far end of the room. After three attempts he pushed himself off the sofa and to his feet. The room began another circuit around him, but he'd long mastered the art of crossing a spinning room by keeping his eye on the horizon. In this case the horizon was a tantalus replete with more of what had landed him in this state in the first place.

Rain pelted against the glass panes, a gentle tattoo which soothed rather than discomfited his aching head. Autumn. The trees stood half-dressed in shades of red and yellow and orange. Late autumn. The precise date escaped him. His father had been gone these six months, which meant St John should be about the business of acting the earl. He poured himself half a glass of brandy, but did not drink it. He shuffled to the window seat and dropped onto the purple velvet cushioned bench. The rain did not block the view entirely. The wide expanse of the estate's grounds gave way to faded green fields. He assumed the intermittent white dots were sheep.

Somewhere, past the fields and sheep, lay Bemerton Hall, his family seat. And his wife. Ah! Lady Portia Traherne, Countess of Bemerton. She wasn't the reason for his journey to Wiltshire. Was she? Wait. Oh... Satan's bollocks.

"Pearce, what day is it?" St John downed the brandy, grimaced, and dropped the empty glass onto the window seat. He lurched to his feet. "Pearce!"

"What the devil!" Pearce sat up and clutched his head with his hands. "Why are you shouting?" He sat legs splayed across the carpet and attempted to push himself up with his hands.

"What day is it? We came to Wiltshire for the christening. What day is it?" Images of the past several weeks and months whisked through his mind, flipping back and forth like pages in a book left out in the wind and rain.

"Christening? What christening? Where are my boots?" Pearce crawled about the garish carpet peering beneath the sofa and between the elephant's feet supporting the heavy marquetry table.

"The child's christening, my daughter's christening, remember? The reason we came out from London?" St John spotted his black and gold brocade waistcoat hanging on the back of a chair. His black wool jacket lay on the floor beneath it. For some reason known only to God, he still wore his neckcloth, hopelessly knotted and stained. "Have your butler organize a bath for me. Sims will have me turned out in no time."

"You left Sims in London. Said you had no need of him. We came for the shooting. Aha!" Pearce dragged his boots from beneath a wing-back chair and wrestled his feet into them.

The shooting. St John had a murky recollection of guns and dogs and tramping through the tall waning grass. Yes, they'd done a bit of shooting. How long ago, he had no idea. He had a daughter. She was born in August. He'd missed her birth and had vowed he'd not miss the christening. An event to which he'd not been invited and would have had no knowledge of if not for an offhand remark by his mother in London a few weeks ago.

Dammit!

He stalked across the room, his head throbbing with every step, and hauled Pearce to his feet. "What. Day. Is. It?"

His friend flailed at him and staggered away towards the tantalus. "It is Sunday. I'm almost sure of it."

"Good. The christening is today. Ring for a servant. I need a bath, and clean clothes. If we hurry, we might catch them before they reach the church." Awash in relief, St John made for the drawing room doors.

"The christening was *last* Sunday, old man, the twenty-sixth. We didn't make it back from the races at Epsom. Remember?"

The all too familiar weight of an icy rock set up residence in St John's gut. He pressed his forehead against the cool surface of the eight-paneled oak door. His stomach roiled with a mix of brandy, a little food, and a great deal of passive regret. The sort of regret one had to cast back in memory to identify. It did not stir nor burn. It merely sat waiting to be visited from time to time, like a Christmas pudding forgotten in the far corner of a seldom used pantry.

Last week. His daughter was to be christened on the twenty-sixth of October. It was now November. Had he missed the anniversary of his wedding as well? Not that it mattered. And now he'd missed the christening. His entire life consisted of misses and near misses and the eternal attempt to outrun his sins. His failures. His—

"No need for all this fuss, Thornley, for a girl child of all things. I'll ring for some food and we can get some shooting in before dark if the rain lets up."

St John heard Pearce. His words even wiggled through the fog thinning and thickening in turns over his brain. His daughter had been christened seven days past, with only her mother to hold her and vow to raise her to be a decent God-fearing child. He didn't even know who had stood as godparents, if anyone had. Lady Portia had a brother and several sisters. Perhaps they had attended. But he had not. He'd gone to Epsom with Pearce and a number of their friends. And here he stood, leaned against a door, smelling of liquor, horses, and sweat. Doing nothing, just as he'd always done.

"Damned pity the brat's a girl," Pearce said and punctuated his disdain with a loud, ragged belch. "I don't envy you having to bed Lady *Porka* again to get a son off her. Bad enough she holds the purse strings. Perhaps you should charge her for your favors. Might be worth a bit of the ready for you to bed her more than once a year. I know you couldn't pay me enough to—"

"Stubble it. And don't call me Thornley. I have been Bemerton these six months." A red haze blurred his vision as

St John strode across the room and knocked the glass of brandy from Pearce's hand. "You are speaking of the Countess of Bemerton. My wife."

"What the devil?" Pearce gave him a shove. "A wife you haven't seen since the day you married her. *Lord Bemerton.*"

"Whose fault is that?" St John swiped a hand over his face. The answer to his question skewered him as surely as a cavalryman's saber.

"Your father's, for saddling you with a fat, spotty sow of a bride no matter how large her dowry. For all the good it did you. Who signs marriage settlements without reading them first? You really—" Whatever further insult Pearce intended to offer went unsaid, stoppered by St John's fist to the man's jaw. His friend went down like a sack of potatoes and did not stir.

He'd lost his wits. Nothing else accounted for this sudden infinitesimal stab of conscience. Lady Portia might not let him in the door, but for some inexplicable reason, he needed to see her. Needed to meet his daughter. Whilst Pearce began to moan his way back to the world of the living, St John stalked quickly to the door and went in search of Hindon Abbey's butler.

It took less than an hour for St John to complete an abbreviated bath and have Pearce's valet put him in some semblance of order. By the time the butler helped him into his greatcoat and handed him his gloves, the view outside the open front door was painted in shades of purple and grey with a sliver of faded yellow along the edge of the abbey's extensive lawn. The rain fell heavily enough to evade a definite rhythm, singing a continuous song of thick splashes against the cobblestones before the portico.

"My lord, the roads between here and Bemerton are no doubt thick with mud and it is nigh dark," the butler advised. "Are you certain you do not wish me to have a carriage made ready?"

"Then it is a good thing I won't be traveling the roads, isn't it, Smythe?" St John left the house and mounted his gelding, Zephyr, before he turned back to the concerned servant who stood on the steps wringing his hands. "I have traveled the woods and fields between Hindon Abbey and Bemerton Hall since Bigsby put me on my first pony. Tell Lord Pearce I shall return tomorrow." He urged Zephyr into a trot and circled the house towards the stables. "If not sooner," he muttered to no one in particular.

Once he'd traversed the various paddocks behind the stables, he pointed the big bay gelding towards Hindon Abbey's home woods. St John had ridden Zephyr for over ten years. Once they entered the woods, the horse picked his way along the various paths with little direction from him. Which gave St John time to reconsider his current plan. Plan? If only he had one. A wild notion had entered his head, and he'd acted upon it. He had no memory of the last time he'd done something so unpredictable. He had no idea why he'd done it this time, save for the vision of his daughter, a child he'd never met, being christened without godparents or any family to honor the occasion.

Honor.

As if his presence would have lent any honor to the event. The Earls of Bemerton had sold their honor several generations ago when they began the tradition of spending their heirs into bankruptcy only to marry the next generation off to an heiress to refill the coffers. Unlike St John, who had been shackled by the marriage settlements his bride's brother had drawn up, St John's father had allowed the now Dowager Countess of Bemerton to cajole, wheedle, and demand her way through the fortune her father had placed in his hands to marry her.

Most of the trees had shed their leaves, but enough yews and hawthorns remained to send cascades of water down his neck as he brushed beneath them. A more aware man might have been frightened by the bare skeletal limbs of the oaks and elms reaching for him, pulling at his clothes. Tugging nearly as hard as the need for a drink to keep the lovely haze in which he'd lived his life these six months since his father's death. *Six months?* Longer than that. He'd succumbed to the siren call of spirits long before the previous earl's demise.

Coward.

The rain increased once they left the confines of the woods and crossed onto the lands held by the Earls of Bemerton since the Conqueror. Thunder rolled across the fields lit by an occasional flash of lightning splitting the rainswept clouds. St John, not to mention his horse, was soaked. A fool's errand. He needed a drink, and a warm fire, and time to come up with a better plan than simply arriving on his wife's doorstep. Zephyr slowed his pace as they climbed the hill overlooking the Hall.

St John pulled the gelding to a halt and gazed at the spread of pastures delineated by walls of stone, hedges, and the occasional wooden gate. The lightning flashed so often now the view was nearly as clear as if it were daylight. It did, however, make the darkness far blacker and impenetrable. With the next flash, he made out the edge of the lawns and gardens before Bemerton Hall. A few lights winked at him in the distance. He gathered the reins and started to turn back.

"It is my house, dammit," he muttered. "My wife. My daughter. My damned life." He goaded Zephyr down the hill. By the time they reached the bottom, he was in a full gallop. The deluge fell in sheets that stung St John's face and drenched his hair. A sense of frantic peace settled over him. He moved low over the gelding's neck, a far distant recollection of the brief joy of his youth teased him, only a little out of reach. The fog of too much liquor and too much useless living lifted like a veil. He threw back his head and closed his eyes against the rain.

Which is why he did not sense the bunching of Zephyr's withers beneath his knees. St John's eyes snapped open just as the gelding rose to clear the wall and ha ha between the last pasture and the first horse paddock. He scrabbled with the reins and fought to adjust his seat. Thunder began to roll from across the way and increased in volume the closer it drew. Lightning illuminated the way ahead in three quick lances through the dark. Zephyr's forelegs landed. The horse hung in the air, as if suspended mid-stride. St John, his reflexes long dormant, was not so fortunate. He pitched over the gelding's neck into the darkness. The sensation lasted an eternity, or perhaps for only a moment. The landing, however, went on forever. His body snapped, and bounced, and jolted *arse* over tea kettle until it stopped, his head cracking against something hard, sharp, and icy cold. So cold.

He lay there he knew not how long. Not long? It couldn't be. He'd heard Zephyr land, scramble at bit and then slow hoofbeats as the nervous animal came alongside him. A soft equine muzzle snuffled his face. St John raised his hand to push him away. The slightest touch sent agonizing pain cutting through his head. He reached out blindly to run his hand up the horse's forelegs.

Sound. Nothing broken.

He patted around the mud and grass and found the reins, which he wrapped around his hand. "S-sorry, boy. My f-fault. My..." Pain, and cold, and darkness dragged him into a deep hole.

₨Ⅎ

Voices. Words muttered then shouted above the place the pain had put him. How long? He licked his lips. He tried to speak. Someone tugged at his hand. He tightened his fingers, at least he thought he did. Something slid from his grip. Reins. Zephyr. Two voices. He fought to open his eyes. A lamp neared his head. The little bit of light that slipped through his slitted eyelids hurt like hell.

"Go fetch a cart, boy. Be quick about it. 'Tis his lordship. Hurry."

St John recognized the voice. He cast about his mind for a name. He swallowed and even that hurt. What the devil had happened? He was wet, cold, and every inch of his body hurt, nowhere worse than his head.

"Lie still, my lord," the familiar voice said. "The cart is coming. We'll have you home in a thrice. Don't move."

Excellent advice. Damned redundant, when a man had neither the ability nor the desire to do so. Where the hell was he? Other than on the ground, in the mud, wet and cold to the bone, and beaten within an inch of his life. London? No. Didn't smell of piss and coal dust. Bath? Brighton? It came to him.

"Bigsby?"

"Yes, my lord. Lie quiet now. We're going to lift you into

the cart."

"I'm at Bemerton." St John gasped as searing pain roiled through him like the distant thunder. Other voices now. Strange ones. They carried him a few feet and lifted him onto a hard surface.

Bemerton. Why am I at Bemerton?

"Zephyr," he croaked.

"We've got him, my lord. Jem is leading him home," the familiar voice assured him.

Bigsby. That's right. Bigsby. At Bemerton. Home.

He'd come for a reason.

What day is it?

It was now November.

He'd come to Bemerton in November. For what? His head throbbed, pulsed, and swelled in and out like a bellows. St John prayed for it to drop off his neck if it meant the pain might abate for even a moment. What the hell had happened? Darkness descended once more.

୧୦୯୨

Put out the damned lights.

St John woke to a blinding glare attempting to pry his eyes open. The rain had stopped. No. Not stopped. Indoors. Warmth. Dryness. The smell of beeswax candles and wood polish. More voices. Women's voices. Dainty feet on marble floors. The smell of starch and fresh linen. Orders barked in a firm, feminine voice. Another voice he knew. Lemon verbena. A soft hand on his neck. Gentle fingers touched the side of his head. He winced in spite of himself.

"What the hell have you done to yourself?"

St John opened his eyes wide. He blinked past the pain and blurred vision until a face, a heart-shaped face and moss green eyes came into view. Leaves of memory rushed at him on a rushing stream of cool water.

"Lady Portia," he whispered in a hoarse rasp. "I'm not too late, am I?"

"Too late for what, you great looby?"

"Our wedding."

Chapter Three

He was thinner than Portia remembered. Not that her memory of him was to be trusted. Neither the silly, sheltered girl of twenty-two who'd believed the sincerity of his courtship nor the eons older woman of twenty-three who'd borne his child had an informed, intimate knowledge of Lord St John Traherne, Earl of Bemerton. She'd never even seen him unclothed. Until now.

His neck cloth had been lost somewhere between the far paddock and the house. Portia handed the soaked and mud-stained shirt, waistcoat, and jacket to Mrs. Whitby, the housekeeper. The tall, grey-haired servant *tsk'ed* and draped them over the mahogany and mother-of-pearl inlaid screen in the corner of Portia's bedchamber. The fine lawn shirt, silk brocade waistcoat, and blue wool jacket were ruined. Clothes fit for the rag bin were the least of Portia's worries.

"I'm not too late, am I?"

"You have no idea," she muttered as she tackled the buttons of his falls.

"Talking to yourself?" Nanny Rose asked from the end of the bed as she worked to remove St John's boots and stockings. "If you're too shy to undress your husband, perhaps you should have Mrs. Whitby and I do it." She gave the housekeeper a wink, which Mrs. Whitby answered with a half-grin.

"Don't be ridiculous." Portia struggled to remove his skin-tight buckskins. The fabric, made taut by the icy rain, clung to his chilled flesh. She squared her shoulders and ran her hands beneath the waistband, working the breeches down his legs whilst trying not to dislodge his smalls. "I am a married woman who has given birth to this man's child. Why would I be missish about seeing him naked?"

"A man doesn't have to be naked to get a woman with child," Nanny Rose observed. "A man who knows his business doesn't even have to remove his boots."

Portia busied herself spreading the buckskins over the screen. She didn't want these two women to see the red-hot blush that suffused her face, nor the resigned anger in her eyes. When Bemerton's stablemaster, Mr. Bigsby, and his men had carried her husband into the foyer, she'd reacted as any mistress of the house might. She'd sent a rider to Salisbury for the doctor and had St John brought upstairs to her own bedchamber, where a blazing fire burned in the hearth.

She watched now as Mrs. Whitby and Nanny Rose used soft cloths and basins of hot water to clean the mud and blood from his face, neck and shoulders. His complexion was a chalky shade of white. One eye had swelled shut. His lip was split. Several scratches drew ugly crimson lines across one cheek, his forehead, and his chin. His dark brown hair, matted with blood, covered a nasty, ragged slice from his temple, behind his ear, and back nearly to the nape of his neck. He looked… helpless. Portia didn't want him helpless. Even drunk and smelling of some tavern wench's perfume, he'd not been helpless the night he'd crawled into this very bed and made her his wife.

Portia had planned several pointed, profanity laced speeches for her husband the next time he crossed her path. A clever lady like herself might plan a veritable sermon book of speeches in the year since she'd last seen him. What did he do? He'd arrived on her doorstep half dead and out of his senses, effectively spiking her guns and depriving her of delivering the set down he so richly deserved. Which confirmed what she'd suspected all along.

"Having a husband is a damned nuisance." Shocked she'd expressed those sentiments out loud, she glanced quickly at the other two women in the room. They merely smiled and shook their heads.

"Rather less a nuisance when he stays away for a year and arrives home knocked senseless," Nanny Rose observed as she walked to the bedchamber door and handed St John's boots to a footman.

"Bit more convenient than the last earl, God rest his soul," Mrs. Whitby added.

Portia padded to his bedside. A lock of his hair, now washed clean of blood, had fallen over his eyes. She pushed it back off his forehead, then snatched her hand back as if burned. "I daresay it'd be a bit more convenient for all of us if he stayed this way." The words tasted as bitter as wormwood. She'd never have said such a thing a year ago, not even in jest.

A clumsy, stifled silence enveloped the room. Even the fire burned without making a sound. The rain against the windows had ceased. Her husband's breathing rattled at intermittent intervals, though the evidence of it was clearer when she followed the rise and fall of his whipcord defined chest above the sheet and counterpane drawn to his waist.

When she finally dared to turn her attention to Nanny Rose and Mrs. Whitby, the cruel indifference of her statement lashed at her conscience. They had not said a word. There was no need. Portia crossed her arms and stepped away from the bed.

"I will go and see what is delaying the doctor. Salisbury is less than five miles away and—"

"You stay, my lady." Mrs. Whitby gave a stiff curtsy. "I will see to it." She bustled out the door.

"Not well done of you, my girl," Nanny Rose said, her lips pursed in the familiar fashion with which she'd expressed disappointment in Portia and her siblings over the nearly thirty years she'd served the Chastleton family. She went to the far side of the bed and placed the back of her hand against St John's neck.

"I didn't mean it." A weak excuse even to Portia's own ears. She edged cautiously toward the large oak canopy bed that reigned over the countess's bedchamber, a carved presence designed to pay homage to the brave, and shame the timid, women who'd held the title before her. The posts had been sculpted of richly stained oak, each created to appear as a tree erupting from the rose, gold, and green Aubusson carpet. The canopy and bed curtains had been crafted of gold brocade fabric, the embossed lions glinting in the light of the fire and candles.

Against her every self-preserving instinct, she settled onto the bed at his side and studied her unconscious husband. His pallor had grown worse. Lines of pain drew his face tight. Her lungs closed against the drawing of breath. Her heart did a slow flip in her chest. She covered his hand with hers, curling her fingers around his and tucking them beneath his palm. His hand was cold. So cold. She clasped it between her palms, as much as she was able. His hand was large, with remarkably drawn sinews and roughened places most gentlemen did not possess. She chafed it gently, urging warmth back into his flesh with her own. After tucking it beneath the heavy, quilted, hunter green velvet counterpane, Portia reached for his other hand. It bore scratches and even a few scars. How odd she'd never noticed those scars during their brief courtship, though from their state it was obvious he'd carried them long before she'd met him.

A highly indignant, though infantile cry issued from behind the door into her dressing room. In the absence of her husband, Portia had set up her daughter's nursery in the earl's bedchambers. The space was ample enough for all the furnishings necessary to keep an infant in comfort and still provide space for Nanny Rose to have her own quarters. The earl's sitting room had been turned into the older woman's bedchamber, which allowed for Lady Alexandra Eloise Traherne to have both her nanny and her mother within earshot.

St John's fingers tightened around her own, though his eyes remained closed and his breathing raggedly shallow.

"I'll see to her." Portia quickly set St John's hand atop the counterpane and practically leapt off the side of the bed.

"You will see to your husband, my lady," Nanny Rose commanded, her lips drawn tight enough to close a miser's purse. "I will see to the little one." Far more quickly than Portia might have credited, the older woman bolted through the dressing room and into the nursery, closing the door with a punctuating slam.

"I was under the illusion I am mistress of this house,"

Portia muttered and returned to St John's bedside to study his prone and worrisomely still form. "How presumptuous of me." She turned back to the dressing room door briefly and stuck out her tongue. "I'm only the Countess of Bemerton." A flash of shame showered heat over her body. She'd married this man for better or worse. She'd not counted on the *worse* being quite so painful, but she'd wanted her independence, not to be a burden to her brother and sisters.

"Oh, very well." She retrieved a cloth from the clean basin of warm water on the bedside table. Once she'd wrung the excess water from it, she sat back on the edge of the bed and wiped the perspiration from his face. St John Augustus Traherne was a handsome devil, even lain low as he was now. A strong, square jaw, with a dimpled chin, sculpted beneath elegantly sharp cheekbones, and centered by a perfectly proportioned nose. *Drat him!* Her nose was her least lovely feature in a long list of least lovely features.

She'd dreaded meeting him. Her father had informed her he'd found her a husband, a man willing to take her on in spite of her plain looks. The moment the Duke of Wharram— none of his children called him Father, or God forbid *Papa*— had informed her, Portia had been overwhelmed with abject terror and abysmal regret of her decision to go behind her brother's back and ask their father to marry her off. Then she'd met St John, and every bit of sensibility and doubt had disappeared. Right up to the moment she'd overheard that fateful conversation the night before her wedding. Young women were supposed to be foolish, or so she'd been told. She'd abused the privilege.

"Lady Portia?" His voice, though nearly devoid of sound, startled her. His eyes fluttered open, as much as they could, that is. One was well on its way to sporting a black eye any pugilist in Britain might envy.

"I am here." Well that was an obvious thing to say. "The doctor should be here any moment." She gave his bare shoulder an awkward pat.

"Don't need a doctor," he mumbled even as his eyes fell closed once more. "A bit under the hatches is all. Be right... as rain... in the morning. Tell Pearce not to forget... the ring." His head lolled to one side.

"What ring?" She gave him a shake. "What ring, my lord?"

"Wedding ring. Tying the parson's knot... in the morning. Didn't... forget."

"Well, that is hardly a good sign."

Portia looked over her shoulder to find Dr. Pratt directly behind her, a somber expression on his normally affable countenance. She stood and allowed the physician to take her place.

"Correct me if I am wrong, my lady, but your nuptials were nearly a year ago," Dr. Pratt said calmly, even as he examined St John, and furrowed his brow more deeply with each passing moment. The physician was barely over forty year of age, though the hair at his temples was white as snow against the black of the rest. He was tall and thin with acutely sharp features and kind brown eyes. She'd never seen him anything save serene and hopeful. Tonight, he looked deeply concerned.

"Nearly to the day, sir. Tomorrow is the anniversary of my wedding."

"His lordship has taken a nasty crack to the head. There is more swelling than I would like. Are there any other injuries?" He stripped the bedclothes down to the foot of the bed and made a thorough check of his patient's limbs whilst Portia did her best not to watch. Too much.

"Has he said anything else?" Dr. Pratt asked as he covered St John and returned his attention to the head wound.

"He made similar remarks when they brought him into the house, about the wedding and not being too late." Portia sank her teeth into her bottom lip and forced her hands to her sides.

"I see." The physician lifted the candle from the bedside table and brought it close to St John's face. He pried his patient's eyes open and shone the candlelight into them, each in turn. A nearly imperceptible change in Dr. Pratt's breathing did nothing to assuage the sudden sense of panic rattling Portia's bones. He handed her the candle, which she returned at once to the table. Her hands had grown nerveless.

The rain began to pound against the windows. Lightening lit the darkness outside her chamber. She paced to the French windows that led to her balcony and gazed out at the flashes of light, the trees in the grip of the storm's fierce winds. St John might have lain out in this all night. A young ram had escaped the sheep barn and Bigsby and some of the stable boys had joined the search. Otherwise, she might have been a widow by morning. A widow with a three-month-old daughter who had never met her father. The idea made her terribly sad.

"I believe I will stay the night, if it is not an inconvenience, my lady," Dr. Pratt announced from St John's bedside. He was returning a number of items to the large satchel he always carried. She'd never even noticed his use of them, so economical were his movements and manner. A thick, white bandage covered the ugly wound to the side and back of her husband's head.

"Of course, Dr. Pratt. I will have the chamber across the corridor prepared if that will suit."

"That will suit very well. I shall check on him through the night." He indicated the two chairs before the fire. Portia's legs turned stubborn. They wished to carry her to her husband's bedside. She forced herself to settle into one of the white and gold striped low set chairs. Dr. Pratt sat opposite her, his hands clasped between his knees.

"How badly is he hurt?" Portia blurted.

"I have no wish to alarm you, my lady. He may awaken in the morning as if nothing at all has happened, save for a bump on the head and some bruises, scrapes, and scratches."

"And if he does not?" The room was warmed by the fire blazing away in the hearth, but Portia's skin turned cold and damp. Her heart hammered against her ribs. St John Traherne, Viscount Thornley, and now the Earl of Bemerton, had been well out of her life for a year. He'd given her a title and a child and left her alone. She'd wanted nothing more from him. Until now.

"He has fallen into... a stupor, if you will. I do not say coma because it has only been a matter of hours." When Portia opened her mouth to protest, he raised his hand. "With head wounds, it is difficult to say. I am concerned with this memory slip. It is possible he might awaken tomorrow, but not remember his own name, let alone the past year. But with his state of health, there could be any number of reasons for it."

"His state of health?"

"He has been lying in the rain, stripped and washed by the utterly thorough Mrs. Whitby."

Portia nodded and had to smile. Dr. Pratt and Mrs. Whitby were often at odds over the best treatment for the various illnesses and injuries on the estate.

"His skin still reeks of brandy and ale. He is thin, and beneath the pallor from tonight's misadventure his color is the sallow of a man lost to drink. He has been... unwell for some time."

"I will not do you the discourtesy of dissembling. What can we do?" She fought the terror rising from her belly up through her lungs and into her throat. This was the last way she'd expected to spend her wedding anniversary. She'd not expected to spend it any way at all. Alexandra had been appropriately christened. In no time at all Christmastide would arrive. She did not want to think on planning a—

"Do not rush into the abyss so swiftly, my lady." Dr. Pratt leaned forward and patted her hands, clasped tightly in her lap. "God had him found in that paddock for a reason. I cannot help but think that reason is more than to simply provide the earl with a proper burial."

"It is a pity God did not see fit to find his lordship *before* he tried to take that wall in the dark in the middle of a rain storm." Portia pushed out of her chair and returned to the bed.

"Yes, it would have been far more convenient for all concerned," Dr. Pratt said and walked to the bedchamber door. "But sometimes, a bit of inconvenience is just what we need to set things to rights. I shall go and beg Mrs. Whitby to prepare that chamber for me. You stay with his lordship."

Then, once again, she was alone with her slumbering husband. Which seemed to be the intention of every interfering busybody in her life. She gazed down at him, his dark brown hair in stark contrast to the white bandage and the pallor of his skin.

"What did the doctor say?" Nanny Rose asked from the dressing room doorway.

Portia continued to watch St John sleep. In the fairy tales it was the princess who fell into a stupor and needed her prince's kiss. She could not remember if he'd ever even kissed her. An odd thing to come to mind tonight. Whatever she wished to bestow on him now, a kiss was not the first thing that came to mind. He had no right to hold his life so cheap he'd toss it away over a wall he had no business taking. She drew in a long breath. To prove herself capable to her family, she'd married the first man who'd offered for her hand. By God, it was time to be capable.

"Please bring Alexandra to me, Nanny. I will be spending the night in here. Dr. Pratt is staying in the blue bedchamber." She settled onto the side of the bed.

"Let the little one sleep. I'll sit up with you."

Portia turned to meet the nanny's puzzled expression. "It is time my daughter meets her father."

A thousand questions crossed Nanny Rose's face. She asked not a one. It took no time at all for her to go back into the nursery and return with a deeply sleeping Alexandra. Portia took the infant into her arms and held her close. She was warm and safe and smelled of heaven and the chamomile soap from her bath. Portia leaned across the bed and placed Alexandra, blankets and all, next to St John.

"My darling girl, may I make known to you, St John

Traherne, Earl of Bemerton. Your father. My lord, this perfectly beautiful creature next to you is your daughter, Alexandra. You *will* wake from this stupor in the morning and apologize to her for missing her christening. As pitiful a father as you have been to her thus far, you are still better than my own pater. But not if you insist on succumbing to a bump on the head a scant six weeks before Christmas."

"Let her lie there until she is wet or hungry. In full cry, that child can wake the dead."

"I hope we do not have to put her to the test," Portia said softly. They slept on together, father and daughter, completely unaware of the cracks and tears forming in Portia's heart. Appropriate that Dr. Pratt had cautioned her against falling into the abyss. She'd started a slow slide the moment she saw the face of the man they carried into her foyer. Now she held onto the sides of the crevice, fighting a peculiar despair with an even more peculiar hope.

"Don't you worry, my lady. The bad ones never die young," Nanny Rose said as she collapsed into one of the fireside chairs and toed off her shoes. "They stay about to plague a woman's heart into her old age."

"I sincerely hope his lordship enjoys a complete recovery," Portia said as she touched the backs of her fingers to Alexandra's cheek. Her other hand rested on St John's chest. "But as he has not *stayed about* this year past, I hold no hope he'll do so once he is well."

"Would you want him to?" Nanny Rose asked, just before she closed her eyes and leaned back in the chair to sleep.

Chapter Four

Bemerton Hall, Wiltshire
Early December, 1817

Snow. St John smelled snow. And beef broth? Whatever amount of brandy it took to sink him into the thick fog from which he'd been striving to escape, he vowed never to drink that much again. He forced his eyes open. Blurry. Itching as if he'd ridden into the wind over a rainswept moor all day. He raised his hands to swipe away the detritus of too much drink, too much sleep, too much… His head began to swim. Familiar. Of course, it was familiar. It happened to him all the time. Not like this. In fits and starts, he pushed himself up to sit against the headboard of the bed. Why was he so damned weak?

Bed.

Whose bed?

A careful perusal of his surroundings did little to help. The room bore a vague resemblance to his mother's bedchamber at Bemerton Hall. It had been altered, however, and the colors and furnishings had a more cheerful tone. Cheerful? He *had* consumed far too much liquor. Movement and voices issued from behind the door into the dressing room.

"Come along, pet. We'll take a turn with your father

before your mother comes back above stairs."

He didn't recognize that voice at all. *Father? Mother?*
Where the devil was he? And why? Late. He was late for
something. Again.

Bollocks! Time to leave the warmth and comfort of this
bed and find some answers. St John wrestled the sheets,
blankets, and counterpane into submission and finally swung
his legs over the side of the bed. Pale. And thin. His feet sank
into a thick Aubusson carpet, but when he stood, his knees
nearly gave way. He clutched the bedpost for support. When
he looked down, to his horror he saw he was clad in a heavy
cotton nightshirt. One thing was certain, he'd not spent the
night in a woman's bed. He normally slept naked, especially
when he had a woman in his bed.

The voice from the dressing room started again. "Oh
bother. Could you not have waited a bit longer to do that, you
naughty girl? His lordship will have to wait. He's not going
anywhere." The woman continued to speak, but her voice
faded. Perhaps she'd returned to a bedchamber beyond the
dressing room. He took a step towards the sound of that
voice. No. There was a child in that direction. There were few
things he scrupled, but involving a child in his scandalous life
was one of them. Across the way, a set of double doors
beckoned. His limbs still rebelled and refused to act as they
should. At a slow pace, he managed to reach those doors.
They opened into a wide corridor. A Turner landscape hung
on the wall opposite where he stood.

He *was* at Bemerton Hall. The smell of snow and the chill
in the corridor said late fall or even early winter. At least he'd
only be frightening his own servants when they discovered
him wandering the house in a nightshirt and his bare feet.

Late fall. At Bemerton Hall. He was here for a reason. An important one. He rubbed his temple. His fingers brushed over a long scar. When did he acquire such a scar? Dammit! His mind danced like a patchwork quilt hung out to dry in a gale.

Once he reached the second-floor balustrade, St John leaned over in time to see a quartet of footmen dash down the steps from the first-floor to the foyer. *Trouble?*

"I don't answer to the likes of you, *Lady Bemerton*."

Pearce?

"It is none of my concern whom you answer to, but if you do not state your business in your very next breath, I shall have my footmen boot your *arse* to the gates of Bemerton forthwith."

Definitely Pearce. Only he could drive a woman like Lady Portia to speak to him as if dismissing a vagrant on her doorstep.

Lady Portia? Lady Bemerton? Wha—

A searing pain lashed his head from temple to temple. He sank to the floor, his hands clutching the thick marble balusters. He tried to peer down into the foyer, but his view was blocked. Fortunately, the vaulted ceiling rising high above where St John hid carried voices as clearly as if those who spoke stood right next to him.

"Allow me to see if I have heard you correctly." An iron will St John had never heard in Lady Portia before laced her every word. "You misplaced your closest friend nearly a month ago and you have only now come here in search of him?"

"I had no reason to search for him here. Why would I? Surely you did not think he'd bother with the christening of a daughter. He most likely went down to London. I don't know why I thought it possible he stopped here no matter what Smythe said." The acrimony in Pearce's voice confused St John. The man had ever been rude, but not so vehemently hateful as this.

"Then why are you not in London?" Lady Portia demanded.

"I have been in London."

"It took you a month to search London? The number of gaming hells, brothels, and willing widows must have increased greatly in the past year if it took you so long to search them for your friend."

St John winced. His memory of his courtship with Lady Portia came back in bits and pieces, but he did not think she knew him quite so well as this. His head throbbed, a steady drumbeat of lightning pain. The past... month, did she say? His thoughts were a miasma of places, voices, and questions.

"Come now, my lady. We both know why he married you, and a bad bargain it turned out to be. Surely you didn't expect him to be the attentive husband. Your family may lie to you, but your mirror doesn't."

Crack!

St John recognized the sound of a well-earned slap when he heard one. He looped an arm over the top rail of the balustrade and tried to pull himself upright. He could not allow Pearce to speak to a lady in such a fashion. Especially not the lady who was... was to be the Countess of Bemerton. Which was it?

"Get out of my house or I'll have you thrown out."

"You'll regret this. Thornley won't stay gone forever. When he returns—"

"My *husband* is not Thornley. He has been the Earl of Bemerton these seven months, which makes me the Countess of Bemerton. Lady *Porka* might owe you an answer. The Countess of Bemerton does not. And you can give that selfsame message to my mother-in-law when you see her. Good day."

Lady Porka?

St John gained his feet in time to hear footsteps across the marble parquet floor and then the punctuation of a firmly slammed door. *He* was the earl? And why had she not told Pearce he was here? He needed to think, to sort it all out before he confronted her or anyone else. With halted steps, and one arm out to balance himself, he made his way back to the bedchamber in which he'd awakened. It remained empty, and as no alarm had been raised, he assumed no one knew he was awake. He slid back into the bed and closed his eyes against the bright winter light from the French windows. He'd done very little, yet his body ached as if from a week-old beating and a night of debauchery. His life had become a puzzle to which most of the pieces were missing, save one.

Portia.

He pulled the counterpane up and assumed the position of one in a deep sleep just as two female voices issued from behind the dressing room door.

"You've done it now, my girl. What were you thinking?"

The door opened. Two sets of footsteps—one light and dainty, the other slow and plodding.

"I was thinking I wanted to punch Lord *Arse* in the nose, but ladies are not allowed to punch," Lady Portia said.

St John suppressed a chuckle.

"Cut line, my lady. Why didn't you tell Lord Pearce his

lordship has been here all this time?"

It took all of St John's fading presence of mind not to react when a warm and well-curved bottom settled onto the mattress next to his hip. The slightest scent of lemon verbena teased his nose nearly as much as the gentle heat pressing against his body.

"The truth?" Lady Portia asked softly.

"If you please."

"You asked me that night, if I wanted him to stay." Her voice slid along his skin and into his aching bones like a balm, though he had no idea why. "I don't know if I want him to stay, but I want the right to decide. I want the time. And I don't want Lord Pearce or the dowager countess or anyone else to take that from me until I am ready."

"And if he never awakens?" The other woman's voice was older, and though not crude, held none of the cultured ring of Lady Portia's. "What if he has forgotten his name, or the past year, like the doctor said he might?"

Never awakens? How long had he been asleep?

"I will cross that bridge when I come to it." Her weight shifted against him. Her fingertips stroked St John's face. When she lifted them, he nearly leaned up to follow her touch. A moment later, a cool cloth was dragged carefully across his brow and cheeks and then down to his neck. "If he has forgotten this past year, he is far more fortunate than I."

"What if he wakes up tomorrow and remembers everything. What is your grand plan then, my lady?" the older voice demanded.

"I haven't the faintest idea." Lady Portia finished her ministrations. St John heard a small splash as she returned the cloth to the water from which she'd drawn it. Her hand came to rest on his chest. His heart stuttered. He reminded himself she'd lied to Pearce. She had an advantage over him, many in fact. She knew precisely where all those missing puzzle pieces were, and exactly how they fitted together. As sleep finally overcame him, St John decided whether Lady Portia had a plan or not, he needed to come up with one. And quickly.

ဆလ

St John erupted from sleep with a stifled oath. The clock in the corridor hammered out three eerie chords and went silent. A quick search with his hands and he oriented himself. He was in a large bed, the hangings drawn on the far side, but open on the side closest to the fire, the side on which he'd slept. Slept for what seemed like ages. He threw his legs over the side of the bed and slid from beneath the bedclothes. In spite of the thick carpets the floor sent shards of cold through his feet and up his bared legs.

Where the devil is my dressing gown?

His eyes, accustomed now to the soft warm glow from the fireplace and candelabras lit on either end of the mantel, settled on an odd sight. Beneath a heavy quilt curled up on one chair with feet and legs resting on another, lay a distinctly feminine form. A thick, single braid hung to the floor, partially obscuring the face. Portia. His... wife. He took a step closer. Her hand rested on the side of a cradle. St John's heart took up a hammered tattoo in his chest. He moved so quickly he nearly tripped. Only his steadying hand shot out to the back of the far chair at the last minute stopped him.

Peering up at him from the various blankets and coverlets, a round little face with dimples in either cheek and a pink pursed mouth regarded him solemnly. He extended his hand inch by inch and brushed his knuckles over the softest skin imaginable. A tiny hand flailed about under the covers and eventually worked its way out to bang against his. He touched the dainty mouth with his forefinger. A mistake, as the fey creature gripped it far more tightly than he might have credited.

Alexandra. His daughter.

His knees threatened to give way. He stood there, waves of terror and wonder taking turns at battering against him. After several moments, the infant's grip relaxed and with a tender sigh, she resumed her slumber. St John stepped back until he bumped against the chair on which his wife's feet and legs rested. A Scot's plaid rested on the back of the chair. He lifted it and draped it across Portia's body. A foolish gesture, one he would be hard pressed to explain. She appeared warm enough beneath her quilt. He withdrew to the French windows and pulled one of the heavy drapes back just enough to look out into the night.

Beneath the moonlight, the view stretched on, an endless swath of white. He'd smelled snow earlier. Bemerton Hall. He was home. He'd spent most of his childhood here, listening to his mother's demands for money and his father's ineffectual attempts to stay the bloodletting of funds from the estate. And when he could listen no longer, St John had fled to the fields and hills of this magical place. After all this time he had returned, but not to the same sad and confusing place he'd always known. The very air he breathed was different now. Clean and pure and… at peace.

Unable to remain still, he strode silently past his sleeping wife and child, took the nearest candelabra off the mantel, and like a wraith slipped out into the corridor.

His wife and child.

He turned the words over and over in his head as he traversed the stairs all the way down to the entrance hall. A footman snored softly from a chair next to the front doors. St John wandered into the front drawing room. Gone were the faded carpets and worn furnishings. Gone was the dark, hideous wallpaper. The room had been done over in a pale blue with white, navy, and gold furnishings. It was tasteful and elegant and… happy.

He'd lost his wits in addition to no small portion of his dignity. Sneaking about his own home like a common thief. Mooning over wallpaper like someone's maiden aunt. He made quick work of the other rooms on the ground floor until he came upon his father's study. The earl's study, now his. Right. He was the earl now. The servants had found Father sitting on the bench in the little garden of their London townhouse. St John's mother and sister had been out shopping with money they did not have. St John had been drunk in a gambling den in Seven Dials. His father had died in a place he loved, but he had died alone.

St John placed the candelabra on a small library table and collapsed into the chair behind the desk. At least the décor in this room had not been changed a great deal. Order had been restored. New shelves lined the walls and held what looked to be the estate ledgers and record books back to the Conqueror. The room smelled of wood polish and lavender. The heavy oak desk was neatly appointed. An elaborate inkstand stretched across the front of it, bearing two inkwells, a quill rest, a silver cup full of sharply trimmed quills, and numerous containers of letter sand and wax for sealing. He spied a silver salver on which several sealed letters rested. A large leather-bound ledger lay in the middle of the highly polished surface.

His head began to throb. He rubbed his hand over the scar behind his ear. He'd fallen from his horse like the greenest of riders. His thoughts had not been on his horse or the rain or anything sensible. His mind had been filled with Lady Portia, the missed christening, and everything else he'd missed. It came to him, a black cloak smothering light, and pain, and the frenetic debauchery of his life. Leaving a blinding realization from which he only wanted to flee.

St John shuffled through the missives on the salver. Letters to her family, if he remembered their names rightly. Remembered. He chuckled dryly. Perhaps he'd awaken in the morning and not recall a thing. Oblivion without the aid of spirits might be a welcome change. A letter to one of the banks under the control of the Rothschilds family. A letter to Lady Portia's London solicitor. He recognized the name, as the man was the very one who issued the monthly checks to those dependent on the lady's largesse—St John, his sister Lavinia, and the Dowager Countess of Bemerton.

The ledger revealed far more. The estate was doing well. Extremely well if the figures written in a meticulous feminine hand were to be believed. Their coffers were fair to bursting with the ready. Their coffers. *His* coffers. Thanks to her devilishly clever brother, she held the purse strings of the money she'd brought to the marriage. The money the estate earned, however, was another thing entirely. Had to be.

He needed a drink. Badly. Not the normal hum of need, but a sudden sharp pang as if from a wound thought healed ticked at the back of his head. He shot out of the chair and slammed the ledger shut. Too much memory, too much information, too much sudden longing for an intangible *something* tumbled over and over in his aching head. The date of the last entry in the ledger leapt off the page.

3rd December, 1817

He'd slept nearly a month. No wonder his wife and her servant talked of him sleeping forever. An entire month abed. A month without a drink.

He fairly sprinted to the sideboard at the far end of the study. It ran along the wall next to the fireplace. Tray after tray of decanters lined up like so much useless statuary yielded... nothing. Empty. Every. Last. One. His feet began to feel the cold. He stamped them a bit and made his way out of the study and back up the stairs to the first floor. A footman disappeared around the corner towards the dining room.

Damn!

With no idea when the servant might return to the chair and lamp at the end of the corridor, St John elected not to search for brandy in any of the customary places it might be found. Instead he padded across the burgundy and blue patterned Turkey carpets along the balustrade and took the stairs back up to the second floor from whence he'd come. The case clock on the second-floor landing struck the hour. Four in the morning. He'd spent an hour creeping about his ancestral home as a ghost, he suspected a most unwelcome ghost.

He needed a brandy and time to consider what the morning was to bring, to him and to his wife. His wife. His daughter. Actually, he needed two brandies, one for each hand. Lying abed in a state of injury-induced forgetfulness suddenly acquired an entirely new and favorable appeal.

Coward!

The overlarge portrait of his grandfather glared down at him in frozen disapprobation.

"Stubble it, you old reprobate," St John muttered as he opened the next door down from his judgmental ancestor. "You didn't do any better than the rest of us."

The chambers he'd used once he'd finished at Oxford had been made over as well. The dark blues and greys had been replaced with greens and a cream color. How hard had he hit his head? Admiring the décor again? Brandy. He'd been tucking brandy and port away in this room since he'd attained the age of sixteen. He placed the candelabra on the mantel and systematically searched every single cubby hole, drawer, and loose floorboard. Nothing. A temperance-minded governess could not have done a better job of fleecing him of his favorite source of comfort.

His mouth went dry. A slight tremor, not there before, and St John had to steady his hand before he reached for the candelabra. Tomorrow. He needed to plan, and tomorrow he would have an entire bottle of brandy brought to him, perhaps in *his* study, where he would go over the estate books more thoroughly. Now he'd gathered most of the wits he'd left scattered at the foot of a paddock wall, he'd do what he must to set things to rights. His little respite was over, and he had no business dallying in a world, in an idea, that was not to be. With a swift check outside the bedchamber door, St John traversed the corridor and re-entered the room in which he'd awakened nearly a day ago.

The candelabra cast a golden glow onto the sleeping form before the fire. St John returned the candelabra to the mantel. He circled the two chairs of Lady Portia's patched up bed and settled onto the arm of the one on which her feet and legs rested. She'd kicked the plaid he'd added off to the side. He lifted it carefully and tucked it around her. With a now steady hand, he lifted the braid from across her face to better study the woman he'd married, the woman who controlled nearly every aspect of his life.

She was prettier than he remembered. Not beautiful by any means, but lovely in the way the sight of Bemerton Hall was after a long journey. She had a round Madonna's face with a slightly upturned nose—not pert, but rather decisive. A dusting of freckles across the bridge of it prevented that nose from being too stern. Her hair was a rich brown and from the thickness and length of her braid there was a great deal of it. She was a curvaceous woman, but small of stature. Few women of his acquaintance were short enough to sleep comfortably in two pushed-together chairs.

He'd slept for a month. How many nights had she spent watching over him? That undefined longing raised its head and let out a lonely howl. A snuffling noise drew his attention to his sleeping daughter. He leaned over and gazed into the cradle. The child slept fist firmly ensconced in her mouth. *Alexandra.* Named for her mother's only brother or so his mother had informed him in the voice she reserved for the most inconsequential and distasteful of matters.

"I received an invitation from that cow you married, Thornley. She is having her daughter christened and expects us to attend. As if I would leave London for anything less than the son her father promised she would produce. The brat's to be christened Alexandra, after the Marquess of Winterbourne. Little good it will do her."

His father had been gone six months and still she called

St John Thornley.

"My husband is not Thornley. He is the Earl of Bemerton..."

A log shifted in the hearth and sent sparks dancing up the chimney. St John tucked the coverlet around the infant and in a few steps was back in bed, the counterpane drawn up to his waist. He closed his eyes and drew in a long, deep breath. When he opened his eyes once more his gaze fell to his wife's face, serene and angelic in slumber. With any number of comfortable beds in the sprawling expanse of Bemerton Hall, she chose to sleep in the bedchamber where he'd lain unconscious for a month. A gnawing stab of annoyance dug in his gut like cheap gin or a greasy tavern pasty.

He slid down into the bed and turned on his side so he might watch over her and his daughter. A strange sensation settled around him, warmer than the warmest blanket. Stranger than the most foreign creature he'd ever seen in any menagerie. St John conjured a plan, pondered it, changed it, and finally decided. He'd gone mad as a hatter. And he didn't give a damn.

ഇന്ദ

He'd slept again, but not terribly long. The light from the French windows was bright, but not quite intrusive enough for a December noontide. Early morning then. A quick peek from beneath the counterpane revealed his nighttime nurse and her tiny companion had absconded, taking the cradle with them. St John, however, was not alone. A maid stood with her back to him, humming *Barbara Allen* and mincing over a tray of food on a small table near the foot of the bed. As much as he hated to do it, she was about to experience quite a shock. He had to piss in the worst way, and she stood between him and the chamber pot behind the screen in the corner. Perhaps he might temper the surprise.

"Good morning," he announced as he threw off the bedclothes and sat up on the side of the bed. "What is your name?"

The tray went flying. The maid shrieked, covered her mouth with her hands, blanched, and fled screaming into the corridor.

"That went well," he muttered as he strolled behind the screen and made use of the chamber pot. He stepped around the remains of what looked to be an insipid breakfast and sat down on the edge of the bed. Time to put his madcap plan in motion. God help him.

Chapter Five

Mrs. Whitby hurried the sniffling maid out of the nursery. Even seated across the room from the open doorway, Portia saw half the servants in the house milling about, staring and pointing at the doors to the bedchamber next door. The appearance of Bemerton Hall's stern housekeeper quickly scattered the crowd and set them to seeing to their duties. One of which was to send a rider to fetch Dr. Pratt at once.

"What do we do with him now?" Nanny Rose asked as soon as the doors closed behind the housekeeper.

"What would you suggest? Lock him in the wine cellar? Drop him down a well?" Portia adjusted the cloth shielding her nursing daughter from view. Other women might eschew modesty when feeding a child, Portia's opinion of her own body did not allow her such a free attitude.

"None of your cheek now, my lady. You've landed us in a right pickle. Lied to a lord. Kept his lordship here without a word to a soul." The old nurse stopped her pacing long enough to take the now sated and sleeping Alexandra from Portia. She returned the baby to her cradle whilst Portia adjusted her blue wool morning dress and rose from her chair.

"Pearce is barely a lord, and other than his much belated inquiry, no one has asked after his lordship." Portia stared at the door into the dressing room between this chamber and the one where her husband, now awake, awaited her.

"And don't I know you've sworn the entire household to secrecy with not a word as to why." Nanny Rose moved to stand next to her.

"As soon as I know the reason why, you shall be the first to know."

"Saints preserve us," Nanny said under breath. "Are you going to beard the lion in his den or wait for the doctor to do so?"

"He's been sleeping for a month," Portia replied as she opened the door and stepped inside the spacious dressing room. "Which makes him more a garden slug than a lion."

"Make no mistake, my lady," Nanny said as they stopped before the door into the countess's rooms. "A sleeping lion is still a lion." She leaned in close. "And just as dangerous."

"You are not helping."

Nanny snorted. "The devil himself cannot help you now, my lady. I don't know where this plan of yours will land you, but I'll wager it is nowhere you want to be."

"I'm already there," Portia mumbled and lifted the latch on the door into the chamber where she'd watched over her sleeping husband for the past month. Nanny was utterly wrong. She had no plan to deal with St John awake and in her life. He was supposed to sleep—through the Christmas she had no intention of celebrating, through the winter's chill and into the spring lambing, through... Oh, hell through everything until she knew what she wanted of him, of marriage, of life. She squared her shoulders, opened the door, and stepped into the bedchamber.

"Oh!" Portia stopped so suddenly Nanny nearly bowled

her over. St John had divested himself of the thick cotton nightshirt they'd dressed him in and was shouldering his way into the quilted velvet dressing gown they'd found in the bedchamber down the hall. Not before she was afforded a spectacular view of his naked back and buttocks. Some of his muscles had survived the predations of a month in bed very nicely.

"Lady Portia." He spun, swayed slightly on his feet, and wrapped the dressing gown tightly around his thin frame. "Good morning." He executed a creditable bow. "I seem to have misplaced my clothes."

"Not to mention his wits," Nanny muttered as she retrieved the discarded nightshirt from across the chair behind Portia.

"Stubble it," Portia shot back under her breath. She'd spent the better part of the last four weeks in the same room as her husband contemplating exactly what she might say to him should he awaken. Then he had to go and spoil it all by actually waking up.

"So long as I haven't misplaced my wedding clothes," St John said as he settled onto the side of the bed.

Portia and Nanny exchanged a glance. "Wedding clothes?" Portia offered, a lump began to form in her stomach, half hope and half terror.

"For our wedding, my lady. It is tomorrow, is it not?" His boyish smile might have been endearing had it reached his eyes. That lump in Portia's stomach began to turn to stone.

A brisk knock at the door saved her from having to answer his question. It did not save her from what sounded suspiciously like *"Dicked in the nob and no mistake."* being whispered in her ear. She swatted behind her and was rewarded with an inelegant grunt as she scurried to open the door into the corridor.

"I hear Lazarus has arisen," Dr. Pratt announced as he stood in the doorway, medical satchel in hand.

"I don't know about Lazarus, sir, but my..." Portia lowered her voice and hid her mouth behind her hand. "husband is awake and a bit confused."

"Confused, my lady?" The physician leaned down and adopted her quiet tone even as he eyed his patient, brow furrowed and eyes slightly narrowed.

"He thinks he is to marry me tomorrow."

"More than a bit confused, I would say. You have been married more than a year, have you not?" Dr. Pratt continued to study St John who was arguing with Nanny about climbing back into the bed and covering himself as *any decent gentleman would.*

"Shhh! I don't want him upset." She didn't. What an odd thing to say. And feel.

"Someone is upset," Pratt muttered and delivered Portia a side-eyed glance.

"Has anyone ever told you, you are a most annoying physician?"

"Nearly everyone." He straightened and patted her hand absently. "Leave me alone with him. I will examine him and determine exactly what he has forgotten and what might be the cause. I'll sort this out."

"Leave him?" Portia said as she followed him to St John's bedside. "Why?"

"Come along, my lady." Nanny grabbed her arm and dragged her toward the dressing room door. "His lordship is safe with Dr. Pratt, even if Mrs. Whitby says he is little more than a barber with a bag of potions."

"Yes, but I have yet to concoct a potion to turn Mrs. Whitby up sweet," the physician said as he held a lit candle before St John's face and asked him to follow the flame with his eyes.

St John muttered something to provoke a bark of laughter from Dr. Pratt. Portia tried to peer around Nanny Rose who continued to push her across the dressing room. St John gave a little wave even as Pratt drew his attention back to the moving candle.

Portia snatched her arm free and strode through the door into the earl's chambers, now her daughter's nursery. A quick check of the large, intricately carved cradle set Portia's racing heart somewhat at ease. Alexandra, her beautiful daughter, slept on unaware of the turmoil awakening in all their lives. Portia, however, was very aware. Of the trouble, the lies she'd already told, the lies she contemplated telling even now, and the inexplicable pull the sight of her husband smiling and vital had awakened in her.

More fool she. If he did not remember now, he soon would. Expecting anything to change, expecting him to change was folly of the grandest nature. Did she want him to change? Change how? Portia had learned how to live with a husband who despised her and avoided her like the plague.

Rather, she had learned how to live without him. She'd done well. She'd married St John to declare her independence from her family. No longer *poor dear Portia*, the plain sister for whom her other sisters or even her scapegrace brother would have to find a place, she'd taken control of her own life. She needed no husband to care for her estate, her child, or her fortune.

Portia caressed her daughter's cheek and tucked the petal soft blanket her husband's old nurse had knitted for Alexandra's christening around her. She made her way to the tall windows looking out over the back gardens and beyond to the pastures faded by the winter's cold. With the door into the dressing room open she heard snatches of voices from the other room, but could not make out the words.

A soft India shawl dropped around her shoulders. "All will be well, my lady," Nanny said and squeezed her shoulders. "You'll see."

"And do you have an inkling exactly what form *well* will take?"

"That's up to God, and he hasn't seen fit to share that information with me." Nanny settled into the rocking chair next to the cradle and took up her needlework.

"How dare He," Portia murmured as she pressed her hand to the icy glass of the window. The chill of early December seeped into her fingertips. As a child she'd always loved this time of year. Her mother and later her sisters and brother always made a great fuss of Christmastide in the country. And her father usually remained in London, making the holidays more than merry.

Last year Portia had spent a miserable holiday alone, save for the knowledge her husband had done a poor job of consummating their marriage, but a more than decent job of getting her with child. Her family had assumed she was still in the honeymoon phase of wedded bliss and had not bothered to visit. With St John in a perpetual stupor, she'd hoped to pass an equally quiet and insignificant Christmas this year. Now what?

"Beg pardon?" she turned from the window. Nanny had

said something and she'd missed it.

"Don't beg my pardon. Beg God's *How dare he.* Blasphemous girl."

Portia smiled.

Nanny Rose spent most of her time fretting over Portia's consequence as the Countess of Bemerton, her proper behavior or lack thereof, and the household maids' attendance on the fires throughout the house. Every now and again she made an attempt to ensure the safety of Portia's immortal soul. Portia's worries centered on what happened on this side of the grave. And this morning her worries had multiplied ten-fold.

A brisk knock at the door from the corridor into the chamber startled Nanny and Portia both. Alexandra stirred for a moment and then settled back into sleep. In that respect she was very like her uncle and namesake. A full belly was cause for a long nap.

"Enter."

Nanny nodded at Portia's imperious tone and settled back into the rocking chair.

Dr. Pratt opened one of the double doors enough to poke his head in and glance toward the dressing room between this chamber and the room where St John no doubt awaited Portia's pleasure. She cringed inwardly. Not her best choice of words. Taking his hint, she padded silently across the room and closed the door against her newly awakened husband hearing her conversation with the physician.

"How is he?" she asked as she settled into a green and gold chintz armchair before the hearth and indicated Dr. Pratt should take the matching chair opposite her.

"Far more hale and hearty than he has a right to be,"

Pratt announced frankly. "A month of rest from pernicious living and liquor has done his lordship a world of good."

"I daresay his lordship might not agree. Especially as his abstinence was not voluntary, but the result of poor horsemanship." Portia's mind was in a whirl. Her breath fought to come in decorous even counts. Her breakfast threatened to make a reappearance. "What of his memory? Has it returned?"

"I do not think he would appreciate your assessment of his horsemanship, but as he remembers very little of the past twelve months—"

"Very little? What does that mean? What does he remember?" Portia refrained from clapping her hand over her mouth. She wished desperately she had done so before revealing so much to the physician.

Dr. Pratt studied her over the rims of his spectacles. He tilted his head slightly. "What do you want him to remember, my lady?"

"I... What sort of question is that? I want him to remember he is already my husband, of course. Marrying him once was quite enough."

"Ah. Well," Dr. Pratt stalled as he removed his spectacles, pulled a handkerchief from his pocket, and applied it to what appeared to Portia to be spotless lenses. "I have convinced him of that. The fact he is married to you, that is. And the unfortunate news of his father's death and his own ascendancy to the earldom."

"Oh." Portia had not considered St John would have to experience the death of his father once more. "It was... difficult for him to hear?"

"Which?" Dr. Pratt redonned his spectacles and carefully

tucked away his handkerchief.

Nanny Rose chuckled, never once looking up from her needlework.

Portia rolled her eyes. "You mean to tell me he remembers nothing of the past year? Neither being my husband nor being Alexandra's father? Nothing? What did he say?" She'd determined not to turn into a hysterical female, a damned hard endeavor with a physician as tight-lipped as a Wiltshire tavern keeper questioned by a farmer's shrewish wife.

"He has accepted my explanation of his circumstances with precisely the equanimity I would expect of any English lord."

Portia narrowed her eyes and pursed her lips. She didn't give a damn about any English lord. She was about to show this man of medicine how an English lady responded to responses even a Sphinx would deem cryptic.

"He is far more interested in the answers with which I could not supply him, my lady."

Portia stood and threw up her hands. She was a countess. Surely, she could beat a mere physician into being more forthcoming without being brought before a magistrate.

"He wishes to know what sort of husband he has been." Dr. Pratt rose and picked up his medical satchel. "And what sort of father he has been to Lady Alexandra."

Nanny Rose swore and stuck her finger into her mouth. Portia glanced at her and then at the dressing room door. An odd sort of chill came over her, not cold nor hot, simply... a sense of eerie calm.

"What do I tell him?" she asked softly.

"That is the question, my lady. And you are the only one who can answer it. You will have to decide what you want to tell him. What sort of husband do you *wish* him to remember being?" He bowed and strode to the double doors.

"Will his memory return, Dr. Pratt?"

"I cannot say, my lady. It depends upon the full recovery of his health and even that may not help."

"What shall we do?" she asked, more to herself than anyone else. The silence in the room was a living presence. Nanny Rose and Dr. Pratt existed as mere afterthoughts. Curious, questioning without saying a word afterthoughts.

"Routine, my lady. He needs a regimen of good food, exercise, and the sorts of activities which will evoke memories." He opened the door and stepped into the corridor. "Or perhaps the activities that will create new ones. The choice is yours. Good day, my lady. Send for me should you need me." He was gone before Portia uttered another word.

She turned and checked the cradle once more. Alexandra slept on, oblivious to the changes in her young life.

"What the devil—"

Portia held up a staying hand. For once, Nanny Rose closed her mouth without uttering another sound. Though she did roll her lips in and set the chair to rocking furiously. Portia paced to the door into the dressing room and then back across the room to the hearth. She went over Dr. Pratt's words, the few he'd uttered, again and again.

"What do you want him to remember, my lady?"

Every slight, every absence, the unkind words of her wedding night tumbled into her mind to mix with the physician's assurances and suggestions. She continued to pace and as she did the events of the last twelve hours melded into the events of the last twelve months. The skirts of her light wool morning gown whipped about her feet to the point of nearly tripping her.

"What sort of husband do you wish him to remember being?"

The chilling serenity fled, replaced by the same sort of singular determination she'd donned each time she'd wanted to give in and send for her brother over the last year. She'd taken a husband without Alexander's approval. She'd become a mother and turned her estate into a profitable concern without his help as well. She ran to the doors out into the corridor.

"John, find Farnham and have him come to me at once," she ordered the footman at the top of the stairs. "And find Mrs. Whitby as well."

She stepped back into the nursery. Nanny Rose slowly pushed to her feet.

"What are you about now, my girl?"

"You will need to move your things into the blue room across the hall," Portia said as she set about gathering the older woman's clothes, needlework, and other possessions.

"Have you lost your wits? There is not enough room in the blue chamber for me and the little one." Nanny Rose tried unsuccessfully to retrieve a worn woolen shawl from Portia's grip.

"Quite so. Alexandra will remain here. You will be close enough should she need you." Portia piled the accumulated items onto a chair and began to strip the bed.

"Close enough to— Who will be sleeping in here with her?"

"Why her father, of course. He has insisted on seeing to her care himself from the day of her birth." Portia's mind balked and bolted, headlong like a runaway horse. Frightening, but she held tight.

"He what?" Nanny Rose reached for Portia's elbow and missed.

A tap at the door and the staidly attentive entrance of Bemerton Hall's butler, Farnham, saved Portia from having to explain herself. For now.

"Yes, my lady?"

"Farnham, are you well-acquainted with the butler at Hindon Abbey?" Her thoughts picked up speed. Plans popped up and were formed or discarded. She dared not stop to think.

"Most assuredly, my lady. Smythe is my mother's brother." Farnham, a tall, spare man of some fifty years, clasped his hands behind his back, his expression very nearly devoid of curiosity.

"Better and better," Portia muttered. She bit her lip. Took a long deep breath. Her shoulders squared and chin up, she continued. "Would it be possible for you to retrieve his lordship's belongings from Hindon Abbey without alerting the staff there? Or any members of the family in residence?"

Farnham's left eyebrow twitched, but immediately subsided. He swallowed and inclined his head. "Of course, my lady. I will see to it myself." The butler bowed and turned for the door.

"As quickly and unobtrusively as possible, please." Portia did not hear his reply as she hurried to the desk in the corner of the room, dropped into the chair, and dragged foolscap and pen to her. She began to write, even as Nanny

Rose came to stand across the desk from her, arms folded across her chest.

Portia had long grown immune to disapproving glares, pointed *tsk's*, and other expressions of disapproval. She'd decided on a course of action. And like that runaway horse, she fully intended to let it run until it exhausted itself, she gained the sense to slow it to a walk, or it ended up tossing her on her *arse*. She continued to write, ignoring Nanny Rose's silent censure, until Mrs. Whitby hurried into the room. The housekeeper took in the somewhat disorganized appearance of the nursery even as she bobbed Portia a curtsy.

"You sent for me, my lady?"

Portia held up a finger and continued to write. Nanny Rose tapped her foot. Once she had finished her list, Portia poured a bit of sand over it, waited a moment and then handed the piece of foolscap to the housekeeper. As Mrs. Whitby read her eyebrows rose higher and higher until they nearly disappeared into her hairline.

Nanny Rose cleared her throat. Forcefully. Then returned to tapping her foot.

"You spoke with Dr. Pratt about his lordship's condition?" Portia asked the housekeeper.

A slight flush suffused Mrs. Whitby's face. She'd been the housekeeper at Bemerton Hall since St John was a boy. It was not her place to ask for a report from the physician concerning the health of the master of the house. Which meant she'd probably lain in wait for the poor man and pounced on him the minute he'd left Portia's bedchamber.

"Yes, my lady." Mrs. Whitby folded her hands at her waist and tightened her lips into a straight line. Portia bit back a laugh. There were tombs incapable of keeping their own counsel better than Bemerton's enigma of a housekeeper.

Portia stood and moved to the cradle once more. Alexandra did not stir. She envied her daughter the serenity to sleep through the farcical barbs Fate continued to toss their way.

"Then you know Dr. Pratt has recommended his lordship maintain a routine in the days and weeks to come. It will help him to heal and perhaps regain his memory." Portia slid one hand into the pocket of her dress and crossed her fingers. "We need to establish this routine at once, and the entire household must assure his lordship it has been his long- established habit. Do we have... an understanding, Mrs. Whitby?" Portia leveled her most imposing, no-nonsense gaze onto the older woman.

Mrs. Whitby read the neatly penned list of instructions over again, this time with a great deal of care. Her eyebrows remained unmoved. Her lips, however, twitched at several points. She handed the foolscap back to Portia. With her head at a slight angle, she gave Portia an assessing perusal.

"We have an understanding, my lady. I will see to it at once." She curtsied and went to the chamber door. "Good luck, my lady."

"To all of us, Mrs. Whitby," Portia replied as the housekeeper made her way into the corridor and began summoning the staff to the servants' dining room at once. Portia studied the closed doors and fought the urge to run after her. She'd taken a flash of an idea, a portion of hurt, and the smallest sliver of hope and created a hen-witted scheme even her wicked brother would not countenance. She turned to the door into her own bedchamber, her husband's bedchamber, these past weeks. Her hand holding the written evidence of her scheme bounced noisily against her skirts. Her entire future now rode a runaway horse of an idea and she'd just let go of the reins. What the devil had possessed her?

The piece of foolscap was snatched from her limp fingers. She'd been so distracted by the spinning top in her head that Nanny Rose had managed to slip up behind her unheard. She refused to try and wrest it from a woman of Nanny's advanced years and sharply honed cunning. The old woman plopped into the rocking chair, looked from the paper to Portia and back to the paper.

"You *have* taken leave of your senses. This," she shook the list at Portia. "Will not prod his memory. If you do this to him, it may very well steal what few wits the man has left."

Portia smoothed her skirts in an attempt to dry her damp palms. "Let's find out."

Chapter Six

St John stared at the newly arrived breakfast tray and peeled his lips back into a congenial smile. At least he hoped it was congenial. Had he known the contents of the second tray, he'd never have startled the maid into flinging the first one across the room like a bowler at a cricket match.

Dry toast. A cup of lukewarm beef broth. And coffee.

Coffee so dark it might be mistaken for a cup of tar.

Of course, he'd been ill for weeks. Perhaps this was sickroom fare, and those in the kitchens had not been informed of his *miraculous recovery*. He picked up the toast and tapped it against the side of the tray. The footman who had delivered it flinched. He didn't blame the man. If St John decided to throw it at him, the servant might very well lose an eye. He elected to attempt to eat it instead. He was still chewing the first bite when the dressing room door banged open and Lady Portia marched into the room.

"Thank you, Georgie," she dismissed the footman with a smile. "Please come back in an hour to help his lordship dress for his morning constitutional."

"Yes, my lady." The footman gave St John an oddly pitying look, bowed, and quit the room. Quickly.

Lady Portia came to his bedside. "I am pleased to see you eating your customary breakfast under your own power, my lord. We had a great deal of trouble force-feeding you the gruel Dr. Pratt insisted upon whilst you were asleep."

"My… customary breakfast?" St John studied his wife over the rim of his cup. In spite of the powerful fumes marauding up from the black brew, he took a sip of the coffee. His eyes crossed, and he fought not to spit the hot liquid all over the bedclothes. He swallowed, which set off a barrage of coughing that only ended when the lady serenely took his cup and handed it to the older lady hovering behind her. She snatched his wrist and raised his hand over his head, all the while pounding his back as if it were a particularly dirty rug. He waved her off, but did not withdraw his arm from her clasp.

"Do… I… always… drink… it…"

"I assure you, husband, everything is as you have ordered it each morning since we married. It does my heart such good to see you returning to us just as you were before."

Her smile and tone of voice reminded him of his mother at her most ingratiating. This was not the Lady Portia he knew. Save for the eyes. They shone a deep jade green with a glint very like amusement in their depths. He remembered those eyes. Something about those eyes. A slow building of heat radiated from where her bare hand touched his skin. He saw the moment she realized she was still holding his wrist. Her eyes locked with his. She lowered his arm slowly to the heavy green velvet counterpane. A tiny fissure of ice traced its way down the side of his neck, then down his spine.

"F-finish your breakfast, my lord," she said softly. "Georgie will be up in a thrice to help you dress. You are already hours late for your morning walk, and I know how it grieves you to miss it."

"My… morning walk?" What the devil was she about? He

never walked. Anywhere.

"Of course. You are most insistent upon it. Perhaps it will help to jostle your memory." She patted his hand and turned to go. He caught her fingers.

"Will you walk with me, my lady?" He needed to discover how far she intended to carry this pretense. And why. A turn about the gardens would give him the chance to speak with her away from the prying eyes of servants and loyal retainers like the sharp-eyed old shrew she'd brought with her from Suffolk.

"Told you so," the old shrew muttered. Lady Portia tossed her a glare even he might fear should it be turned on him.

"You are accustomed to walking alone." She twisted her hand slightly in an inobtrusive effort to free it.

"Ah," he said and rubbed his thumb across the heel of her hand. "But I have been ill, and my memory fails me. I might become lost or confused. A shame after being on death's door for so long."

"A great shame indeed," she ground out. "I will meet you in the foyer in an hour." Lady Portia tugged her hand free and left the room by way of the dressing room. Her elderly shadow handed him his cup of coffee.

"Drink this, my lord," she said with an eerie smile. "I suspect you'll need it."

஋௸

More than an hour later, St John paced the perfectly appointed entrance hall of his ancestral home and contemplated fleeing into the bracing winter morning to avoid even one more servant prosing on about his recovery and the joy it brought to one and all. Especially her ladyship.

If he had a conscience, he might ascribe his irritation to guilt. As he was fairly certain his conscience had fled years ago, he chalked it up to the strain of keeping up the farce of his lost memory.

Or perhaps the new furnishings annoyed him. A beautiful mahogany long-case clock stood against one wall. Large Grecian urns atop tall Doric marble columns accented either side of the staircase. The walls were painted a soothing pale green. Every inch of the house he'd seen thus far had gone from the shabby desperation of depleted fortunes to the well-kept newness of the terminally cheery. Cheery. The very word twisted in his gut like a potent curry from a disreputable London tavern.

"Shall we, my lord?"

St John started and whirled around to find Lady Portia being helped into her cloak by Farnham. She descended the stairs without making a sound. Never a good quality in a wife. Or at least he suspected as much. He'd never had a wife before, in spite of his marital state. Not so anyone, least of all he, might have noticed. She drew on the heavy gloves the butler handed her and marched out the front door.

"Best hurry, my lord," Farnham suggested. "Her ladyship is not known for setting a slow pace. At anything."

St John snatched his gloves from the man and hurried after his countess. He finally caught her at the bottom of the steps leading into Bemerton's front gardens. Damn! Lying abed for a month had sapped his strength. For a while he struggled simply to match her pace as he had no breath left to speak. They walked briskly down the stone-inlaid paths between neatly trimmed walls of yew trees.

"I suggest we do one time along your usual path this

morning, my lord. It is your custom to do six turns around this same path beginning at eight o' clock at the start of every day." Arms swinging, Lady Portia sailed along the path in a cloud of slate blue wool, the bottom of her cape fluttering out around her feet to reveal remarkably sensible half-boots. And an occasional flash of a rather attractive ankle.

"Might we slow down a—" St John stopped in his tracks. "Six times? At eight in the morning?"

She glanced over her shoulder, her green eyes wide and the color of jade in the clear December sunlight. "Every morning, my lord. Even Sundays. Shall we continue?"

He did not know his wife well. Hell and the devil, he did not know her at all. Most women found him attractive. He could not remember a woman ever going to such lengths to escape conversation with him. Nor could he recall a woman going to such lengths to punish him for... What had he done to his wife in the less than twelve hours between their vows and his hasty retreat to London?

"My lady? Portia," he barked.

She halted. Slowly, she turned to face him. She raised a delicately curved eyebrow at him. St John suppressed a laugh. His wife was a feisty little thing. He indicated a stone bench set into an arch carved into the wall of yews. "Shall we sit for a moment, wife?"

"Dr. Pratt said—"

"Dr. Pratt said for me to rely on you for my health and my memories."

She settled onto the edge of the bench and folded her hands in her lap. "And we are to sit here in aid of..."

He dropped onto the cold stone next to her. "Both. If I walk much longer at your pace, I fear a relapse."

"We can't have that," she said beneath her breath.

"I suspect any number of wives might prefer husbands in a perpetual stupor. We are ever so much easier to tolerate in such a state."

"I would not dare to naysay you, my lord."

St John threw back his head and laughed. A half dozen thrush erupted from a nearby hawthorn bush.

She gave a half-gasp and shook her head. "I did not mean that the way it sounded." She reached over and began to button his greatcoat, which he'd neglected to button in his haste to catch up to her. "You really should take more care. We were fortunate you did not contract a lung fever when you fell from your horse. It was pouring rain that night."

He angled himself towards her. He wanted to see her face. Oddly enough, her face had grown more mature than a mere year might make it. He'd married an innocent, reticent girl. His wife evinced a sort of wary defiance, and far more perception than he credited.

"Why was I riding out so late at night?" St John decided the direct approach was best.

"You went to visit Lord Pearce," she replied and immediately closed her lips in a tight line.

"Ah. Perhaps I should speak with him about that night."

"I... don't believe he was in residence. He has been away in London for several months now." She picked at a frayed seam in her gloves.

"A pity. Were you worried when I did not return home?"

"Of course, I was. It was most unlike you. We are fortunate Bigsby and his men found you."

Most unlike you. To ride out drunk with no thought to the consequences. To arrive too late for his only child's christening. He drew in a painful breath. "And my horse?"

She snorted, which gave her nose a delightful crinkle. "Has been eating his head off and enjoying a life of leisure according to Bigsby. Demanding the care of every groom and stable boy available to him."

"And you have been caring for me," He searched her face. She did not like to lie, that much he had learned. A woman who did not like to lie only did so for a good reason. "Dr. Pratt said he has never seen a more attentive wife."

"Dr. Pratt is too effusive with his praise. I did what any good wife might do. And the servants have also been most devoted in their care." A slow flush crept up the portion of her neck and face bared by her cloak.

Any good wife...

"And have I been a good husband, my lady?" He startled himself with that question. He'd not intended to ask. He only wanted to know how far she intended to string him along and why. But, dammit, he wanted to hear what she'd say.

She turned towards him, her expression open and her eyes over-bright. "You have been the perfect husband, my lord, and an exemplary father."

What the devil? The hairs on the back of his neck stood on end. "Doing it up too brown, my lady. My illness has not made me so frail as that. No husband is perfect. Especially not the Earl of Bemerton's incorrigible heir. Now is the time to tell me every terrible thing I have done since we married. I will have no choice but to believe you." He gave her his most unconcerned grin. To his amazement, her heretofore bland expression softened. A comforting beauty shone from her gaze.

"You are no longer his heir. You have been the earl these

six months and more." She placed a firm, long-fingered hand on his arm. "I am sorry. Sorry you had to suffer his loss twice."

His heart stuttered. For a few breaths it hurt to breathe. "As am I. He did the best he could for me." St John covered her hand with his own. "Just as I will try to do for our daughter."

"Oh, I assure you, you are a most attentive and loving father to Alexandra. In fact—"

"You did not answer my question, Portia. Have you had no cause, not even a moment to regret taking me as your husband?" His gaze locked with hers.

She swallowed, but did not look away. "I will tell you this, my lord. Since the morning of our wedding I have not received an unkind word from you. Few wives in England can say the same."

Few wives in England have a husband disappear the morning after their wedding only to return to spend a month in a stupor. Suddenly he did feel ill, or tired, or God forbid, guilty. Dammit, *she* was lying to *him.* He had every reason to continue this ruse in order to discover precisely what her game was.

"You look a bit pale." She leapt to her feet and dragged him to his. You can try your walk again tomorrow. I am certain you will feel much more like completing your six rounds after some good food and a good night's sleep in your own bed."

He offered her his arm, which she took albeit after a moment or two's hesitation. "My own bed? Have I not been sleeping in my own bed?" They strolled slowly back towards the house. Her hip brushed against him from time to time.

The shock of sensation the contact sent coursing through his body was strange, new, and... irritating.

"Actually, my lord, you have been sleeping in *my* bed. It was easier for the servants to see to your care in the countess's apartments." She peered up at him, her complexion an intriguing shade of pink.

"We do not sleep together?" He found he rather liked teasing her.

"Not for quite some time, my lord. You snore. Loudly."

He loosed a shout of laughter. "Well played, wife. I shall repair to the earl's chambers to lick my wounds."

They entered the house and handed their coats and gloves to Farnham.

"I suspect both of our chambers have been set to rights by now. I will take you up and acquaint you with your arrangements." Her lips, plump and inviting curved into a smile Machiavelli might envy. "Come along, my lord."

"St John," he replied as they started up the stairs. "Though I do not remember it, we have shared far too much for you to address me so formally. Portia."

She missed a step and he cupped her elbow to steady her. "We have never—"

"I insist." Before they even reached the second-floor landing a plaintive shrieking wail pierced the air. The closer they drew to the earl's apartments, the louder the noise grew. Involuntarily, St John's footsteps began to drag. Portia strode forward and threw the doors to the earl's chambers wide. The cries of a very angry baby roared out of the room like a banshee out of the highlands of Scotland.

"Good God." St John stood in the corridor, awash in an emotion he'd never had occasion to feel before today.

Absolute terror.

Portia came back to take his arm and drag him forward. The sitting room appeared fairly normal. The sparse furnishings were of a blue and gold brocade. An overstuffed brocade rocking chair sat before the massive fireplace in which a well-built fire burned. On one side of the room a long table loaded with folded blankets, sheets, towels, flannels, and other fabric items stood. The doors to the bedchamber stood open. The room within was… pink. Frighteningly pink considering the caterwauling wafting from within it.

St John slowly crossed the sitting room and took two steps into what had been the earl's bedchamber for centuries. His wife's elderly companion paced back and forth before the hearth making soothing sounds to the squirming blanket-wrapped bundle against her shoulder. An ornately carved cradle sat where the earl's four poster bed had once stood. The room was decorated in frilly curtains, lace doilies, thick pink carpets and a pair of brocade cushioned rocking chairs. Against one wall was a simple bed just large enough for one person. His dressing gown was draped across the foot of it. An open wardrobe stood nearby. In it were clothes that looked entirely too familiar to St John. Before it several pairs of boots rested. How the devil had she retrieved his entire travel wardrobe from Hindon Abbey?

His head began to spin and it had nothing to do with his fall nor the month he'd spent asleep. The grey-haired harridan smiled broadly and hurried over to thrust the squalling infant into his arms.

"Thank goodness, you are up and about, my lord. I confess I am not up to caring for a little 'un these days. This one has missed her Papa and no mistaking it."

St John barely heard her over the unnervingly indignant screams assaulting his ears. He clutched the bundle beneath the arms and held her out in front of him. Babies were supposed to be angelic and sweet and... pretty. This red-faced, furious creature was anything but pretty.

"She's... very healthy," he admitted when he finally turned to Portia, still holding his daughter like a squirming puppy. "Whose idea was it to move the nursery here? On the floor with the... rest of us?" His daughter hiccupped, sniffled, and then went silent, studying him from tear-shined eyes exactly the same shade of blue as his own.

"Yours, my—St John. You have insisted on caring for Alexandra yourself from the moment of her birth." The benevolent tone of her voice belied the triumph in her face. "As I said, you have been an exemplary father. I daresay I am the envy of every woman in England."

"You— I—" Falling off his horse was nothing compared to this.

"And, of course, now you've sworn off spirits of any kind—"

"I've what?" He dropped into the nearest chair as if he'd been shot. His head began to pulse like a Christmas pudding kept in the pantry too long.

The baby began to howl once more. Never had he understood another person more.

Chapter Seven

One week later

"Dear God, what is that smell? This cannot be… What is wrong with her?"

"Nothing, my lord. 'Tis the milk. When she begins to take solid food, the smell will be less…"

"Like the Thames at low tide in August? Can we not simply dip her entire bottom in the basin of water? Who knew caring for one little girl could be so odiferous?"

"It's what babies do, my lord. You'll grow used to it."

"What babies do is all over my shirt is what it is. That makes the third one today."

"Shall we try again, my lord?"

"Why not? I have at least six more perfectly clean shirts in the wardrobe."

Portia stifled a snort and shook her head.

"What are they doing now?" Nanny Rose whispered as she tried to peek over Portia's shoulder. The dressing room door was cracked just enough for one person to peer into the nursery, two if one of those doing the peering stood hovering nearly on top of the other.

"Shhh." Portia swatted blindly at the older woman. "They'll hear us. Are you certain Georgie knows what he is doing?"

"Of course, he does. He's the oldest of fourteen. He's as dab a hand at changing a baby's clout as I am. This was your idea, my lady, not mine."

Portia chewed her lower lip and pressed her eye to the space between the door and the jamb. "I didn't think it through. I never dreamed I'd have the blind leading the blind when it came to caring for my daughter."

"If you ask my opinion."

"I didn't."

"The only blind one in all of this is you."

"You have a perfectly lovely chamber waiting for you across the corridor, Nanny. And an entire evening to yourself," Portia started. "Why don't you—"

"If you think I could sleep a wink knowing that scoundrel is looking after my girl you *have* taken leave of your senses."

A string of colorful language ensued in the nursery.

"Go to bed, Nanny." Portia straightened and pushed the dressing room door open. "Good evening, Georgie. Husband. What's the trouble?" She pasted her most blandly innocent smile onto her face.

"My lady," the footman bowed and eyed the doors that led into the sitting room and eventually the corridor. And escape. "No trouble at all. I was…"

"Refreshing my memory as to the proper way to change a clout," St John said. "I have had some difficulty recalling the knack." The handsome Earl of Bemerton managed to look endearingly sheepish as he indicated the pile of discarded clouts at the end of the sideboard onto which he'd spread a thick pallet of blankets. Alexandra lay on the blankets, happily kicking her feet in the air. St John had one hand on her little belly, holding her in place. In his other hand, pinched between his thumb and one finger, he held a distinctly wet and pungent garment.

"And has it come back to you?" Portia asked as she wandered in pretended aimlessness about the nursery. "It has been a week, after all."

"Thank you, Georgie," St John said and nodded toward the sitting room. The young man did not have to be told twice. He fled the nursery with as much dignity as a scrambling clout-changing footman could muster.

"Has our daughter always had a proclivity for wetting herself immediately after someone changes her, or is that a privilege she only affords her father?"

Portia glanced at him and slapped a hand to her mouth. He wore no coat nor waistcoat. The entire front of his linen shirt and buckskin breeches was soaked and horribly stained. He dropped the wet clout in his hand into a bucket at the end of the sideboard. She moved closer as he turned back to Alexandra. He stuffed a clean flannel into a bowl of water, squeezed it out with one hand and gently wiped the baby clean. He lifted her little bottom and gently tucked a clean clout beneath her.

"Let's try this again, shall we, Lady Alexandra?"

He actually managed a fairly decent job of wrestling the wriggling little girl into her clout. One might consider him an expert if not for the trembling of his hands. With fists on his hips he stood over her and gave Alexandra an anticipatory study. Seeing the two of them so closely together, Portia admitted, probably for the first time, how very much her daughter resembled St John. A jumbled mix of anger and relief washed over her.

"What are you waiting for?" Portia asked.

"For her to christen this one the way she has the last half dozen or more." He rubbed Alexandra's belly with his fingertips which caused her to chortle and kick her legs. "She is so small. I never imagined she would be this small."

"She is not quite four months old. Of course, she's small. She'll grow." Portia reached for her, but St John beat her to it. He pulled a warm gown over Alexandra's head and worked to put her little arms through the sleeves.

"I do not remember her christening." His face grew grim. He lifted their daughter into his arms, careful to prop her against the cleaner portion of his shirt. "Was I there? Who are her godparents?"

She wanted to tell him the truth, to end this farce. Not today. Not yet. "You were there. She wore your christening gown. My brother, Alexander, is her godfather. And my sister, Helena, is her godmother."

He handed the baby to her and strode to the wardrobe. "My mother and sister did not come." It was not a question.

"They were much engaged in Town." She did not have the ability to make the excuse any more than what it was, an excuse, and a poor one at that. He stood before the wardrobe, unmoving for several moments. She thought she heard him chuckle.

Then to her surprise he pulled his shirttails out of his breeches and whipped his shirt off over his head. Rather than don another shirt, he plucked his dressing gown from the foot of the narrow bed and pulled it on over his breeches. Only then did she notice he wore neither stockings nor shoes. How was it a man's feet and legs could be carved in such sinewy detail and hers resembled those of a peasant woman

374 • Louisa Cornell

plowing a field behind a pair of oxen?

"You have eaten little of your dinner, my—"

He turned and met her gaze, one eyebrow raised.

"St John. Are you not hungry?"

He glanced at the small table set before the hearth. "Boiled beef and boiled cabbage." His expression said it all.

"They are your—"

"Yes, my customary fare. How did you marry such a dull and lazy fellow, Portia?"

"Dull?"

"The same food every meal. The same walk every morning." He plucked a piece of bread from a plate on the table and began to spread it with butter from the crock next to the mug of coffee.

Little did he know the servants had begun to take bets amongst themselves as to how many times his lordship would follow the path her ladyship had outlined around the gardens. He'd even walked in the light snow which had fallen two days past. He'd stomp into the house bellowing for a bath. After which he'd wolf down his dry toast and beef broth breakfast, bathe and change Alexandra, and lay down for a nap until she bawled for Portia to feed her again. She'd find it amusing if he did not do it all with such earnest good grace. Damn him. She'd not expected it of him.

"Is it dull to have some order to one's life?" She lowered herself into one of the rocking chairs and lifted Alexandra to rest against her shoulder as she rocked.

"Perhaps not." He sat on the arm of the horsehair chair before the fire. "But you must admit a husband who does nothing but stroll his gardens and play with an infant must count himself as lazy. Perhaps if I were to help you with the running of the estate..."

"Do you think tending your daughter is less important than the management of your estate?" An inkling of warning tickled the back of her neck.

"Not at all. I rather enjoy being spat upon, pissed upon, shat upon, and awakened all hours of the night." His careless grin was genuine. His tone was replete with unasked questions.

"I assure you, managing this estate is very like that on more days than I care to count." Portia rose from her chair and placed a sleeping Alexandra into the cradle. She gazed into her daughter's cherubic face. An overwhelming urge to weep assailed her. What was she doing? And far worse, why?

"St John, I must tell you—Oh!" He'd come to stand behind her so quietly she nearly fell over him. He gently clasped her upper arms, his long fingers sending fissures of heat up and over her shoulders, along her spine, and wheeling around her body.

"What are you planning, wife?" His rich baritone entranced her.

"Planning?"

"For Christmas. It is nearly upon us. What festivities did we enjoy last Christmas?"

"Last Christmas?" She truly needed to stop gazing into his blue eyes. She couldn't think. Not a wise place for a woman to be when trying to carry off a scheme such as hers had grown to be. "We... we did not even have a turkey. I was ill and you... well, you celebrated with Lord Pearce as I recall. I had not planned to celebrate this year. You were ill and well, I have not had the time."

"All the more reason for us to celebrate this year. It will

be our daughter's first Christmas. Our first Christmas as a family." He pressed a sudden kiss to her lips.

Portia gasped. She'd been in an apple orchard on her brother's Suffolk estate when lightning struck the ground not far from where she stood. Her husband's kiss was like that—unexpected, staggering, searing the air around her. He stared at her, eyes wide and mouth slightly agape. His arm was curled around her before she knew it, his hand pressed warm and firm against her back. He drew her close. The fingers of his free hand traced the curve of her eyebrows, the length of her nose, the curve of her lips.

He kissed her. Softly at first, tentatively. If he kissed her on their wedding night, she did not remember it. Imagine. Her with a faulty memory. This kiss she would remember all her life. Even if he didn't mean it. He teased and tempted with little nips and sweet brushes of his lips against hers. She sighed and he pulled her even closer, slipping his tongue slowly and deliciously into her mouth, tasting and caressing in languid strokes.

A sudden noise from the dressing room startled them both. Portia stepped back and bumped into the cradle. He appeared a bit dazed, which oddly enough pleased her. She was playing with fire and lies. Nothing good ever came of such a mix.

"I'll speak to the steward," he said, a hoarse rasp softening his sudden words.

"The steward?"

"About Christmas. We have not celebrated here since I was a child. He will know where to find a yule log and mistletoe. And I will check the ledger books to see what monies we give to the church, and the servants, and such." He squeezed her hand. "I will see to all of it."

His face was lit with enthusiasm. For a family Christmas with her and his daughter. The man who had spent last Christmas gambling and whoring all over London, thanks to a bump on the head and her web of lies, was now planning the perfect country house Christmas.

She had to get out of this room. "You will bring her to me should she wake hungry?"

"Does she wake any other way?" St John teased.

Portia laughed in spite of the stinging sensation in her nose and eyes. "Good night... St John." She kissed her fingertips, pressed them to Alexandra's downy cheek and hurried into the dressing room between his room and hers. Nanny sat on his now empty trunk, arms crossed and eyebrows raised.

"Oh, do be quiet," Portia snapped. "Why have you not found your bed?"

"I chose not to until I discovered who would be sleeping in yours."

"Don't be ridiculous."

"That kiss didn't look ridiculous."

Portia threw up her hands and marched toward her chamber. A plaintive cry from the nursery brought her up short. She and Nanny stumbled over each other to reach the door and open it just enough to see...

"Jupiter's pizzle, shoot me now! Alexandra, this is my favorite dressing gown. Did you really just— Holy hell! Go ahead and laugh, you little fiend. It's Papa's turn to cry."

Portia stared through the crack in the door as her wayward husband stripped to his breeches, tested the water in the basin on hob with his elbow, washed her daughter clean and redressed her for bed, all while singing an off-key *Barbara Allen.*

How could she continue to lie to him? And what would he do once she told him the truth?

Chapter Eight

St John shoved his hands into the pockets of his greatcoat and started down the aisle of yew trees for the sixth time. It was colder than his mother's heart outside, and he'd already covered Portia's helpfully drawn path five times. He knew this entire endeavor was designed to torture him. Just as he knew she stood watching him from one of the windows overlooking the gardens. Still he trudged on, never once looking back at the house. Truth be told, the walking helped. With rebuilding his strength after a month lying abed. With the incessant tug of need any thoughts of a drink brought forth.

He'd spent the first week of his *resurrection* searching the house every spare moment he could steal. She'd done an excellent job—coaching the servants on exactly what to say and do, ridding the house of every drop of spirits save the ale which magically appeared with the servants' meals only to disappear once more. He suspected it resided in the butler's pantry. And whilst he was certain he could take Farnham, St John had not descended to the level of wrestling a key from his butler.

This week he'd divided his time between caring for his daughter and discovering everything possible about Bemerton's improved fortunes. Under the guise of making preparations to celebrate Christmas, he'd studied Portia's ledgers, questioned the steward, and ridden the estate from one end to the other. Only last night he'd found what London banks held the estate's monies. His wife had made him a wealthy man. He could make for London tomorrow and not a one of those banks would refuse him.

Still he stayed. To avoid suspicions he'd told himself. No need to tip his hand. He'd even ridden the border between his and Pearce's estate, contemplating paying his friend a visit. Yet he'd turned and ridden back to Bemerton Hall in time to attempt to feed his daughter one of her first bowls of gruel. When he finally made it back to London, he'd be forced to use some of the money his wife's management had afforded him to replace his shirts.

He cleared the avenue of yews and braced himself against the December wind sweeping across the neatly appointed beds of dormant roses. These gardens had been his grandmother's pride and joy. His mother had never cared for them. The money to pay for their upkeep was better spent on her or his sister, Lavinia's, wardrobes. Portia had set the gardens to rights as well. He turned and studied the front of his ancestral home.

She had a gift for such, his wife. A gift for setting things to rights. Gardens. Houses. People. Him. He didn't know how he felt about it. He didn't want to know. The woman who had done all these things with a gentle smile and an easy, chiding manner was also lying to him about every aspect of their marriage. She'd created their lives together, their marriage, out of whole cloth, and he had no idea why.

Brilliant rays of valiant sunlight glinted off a large marble structure on the hill behind the hall. The family mausoleum. They'd laid his father to rest there over six months ago. They. His mother and sister had managed the journey, along with a good portion of the London house staff. He'd been in London, drunk and miserable. Alone. Hands still in his pockets and shoulders hunched against the cold, he headed up the hill. In spite of his weeks of daily exercise, the climb proved more taxing than he'd expected. He had to stop halfway up to catch his breath.

Once he'd reached the mausoleum, he hesitated, his hand flat against the heavy, ornate iron gates. With a long, bracing breath he pushed those gates open and stepped inside to find an urn filled with fresh hot house flowers and Christmas greenery before his father's black marble tomb. He lowered himself onto the little stone widow's bench next to the massive monument to the last Earl of Bemerton.

"I suppose I should thank you," he mused out loud. "I was less than grateful when you offered the Duke of Wharram's daughter as my bride." He leaned back and rested his head against the cool, marble wall. "She was a good choice. Far better than I deserved."

His only answer was the wind whistling around the mausoleum and the occasional bird call. He'd never been one to appreciate the silence. Until his daughter came into his life.

"You have a granddaughter, you know. She is an utterly adorable tyrant. With a voice like a Yorkshire fishwife. And an uncanny ability to know when I have on a clean shirt. You'd like her, Papa. I am sorry she has no chance to meet you."

"You can tell her about him."

St John shot to his feet. Portia, dressed in the slate blue cloak he thought so becoming on her, stepped into the mausoleum. She perched on the end of the bench and motioned for him to join her.

"I am not disturbing you, am I?" she asked in that soothing, solicitous tone he'd come to appreciate.

"Not at all. Papa and I are simply enjoying a little conversation. Decidedly one-sided, but congenial nonetheless." The slight press of her body warmed him, nearly to his bones. He'd said he didn't mind her presence, and he didn't. Not at all. In fact, having her next to him was a comfort. Like none he'd ever known.

"You were telling him about his granddaughter," she observed. She always studied him so closely. What did she see when she looked at him? He shuddered to think.

"He would have spoiled her dreadfully, you know. He—" He sat up. "Who is watching Alexandra? I should put her down for her nap."

Portia reached for his hand and squeezed it. "Nanny Rose will see to it." She tilted her head, her expression both quizzical and a bit amused. "Some children are actually put into the care of nannies and nursemaids from time to time."

"Not our girl." He relaxed, hands clasped between his knees. "Queen Alexandra demands obeisance from only the highest ranked courtiers in her kingdom."

Portia laughed, a deep, throaty, alluring sound that sent a thrust of heat and animal lust straight to his cock, swathing his brain in a pleasant haze. He dared not risk touching his wife nor even turning to face her in his current state. His thoughts had been so scrambled of late he wasn't certain he was capable of intelligent conversation with the curvaceous siren he'd married. Talking with his dead father was far simpler.

"Queen, no less. I suspect you will do a handy enough job

of spoiling our daughter yourself, Lord Bemerton."

"I have no memory of her birth. I think that may well be the thing I regret most." Yes, he truly was in no condition for conversation. Especially with this woman. More and more he found himself incapable of keeping the truth from her. If he had any hope of securing access to the estate's funds, his funds, he needed to maintain the charade he'd begun the moment he awoke from his stupor.

"Your... loss of memory is not your fault." She let go of his hand and tucked hers into the pocket of her cloak.

"No? My father's funeral. Was I in attendance?" Where the devil had *that* come from and what possible good could it do him?

"You saw to it all was done to honor him as he deserved." She nodded at the urn of flowers—red and white and green and gold in honor of the season. "Fresh flowers are placed here every day by your order."

His chest squeezed to the point he believed he might never breathe again. He shook his head. "Portia, I need to—"

"You loved your father very much. You told me so before we married. It is one of the things I admired most about you."

"Not my dancing. Nor my sparkling wit nor amiable friends." St John closed his eyes and slumped against the wall. Her attempts to comfort him and make him appear more than what he was stood every chance of undoing him.

They sat quietly. Perhaps she did not intend to answer him. He might hardly blame her.

"Your dancing? Most definitely. You made even me appear graceful. Your wit? On occasion, when not directed at yourself. Your friends? Definitely not." She bit the last words off so sharply he pushed himself up and studied her face, mottled with fury and something more. A niggling, whisper of a thought slithered through his memory and was gone. He needed to move before maudlin sentiment had him in tears. He stood and offered Portia his hand.

"Shall we go and relieve Nanny Rose of duty? Even the most stalwart of attendants deserves a respite." Portia smiled and placed her hand in his. He drew it through his crooked arm and stood before his father's tomb for a moment more. "I am glad he was given a good sendoff. Had it been left to my mother, he'd have been bundled into a wooden box and shoved into the tomb with some other Bemerton ancestor."

"Really, St John. Your mother is—"

"The reason my father is dead. The Countesses of Bemerton have a long history of hounding their husbands into an early grave. And their sons have a history of turning a blind eye to it. Shall we?" *Damn!*

They left the mausoleum and made their way across the icy lawns to the house.

"I hope you do not include me in that number," Portia said quietly after they'd walked for a while.

"Definitely not. You are unlike any countess I have ever known." He covered her hand resting on his arm and held it fast. The strength and warmth of her touch reached him even through the leather of her gloves and his.

"Doing it up a bit brown, my lord, and there really is no need. Your daughter has learned her tyranny at my knee, and I am well aware of it."

He stopped and dragged her close. She met his gaze, unblinking and yes, curious.

"You are nothing like my mother. You are a tyrant, but a benevolent one. You look after everyone on this estate from the boot boy to our daughter with the same sensible care and forethought. I don't understand it. I never will, but I am grateful for it. I don't understand how I missed it, how I could have ever not seen..." His breath came in short bursts, little puffs of air visible in the morning sun. She licked her lips.

"Not seen what?"

"How beautiful you are." He hauled her into his arms and kissed her for all he was worth. To his amazement and delight, she lashed her arms around his neck and matched him kiss for kiss. Her lips were full and soft, and he could not get enough of them. She teased him with the tip of her tongue and squeaked when he drew it into his mouth to suck, then lick and stroke with his own. Her breasts and thighs pushed against his, searing him and nearly taking him to his knees.

"Wait!" she gasped and tried to push out of his arms. As quickly as her passion ignited it was doused and replaced with the same wariness and confusion he saw on her face all too often. "We should get back. Alexandra will be fussy and perhaps hungry." She backed away and stumbled towards the house.

"I—" St John hurried after her. What had he done this time? He caught her and drew her arm through his once more. They walked the rest of the way to the house without saying a word. Once in the foyer the smells of Christmas baking lured them both down the corridor to the baize doors into the kitchens, with Farnham trailing after them to take their coats and gloves. The servants paused to make their bows and curtsies, but went back to work the instant Portia waved her hand.

"We need to discuss..."

She cut him off with a mere glance. He wanted to laugh.

He had to agree with her. Alexandra gave him the same look when he failed to shovel that awful gruel into her mouth quickly enough. Portia backed up until her body was flush with his. St John suppressed a groan.

"We need to discuss how to sneak some of those little mince pies off the table without Mrs. Cole catching us. I tried this morning."

He bent to touch his lips to her ear. A shiver raced through him. "And?"

"She smacked my hand and reminded me they were for Christmas Day."

St John reached around her, snatched two pies from the work table and stuffed them into his coat pockets. "Up the back stairs, wife. Make haste."

They raced to the door across the kitchen and stumbled up the stairs like guilty children. Once they reached the earl's chambers cum nursery, they ducked inside, propped themselves against the closed doors, and fell upon the pies like ravenous dogs. Which is exactly how Nanny Rose found them as she came into the sitting room, a very disgruntled Alexandra in her arms.

"There you are." The harried woman marched up and handed the now crying baby to St John. "You have ruined this child, my lord. She refuses to settle down for a nap."

"Have you tried reading to her?"

"Bah! She's been fed and changed. It was all she needed before you came along and—"

"Nanny!" Portia stepped around St John and pressed a sticky hand over the old woman's mouth. His wife's face had gone white.

"Before I came along and?" He raised his daughter above

his head and made a face at her. And she promptly cast up her morning gruel all over him.

Chapter Nine

Christmas Eve

Portia glanced around her study and frowned. All appeared as it should, but something wasn't quite right. Had not been quite right for weeks now. Perhaps as Mrs. Whitby had said, she was merely disconcerted by his lordship's presence in the house. His presence in the house was not the issue. His presence in Portia's life was another matter entirely.

She enjoyed her independence. She'd made the daily decisions of her life and the lives of everyone on the estate without having to consider the opinions or feelings of anyone else. Now she found herself wondering at every turn, and she didn't like it. Still ill at ease, she checked the account books on her desk. She opened first one drawer and then another. Everything lay just where she'd left it. A peel of feminine laughter drew her attention to the corridor outside the study. By the time she snuffed the candles and opened the door the corridor was empty save for the sweep of a maid's skirts around the corner. She glanced up and spotted a kissing ball hanging strategically above the doors into the kitchens.

The servants, both inside and outside of the house, had spent the better part of the day bedecking the house with greenery, ribbons, and kissing balls delivered courtesy of

Lord Bemerton, Bigsby, and a good number of the grooms and a few of the tenants' sons, sweet, no doubt, on a few of the maids. They'd been rewarded with mulled wine and mince pies. The house looked and smelled heavenly. Like the Christmases of her childhood, but far more merry and grand.

She'd carried Alexandra around to see it all. Her first Christmas. Their first Christmas as a family. All Portia had to do to bring it about was lie to a man who'd lost his memory and cajole her servants into playing along. Suddenly, the glow of the decorations faded. She opened and closed her fists and shook her head. After Christmas. She'd tell him after Christmas and to hell with the consequences.

The kitchens had been a noisome flurry of activity, especially these last few days. This evening very little sound escaped the double baized doors. Portia stepped inside to find Mrs. Cole and a few of the kitchen maids putting the finishing touches on the many dishes to be served at Christmas dinner tomorrow.

"My goodness, Mrs. Cole, where is everyone?"

"Oh!" The round little cook turned and pressed a hand to her chest. "My lady." She dipped a belated curtsy. "I was not expecting you." The others curtsied and glanced at the cook nervously.

"No need to worry. I simply stopped in to see that all is in readiness for tomorrow." Portia adopted her most reassuring tone. She'd done all in her power to treat the servants at Bemerton with the respect and kindness her father's servants never knew. "Where are the younger servants? The pot boy and the scullery maids?"

Mrs. Cole and the maids turned their eyes to the narrow door on the far side of the kitchens. Portia had only lived in the house a little over a year, but she'd made it a point to learn every hidden door and every servants' staircase. She plucked a candlestick from the kitchen mantel and lit it from the fire. Her skirts in one hand, she went to the door, fumbled it open and started up the narrow wooden steps.

Like all servants' staircases it twisted and turned with landings in odd places and another set of steps at one point leading down towards the wine cellar. She bypassed those and continue up until she spied half a dozen of Bemerton's youngest servants sitting huddled against a door with an open carved lattice panel at the bottom of it. Portia stepped out of her slippers and continued up the steps. When the young scullery maid spotted her and made to rise, Portia put a finger to her lips and joined her on the step where she sat. She smiled at the young servants and leaned in as they had done.

St John's voice drifted into the staircase from the nursery. He was reading aloud. After a few lines she recognized the story. The *Tales of King Arthur*. Tonight, he was reading *Sir Gawain and the Green Knight*. She doubted Alexandra understood the tale, but he read it with such enthusiasm, changing voices for the characters and reciting the daring deeds with a heroic flourish. Something stirred in her heart. A flicker of a flutter that had been growing stronger and more disconcerting the more time she spent with St John. A foolish notion. The last thing she needed was to fall in love with a man who didn't know who he was. Who would not care to know who she was, once he remembered himself.

St John had the perfect voice for storytelling. No wonder the youngest members of Bemerton's household were drawn to it. They all sat in rapt attention until the green knight was vanquished and the book was closed with a resounding thud. Then they melted away down the staircase, smiling and waving at Portia to the point her heart nearly burst. The scullery maid hurried back up with Portia's slippers in hand. She delivered them, curtsied, and hurried back down to join the others. Portia put her slippers back on and started down the stairs. Something held her back.

She stood at the door and contemplated what to do next. She sank her teeth into her bottom lip and pushed the door open. Only to find the cruel reprobate she'd married gently rocking their daughter's cradle as he attempted to sing *Greensleeves*. Once he saw her, he grimaced and ceased singing. He slowed the cradle until it finally stopped. He unfolded from the footstool on which he sat and padded across the room in his stockinged feet.

"I'd forgotten about that door," he said quietly as he peered behind her. "Pearce and I fell into a great deal of trouble using it and the one in the nursery."

"I can believe that of Lord Pearce. What sort of trouble?"

The side of his mouth kicked up. Dear Lord, he had no right to be so handsome, so endearing, so... everything. "I'll show you." He took her hand and pulled the door open wider. "Are you up for a bit of adventure?"

She rolled her eyes, but raised her candle and followed after him. He reached the stone steps leading down, turned and winked at her, and squeezed her hand.

"Keep the candle up. I would hate for you to have to explain my dead body at the bottom of these stairs," he teased.

"Who says I would explain? I could simply leave you

there and have the staircase walled up like King Edward did to the little princes."

"Heartless wench. You would miss me. Confess it now, Portia. You would and you know it." He turned and smiled at her in the candlelight.

"I would." It was the truth. God help her it was. She'd not missed him for a moment after he'd abandoned her the morning after their wedding. When he left again, once she told him the truth, Portia knew she'd miss him forever.

He swallowed and continued down the stairs, still holding her hand. When they reached their destination, he took the candle from her and used it to light a series of sconces embedded in the walls. They were in the wine cellar. She'd visited it a number of times since her marriage. In fact, she'd visited it recently when she'd supervised the removal of all of the liquor in the house. An array of the various decanters filled a series of shelves on the far wall. St John strolled over and picked up a bottle of brandy, and then a bottle of port.

"My idea?" he mused.

Portia nodded, not trusting herself to speak.

"Very wise of me, hiding it in plain sight."

"St John, I..."

"I have wanted a drink nearly every moment since I... awakened from my stupor. The need is always there." He returned the bottles to one of the shelves. "I didn't dare come down here in search of something, anything. I did not trust myself. I had to depend on the trust of another."

"Another? Who?"

He glanced in the direction of the stairs and smiled—a sad, regretful smile. "Our daughter. She trusts me. I have no idea why, and when she is older, we shall teach her better. She cries and trusts I will come to make it right."

"She cries because she has you well-trained," Portia assured him, her heart aching for him, his words, and all he was learning in spite of her lies. Or perhaps because of them.

St John laughed. "As is a lady's prerogative." He shook his head. "I see it in her eyes, Portia. She trusts me to care for her, to feed her, to comfort her, and I cannot do that worse the wear for drink."

Portia's eyes itched and burned. Her heart pounded like a regimental drum. "You are a good father, St John. Never doubt it."

"I must believe you. You would not have entrusted me with her care otherwise. Even with Nanny Rose lurking around corners and peeping through keyholes."

It was Portia's turn to laugh, in spite of the tightness of her throat. "She does the same to me."

"This last month is the longest time I can remember being completely sober since the day I took my first drink." He sat down on an upturned ale barrel and studied his clasped hands.

"When was that?" Portia chose a barrel across from him and sat to face him.

"I was twelve. I was home from school for Christmas. It was the first time I realized being an earl did not mean an endless supply of money." He glanced up at her and smiled. "My mother threw a house party. She spared no expense. When it was over, I heard them arguing. Or rather, I heard her screaming at him. He did not argue with her. He never did. The money was hers you see. Her dowry. A family tradition, so to speak."

"I am sorry." She tried to imagine him at twelve, learning such a hard lesson with no sibling to confide in, with whom to commiserate. Her life with the Duke of Wharram had been miserable, but she'd had Alexander and her sisters. St John had faced it all alone.

He shrugged. "There are people in England with no food, no roof over their heads. I have been fortunate. A sot drunk since I was sixteen, if the truth be told, but fortunate. My father was not so lucky." His voice cracked on the last word. "She drove him mad. She insulted him, harangued him. And she raised Lavinia to do the same. I think... I think he was happy to die."

"No one is happy to die, St John. He had you. I am certain he was proud to have you as his son."

St John snorted. "Sent down from Oxford. Sent down from Cambridge. In every scandal sheet in London. The only day he was proud of me was the day I married you."

"I am certain that is not true."

"It is. He told me so." St John slid to his knees before her and took her hands. He kissed each one in turn. "No matter what happens, Portia. I want you to know how proud I am to be your husband."

Tears pricked at her eyelashes. "You don't have to say that, St John."

"No, I don't, but I mean it. Promise me you'll remember that. No matter what." He lay his head in her lap with a sigh and curled one arm around her waist.

She stroked his hair and fought back the sobs that clogged her throat. When he finally lifted his head, she kissed him. She took and took and reveled in the powerful clasp of his arms around her. She tugged his neckcloth free and slid her hand inside his shirt. He stroked the side of her breast and cupped it, running his thumb across the nipple straining against the wool of her dress.

"St John," she murmured against his lips.

He stilled. "Wait. We're not doing this."

She nipped his earlobe and kissed the side of his neck. "We're not?"

"No, we… woman, stop or I will not be held accountable for my actions." He leaned back and wrapped his hands around her wrists.

"I thought you didn't want to be thought of as dull." She tried and failed to catch her breath. Her heart thundered against her ribs.

"I don't want to be thought of as a ruffian either." He stood and pulled her to her feet. "Nor do I want to end up with cellar dirt in my drawers."

"You no longer wear drawers."

"Lady Bemerton!"

"I peeked."

"You what?"

"I watch you undress for your bath every evening. The dressing room door provides an excellent view."

"Scandalous minx. I don't wear them because our daughter is capable of wetting through my best buckskins *and* my drawers in one sitting. We have a perfectly comfortable bed upstairs and I am reasonably certain neither of us will find dirt anywhere once we are done." He started up the staircase, pulling her along in his wake.

"Are you proposing we do… this in your bed in the nursery?" Portia inquired as they hurried up the stairs.

"This?" He turned and pulled her close for a searing kiss.

"Not unless you wish to spend half our time on the floor. I have bruises on my fundament from the falls I have taken from that miserable contraption."

She laughed as they continued. They reached the narrow passage that joined the series of servants' stairs and hidden doors. Shouting and running feet emitted from the inset panel into the foyer. St John tried to pull her forward. Portia put a finger to her lips and an ear to the panel.

"I am telling you he sent for me. Now step aside, you old rummy, or I'll have my men push you aside."

Lord Pearce. Something struck Portia. Her heart flopped over. *He sent for me.* She stared at St John. Even in the dim light of the candle his face appeared grey. He opened his mouth. Closed it.

"Go upstairs, Portia. I'll take care of this." He stepped past her and pushed the panel open.

"My lord, I—"

"It's fine, Farnham," St John said. "Lord Pearce was just leaving."

The butler stepped back and moved in front of Portia in an attempt to shield her. She moved around him, but not far from the servant's side.

"The hell you say. You sent for me. And about time too. This chit." He pointed at Portia. "Lied to me. She told me you were not here. What the devil is going on, Thornley?"

"You sent for him?" Portia said softly.

"This *chit* is the Countess of Bemerton and my *wife*. You owe her an apology," St John demanded. "And stop calling me Thornley, you imbecile."

Portia glanced down and caught the closing and unclosing of his hand. It didn't make sense. Something was terribly wrong.

"An apology? To *Lady Porka*?"

St John's fist flew so swiftly to Lord Pearce's chin Portia nearly missed it. The chin in question, however, did not. The heir to the estate next door glared up at her from the foyer's parquet floor.

"Get out of my house," she ordered and stepped towards him.

"Your house?" Pearce cried even as he slid backwards away from her. "Your dowry may have bought the title, but it didn't buy anything else. He's discovered where all the money is, bitch. Every shilling you stole from him. He'll—"

"Get out!" St John roared. He picked Lord Pearce up by his neckcloth and dragged him out of the house. Portia started after him. Farnham grasped her shoulders and held her in place. The front door stood open. Though darkness had fallen, the sounds of a man receiving a sound beating could not be mistaken.

After what seemed like hours, St John strode back inside and slammed the door with all his might. The sound reverberated to the tall ceiling of the foyer and back down again as he and Portia stood staring at each other. Farnham let go of her and shepherded the gawping footmen down the corridor.

St John's clothes were torn. He had a bruise on his cheek and a cut on his bottom lip. Portia forced herself not to go to him. She doubted she had the strength. Everything that had been said, bits and pieces of suspicions and niggling doubts flooded her mind and washed down her body in icy streams.

"You sent for him?"

He reached for her. She backed away. "A week ago. I...

wasn't thinking clearly. I made a mistake, Portia. A horrible mistake."

"How long?" she finally croaked. She cleared her throat. "How. Long?"

He stared at her, his face expressionless, but he knew. He ran a hand through his hair. "From the beginning," he replied, head up and eyes painfully clear.

"Then it was all a lie. Every day. Every word. All lies." She backed towards the stairs.

"No, Portia. Let me explain. It wasn't... I made a mistake. I should never have—"

"Neither should I, my lord." She looked around at the greenery, the signs of a Christmas she'd never expected to celebrate. A Christmas she no longer wished to celebrate. "Neither should I." Before the tears started, she fled.

Chapter Ten

St John picked up the glass of brandy for the hundredth time since he'd poured it from the decanter beckoning to him from the sideboard across the library. He'd fetched it from the wine cellar soon after beating his best friend to a bloody pulp on the front steps of Bemerton Hall. He had yet to consume a drop, but he wanted to. Dear God, he wanted to. He placed it back on the fireside table.

Lady Porka.

Part of his lost memory was true. He had little memory of the day and night he'd married Lady Portia. His recollection of the night before had been hazier still. Until he heard Pearce call her that horrid name. It all came back to him. Portia had thrown it in Pearce's face the day St John realized she intended to lie about his presence at Bemerton Hall. She'd heard it somewhere before and after last night's events, St John knew in his heart when and where she'd heard it.

And she'd married him anyway. What should have been one of the most memorable days of her life had been the very worst. And then he'd crawled into her bed, drunk and smelling of some tavern wench's sweat and perfume. He shuddered. He didn't want to think about it, and he was damned certain she had no desire to think on it again. And yet, they'd been given the greatest gift imaginable from that night.

He'd just spent his first night away from his daughter. Her absence hurt like a wound. He'd lain on the long leather sofa before the library fire and slept not a wink. His thoughts flitted from Alexandra to Portia, back and forth until dawn streaked through the stained-glass windows above the window seat and he'd returned to contemplating the brandy.

Somewhere in all his questioning and anger a truth came to him. Portia had lied to him and forced him to live a life he'd never lived. And he'd resented it, played it, and finally come to love it. He'd lied to her to discover the source of the money for the newly refurbished Bemerton Hall. He'd seen the financial ledgers of the failing estate he'd been left and the changes she'd wrought, and all he'd considered was how to get his hands on the money. That's why he'd played along with her lies. For the money.

I am certain he was proud to have you as his son.

St John laughed, loudly and long. How could his father be proud of him when it was abundantly clear he was his *mother's* child? He'd hurt the woman he loved in order to steal money to which he had no claim nor right.

Raised voices and footsteps announced an interruption to his misery. He recognized his butler's voice at once. It took a moment to make out … it couldn't be. St John groaned and swore under his breath. *Could this day grow any worse?* The library doors burst open and in strode the very *last* person with whom he wanted to spend Christmas, or any other day for that matter.

Alexander Chastleton, Marquess of Winterbourne, marched across the thick Turkey carpets, snow still clinging to his Hessians. "I am glad to know someone is having a

Happy Christmas. No need to announce me, Farnham," he said to the butler close on his heels. "Run along and make certain Mrs. Cole doesn't butcher that turkey. The damned thing was cooked in London and my chef insisted it ride all the way here inside my carriage. And remember, not a word to her ladyship. I want to surprise her."

St John rolled his eyes, but waved Farnham off to do as the marquess bid. Said marquess picked up the glass of brandy St John had poured and drained it in one draught.

"You weren't going to drink that, were you, brother-in-law?" He flounced elegantly into the chair across from St John and threw one leg over the chair arm. "Rumor has it you have given up spirits and taken up beating perfectly innocent gentlemen nearly to death on the front lawn."

"Where did you hear that?"

"Tavern in the village. You serve a very fine brandy, Bemerton. French?"

"Yes. And I didn't beat a gentleman. I beat Pearce, and it was hardly to death. I broke his nose. And perhaps a few ribs."

"Poor fellow."

"You are acquainted with Rupert Pearce, Winterbourne. Innocent is not a word I would use to describe him."

"Yes, well. I did say it was a rumor."

"You brought a turkey?"

"Yes. My sister informed me too late last year that you do not raise them on the estate."

"My father's edict." St John could not help but smile. "Had one attack me when I was four. He never allowed one on the place afterwards."

"A good father," Winterbourne mused. "Speaking of

fathers, heard you had an accident on the way to your daughter's christening."

"Do you have a spy in my household or are my affairs being printed in the London gossip rags?" St John spotted one of his wooden horses under a table where Alexandra had flung it. He retrieved the old toy and settled back into his chair to run his fingers over the wood his daughter had polished with drool and God only knew what else. "Why the devil are you here?"

"Had a letter from my sister." Winterbourne rose and went to the sideboard to pour himself another brandy. "Actually, my sister, Catherine, had a letter from Portia a fortnight ago. She was good enough to share it with me."

"I suspect Portia thought that letter was private," St John suggested once Winterbourne was seated across from him once more.

"I grew up in a house with five sisters, Bemerton. Nothing is private."

"Then I suppose you know everything." St John glanced up to find Farnham entering the library with a tray bearing a coffee pot, two mugs and a plate of mince pies. He placed it on the low table next to where St John and Winterbourne sat.

"Your breakfast, my lord," he droned even as he gave the marquess a censuring look and retreated back the way he came.

"Mince pies?" St John called after him.

The butler froze, one hand on the library door. "Don't tell her ladyship, my lord."

A bitter smile teased St John's lips. "She won't hear it from me."

Winterbourne raised an inquiring brow as the doors

closed silently behind the butler.

"Whatever Portia wrote I am certain it is true," St John said as he filled the mugs from the still hot pot of coffee.

"Suppose *you* tell me." Winterbourne had oddly colored eyes, an icy shade of blue. Something in them, however, put St John in mind of Portia.

"What did she write?" St John had played cards with Winterbourne. He knew when he was being baited.

"Only that you had fallen from your horse, spent a month in a stupor, and had suddenly awakened."

"That's all?"

"Well, she did say she'd done something foolish. When one of my sisters says she has done something foolish, and a man is involved, that man is usually in dire need of my help."

St John snorted. "Have you asked Portia what foolish thing she has done? Besides marry me, that is?"

"If your man Farnham is a man of his word, my presence has yet to be announced to our dear Portia. Ask her what foolish thing she has done?" Winterbourne exchanged the glass of brandy for the mug of coffee. "And have her accuse me of interfering? I am a fool when it comes to choosing women, not when it comes to dealing with them. What foolish thing did she do?"

St John sipped his coffee and studied his brother-in-law over the rim of his cup. Slowly, something unfurled in him. He began to talk. He started with his decision to ride to Bemerton after missing Alexandra's christening. Whilst St John spun out the tale of the last few months, Winterbourne sipped his coffee and grimaced. He did not interrupt, though it was apparent he fought not to smile from time to time. By the time St John finished with the events of the previous evening the marquess had finished his coffee and his expression was anything but smiling. When he opened his mouth to speak, St John lifted a staying hand.

"There is nothing you can say I have not already said to myself. I am leaving for London in the morning. I think you will agree it is for the best. I have hurt your sister enough."

"For the best. Yes, I suppose it is. I always knew this would happen."

"This?" St John was quickly growing tired of Winterbourne's cryptic remarks. He'd not been able to draw a complete breath since Portia had locked him out of her chamber and the nursery. He doubted he'd ever be able to do so again.

"We always knew Portia would be the one we'd have to take care of. She was determined to take care of herself and look where it landed her."

"Portia? Taken care of?" St John pushed to his feet and began to pace. "Do you even know your sister? She has brought Bemerton back from the brink of ruin. She gave birth to our daughter and cared for her all while managing the estate and sending money to me and my mother and sister. This house was a tatty ruin when she moved in and look at it now. Perhaps had you and the rest of her family seen her for the magnificent creature she is, she might not have ended up married to a worthless scoundrel like me." He came to a stop before Winterbourne's chair, shouting at the top of his lungs. The bastard had the audacity to smile.

"You'll do."

"Do for what?" St John demanded.

"For her."

"Don't be ridiculous. I am the last thing she needs. Your

sister and niece are far better off without me."

"Leave if you like, Bemerton, but don't lay it at my sister's doorstep. Your decision to cry craven has nothing to do with her and everything to do with you."

"I lied to her."

"She lied to you. It happens. Even when you love someone. She lied to show you the kind of husband you might be."

"And I lied to steal her money and run back to London."

"Yet here you stand. And about that money. I went by my sister's banks last week after Catherine shared Portia's letter with me. Damnedest thing. Someone ordered all of the estate's funds be moved from the estate's accounts directly into my sister's personal accounts, completely out of your reach. They refused to tell me who ordered it done, but it does not strike as something Portia would do."

"The money is safer from my mother and sister in Portia's control. One of the dowager countess's lovers is her banker."

"*One* of her lovers?"

"Your father and my mother have a great deal in common," St John assured him.

Winterbourne shuddered. "Do you love my sister?"

"I'm afraid so." The moment he said it, St John knew it to be true.

"Yes, well. You should be. Chastleton women are terrifying. Never more so than when they are in love."

"Your sister does not love me. She left me in no doubt when she slammed the door in my face, cast aspersions on my ancestors, and critiqued our wedding night for the entire household staff to hear."

"Good God."

"Oh, He heard it. There are people in Scotland who heard it."

"Portia always did have excellent lungs."

"So does your niece."

"Why didn't you drink the brandy?"

"What?" St John shook his head. The ability to change subjects in conversation at blinding speeds had to be a Chastleton family trait.

"The brandy I drank had been out of the decanter for quite some time. Why didn't you drink it?"

"I have been caring for Alexandra. I could not allow myself to become muddle-headed while… what are you smiling at?"

"You will be caring for her for the rest of your life. Are you willing to forego spirits that long?" He made a face and put his half-drunk mug of coffee onto the table. "Even if it means drinking this swill? She really said you *preferred* this?"

St John nodded, his mind a whirl of questions, answers and none of them matched.

"She is far crueler than I ever credited her."

"What did you expect of a woman you've underestimated her entire life?"

Winterbourne laughed. "You *are* in love. Poor bastard."

"I…" He knew the answer. Even without saying it, he knew. "I've made a monstrous mess of my marriage, Winterbourne. How can I ever make up for that?"

"By refusing to raise turkeys on the estate. By trusting her with your fortune. By forgoing spirits for the rest of your life. And a thousand other little things. Fortunately for us a thousand little things make up for one monstrous thing so long as we keep doing them."

"Us?"

"Men. We are the ones who tend to make the monstrous messes."

St John strode to the library doors. He gripped the handles so tightly they shook. "What do I say to her?"

"Whatever comes into your head. In addition to an appreciation of the little things, women have very low expectations when it comes to what we say."

"I don't even have a Christmas gift to offer her."

"A few of your Mrs. Cole's mince pies would not go amiss."

St John flung open the doors and stood in the threshold a moment. "Thanks, Winterbourne."

"Hurt her again and I shall be forced to kill you. And they'll never find your body."

A comforting thought to be sure. St John ducked into the kitchens before he headed up the back stairs.

⁊ᴖᴑ⧽

She truly was the most pitiful of creatures. Portia picked up the prettily wrapped package for the hundredth time and drew back as if to fling it into the fire. With a heartfelt sigh she dropped it back onto the tea table and collapsed into the brocade chair she'd just vacated. She'd spent the night crying and rocking Alexandra. She'd spent the morning pacing and sitting, sitting and pacing until she was nearly dizzy. Nanny Rose would peek in on her from time to time, *tsk* loudly, and withdraw muttering to herself.

Enough!

St John had sent her a note by Georgie late last night. It was a very pretty apology for pretending to have lost his memory, for digging into the estate accounts, for lying to her, for hurting her, for practically everything save marrying her. There was that, at least. He informed her he would leave for London the day after Christmas. What had she expected? That he'd fall madly in love with her, give up a life of debauchery for dirty clouts and farming, never to return to the allures of London again? Portia knew she was not the sort of woman for whom a man made sacrifices. Which was perfectly fine with her. She wasn't the sort of woman to make sacrifices for a man.

She liked managing the estate. She liked being the person the tenants and servants came to with their questions and problems to be solved. She'd married a man she hardly knew to gain her independence and she wasn't about to give that up by begging St John to stay.

Portia snatched up the package and marched into the nursery. Nanny Rose had Alexandra in her arms, rocking the baby to sleep.

"Your brother is here. He brought a turkey for Christmas dinner. That French chef of his cooked it, so God only knows if it will be fit to eat."

"I'm certain it will be perfectly fine, Nanny. It was kind of Alexander to bring it, though I suspect Catherine's hand in his arrival. Not to mention his own need to interfere where he is not wanted. Perhaps next year he can bring some Christmas cheer along with the turkey. One more disappointing Christmas at Bemerton and I will be forced to ban it altogether. Like the earl banned turkeys."

"You may be queen of this little kingdom, my lady, but you cannot ban Christmas," Nanny Rose declared as she increased the pace of her rocking. "It's blasphemous."

"Blasphemous or not, Lady Portia can ban Christmas if she wants to," an all too familiar baritone voice announced. "But she is not the queen. That honor belongs to Lady Alexandra."

"*Humpf!* You are spoiling this child and no mistake, my lord."

"A father's prerogative."

"As you say." Nanny placed the baby in the cradle and snatched a mince tart from the plate in St John's hand as she made her way out the doors into the corridor.

"Your brother recommended I bring these." He offered Portia the plate.

She took it and placed it on the tea table next to the discarded parcel. "I thought you were leaving." Portia wanted to kick herself. Half for indicating she'd read his note and half for wishing he'd stay.

"Do you want me to?"

"This is your home, my lord. You may stay or go as you please."

"That is what got us into this mess," he offered.

"I beg your pardon?"

"I left. After I married you. I left."

"I remember. I was there."

He winced. "Portia, I—"

"St John—"

"You first." He waved in her direction.

She could not think of what to say. He'd lied to her, but she'd lied to him. As awful as that was, they'd learned something about each other. They should have done so before they married. He might never love her the way she loved him. She started. Wait! She loved him? When did that happen?

"I love you, Portia."

Her ears began to ring. She narrowed her eyes and stared at him. "What did you say?"

"I love you. I'm not quite certain how it happened. Or when. But I love you and I don't want to leave. Unless you want me to. I mean. I'll do whatever you want me to do because that is what you do when you love someone. Isn't it?" He was babbling. Her elegant, smooth-talking rake of a husband was babbling. About loving her. *Her! Lady Porka!*

"St John, you don't have to say that. I mean, I know I am not the sort of woman a man like you marries. And I—"

"Well thank God for that."

"What?" Was this how he felt when he fell off his horse?

"Men like me generally marry empty-headed shrews who spend money like water and give their children over to someone else to raise. I don't think I'd like that very much."

"What would you like?" She shook her head. "I mean who?"

"Well," he drawled. "I'd prefer a wife who manages the money, and the estate, and looks after me, and provides me with children to play with and clean up after and tend."

"I might be able to do that," she said cautiously.

"I made a muddle of this, Portia. From the day we married I've done nothing but bollocks things up."

"I'm not blameless in all of this. I lied to you. I made you eat boiled cabbage. Every day."

"Well, there is that." He stepped closer and took her in his arms. "It's fine if you don't love me, Portia. I don't deserve it, but I reserve the right to try and be the sort of man you could love one day."

"You compared me to bedclothes," Portia accused, only half-teasing.

"Do not discount the charms of bedclothes. They can keep a man abed for days."

"There is some comfort in that." Portia slipped her fingers between the buttons at the top of his shirt.

"I take comfort in you," he said, his eyes, hungry and yearning, never leaving her face.

"Me?" A shivery sensation came over her from the heat and truth of his gaze.

"Every day you give me reason. You are there to remind me of all the things I have to lose should I stumble into drink and ruin again. When I think I cannot possibly be the father our daughter needs. Every day a new reason, a new comfort. I suspect it will be so every day for the rest of our lives."

She pressed her fingers to his lips. "I love you, St John."

He looked very much as he had the night he landed on her doorstep, soaked and *dicked in the nob*, as Nanny Rose put it.

"You do?"

"I have suspected it for quite some time. Rather like an ague coming on, but I knew it when I found out you broke Pearce's nose."

St John threw back his head and laughed. "How did you find that out?"

"When Pearce's butler sent word this morning, along with the five pounds he lost to Farnham."

"Farnham wagered on me?"

"He will always wager on you. As will I."

"I will never give you cause to doubt me again, my love."

"Never?" She raised an eyebrow and began to untie his

neckcloth.

"Never."

"Say it again." She dropped his neckcloth to the floor and stared into his eyes, blue and bright and lit with fire.

"I love you."

"What a coincidence. I love you too." She backed up tugging him towards the narrow bed against the wall.

"We're going to wake the baby—" he protested, though his rakish grin and nimble fingers expressed no such concern.

She pressed her fingers to his lips. "Then stop talking and kiss me."

He nipped at her fingertips. "What's in the pretty package?"

"Your Christmas gift."

"What is it?"

"Half a dozen new shirts."

He chuckled as he plucked at the lacings at the back of her dress. "I did not purchase a gift for you. My wife controls my purse strings, you know."

"Heartless wench." She fell onto the bed and dragged him with her. "There is something you can give me."

"Anything, my love. Anything at all."

"A much-improved wedding night?"

He kissed her, a slow, delicious, sensuous kiss. "I can do that."

"And perhaps another baby for next Christmas?"

"That may take more than one night," he said as he struggled to free her from her dress.

"For you, husband, I have all the nights in the world. Shall we send down word we'll be late for Christmas dinner?"

He tugged her dress down around her hips and down her legs to kick it onto the floor. He ran his hands over her naked body. "I have all the feast I need right here. Happy Christmas, my love."

Portia sighed and closed her eyes. "Happy Christmas, darling. Happy Christmas for the rest of our lives."

About Louisa

After retiring from a European career as an opera singer and returning to the United States, Louisa took up her pen and set sail on her second career, but first love, writing Regency romance. A two-time Golden Heart finalist, three-time Daphne du Maurier winner, and four-time Royal Ascot winner—she is a member of RWA, Southern Magic RWA, and the Beau Monde Chapter of RWA. Her first published work, *A Perfectly Dreadful* Christmas, won the 2015 Holt Medallion for Romance Novellas. She is both indie published and published by Scarsdale Publishing.

She recently released her tenth book, *Her Unrepentant Rogue*, and is currently working on *Thief of Wicked Desires*, the sequel to her December, 2018 release, *Thief of Broken Hearts.* Her Christmas Revels VI story, *A Perfectly Unexpected Christmas*, is the fifth of her *Perfectly* novellas, one of the many series she needs to finish! You can catch up on those various series on several online venues where she pops up to post Regency trivia, Regency research, and listings for English stately homes she'd love to own.

https://www.facebook.com/RegencyWriterLouisaCornell
http://numberonelondon.net/
https://www.facebook.com/groups/TheRegencySalon/

Our Thanks

This is the sixth in the Christmas Revels series, and each new edition has been more successful than the last. For this, we would like to thank our readers, many of whom have said they look forward to the arrival of each new collection. We do our best to offer you thoughtful stories with Christmas at their heart and hope to continue to be worthy of your interest. Do we guarantee that you will "love" each and every story? Of course not. We all have different tastes. But we *can* guarantee that we have all taken great care to present the best tales possible.

We hope you enjoyed our efforts and that they have enhanced your Christmas spirit. If you missed any of the earlier volumes of *Christmas Revels*, be sure to check them out—*Christmas Revels*, *Christmas Revels II*, *Christmas Revels III*, *Christmas Revels IV*, and *Christmas Revels V*. Each contains totally different, but equally delightful, novellas.

Also, please consider leaving an honest review for *Christmas Revels VI*. This helps other readers decide if this book will meet their needs. We're glad you chose to visit with these pieces of our imaginations.

Thank you,

Kate Louisa Anna Hannah

Printed in Great Britain
by Amazon

30040871R00235